Project Epiphany

Alien Emissaries Landing or Shadow Government Ambush?

An exciting UFO/Mystery/Spy novel
by a noted behavioral scientist and specialist
on extraterrestrial-human encounters,
dealing with the dramatic events leading
to open acknowledgment of
extraterrestrial visitation to Earth.

First Edition — November 1996

ISBN 1-885395-21-3

Copyright © 1996 by Richard J. Boylan, Ph.D..

Published with permission by
The Book Tree
c/o P.O. Box 724
Escondido, California 92026

PRINTED IN THE UNITED STATES OF AMERICA

Project Epiphany

Alien Emissaries Landing or
Shadow Government Ambush?

by

Richard J. Boylan, Ph.D.

The Book Tree
Escondido, California

Dedication

Project Epiphany is dedicated to Lee,
my ever-loving, steadfast and supportive wife,
to my most loyal fans, my kids
Jennifer, Stephanie, Darren and Matt,
to my doctoral program mentor and gifted principal
Psychology professor at U.C. Davis, Dr. Glenn Hawkes,
and to all those friends and supporters who have helped
me stay the course in withstanding withering harassment
to unravel the extraterrestrial phenomena
and uncover the UFO cover-up.

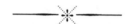

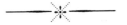

Preface

Welcome to the paradigm-disrupting world of extra-terrestrial visitation, governmental and paragovernmental cover-ups, the war for the right to the truth, and the societal upheaval which occurs when the truth escapes. This book can serve as a primer on the emerging immediate future.

Project Epiphany is a work of fiction. The characters and scenes depicted are inventions. Any perceived resemblance to actual people or events is coincidental and unintentional. No inferences or conclusions about actual persons, situations or events are warranted, nor should they be drawn from this book.

And yet, as with the world itself, there is another level of message which this book may serve. The discriminating reader may choose to find herein a useful scenario of possible future events, some of which, in the author's estimation, have a fair probability of occurring soon.

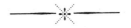

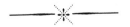

Chapter 1

IN the half-light that crept over the desert a little before dawn, a tawny four-wheel-drive utility vehicle hurried westward down a dirt road. Crossing Chaco Wash, the Pathfinder left a billowing plume of reddish-brown dust trailing a hundred yards behind. Behind the wheel was a tall, tanned athletic man in his early forties with craggy handsome features. He was wearing faded Levi's, a dark "X-Files" tee shirt, sunglasses, and an Aussie bush hat which revealed medium-length sandy hair mixed with gray. Roger Maguire stared intently at the crossroads a mile up ahead. He had to arrive at an ancient Indian ruin on the rim above Chaco Canyon before sunrise. Today was June 21st, the Summer Solstice, a highly significant date to the ancient Anasazi Indians. Maguire had been studying the complex they had built, a city now known as the Pueblo Alto Ruin.

Maguire, a cultural anthropologist, was finishing a National Park Service contract to survey ancient astronomical sites in northwest New Mexico's Chaco Culture National Historic Park. After careful research, he had identified a partially crumbled tower, which he suspected contained a solstice marker. The solstice sunrise this morning was his only opportunity for a year to find out if his calculations were right.

He took no notice of a late-model blue sedan parked alongside the dirt road. Nor did he pay any particular attention to a thin man in his early 30's with a jet-black crew cut, sitting behind the wheel. After Maguire drove past him, the man reached for a microphone under his dashboard. "Zeta One, this is Zeta Four. I have 'Fellow Traveler' in sight. He just passed me. He's headed for the road up to the north rim."

As Maguire neared the parking turnout to the trail head leading to Pueblo Alto Ruin, a faded red Toyota Corolla came towards him from the opposite direction. It zipped by, trailing its own plume of dust. Rolling up his window to avoid the dust, Maguire got a brief glimpse of the woman driver. She had lightly-tanned skin, long, dark hair below her shoulders, and chiseled facial features. She was staring intensely ahead as she drove. Boy, she's up awfully early, he thought. Why would anyone be driving into the Park before daybreak, with the nearest city two hours away? Maguire pulled up to the trail head, unloaded his gear, and began the climb to the rim.

It was that special time in the desert just before sunrise, when indescribable shades of rosy and orangish pinks wash the landscape. The air was cool and still, and the silence almost palpable. Clumps of desert scrub brush and cactus dotted the flat landscape spreading out for miles from the canyon rim. Maguire had positioned himself behind a keyhole slot in the one intact wall of a tower at the northeast corner of Pueblo Alto Ruin. The slot faced the direction where the sun would rise in a few minutes. He had carefully measured the angle from the keyhole slot to a petroglyph inscribed in the partially-crumbled opposite wall. He waited anxiously to see if the first shafts of light from the solstice sunrise would travel that path. As he waited, a distant clunking and scrunching sound resonated across the hard sandstone tablerock that lay atop the canyon rim. Someone's approaching; sounds like hiking boots, he thought to himself. He hoped that they would just keep hiking past his spot. He had just a few minutes remaining before the sunrise test.

"Hello!" a cheerful voice boomed out. "Whew! That's quite a climb up from the canyon floor."

Maguire looked around and recognized the woman who had driven past him near the trail head a little while earlier. As he got a better look at her, he saw a trim, medium-height woman in her latter thirties, with a mixture of Caucasian and Native-American features. Her face was flush from climbing, but radiated a pleasant smile. She was wearing a sleeveless turquoise top, a crystal pendant necklace and black jeans.

"I'm Barbara Catalina. Nice morning." She extended her hand.

Maguire shook hands. "I'm Roger. Glad to meet you. But I

have to let you know that I'm one minute away from an important measurement of an ancient astronomy site. Could you bear with me until I finish this?"

"Sure. No problem." Catalina's smile was cheerful. "Don't want to get in the way of science." She took a seat on a ledge formed by a partially-fallen stone-block wall.

Maguire turned back to the keyhole and stared through at the eastern horizon. A few moments later, as the first rays from the sun peeked above the horizon, a dagger of light shone through the keyhole slot, and precisely illuminated the sun pictograph on the opposite wall. Maguire sucked in his breath. He had definitively identified a primitive astronomical observatory at Alto Pueblo Ruin. This finding would also fill in an important piece of information about the archaeo-astronomy skills of the Anasazi. He had just realized the crowning achievement of his research work at Chaco Canyon. He let out a "Yee-ow!" Normally, Maguire was of even temperament, but at this moment he could not contain his excitement and pleasure at the discovery.

Catalina, who had been sitting quietly, rocked back startled, and then smiled. "Sounds like you just found gold!"

"Just as good in my line of work," Maguire replied. "Barbara, come here and look at this." He showed her the precise line-up of the first shaft of sunlight through the slot as it fell onto the Summer Solstice pictograph on the opposite wall. He explained to her how he had been working for months trying to identify the various suspected astronomy points amid the complex of ancient stone buildings in Chaco Canyon. He told her how the Anasazi used accurate measurements of the sun's seasonal positions to precisely determine when to plant their crops and when to expect rain. Such knowledge was vital in this high desert country, with long winters, short growing seasons, and marginal rainfall. He told her that this morning's discovery completed his last survey, and was his most exciting success.

"Well, I'm happy for you," Catalina said. "Since it looks like you're going to be famous, what's your full name?"

Now that his project was complete, Maguire was in a relaxed mood, and more inclined to chat. "Oh, I won't be famous. My name is Roger Maguire. I'm an anthropologist. I'm doing contract archaeology work for the Park Service. My job is to identify Anasazi astronomy sites here at Chaco."

"And I'm a professional psychic, from Boulder, Colorado. Pleased to meet you. Do you teach anthropology somewhere?"

"I used to teach at the University of California, Davis, while I was doing my pre-doctoral anthropology field studies," Maguire replied. "But since I got my Ph.D., I've wanted to be out in the field, applying what I learned. So, aside from a brief stint teaching Anthro at the University of New Mexico, here I am in the field." His grin betrayed a certain shyness.

"So, it's *Dr.* Maguire," Catalina teased mock-seriously.

"Oh, you can just call me Rog," he replied casually. "What brings you to Chaco Canyon so early on a summer morning?"

"Well, if I tell you, my being a psychic and all, and you being a scientist, do you promise not to laugh?" Catalina replied.

"Sure," Maguire grinned amiably. "Remember, anthropologists are used to dealing with different cultures. We're broad-minded."

"O.K. But remember, you promised." Catalina went on tell Maguire about a vision she had had while asleep about a week ago. In it, she was shown a power spot at a complex of ancient Native American ruins by a sandstone canyon. She was shown that it was very important to go there. There she would learn what she was supposed to do next in her life. She recognized the ruins from photos she had seen before as being in Chaco Canyon National Park. She told him that she had received an incredibly strong pull to travel to that power spot at once, and to be there in time for the Solstice. After she arrived, she identified the power spot as Pueblo Alto. "I made the drive from Boulder to Santa Fe yesterday, and got up at 1:30 this morning to finish the drive here. "So, here I am. And I made it in time for the Solstice." She debated whether to tell him the other element of the dream, and then decided she might as well test just how broad-minded this anthropologist was.

"There was one other detail. The person who was in this vision, showing me the power spot and indicating I should go there, was not human," Catalina said.

"What do you mean?" Maguire asked.

"She was an alien." Catalina waited for the patronizing smile or raised quizzical eyebrow that she had come to expect, when she shared her extraterrestrial contact experiences with professionals.

"Which race of extraterrestrial was she?" Maguire inquired, without a break in the conversational pace.

Catalina was astonished. She had never before encountered a scientist who took extraterrestrial contacts in stride. She would have to reevaluate her opinion about scientists, she thought. At least, about *this* anthropologist. She fumbled for an answer. "I didn't know there was more than one race. I just know the ones that come to visit me. The main one who communicates with me is a little under five feet tall, has a large head, large, slanted, almond-shaped eyes, mushroom-white skin, a very thin body, and delicate hands with three long fingers. She told me that I can call her Arica." Catalina still felt a little sheepish, confiding to a person whom she had just met that she had had visitations by beings from another star system. She was almost afraid to meet Maguire's calm gaze after she finished.

"Oh, I've heard a lot about that race group," Maguire said matter-of-factly.

"You have?"

"Sure. By the way, how many times have you been visited?"

Catalina thought a moment. "I guess about five times." Her surprise was now becoming replaced with curiosity. As Maguire paused to remove his sunglasses and wipe some dust from one eye, Catalina got a better look at his face. What kind of a person *was* this casually-dressed scientist with the pale blue-green eyes?

"How do you know about aliens?" she asked.

"I've been involved with my personal research, interviewing people who have had extraterrestrial encounters. I've talked to more than a hundred such persons. You learn quite a lot about the extraterrestrials when you interview enough people who have spent time with them."

Catalina was all ears. "Tell me more about your work."

Maguire went on to tell her about his volunteering to serve as a professional consultant to MUFON [Mutual UFO Network], a large civilian UFO investigation organization. He told of being called at all hours by people who desperately needed to tell their extraterrestrial experiences to someone professional who would believe them. He spoke of the long hours he spent, using skills from the psychiatric anthropology classes he had taken, listening and trying to help distraught people make sense out of the impossible, other-worldly experiences they had had. "But you know what the toughest part of this extraterrestrial encounters business is?" Maguire asked, and then answered his own question. "It's my fellow professionals. A lot of them have their head up their . . .," he deftly caught himself, "uh, have a narrow viewpoint."

Catalina drew him out. "So, you mean that you have actually presented your research work on aliens to some other scientists?"

"Yes. As a matter of fact I presented a scientific paper at the Abduction Study Conference held at M.I.T. in 1992. There were over 50 of us scientists invited there to quietly exchange information for five days. But you know, not all of them were open-minded. When I made the point that the extraterrestrials have their own mentality and cultures, and that there's a real risk of interstellar racism if we humans define them from just our point of view, a number of the other scientists found that unacceptable." Maguire's voice grew emphatic. "As though it were *okay* to consider an extraterrestrial as some kind of overgrown bug, and to use insensitive language to describe them. I bet that those professors wouldn't dare talk like that about an ethnic-minority human."

Catalina was starting to grow to like this sensitive but outspoken Roger Maguire. "Your empathy for the aliens is unusual, Rog. You know, so many people think of aliens as scary."

"*Extraterrestrials*," Maguire interjected. "I'd prefer you'd call them 'extraterrestrial.' 'Alien' has a negative connotation, you know, as in 'undocumented alien'."

"Well, they *are*," Catalina teased.

"Are what?" Maguire asked blithely.

"They are undocumented. I've never seen one yet show me a green card."

They both broke out laughing.

"But there's still something different about you, Dr. Maguire," Catalina said playfully. "You come at this matter of aliens, oops!, extraterrestrials, with a certain inner feeling that I just don't pick up from just open-minded people. Do you mind if I ask you a personal question?"

"Shoot."

Catalina held her gaze steady at his eyes. "Have you ever had an extraterrestrial encounter yourself?"

Maguire coughed nervously. He developed a far-away look, staring over Catalina's right shoulder. Then he snapped back to the present. "Hey, you're supposed to be the psychic. Suppose you tell *me*," he said in part-tease, part-evasion.

"Oh, no! You don't get out of it like that," she grinned in feigned irritation. "Come on, Dr. Maguire. I asked you fair and square."

"Okay, okay, fair enough." Maguire sat down on a large rock and faced Catalina. "You know, the funny thing about this work of research with extraterrestrial encounters," he said with a wry expression, "is that I can talk on and on about what happened to other people; but when it comes to telling about my own experience, it's hard."

"Why is that?"

"I'm not sure. I guess it has to do with the difference between looking at someone else's experience from the nice safe distance of objectivity, but when it happens to you ...." His voice trailed off and he paused. "Well, if you've had it happen to you, you know how it is. It's so unexpected, and amazing, and mysterious, and ... cosmically tremendous. I think you know what I'm trying to say. You said you're a fellow experiencer of ET contact."

"*Sister* experiencer," Catalina teased, "as long as we're being politically correct." A broad smile spread across her face. "But come on. Tell me all about your contact."

Maguire proceeded to tell her about his extraterrestrial encounter experience three years earlier. He told her that he had been researching pictograms at Gila Cliff Dwellings National Monument, searching for any record of Anasazi contacts with the Star People. It had been late one night, as he was driving north on NM State Highway 15, returning from dinner in Silver City to his campsite at the Cliff Dwellings. As he drew near the narrow bridge over the Gila River, he noticed that a thick mist had settled into the valley. He had never seen that happen before. Up ahead, where the mist was the thickest, there was a mysterious indistinct amber glow.

As he crossed the bridge, he looked ahead and to his left, and saw a horizontal row of three porthole-sized windows, back-lit with yellowish-orange light. The windows were about 75 yards away, and about 50 feet off the ground. Curious, he pulled his vehicle over to the side of the road, stopped and turned to stare out the driver's side window at the floating row of lights. As he stared, he could vaguely make out a dark oval shape, with the lights across its middle. Maguire then felt a presence, and turned around to see an extraterrestrial with large dark oval eyes, staring in the passenger door window. He told Catalina that after that, his memories became fragmented. He remembered a scene of being inside a craft, in a reclining-type chair, with an extraterrestrial running a wand-type object over his body. The "wand" had a small light at one end. Maguire recalled some long tube being inserted way up his nasal cavity. Another memory fragment he recalled was of a very strong, three-fingered hand taking his arm and helping him up from the chair.

"The last thing I remember is sitting back behind the driver's wheel, and looking out the window at the oval shape with the lights. It had risen to about 100 feet, and then shot off like a bat out of hell." Maguire looked up at Catalina to gauge her reaction.

Catalina looked at him with a faint, knowing smile. "Hello, fellow experiencer. I feel as if I've found a new friend. You know, I *knew* I felt something special about you when I first met you."

Maguire smiled back. "I call that 'experiencer bonding.' A lot of the people I've interviewed talk about it. It seems that experiencers can spot each other across a crowded room."

"Say, are you doing anything particular for dinner tonight?" Catalina asked.

"Oh, nothing special. Just the usual campfire chow," Maguire replied.

"How about joining me for dinner? I'm really a good cook."

"Well, that's very kind of you," Maguire replied.

"About seven-thirty, then. See you. Gotta get a campsite before they're all taken." With that, Catalina took off back down the trail, with a final glance and wave back over her shoulder.

As the sun set over the Park's West Mesa, Maguire pulled out of his base camp near the Park Ranger quarters, and headed east toward the public campground. His thoughts were on the pleasant prospects of the dinner invitation, and getting to know this Barbara better. He did not particularly notice the blue sedan still sitting in the Visitor's Center parking lot as he drove past. Nor did he notice the man with dark crew-cut hair sitting inside, pretending not to look at him. Captain José DiGiorgio was attached to Kirtland Air Force Base's Office of Special Investigations (AFOSI), Security Operations Division, Directorate of Counter Intelligence. As Maguire drove past, he radioed his supervisor, Major Bryce Eberhardt, at AFOSI Headquarters, Albuquerque.

"Zeta One, this is Zeta Four. 'Fellow Traveler' is headed east. I'm on him."

The blue sedan waited until Maguire's car was just out of sight, and then pulled out and followed him.

The wood fire at Catalina's campsite had burned down to a circle of glowing orange coals. Maguire was seated on a metal ice chest, picking at his Mexican custard dessert. Catalina, now wearing a salmon-colored squaw dress with a silver conch belt, sat in a camp chair. "I hope you like the flan," she said.

"It's a real treat. I haven't had it in a long time. The quesadillas dinner was delicious, too." Maguire rested his hand on his stomach. "Thank you very much. Best dinner I've had in a long time. And I get tired of my own cooking."

"Then you're not married?" Catalina asked, trying not to sound very interested.

"No. I was once," Maguire replied. "And we had a daughter. Melissa's away at college now, Cal Poly-San Luis Obispo. So I don't get to see her much."

"Where's home for you?" Catalina inquired.

"Chatsworth. It's northwest of Los Angeles. It was a little town when I was growing up. But it's grown a lot. How about you? Being an anthropologist, I have to comment that you look as though you have some Native American ancestry. Which tribe?"

"You're right. Ojibwa, you know, Chippewa. At least half of me is. Mom says the other half is Heinz 57 Varieties, but mostly Scottish."

"Are you married?" Maguire asked.

"I got married when I was right out of high school. It didn't work out. We broke up after seven years. But like you, I had a child, a son, Jason. He's working as a graphics designer in Denver."

"That's a nice..."

"Rog, I'm sorry to interrupt," Catalina said, pointing up at something above and behind him, "but what do you think that is?"

Roger turned around to see what she was looking at, and gazed up at the night blackness and its star-filled canopy. He stared a bit and then noticed three lights, about the size of stars, forming a perfect equilateral triangle. He was about to dismiss it as just a constellation, when he noticed that the triangle was slowly wobbling. As Catalina and he continued to stare at the formation, it slowly rotated until the flat base of the "pyramid" was now where the top had been. Then the bottom light winked out. Thirty seconds later the left top light turned off. A minute later the remaining light went out.

"Wow! That's pretty impressive!" Catalina enthused. "Do you think..."

Maguire finished her question, "...that they were UFOs? Yeah. And I'll tell you something else. I think that they were letting us know that they are up there."

"This is really special," Catalina said. "I feel like this is some kind of a sign. In fact, I think this is a confirmation of what I was shown in the vision, that it was important to be here on the Summer Solstice."

"Well, I gotta admit that that formation was very impressive," Maguire agreed, then stared down at the slowly-fading coals. After a few moments, he looked back up at Catalina and said, "I'm going to tell you something I haven't told anyone before. Over the last few years of interviewing experiencers, I've gotten a really strong impression that the ETs are going to do a major landing. I mean something pretty formal — on the level of official extra terrestrial ambassadors meeting with representatives of Earth. I also got the impression that it will happen soon. Think about it! That will probably be the biggest event in history! And I'll tell you something else. I feel that somehow I'm supposed to be there. I really want to be there. In fact, now that my project here at Chaco Canyon is finished, I've got some time and some money saved up. What I'm going to work on next is locating that ET Landing, and finding a way to be there. I'm going to figure out some way if it's the last thing I do."

"That sounds like a really exciting plan. Maybe there's some way I can help," Catalina said.

"How would that be?"

"Rog, I *am* psychic. I could try to take a look at where the landing would take place," she replied.

"You mean, do some remote-viewing?" he asked.

"You can call it that. I guess the old-fashioned term is clairvoyance. I'm pretty good at it," she said brightly.

"Yes, I guess that 'remote-viewing' is a military term," Maguire responded. "That's what an Army Intelligence General called it when he delivered a paper at a New Sciences conference I attended. But getting back to the Landing, any information you could find would be most welcome. At this point, all I have is a strong feeling that it'll be soon, and that I am supposed to be there."

"I'll really try to look into it, and let you know."

"Hey, it's getting late," Maguire said. "And we both got up extra early this morning. I'll be heading back to my camp. You heading back to Boulder in the morning?"

"Yes," she replied. "I'm supposed to go rafting this weekend with this guy I met from Longmont."

"Well, I hope you have fun. Barbara, it's been a pleasure meeting you, and getting to know you a bit. Thanks again for dinner. It was great. Good night."

Maguire headed off to his car. He was tired, and didn't

take particular notice of the sound of a twig snapping in the dark up on the hillside above where Catalina and he had been talking. On the drive back to his camp, he was excited thinking about his next project of finding the extraterrestrial landing. But soon after he lay down, sleep rapidly won out.

The next morning temporary coolness was brought in by a broken deck of majestic, towering cumulus clouds, spawned by a weak summer monsoon front. Their tops glowed pink and yellow in the early morning sunlight. Maguire began to pack up his base camp. The clatter of gravel stones thrown up under a car made him look up to see Catalina's red Corolla pulling up.

"Hi, Roger. Good morning." Catalina enthused. "I've got interesting news! Last night I had another vision. It had to do with the extraterrestrial landing."

"No kidding? I really want to hear about that."

Catalina told him about a familiar extraterrestrial coming to visit her during the night, and how Arica had created a mental visualization of the extraterrestrials' landing. Catalina was shown a scene of a very large disc-shaped craft setting down on the desert floor next to a high mountain peak. Adjacent to the landing site there had been a group of perhaps a dozen people. After the craft had landed, a door opened in its side and several extraterrestrials walked out and went over to the waiting group of humans.

"And you want to know what?" Catalina gushed. "Arica showed me that *I* was there!"

"Is that right?" Maguire replied politely, not sure what to make of this vision.

"And you want to know what else?" Catalina continued. "*You* were there, too."

Maguire's interest now perked up. "Was there any more to this vision?"

"No," Catalina replied. "That's as far as it went: the ETs getting out of their craft and walking up to the human group."

"Did you recognize the area where this Landing was to take place?" Maguire asked.

"No. But it was definitely desert. From the plants around, I'd have to say it looked like Sonoran Desert. But that still covers a lot of territory."

"Yeah, I'll say! Like parts of four States, not to mention northern Mexico. Well, I appreciate your sharing your vision, but I must say that your ET friend Arica hasn't narrowed down the location of the ET Landing all that much."

"Oh, wait! I just remembered another part of the vision I got," Catalina added. "After the Landing scene, I got this different picture from Arica. It was of this green valley all in clover. And after I looked at that, I was shown another scene. It was a desert antelope with its head down, lapping up some water. I can't figure out why I was being shown those scenes. It's a puzzle."

"Yeah, that is hard to figure out," Maguire agreed.

"One more thing I just remembered. I mentally asked Arica where the mountain was that the ETs' craft landed next to. But all I got back was a word that sounded like 'soles.' I think it was the plural. But that doesn't make any sense. Could Arica have been referring to the bottom of feet?"

"Or maybe the fish, sole?" Maguire asked. "Or maybe she was getting metaphysical and referring to souls? Hard to say." He grinned, "You know, lady, I'm not sure how much more I know about the Landing place than before you drove up."

"Yes, I know," Catalina responded, frustrated. "But I think it's significant that I should get this visit and vision the night after we met. And it *did* show that you and I are both are involved in the extraterrestrial landing."

"True," Maguire agreed, "that *is* significant. But it only makes me more anxious to learn more about this Landing, so I can be there. By the way, are you still returning to Boulder?"

Catalina told him about the things waiting for her there that she had to take care of, and that she had to leave. She found out from Maguire that he was scheduled to deliver a paper at a scientific conference in Santa Fe. After that, he would be beginning his quest to locate the place and timing of the extraterrestrial landing. Neither of them had any idea about whether they would ever see each other again. Catalina said good-bye and got in her car. As she turned on the engine, she felt a wave of wistfulness come over her. Driving off, she reached for a tissue and dabbed her eyes. She was going to miss this charming Roger Maguire.

Maguire stared at the faded red Corolla as it grew smaller in the distance. Ordinarily, someone he had just met, and only for a day at that, would not have much impact on him. But there was something different about Barbara Catalina. And what could her vision of the two of them present at an extraterrestrial public landing mean? Could it just be wishful thinking on her part, translated into a dream? Maguire was not sure just how much stock he put in psychics, particularly ones whose track record was an unknown. He shook his head. It was all just so obscure. Yet he had to admit to himself that the vision of his actually being at the landing was exciting. He also had to admit to himself that he felt a surprising pang of sadness when Barbara drove off.

He thought back to Julie, a woman he had been seeing for several years. But after the Northridge Earthquake, Julie had moved to Oregon, and they had drifted apart. He thought to himself that sharing the dinner with Barbara had made him nostalgic for the many little pleasures that come from having a girl friend to share life with. Her red car was a dot now, going away from the camp.

Chapter 2

A LARGE, tan, luxury four-door sedan raced down Interstate 25, heading south from Colorado Springs. It had General Services Administration license plates and no other identification. An Army Master Sergeant in his mid-twenties was behind the wheel, serving as chauffeur. His mouth was set in a grim straight line as he stared straight ahead. His passenger was everything they had said about him.

"Jesus! Can't you drive any faster? I haven't got all day, you know. Shit! I've got half a mind to have you stop the car and take over the driving myself. Don't they teach you jerks in motor pool school how to drive? Come on!"

In the back seat sat Colonel Jack Partridge. He was wearing the uniform of an Army Colonel, with the insignia of the Army's Intelligence and Security Command. His uniform and rank were real, but basically served as a cover for his official position as director of a compartmentalized Special Access Program within the National Security Agency (NSA). That unit, code-named PANDORA, was involved in the development and testing of high-technology anti-personnel weaponry. Their special armaments included laser weapons, isotropic energy-field radiators, extreme low-frequency sound, electromagnetic pulse generators, high-power microwave emitters, holographic projectors, and beta wave incapacitators. The non-physical side of PANDORA's program, the one in which Colonel Partridge was most deeply involved, was weapons and intelligence applications of parapsychological abilities. This included mental telepathy, telekinesis, remote viewing, mind-control psychotronics, and the directing of life-force energy to alter the thinking, emotions, or health of a "target" person.

After working on the early-stage development of these techniques at Walter Reed Army Institute of Research in Washington, D.C., Colonel Partridge had been moved to a classified underground laboratory at Sandia National Laboratories near

Albuquerque. There he pursued the further refinement of these psychic weapons. Even his classified work in the PANDORA unit at Sandia was, in a way, a cover for his most secret involvement: as a member of a super-secret group called JANUS.

Colonel Partridge had been in a bad mood ever since his chauffeur had picked him up from a restricted tarmac at Falcon Air Force Base east of Colorado Springs. The night before, he had been in Washington, D.C., enjoying networking with Defense and Intelligence Committee Congressmembers at a lavish reception at Fort McNair. There he got to wear a suit and tie and to be called Dr. Partridge, although few of the Congressmembers present knew that his Ph.D. was in the field of Death Science. Dr. Partridge had just delivered a talk to the guests about classified new advances made in "unconventional" weapons designs by his unit at Sandia Labs. His talk had been well received. He had been enjoying the congratulations and attention from these influential committee members when a military courier had handed him a note. He had been unceremoniously ordered to leave at once to appear at a special meeting the next morning at Fort Carson Military Reservation, Colorado Springs. The courier told him that a car was outside to take him to a waiting military plane. The colonel's uniform they had given him to change into on the plane was in what used to be his correct size. But Colonel Partridge had gained weight doing the political receptions circuit. The tight fit only added to his irritation at General Hal Beardsley for pulling him away from Washington, just as if he was some errand boy. That bastard is pulling rank, Partridge thought, fuming. Beardsley didn't even bother to tell me why I had to come here.

The tan sedan pulled off I-25 onto an unobtrusive two-lane asphalt road that led towards the east fence of Fort Carson Military Reservation. After clearing the sentry gate, the sedan proceeded to a junction, and took a dirt road to the left that headed toward a low hill dotted with scrub brush.

"You know where you're headed?" the Colonel snapped sarcastically.

"Yes, *sir!*" the Master Sergeant shot back politely, but with just a hint of annoyance.

"You're headed right into the side of a goddamn mountain, Sergeant," Partridge persisted.

"Sir, if you'll just be patient, you'll soon see that we're headed in the proper direction," the sergeant said earnestly.

As the sedan drew near where the road ended against the side of the hill, the driver slowed. A hundred-foot square section of scrub hillside moved inward and then lifted upward, like some gigantic version of an automatic garage door. The car proceeded into the hillside and forward into an oversized elevator.

It seemed to Colonel Partridge as though the trip down took forever. When the elevator doors opened, the car drove 100 feet forward and stopped. The sergeant hurried around to the rear door, held the car door open and snapped a smart salute. "It's time to get out, sir."

In front of the car was a wall with two tall gleaming metal doors. Flanked on either side of the doors were two stern, maroon-bereted Blue Light Delta Force sentries dressed in midnight-blue jumpsuits. Each sentry had a red shoulder patch insignia, with a black triangle trisected by three horizontal bars. Each sentry cradled a Heckler and Koch MP-5 submachine gun. Partridge's keen military eye noticed that the guns' safety was off.

Colonel Partridge ignored his driver's salute and shot him a question. "Do you know how far down we are?"

"No, sir! I'm not cleared for that information."

"Is General Beardsley here?" Partridge asked.

"No, sir. The General is at Fort Carson Headquarters topside, sir."

"Well, then," the Colonel continued, "do you know what's through those doors?"

"No, sir. I'm not cleared for that either."

Damn, Partridge fumed. Beardsley tells me to come quick, and now the bastard isn't here himself. I don't even know where "here" is. Colonel Partridge walked forward, identified himself to the sentries, and entered an antechamber. He underwent a security iris-scan match identification procedure. He then felt the tingle of a bio-interactive electromagnetic field passing through his body, as he walked past two Extreme Low Frequency coils, each set about 3-1/2 feet high in opposite walls. Having successfully passed through those screenings, he shook his head to clear the electromagnetic aftereffects. He then stepped forward through another set of doors which opened into a large, well-lit, tastefully decorated room. The walls were paneled in richly hued dark wood. Down the middle of the room was a long oval meeting table of polished walnut, surrounded by nine high-back executive chairs.

Around the table eight men were seated. Although their ages varied, most were in their senior years. Partridge instantly recognized the eight, although he could think of only one other occasion when all nine of them had ever been assembled simultaneously. There had long been rumors among UFO enthusiasts that such a group existed. But this group had seen to it that they were never identified in any government document or reputable press story. Such anonymity was vital, and the group spared no effort or influence to maintain itself out of sight. Although a cover story, generated to throw pesky UFO investigators off the track, had been circulated that the group was called the Majestic Twelve, they were neither, and that was not their name. Currently they went by the code designation JANUS, but there were discussions that the time had come to change the code name again.

This group had originally been chartered by an unpublished, ultra-classified Presidential Executive Order in 1947, in response to the discovery and retrieval of an extraterrestrial spacecraft between Roswell and Corona, New Mexico. Commissioned by President Truman under a finding of extreme threat to national security, JANUS's mission was to find out everything that could be learned about extraterrestrial craft and visitors, while keeping the existence of UFOs and extraterrestrials an absolute secret "by any means necessary." Over the next two decades, the group had evolved in membership and mission. Extreme detachment from the oversight of Congress, the Director of Central Intelligence, and the National Security Council had evolved, as Presidents came and went, into total detachment from White House awareness and control as well. In the later Sixties, it took itself out of any semblance of being a governmental agency, and became an autonomous instrumentality of certain elite Black Budget defense corporation officials, selected retired military chiefs, and ultra-compartmented intelligence officials. Because JANUS "did not exist," there was no one to protest when it took itself private without Presidential authorization.

Once JANUS went private, it had unsupervised control of the tens of billions of dollars which it had accumulated in "black" accounts for use in conducting the UFO cover-up. The JANUS members from certain defense industries and intelligence compartments saw to it that additional huge sums of money were secretly siphoned to JANUS regularly to maintain its funding. In return, these defense corporations gained access to extremely-advanced extraterrestrial science and technology. JANUS also controlled an awesome empire of covert military and intelligence units, operating under old National Security carte blanche authority. This empire was invisibly compartmented within, and parallel to, the existing structures of official governmental military and intelligence agencies. JANUS exercised influence on the Congress and the National Security Council through certain of its politically well-placed members.

With such influence and funding, and operating in secret under color of "National Security" with no public accountability, JANUS's potential for serious abuse of power was inevitable, as were the temptation for personal enrichment, and indulgence in habits which required absolute immunity from disclosure.

At the head of the table sat the octogenarian Henri Fournier, Ph.D., a theoretical physicist on the Board of Directors of the BDM Corporation, a firm which performed considerable classified technology research and development for the government. The oldest and only original surviving member of JANUS, Dr. Fournier was on indefinite loan from BDM to the Joint Chiefs of Staff as Science and Technology Advisor. Only the nine men in this room knew that he was also a member and the chairman of JANUS.

To Fournier's left sat the silver-haired Nathaniel Brown, M.D., Ph.D., Director of the Medical Sciences Department of AT&T- Bell Labs. Previous to that position, Brown had held the position of coordinator of UFO information at the NSA. Rumor had it that Dr. Brown had done unauthorized experiments in medical mind-control during his earlier intelligence career at CIA, and that his last act before leaving CIA had been to have the experiments' files burned.

To Brown's left Colonel Partridge spotted portly Roderick Birdsall, Chief of Special Projects within the Directorate of Operations, CIA. Colonel Partridge had little respect for Rod Birdsall, whom he considered cocky and too loose-lipped, because of Birdsall's habit of spreading fact-laden disinformation through intermediaries to civilian UFO investigators in hopes of confusing them.

Next to Birdsall sat the owlish Hubert Tarnsworth, Ph.D., a high-energy physicist with the Edgerton, Germhausen & Greer Corporation (EG&G). Colonel Partridge had met Tarnsworth underground at the "nonexistent" Area 51 Base north of Las Vegas at the northeast corner of the Nellis Air Force Base Range. EG&G operated Area 51 under a "black" joint contract with the Department of Energy (DOE), the CIA, and the Navy. Partridge recalled that Tarnsworth and he had discussed terawatt-regime Star Wars weapons in a secure room 40 stories down under the Nevada desert floor. Partridge guessed that the subterranean room at Area 51 was located farther down than he had gone today under Fort Carson. Partridge considered Tarnsworth bright, but a bore.

On the Chairman's right was Air Force Major-General Robert Lazarus, Ph.D., whose nominal assignment was to Haystack USAF Laboratory underground at Edwards Air Force Base. But General Lazarus was actually the director of a military-compartment UFO Working Group at Laboratory QQ at Los Alamos. Over the years General Lazarus had earned the nickname "Ramrod" because of his insistence on following military procedure in precise detail. Colonel Partridge had clashed more than once with "Ramrod" Lazarus at Los Alamos. The rumor mill at Lab QQ still circulated the story of one heated exchange during a meeting, at which Colonel Partridge had insinuated that General Lazarus was anal-retentive, and the General had retorted that Partridge was "an asshole."

To Lazarus's right sat the steely-eyed Morris Solomon, Ph.D., a retired Harvard economist. Solomon was chief consultant to the Federal Reserve Board and a financial advisor to one of the three richest families in America. Partridge found Solomon's focus on financial policy tedious, but had to admire the way Solomon could always find Black Budget funds for one of Partridge's off-the-books projects.

Next to Solomon Partridge saw Senator John Knapp. The Senator was Chairman of the Senate Intelligence Committee, although he most definitely was not present in that capacity. In fact Senator Knapp was sure that no one else on the Intelligence Committee knew that JANUS existed. Partridge considered Knapp genial, but deadly if crossed. Seeing only the genial side, Georgia had returned its favorite son to the Senate for six terms, and showed no signs of stopping.

In the next chair was the courtly Admiral Jordan Clannon, U.S Navy (retired). Clannon was now director of the Center for Comparative Psychophysical Studies at Batelle Memorial Institute, a paragovernmental R&D corporation. The Center had done classified research on extraterrestrials, utilizing corpses and even one living extraterrestrial recovered from UFO crashes. On contract to JANUS, Batelle had developed a typology of the various extraterrestrial races. Admiral Clannon's face had an emotionless smile as he looked up at Partridge, masking God knows what, Partridge thought.

"Sit down, Dr. Partridge. We've been waiting for you," Henri Fournier said stiffly with just a touch of impatience, gesturing to the remaining chair. "Now, gentlemen, we can move on to the principal business of this meeting. We have a critical situation coming up. I am referring to a new development within the general phenomenon of extraterrestrial contacts.

"As you know, for approximately the last decade, there has been a steady increase in the number of extraterrestrial contacts with humans. This has considerably complicated our task, because of the difficulty of maintaining secrecy about UFOs and aliens with the emergence of all of those numerous new abductees. The resulting publicity, carried by increasingly bold television and newspaper coverage, has necessitated our using maximum pressure and ever sterner countermeasures to assure that our mainstream-media 'assets' hold the line against disclosure.

"Our analysts within Roderick Birdsall's shop at Special Projects have concluded that this increase in human contacts means that the extraterrestrials are up to something *big*." Fournier paused for dramatic emphasis, and then continued in his incongruously calm and measured tones. "Naturally, we began a comprehensive investigation as to what this might be. Birdsall's unit within CIA made discreet inquiries, through his informants within various UFO organizations and support groups, as to what credible abductees were saying. His agents questioned our friends who operate as UFO 'investigators' to find out what they had learned from hypnotizing abductees who came to them. And we regrettably had to have General Lazarus's Special Operations Blue Light Teams perform a special extensive series of covert kidnappings of contactees in order to interrogate them. Interrogations which they were made to forget, of course, by administration of drugs and hypnotic programming to misremember their kidnapping as an 'alien abduction.' Obviously, we had to undertake these distasteful and extreme measures in order to test and corroborate the available data, relayed to us by our own informants, with the coerced information gained from contactees we kidnapped.

"All the data point to a most disturbing forecast. The aliens' plan is to conduct a preplanned public landing within the coming twelve months. This landing will involve the aliens meeting with a special group of humans. Our information indicates that this landing will be the first of several, in preparation for a follow-up major public landing, broadcast worldwide on television. At that landing, the alien ambassadors will meet with official representatives from Earth. Let me emphasize," Fournier's voice showed emotion for the first time, "that there is *no* indication that *our* group would be involved in either the preparatory landings or the major public landing."

A silence spread across the room. Sudden tension gripped the members of JANUS, as the implications of Henri Fournier's remarks sank in. They had come here on an urgent summons, expecting something important. But *this*! This development could be catastrophic for them all. If the aliens were indeed going to conduct public landings, there was no way that the JANUS group, even with the thousands of operatives it commanded and the billions of dollars at its disposal, could continue to maintain the UFO cover-up.

Furthermore, with the collapse of the Cover-Up, discipline could disintegrate all along the chains of command which had executed orders so smoothly in the past. In turn, that disintegration of discipline would bring even greater dangers. If any of JANUS's operatives went public with what they knew about the Cover-Up, the illegal searches and seizures, wire-tapping, physical and psychological intimidation and threatening of UFO witnesses, the slanders and character assassination used against serious UFO researchers, the kidnappings, drugging, torture and gang-rapes of innocent civilian experiencers during pseudo-"alien" abductions conducted by JANUS's special military-intelligence units, and the assassinations of too-determined UFO investigators and of fed-up insiders who had decided to go public with what they knew, such revelations could spell disgrace and extremely long prison sentences all the way up the chain of command. And if, despite JANUS's precautions of compartmentalizing each command layer and limiting information on a strict need-to-know basis, those next down in the JANUS chain of command became indicted, and they decided to cut a deal with prosecutors by identifying members of the JANUS leadership group, then it was conceivable that every one of the individuals in this room could go down. The faces around the table were grave with concern.

The stillness was broken finally by Senator Knapp. "I'll be damned if we're going to have this whole thing fall apart now, just because some goddamn aliens want to push their way into the spotlight!" he exploded. Senator Knapp looked around the table at everyone assembled. "Isn't there something somebody can do?"

Roderick Birdsall spoke up next. "I'll see what additional information my staff at Special Projects can find. There must be something . . ." he trailed off lamely.

"I can tell you this," Morris Solomon intoned ominously, "if the aliens stage a public landing, there will be a crash in the stock exchanges around the world." He shook his head somberly, shaken by his own grim forecast. "Currency markets will nosedive. We will be looking at global financial collapse. There will be widespread public panic. Our position may become untenable."

"Perhaps an appropriate application of technology could help us ward off any alien public landings," Hubert Tarnsworth interjected. "Many of you are probably not aware of a new weapon that we have successfully operated at the Tonopah Test Range, and is now in place near McMurdo Station, Antarctica. This device, to make it simple, generates an unbelievably strong disruptive electromagnetic energy field in the upper atmosphere. Pumped to sufficient energy levels, the disrupter field could encircle the globe like a spherical shell. In a test, we used one of the Department of Energy's Northrop Mark-6 antigravity craft to try to penetrate the field at 160,000 feet altitude. The weapon disrupted our craft's high-voltage lifting field. As a result its antigravity effect failed and our Mark-6 suffered an uncontrolled descent and total destruction upon impact. Naturally, the loss of a fine test pilot was regrettable.

"We call this weapon the High Altitude Radiative Disrupter Omnidirectional Net, or HARDON. EG&G is proud to have participated in its development," he said, with characteristic corporate boosterism. "It may serve our purposes for addressing the problem which our alien visitors are about to present."

"You call it HARDON, eh? That's great!" Senator Knapp drawled. Never one to pass up the opportunity for profane, humor he added, "I'd like to give those slant-eyed bug-men a hard-on where it'll do them some good!" He chuckled appreciatively at his own humor. The sober faces around him did not join in his laughter. He nervously switched ground. "Ah, General Lazarus, what do you think of such a weapon? Would it repel the aliens from attempting a landing?"

"Senator, as you might have guessed, I have been closely monitoring the progress of the HARDON weapon system. Even more closely than Dr. Tarnsworth has," General Lazarus replied, trying to keep patronizing superiority out of his voice. "While we have not operationally tested it against all the various extraterrestrial craft which have penetrated our atmosphere, I will tell you something which even Dr. Tarnsworth doesn't know. Thirteen days ago, one of our military surveillance satellites spotted a 100-meter-wide disc craft headed towards our atmosphere from deepspace. As it approached altitude 90 miles, I authorized a firing of the HARDON system at a power setting of 50 gigawatts."

"But General," Tarnsworth interrupted, agitatedly, "we've never tested the system above the five-gigawatt regime. At significantly higher levels there are potentially serious dangers to the earth and the atmosphere, which our scientists have not solved yet."

"Well, Hubert," General Lazarus shot back unconcerned, "your weapon has been tested at 50 gigawatts now. You know the old saying, 'You've got to break a few eggs to make an omelet.' The point I was about to make before you interrupted me is that when the alien craft entered the HARDON force field, there was a blinding flash, which lit up the night sky over the northern U.S. and Canada."

"Naturally, Jack, you put out the story that it was some unusually large meteorite," Admiral Clannon interjected with a sardonic smile.

"Of course, Admiral," General Lazarus replied. "Now, gentlemen, since the alien craft did not fall to the earth, I cannot tell you absolutely that it was destroyed. But it did disappear from our satellite screens. And personally I think it exploded. So, I say that one of our options is to fire up the HARDON system to prevent an alien landing."

"Not so fast, General," Nathaniel Brown responded. "I want to hear what Dr. Tarnsworth's objections are to using the HARDON system at higher power."

Hubert Tarnsworth ticked off the various possible negative effects of extreme-power operation. Airplane navigation systems could be disrupted. Potential negative effects on human bodies included memory loss, cataracts, leukemia, birth defects, malfunctioning of coronary pace-makers, and cancer. HARDON's microwave radiation could bounce back from the atmosphere and inadvertently detonate bombs. There could be nationwide failure of the electrical power grids. And there was a serious possibility of destruction of the ozone layer and permanent climatic changes.

"OK, Hubert, enough of the doomsday scenario," General Lazarus interjected, sarcastically. "So you've got a problem with using the HARDON system at extreme power. But what other solution do you have to the problem of our web-fingered 'friends' pulling a public landing? Nothing! Whereas, I *have* actually run HARDON at extreme power. And I think we fried 'Charley'." In his enthusiasm, General Lazarus slipped into a military-intelligence pejorative term for an extraterrestrial. "And, what's more, the world didn't come to an end like Hubert said it would."

Nathaniel Brown pursued his objection. "At Bell Labs we have also done some research on atmospheric energy shields. We're obviously not as far along as Dr. Tarnsworth says EG&G is. We haven't gone operational. But we did find out from preliminary studies that the serious hazards he spoke about are real, and can be quite devastating to the population." Brown shot a sharp glance at Lazarus, ill concealing his low opinion of Lazarus's brute-force mentality. "Just because you got away with a brief firing of HARDON at 50 gigawatts does not mean that sustained operation at that level would avoid catastrophic results. Such results definitely *would* occur! And since we will not, in all likelihood, have precise information about when the extraterrestrials are coming for their public landing, you *would* have to run the force shield for an extended period of time." Brown turned to the rest of the men at the table. "I submit that we have to keep in mind the uproar that arose during the Vietnam War. You remember when a Sergeant Calley ordered a Vietnamese village destroyed in order to save it from Communism. We aren't going to win any sympathy from the populace, if our defense for our actions is going to be that we had to destroy the Earth in order to save it. I suggest that we had better consider other options."

Colonel Partridge saw an opportunity to present his proposal. First he reviewed for the others the problems that open alien contacts would bring. The main problem JANUS had with a public alien landing was the prospect that whoever the aliens met with would be seen as the preeminent human leadership. But because Henri Fournier's information was that JANUS was not involved in the alien landing, JANUS very possibly would not be able control those whom the aliens dealt with. In addition, public alien-human contact would end JANUS's monopoly on advanced alien science and technology. Furthermore, there was the disturbing possibility that the aliens might reveal JANUS's illegal secret activities, including its darkest secret: that it had been waging unauthorized war on the aliens, using Star Wars weaponry.

However, the Colonel offered the group a solution. The alien landing problem was fundamentally one of spin control. Partridge reminded them that his background was in psychological warfare and psychotronic technology.

"What we need to do is take control of the way the general population *thinks* about the alien landing," the Colonel stated.

"And how the hell are we going to do that?" Senator Knapp inquired.

Jack Partridge triumphantly replied, "Simple. We beat them to it."

"What? How?" Senator Knapp exclaimed. "What do you mean?"

Colonel Partridge stood up and proudly presented his plan to the group. "The way we beat the aliens to it is by holding an 'alien landing' *first*. We already have the technology to stage a fake but believable alien landing. Over at NSA, my PANDORA unit has several mock-up saucers that our special effects people have constructed. Extremely realistic! One of them could be suspended from a very long thin black cable running down from a silenced black helicopter. Our 'saucer' could come in for a night-time landing, at a place of our choosing, where we could control how close anyone gets and the lighting conditions. Hell, our Psychological Operations people even ran a test last year of one of our mock-up saucers. They set it down on a farm near a small town east of Calgary. The local civilian UFO investigators fell for it hook, line and sinker."

"Very well, Jack," Senator Knapp interjected, "but where do we get our aliens?"

"We can also create fake aliens, good enough that the public will believe they are real," the Colonel assured the group. "Since we control these 'aliens', we can have them meet with whomever *we* want, and say whatever *we* want them to say. Personally, I suggest that these 'aliens' choose to meet with a respectable group of men who just happen to be members of JANUS. And I further vote that the 'aliens' designate *us* as the official representatives that they have chosen to deal with."

"And what happens to the subliminal propaganda image we have so carefully cultivated over the years for those who believe in UFOs: that the aliens are evil, aggressive, and sneaky, and can't be trusted?" Admiral Clannon asked.

"I've thought of that, too. We'll pull a couple of things during our 'public landing' that will give the public the 'proper' view of aliens. For one, we'll have a confederate in the security detachment which accompanies us to the landing. And, of course, our 'aliens' will be in on the plan. We'll arrange to have a 'misunderstanding' created, during which one of our security detail gets jumpy and reaches for his side-arm. Then one of the 'aliens' beats him to the draw with a beam weapon. A modification to one of the hand-held lasers we have should do the trick as an 'alien weapon.' Should produce nice visuals, too, for the cameras. Our security man goes down and is carried off Dead-On-Arrival. The aliens get shown on worldwide television as high-tech trigger-happy gunslingers.

"Then, we'll have some preliminary negotiations with our 'aliens.' During these negotiations, we'll announce to the press that we presented an agreement for peaceful contact and exchange of scientific and technological information to the aliens. At the conclusion of 'negotiations,' we'll report to the news people that the aliens rejected our peaceful proposal, and revealed their plans to systematically colonize the Earth, taking over one country at a time, and replacing human population with their own. Naturally, the 'aliens' will be starting with the United States. *That* ought to get even the bleeding-heart liberals to come over to our point of view. Then, of course, we ride to the rescue.

"We reveal to the public our secret array of ground-based and orbiting Star Wars weapons systems, which we tell them have a proven ability to shoot down their craft. Then in short order, the public demands protection from these aliens, forgives us for violating the no-weapons-in-space Treaty, forgives us for our previous secret shoot-downs of UFOs, and we get Congressional *and* U.N. authorization to conduct a full-scale war on the aliens."

Partridge sat back in his chair with a wide grin, enormously satisfied with himself. The members paused to reflect on his proposal. As they discussed the idea, first one and then another of the members gave approving comments. For this plan not only offered them a reprieve from the grim prospect of public exposure, disgrace, and prosecution, it also held the promise of allowing them to maintain their covert technology, wealth, and power. It even held the prospect of creating a general acceptance by the population that the members of JANUS were the ones to be in charge in dealing with the "alien menace."

On Nathaniel Brown's motion, they tabled General Lazarus's idea to repel the extraterrestrials with the HARDON force shield. However, the General was able to get the group to agree that he could use the HARDON System in the future if for some reason JANUS's fake alien landing plan did not work. With the General's proposal sidelined, JANUS finally voted unanimously to proceed with the faked alien landing plan.

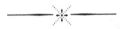

Chapter 3

SITTING up to his neck in 103-degree water in Spence Hot Springs' spacious pool, Roger Maguire stared out from his comfortable vantage-point towards the dramatic jagged ridges of the Sierra Nacimiento Mountains to the west. At an elevation of over 6000 feet in the Santa Fe National Forest, the spectacular view made the steep hike up the dirt trail from the Jemez River worthwhile. Spence was his favorite hot spring in New Mexico, and a welcome pause on his 200-mile drive from Chaco Canyon to Santa Fe. It was Friday afternoon, and surprisingly he had the pool to himself.

He had needed a chance to pause anyway. He had a presentation to go over that he was to give tomorrow at the Southwest Anthropological Association's annual conference. He figured that the title of his presentation sounded innocuous enough: "Star Nation Symbols in Anasazi Petroglyphs at Bandelier National Monument." As he reviewed his notes, he wondered what his fellow anthropologists would think when he presented evidence from 700-year-old rock carvings that the ancestors of the Pueblo Indians had recorded contacts with people from the stars. Or how the conferees would react when he reported that the petroglyph messages indicated that the Star Nations were returning very soon.

After a leisurely soak, Maguire got out of the pool and sat by the edge. As he was finishing dressing, two attractive, college-aged women, a brunette and a strawberry-blonde, came up the trail to the pool's edge. They gave him smiles of greeting, then undressed and slid into the crystal-clear spring waters. As Maguire finished lacing up his hiking boots, the strawberry-blonde, wearing a perfect all-over light-brown tan, reached over with a marijuana joint.

"Hi. I'm Shelley. Want a toke, whatever-your-name-is?" she offered, beaming a broad smile.

"I'm Roger. And ah, no, thanks," he replied. "Actually, I've got a big drive ahead of me, and I've got to be going. I'm headed for Santa Fe, by way of Bandelier."

Neither the women nor Maguire saw a telephoto camera lens barely showing out of a low bushy juniper tree fifty yards up the hillside. Captain José DiGiorgio had stopped staring at the two nude women through his magnification lens long enough to snap a picture of the attractive strawberry-blonde leaning over towards Maguire with her joint. DiGiorgio advanced the film for a clincher photo of Maguire smoking marijuana. He smiled, imagining the commendation and possible raise he would get back at AFOSI headquarters, when he brought in a photo of this surveillance target sitting next to a hot spring, while this gorgeous nude buxom blonde was leaning towards him, as he puffed on a marijuana cigarette. God, he muttered softly to himself, I wish my old lady had some decent tits like those. Then, when Maguire didn't accept the joint, and the blonde sat back in the pool, DiGiorgio silently cursed to himself.

"Oh, yeah, Highway 4 is a pretty winding road," Shelley continued, making conversation. "What are you going to be doing in Santa Fe?"

"I'm presenting a paper at an anthropological conference," Maguire replied.

"Hey, I'm taking an Anthropology class. Do you teach any classes at the University of New Mexico?"

"No," Maguire replied. "I'm a working anthropologist, out in the field."

"Well, what are you going to talk about at your conference?" Shelley smiled, resting her elbow on the rock side of the pool, her chin in her hand.

"I'm going to speak about ancient Indian petroglyphs, which show that extraterrestrials visited Earth a half-millennium ago," he replied nonchalantly.

"Oh, Vina, tell Roger about the UFO you saw yesterday," Shelley said, turning to the other woman.

The brunette slid over to the pool's edge nearest Maguire.

"It was the *neatest* thing!" Vina enthused. "It was dusk, and I was driving back to my house outside of Bernalillo. This shiny metal thing that looked like a top, it had reddish-orange lights all around its middle, anyway it came down and hovered near the road a little ways ahead of me. I stopped the car to look at it better. It must have sat there a couple of minutes. Then suddenly it was gone. Funny thing is, next thing I'm driving again down the road, only I don't remember turning the motor back on."

Maguire smiled, recognizing signs of a possible unremembered extraterrestrial encounter connected to a UFO sighting. But he still needed to finish his drive to Santa Fe, so he decided to pass up talking to Vina at length about her sighting. He said good-bye to the two women, and proceeded down the dusty trail towards his car.

The Southwest Anthropological Association had had a better than average turnout this year. The main conference room of the Santa Fe Radisson was about three-quarters full, as Maguire began to present his evidence from Anasazi petroglyphs for ancient contact between extraterrestrials and humans. He wouldn't have noticed as a portly, middle-aged man, registered as "Dr. Partridge" and dressed in a conservative light-weight tan suit, slipped into a empty chair at the back of the auditorium when Maguire's talk began. Colonel

Partridge had had the title of Maguire's talk brought to his attention by an NSA intelligence analyst in the PANDORA Unit. The analyst was a specialist in Southwest Indian cultures, and knew that the Colonel was interested in evidence of alien contacts found in earlier history.

Nor would Maguire have noticed that Partridge took careful notes, as Maguire deciphered the Anasazi petroglyphs. And Maguire was too concerned with the reactions of his colleagues to notice that Partridge nervously dropped his notebook when Maguire related what the petroglyphs foretold: that the Star Nations were due to return "after thirty-two generations had passed," and that this best estimate of *that* time was the current time.

As Maguire finished, a number of hands shot up around the room. A number of those commenting on Maguire's talk were skeptical of his findings. One anthropologist, a red-bearded man, identified himself as working for the Bureau of Indian Affairs at Dulce, New Mexico, the Jicarilla Apache tribal headquarters. He made the most forceful objection of those who disagreed, claiming that Maguire was taking the symbolism of a primitive Indian origin myth about descent from the gods, and then placing a overly literal interpretation on it. The red-bearded man did not change his mind, even when Maguire pointed out that the Anasazi had a different origin story, completely unrelated to the Bandelier petroglyphs Maguire had described. There were also a couple of anthropologists who rose to express interest in his findings, and to ask for further information. During the question and answer period, Maguire wondered briefly at the unusual number of photographs being taken of him, but then in the press of questions gave it no further thought.

At the end of Maguire's presentation, Dr. Partridge closed his notebook and walked out of the conference hall to his car. As he pulled out of the conference parking lot and headed for his underground office at Sandia Labs, Colonel Partridge got on his secure scrambled car phone and placed a call to Major Eberhardt at Kirtland Air Force Base's Office of Special Investigations.

"Bryce, this is Colonel Partridge. What do you have on one Roger P. Maguire, Ph.D., anthropologist?"

"Give me a moment to bring him up, Colonel," Major Eberhardt replied in his most ingratiating manner. His computer was state-of-the-art, and did not hesitate when Maguire's name was given via voice-activated entry.

"Oh, yes, *this* one. We have kept a low-medium surveillance on him, because of his extensive work interviewing UFO abductees. The latest report from the field probably might not be of much interest here. To summarize, it seems that Dr. Maguire says he has received information passed onto him by abductees, originally from the extraterrestrials. That information is that there is going to be a public alien landing in the near future. Furthermore, our Dr. Maguire has set himself an agenda of finding out the location and timing of this public alien landing. He intends to be there. Whoa! This guy may have gone a little around-the-bend, Colonel. He sounds pretty grandiose to me. Probably one of your New Age fruitcakes," Eberhardt chuckled disdainfully.

Colonel Partridge roared into the car phone, "Bryce, when I want your goddamn opinion, I'll ask for it." With his emotional outburst Partridge betrayed his extreme shock and concern that a mere civilian had learned about the alien landing secret that had JANUS so worried. Then catching himself, he lowered his voice and took a practical tone. "Look, Bryce, you say you've got moderate surveillance on him. What's the highest level of surveillance you boys at AFOSI-CI can do?"

"Well, Colonel, our highest level is A-10: continuous, interactive, high-tech, global, extreme priority."

"Good, Bryce. I want Maguire covered like ants on a picnic basket. You understand?"

"Yes, sir, Colonel. I'll see to it right away. Sounds like he's a hot item, eh?" Eberhardt, his curiosity piqued, tried to draw the Colonel out.

"Bryce, information on this individual is on a need-to-know basis. Listen up. I want you to send any raw information to my office on a continual basis. I don't want any of your people doing any intelligence analysis on it first. This Maguire is strictly a hands-off target, as far as your CI people are concerned. Understood?" Partridge's voiced was clipped and tight.

"Yes, sir," Eberhardt shot back. "Anything else, sir?"

"Yes, Bryce, I want daily reports to my Sandia Chief of Program, more frequently if Maguire's actions require it. Got that? Any screw-ups and you're going to be cleaning outdoor latrines up at Elmendorf with your toothbrush," Partridge added, his voice emphatic with menace. "And I hear the Alaskan winters are really a bitch."

Partridge clicked off his phone in a huff and pulled off the highway to the shoulder. He stopped and sat behind the wheel, soaking in the intelligence which Eberhardt had relayed. Shit, he thought, we've got enough damn trouble with the aliens planning to go public, and now this goddamn civilian abductee investigator is going to poke *his* nose into it. Partridge considered having Maguire terminated at once, but then reflected on the angle that there might be some usefulness to letting him operate a bit longer. There was always the chance that Maguire just might find out details about the real alien landing that could prove helpful to the JANUS group. Besides, the Colonel told himself, by putting continual surveillance on him, we always have the option of terminating the son-of-a-bitch any time we want.

Monday morning was cloudless and mild, with an intense blue vault of sky overhead, framed by Santa Fe National Forest's green mountain ridges lying to the east and west of Santa Fe. Maguire checked out of the conference hotel and headed southwest on I-25. An hour later at Albuquerque, he switched to I-40 westbound, and settled into the six-hour drive to the Hopi Indian Reservation. The long drive would give him some time to think. He wanted to be clearheaded and centered before he talked with Hopi Elder Timothy Katoya.

Maguire had met Timothy Katoya while doing his predoctoral field research on the Hopi Reservation. Maguire had been at the Hopi village of Hotevilla only two days then, when he happened upon a distraught young Hopi mother frantically hurrying up a cliffside trail to her village atop Third Mesa. She was carrying her little girl, who had been bitten by a dark-skinned rattlesnake hiding coiled in some shadows. Maguire quickly drove mother and child the thirty miles to the Indian Health Service Hospital at Keams Canyon, where prompt medical treatment saved the child. It turned out that the little girl was the granddaughter of Timothy Katoya. After the revered tribal elder had learned of the Bahana (White Man)'s good deed, Katoya had been unexpectedly accessible. This was extraordinary, because Hopi traditionals usually held most anthropologists in contempt, as meddlesome and empty questioners who only opened Hopi culture to exploitation by others.

Elder Katoya's revelations had been the focus of Maguire's research for his dissertation topic, "An Anthropological Study of Modern Hopi Oracular Shamanism." In gaining access to Elder Katoya, Maguire had hit the Mother Lode of Native American unpublished oral tradition. The Hopi were considered by other Native American tribes to have kept the purest and most complete spiritual oral traditions. And Katoya was the surviving Keeper of the Hopi Prophecies, the person entrusted with the sacred duty of recalling all the ancient predictions and handing them down to the next generation's Keeper.

These Prophecies were considered private by traditional Hopi, and so sacred that most Westernized Hopi had not heard them, much less any *bahanas*, until Kotoya opened up to Maguire. About the time Maguire had first arrived on the reservation to do his pre-doctoral field studies, Elder Katoya had received a vision telling him that the time had come to share some of the Prophecies with the Bahanas. After the emergency assistance to his granddaughter, Katoya knew that this student anthropologist was the one with whom to begin the sharing with the White Man. So Maguire had learned many things about Hopi spiritual secrets. These secrets included the inner meaning of their legends about the Kachinas, various gods who came down from far away in the sky and regularly visited the Hopi. Maguire heard that the Kachinas came down to do such things as give practical instruction, issue warnings, predict crop outcomes, express compassion, affect the weather, demonstrate invisibility, and teach spirituality. As he listened to the Hopi Elder, Maguire had been struck by the similarities between the characteristics of many of the Hopi's Kachinas and those of the extraterrestrials he had heard about during his research with experiencers.

Maguire felt that during this upcoming visit, there was a good chance that Katoya could fill in the sketchy picture outlined by the petroglyphs Maguire had studied at Bandelier. Those petroglyphs suggested visits by the Star Nations and their promised return. Any more precise information from the Hopi Elder could only help in Maguire's quest for the location and timing of the extraterrestrial public landing.

Maguire left Interstate 40 at Gallup and turned north onto Indian Highway 3. A quarter-mile behind him and 2000 feet above him, a modified small gray single-engine plane with extra-slow-stall-speed wings and a partially sound-suppressed engine, made a similar turn. Captain José DiGiorgio sat in the co-pilot seat across from the pilot, a contract freelancer who formerly flew for CIA's Air America. DiGiorgio frequently glanced at the transponder signal emanating from the left rear chassis frame of Maguire's Pathfinder. The transponder signal was coming in strong. So was the laser audio pick-up signal constantly directed at the Pathfinder's rear window by the plane's optical lock-on technology. So far, no sounds came up the laser signal except the muffled noise of wheels on pavement.

"Kind of boring," DiGiorgio commented to the pilot. "There's no sound coming out of that car. The guy must be a misfit. Doesn't even have any country music on the radio."

The pilot nodded. "These fuckin' national security risks are all a bunch of weirdos. He's probably some goddamn ex-hippie. They should all be taken out. None of 'em would be missed."

"Just don't lose him in that weather up ahead," DiGiorgio

said, looking nervously at the storm brewing in the west. "My ass'll be in a sling if we do."

"Don't worry," the pilot answered. "I flew ridge tops during monsoon season in Cambodia. And I dodged volcanoes during low-ceiling weather in El Salvador." He nodded at the weather front up ahead. "That shit ain't nothing."

Seven miles later, at Ya-Ta-Hey, the Pathfinder took a left fork in the road, as Indian Highway 3 turned west into Arizona toward Window Rock and the Hopi reservation. High above Maguire, the gray plane made a corresponding lazy curve towards the west. Beyond Ganado, the weather front of darkening cumulus clouds towered high, flashing frequently with brilliant strokes of lightning. Dark streaks below the clouds indicated heavy rain near the boundary between Navajo Nation and the Hopi tribal lands. The Thunder Kachinas were rumbling and making their presence known.

Sheets of rain poured down as Maguire crossed Oraibi Wash and down-shifted for the steep climb up the cliff road to Third Mesa and the village of Hotevilla. He stopped at the general store to ask the Hopi proprietor if Timothy Katoya was at home.

"No," the bronze-faced woman said. Then her eyes crinkled with a glance of recognition. "It's Dr. Maguire! It is good to see you again. It has been a while."

"Yes it has. About three years," Maguire replied. "Good to see you. Eleanor, isn't it? It's nice to be back in Hotevilla. Do you have any idea where Elder Katoya is?"

"He's gone to visit his new great-granddaughter in Kykatsmovi. He left early this afternoon, so he should be back soon. He never likes to miss dinner-hour," Eleanor grinned. "You can wait here, out of the rain. His daughter will be driving him in a blue Ford pickup."

The late-afternoon storm swept through rapidly. In forty minutes the rain had stopped, and the sun, now near the western horizon, turned the trailing clouds into a riot of brilliant colors. Red, magenta, tawny, mauve, pink, and a half-dozen other indescribably vibrant shades filtered through the billowing cumulus. Maguire stepped outside to better savor the sunset display. In his opinion, Arizona had the world's most colorful sunsets. A chunking sound of a vehicle navigating the potholes in the dirt road leading to the general store caused him to turn around. The blue pickup was close enough that he could see Timothy Katoya sitting on the passenger side, leaning out the window.

"Is that the *Bahana* anthropologist that Yaponcha, the Dust Devil, has blown in to trouble my old age?" teased the Hopi Elder, head stuck out the window and flashing a gap-toothed smile. His leathery, deeply tanned face was crinkled with deep creases.

"Is that Chaveyo, the Ogre Kachina? I didn't know that he rode in a truck?" Maguire teased back, affectionately.

The blue pickup came to a halt in front of the store. Maguire hopped on the running board, and the truck proceeded forward and then to the right for two blocks. It came to a rest in front of a modest-size cinder-block dwelling. A traditional beehive-shaped outdoor oven stood in the side yard. Maguire stepped off the running board and paused by the porch. Timothy Katoya emerged from the truck with a quickness which belied his seventy years. Katoya stood five-foot-seven, considered on the tall side for Hopi men of his generation. His hair was salt-and-pepper gray, wrapped in a classic Hopi sweat band of deep purple. He wore jeans and a colorful cowboy shirt with a bolo string tie, fastened with a silver clasp, engraved Hopi-style with black inlay. The engraving depicted the Anasazi petroglyph of The Emergence. It showed a human figure (representing the Hopi's ancestors, the Anasazi), emerging from a maze (representing the long migration from the previous worlds into the present world.) Katoya had explained that his mission, as holder of ancient teachings, was to prepare the people for emergence into a new world.

From the truck Katoya's daughter bade them good-bye, explaining that she had to get home and fix dinner for her family. Katoya waved as she drove off.

"Come in, come in," Katoya urged, opening his unlocked front door.

"Thanks," Maguire said, stepping inside onto the smooth floor of closely-fitted sandstone blocks.

The Tribal Elder's house was small, a front room with adjoining kitchen, a bedroom and a bathroom. It was sparsely furnished, but colorfully decorated with clusters of multi-colored corn hanging on the wall, brightly-painted kachina dolls on the mantel, a modernistic picture of a ceremonial dance painted in electric colors, and brick-red pottery objects, hand-painted in black with bold geometric patterns.

Katoya checked on some Hopi stew he had left slowly simmering on the stove. The aroma was wonderful. It reminded Maguire that he hadn't really eaten lunch.

"The stew is ready and I'm hungry," Katoya said, as much for his guest's benefit as his own. "Let's eat."

Over the humble but tasty dinner, followed by after-dinner tea made from a local plant, Katoya and Maguire spent several hours in conversation. They discussed tribal and world events, and caught up on the news in each other's lives. Over the fifteen years they had known each other, a deep level of understanding and respect had grown. Maguire had shown a personal and participatory interest in the tribal culture, and had given careful attention to the Hopi Elder's teachings and responses to his questions. In return, Katoya had shared with Maguire many inner understandings of the Hopi spiritual cosmology and Earth cycles. During some of Maguire's earlier sojourns on the reservation, in an unprecedented privilege, Katoya had allowed Maguire to sit in on selected portions of the training of an apprentice Hopi shaman.

Since Maguire's last visit to the tribal lands, the only other person who knew the entire Hopi Prophecies, a fellow member of the Snake Clan, had died. Katoya was now working intensely with an apprentice Keeper of the Prophecies, to pass on to that young Hopi all the prophecies before Katoya died, or there would be no one to relate the ancient predictions.

Maguire in turn brought Katoya up to date on the significant events in his life. With quiet pride he told the Elder about his discovery of a Summer Solstice observatory at Chaco Canyon.

"Oh, yes," Katoya nodded, "you mean the room with a

wall with a hole, and with the Sun symbol on the other wall. It's the one in the village built by the Ancestor People, the village you call the Pueblo Alto Ruin." Katoya carefully avoided the Navajo term "Anasazi." The last thing he would do is call his ancestors by a *Tavasuh* word. The Hopi still remembered that the Navajo had formerly been a murderous enemy, who had started invading Hopi lands around 1550. Though at peace now, mutual antipathy was still common among many in both tribes.

Maguire inwardly marveled that Katoya knew the intimate details of Pueblo Alto, an ancestor village 200 miles and 800 years to the petroglyphs he had studied at Bandelier Monument. He told Katoya about the star symbols he had seen, and his preliminary attempts to decipher their meaning. He described his own tentative interpretation, but said that he wanted a native expert's interpretation.

"Timothy, you can help me make sure I'm not missing something. I have a hunch that these symbols are saying more than I'm getting," Maguire said.

"You are correct, Roger," Katoya replied. "These symbols are not only a message for friendly eyes, but also a way to hold back a part of the message from strangers' eyes."

"I figured that they were pretty cryptic," Maguire responded.

"Yes. And because you have shown yourself to have the heart of a Hopi, besides your *bahana* heart, I will tell you what else is in the message that it is right for you to know."

Maguire started out by telling Katoya what he got from a reading of the star symbol petroglyph text so far. Maguire deciphered that there had been extraterrestrial contact with the Ancestor People, that the Star Nations had foretold the Anasazi that they would return, and that the predicted time appeared to be in the current era. Maguire also shared with the Elder the information he had obtained from experiencers. They reported that the extraterrestrials had told them that they were going to do a public landing soon.

"Timothy, I want to be there for the Landing. I have this feeling somehow that it is right. The thing I want to know is, where will the extraterrestrials reappear? And when? What can you tell me?"

Katoya's face became solemn, and he leaned forward to speak to Maguire in quiet tones, as though afraid of being overheard. "Your reading of the rocks at what you call Bandelier Monument is pretty good. And what your experiencer people tell you is pretty close to some of what the Star People have told our ancestors. But the rock writings at Bandelier speak of only part of the prophecy given to the Ancestors where the Star Nations will return. What the prophecy says is that the Star Nations will return near a place which divides the waters of the East from the waters of the West, and the Peoples of the North from the Peoples of the South. The 'division of waters' is understood by us to mean what the *bahana* call the Continental Divide."

"Who are the Peoples of the North and South?" Maguire asked.

"That is less clear. But the old Keeper who passed the prophecy on to me thought that the People of the North were what is now called the U.S. He thought that the People of the South most likely meant Mexico, but might include the land which the *bahana* call Central America. Roger, I know you would like things to be real clear, but that is all I know."

"Thank you, Timothy. Actually, that is a big help. I'd like to ask one more question. When will the Star Nations come?"

"Again, the prophecy does not offer the preciseness that is the *bahana* way. It says that there will come a time when a picture of one of the Star People is shown to folks all over the world. And it says that before the Winter Solstice of the year that follows that showing, the Star Nations will come back. That is all I can say, for that is all the prophecy says about the time." The Elder sat back in his chair, and took a sip of tea.

Maguire was stunned and excited by the prophecy information. Here was information to help narrow the area of his search. The landing location was somewhere around where the Continental Divide meets the U.S.-Mexican border. Furthermore, it seemed likely that the triggering event for the timing might well have already happened. He shared with Katoya that the recent world-wide televising of photographs of an extraterrestrial could well have met the criterion for starting the clock on the timing of the Star Nations' return.

The Elder leaned forward again, and said "It may be as you say. I cannot say for sure. But I want to talk to you about another thing, this desire of yours to be at the place where the Star Nations return. Be careful! What you have set out for yourself to do has many dangers. The forces that the Star Nations bring with them are very powerful. Our traditions tell of one man who crept up too close to where they were, when they were not expecting him. His curiosity had gotten the best of him. They say he went mad at what he saw. My advice to you is, be sure it is your heart which tells you that it is all right to be where they land. Do not go if it is just because you are curious. Our tradition says that only one who is right in his heart can get close to the Star People without bringing trouble on himself."

Maguire was about to answer when both men heard a muffled noise, which sounded like an electronic female voice coming from outside the house.

"José, give me a call back. It's been too long since . . ." The sound broke the night stillness, then suddenly stopped.

Outside on the left side of Katoya's house was a figure wearing a flat-black and gray camouflage jumpsuit and a black watch cap with the eye holes pulled down over his face. The figure was crouched below the side window of the front room. A tiny unnoticeable speck was affixed to the bottom corner of the window, from which ran an ultra-thin wire, finer than a hair, down to a tiny recorder no bigger than a wristwatch face.

"Damn it!" José DiGiorgio swore softly at his wife's voice coming over his pager. He desperately fumbled to shut it off. "I told that bitch Juanita a dozen times never to call me at this number."

DiGiorgio yanked the wire, pulling the audio receiver off the window. He turned and began retreating in a half-slouch, half-run towards the neighbors' back yard, an emergency escape route he had checked out in advance. As he retreated, he was muttering to himself. That *cabrona* probably thinks I'm out screwing some decent-looking chick. I oughta do it, just to show the *bruja*. I hardly get any sex at home anyway.

At the sound of the electronic voice, Maguire and Katoya briefly looked at each other. Then Maguire bolted from his chair and went outside to see who was there. As his eyes adjusted to the night, Maguire saw a dark hunched-over figure round the corner into the neighbors' back yard. He advanced cautiously to the back yard, then heard footsteps going around the other side. When he rounded the corner to the other side, he heard a car motor start. While Maguire was racing to the front of the neighbors' house, a dark sedan took off at high speed, a black-hooded figure behind the wheel. Maguire squinted and made out a GSA license plate. The car and the plate looked like the ones used by the federal Bureau of Indian Affairs. As he stared at the BIA car speeding away, Elder Katoya caught up with him.

"It doesn't make sense," Maguire said. "Why would a BIA man be skulking around your house in the dark?"

"Damn BIA!" Katoya exclaimed, spitting onto the dusty ground. He shared the near-universal contempt that Native Americans have for a federal agency perceived as overcontrolling, undermining of traditional life, and self-perpetuating. "I wouldn't put anything past them. At least you scared them off," he chuckled.

"Timothy, you've got connections down at Tribal Headquarters. I memorized that government license plate and I'll write it on a piece of paper. Think you can have someone run an identification on it? Find out who it's registered to?"

"Sure, Roger. I'll do it in the morning. Now, come inside. There's some more tea left. By the way, you can stay at my house as long as you are here. The couch is comfortable enough. I would offer you my bed, but my bones don't do too well if I don't sleep in a bed," the seventy-year-old said.

"Thanks. I'll take you up on that couch tonight. But actually, after I say hello to a few old friends around the village, I'll be leaving tomorrow. But I really appreciate the information you shared from the Prophecies. It will be a great help in my search." Maguire slipped into the formal, respectful manner of addressing a Native American Elder. "And it has been good to catch up on the news with you, and to see that you are in good health, Grandfather."

Katoya bowed slightly in humble recognition of the respectful form of speech. "I see that my *Bahana* grandson has not lost his manners. It is always good to see you, Roger. And now, if you'll excuse me, I'm headed for my bed."

The morning dawned clear and cold at Hotevilla's 5700-foot elevation. Maguire stepped outside of Katoya's house. He walked the short distance over to the south edge of the mesa that Hotevilla village was located on, and sat on the edge of the 150-foot-high sandstone cliff. He stared out at the view of desert and mountain ranges which stretched for a hundred miles. Clearing his mind, he went into alpha state, to better synthesize all the information he had learned the past few weeks.

The cheerful face of Barbara Catalina came to his mind's eye. He thought about how they had met at the Solstice at Pueblo Alto Ruin, and how Barbara had offered to use her remote-viewing ability to help out with the search for the Landing. He recalled her vision that night of the extraterrestrial public landing, and the surprising detail that both of them would be present at it. He reflected on what he had learned from the star petroglyphs at Bandelier, and what Timothy Katoya had told him the Prophecies said about the location and the time of the Star Nations' return. A feeling came over him that today something would happen to help his search. His meditation finished, he saluted the four directions, and rose. He would pay his respects to some old friends in the village before departing.

Agnes Tewaquaptewa's gnarled bronze face broke into a smile, as she prepared to say good-bye to Roger Maguire at the end of his visit. He had been sure to include Grandmother Tewaquaptewa among those he visited on this return trip to Hotevilla. Years before, Agnes had taken pity on him as a young graduate student, and cooked him supper a number of evenings during his field studies. Her blue-corn fry bread and Hopi chili were famous throughout the village. He credited her nurturance and support as a major help over the years.

"May Patusung-Ala, the spirits of the Four Directions, keep you safe on your journey, son," Mrs. Tewaquaptewa said, giving him a farewell blessing.

"And may Kokyang Wu-Uti, Spider Woman, smile on you, Grandmother," Maguire answered with another blessing.

His courtesy visits completed, Maguire headed for the general store, where he had his car parked. As he reached into his pocket for his car keys, he noted with surprise that the car door was slightly ajar. He was sure that he had locked it. Yet the door showed no signs of forced entry. He looked inside to see if anything was taken. His stereo and music tapes were all there. Then he noticed that the hand-woven yarn God's-Eye religious fetish which a Hopi child had made for him was missing from the dashboard. He wondered why would someone break into a car, and then only take an amateurly made weaving with no resale value. And who could break into the car without leaving any marks? Property crime was almost unknown on the Hopi Reservation. He considered whether there was some connection to the dark-garbed figure he had chased last night. As he was musing over this break-in, a faded red Toyota Corolla drove up behind him and stopped.

"Hey, stranger, explored any good ruins lately?" Barbara Catalina jumped out of the car, came up to Maguire and gave him a friendly hug.

"Barbara, what are you doing here? I thought you had gone back to Boulder. How did you find me here?"

"I *did* go back to Boulder," Catalina replied. "But this guy I was supposed to go white water rafting with showed up at the launch site with a female friend. He said she had just come back into town, and they had made up. So, I blew *that* off. Then, when I got home, I tried to do some remote-viewing of that ET landing site you spoke about. You know, to help you out. But I kept getting this very strong image of your face and of the Hopi mesas. Since it kept reappearing, and wouldn't let me focus on anything else. I took it to be a sign that I should reconnect with you. I also figured it meant that I would find you on the Hopi reservation. So I put a message on my answering machine that I'd be gone for a while, got a girl friend to watch my house, and here I am. I'm ready to go with you and help you find the Landing, that is, if you want my help."

Maguire was taken by surprise. He had been thinking of his search as an individual quest. But then he reflected on the synchronicities that Barbara had met him just as he was making the archaeo-astronomy find of his career, and that her psychic sense had demonstrated itself to be very strong. And she had earlier offered to assist him in his search by her psychic abilities.

"Barbara, I really appreciate your offer. But I really don't have a precise idea of where to go."

"Silly!" Catalina grinned. "That's where I can be of help."

"Well, you gotta know that my style of field reconnaissance is pretty spartan," Maguire replied. "Like a sleeping bag on the desert sand many a night. And using a stream for baths. And I'm not in a position to pay you for your help."

"Roger, I've done a fair amount of roughing it outdoors in the Rocky Mountains. The streams in southern New Mexico can't be as cold as some of those creeks in the Rockies. And did you hear me ask for any money? I can operate for a while on some savings I brought with me. You know, Women's Lib, and all that?" she teased.

"Barbara, do you know that you came into my meditation this morning?" Maguire said, his resistance softening.

"What time was that?" Barbara asked.

"Right before nine," Maguire replied.

"Rog, do you know that was about the time I was driving near the town of Aztec? I was thinking about the Anasazi ruins they have at the National Monument there, and I got this strongest sense of connection with you. How's that for a 'coincidence?'" she asked.

"Probably not a coincidence," Maguire conceded. "Tell you what, let's talk about this some more over lunch. There's a great restaurant at the Cultural Center on Second Mesa."

"You're on," Barbara said, smiling.

Secakuku's Restaurant was moderately full, with a typi-
cal mix of Caucasian tourists, Navajos passing through, and
Hopi locals. A Hopi waitress, dressed in the traditional black
and white dress, white boots, and red sash of the Hopi
maiden, showed Catalina and Maguire to a corner booth.
Over a lunch of Hopi stew and blue corn *piki* bread, they
discussed the available facts. He asked Barbara whether she
had obtained any more psychic insights into the location and
timing of the extraterrestrial public landing. Catalina said
she had not. But remembering the Landing visions she had
been given by the extraterrestrials, she reminded him that
they showed the location in the desert mountains, along with
the vision of a valley filled with clover and another scene of
a desert antelope reaching down to lap up some water. And
that in connection with this scene she had heard the word
"soles".

Maguire's face suddenly lit up. He hurriedly pulled out
a map of New Mexico and Arizona, and spread it out on the
table. He invited Barbara to join him in figuring out what
could be pieced together by joining what she had seen psychically with the information Katoya had given from the Hopi
Prophecy. His finger traced down the Continental Divide as
it ran south through New Mexico. He noted that the section
right before it plunged into Mexico was called the Animas
Mountains.

"Barbara, 'Animas' is the Spanish word for 'souls.' You
heard the word 'soles' in connection with the vision of the
mountainous scene near the Landing site. The ETs must have
meant the Animas Mountains!"

"Wow, Rog, this is encouraging! Looks like we're starting to make sense out of the message that Arica gave me. Let
me look at that map." Barbara stared a few moments at the
map, then pointed her finger and became excited. "Look at
this! The town nearest the Animas Mountains is Cloverdale!
Get it? The ETs showed me a valley of clover. They were giving me the picture-name of Cloverdale. And look at the town
that's the next nearest to the Animas Mountains. It's called

Antelope Wells. See! That fits the vision I was shown of an antelope drinking some water. Rog, I think we've got it!"

"That's still a lot of desert area." Maguire made a quick calculation of the area fitting that description, after checking the map's mileage scale. "There still could be as many as 400 square miles where the Landing could take place. For sure these coordinates do help narrow down the search. But we still need to know where exactly the Landing will be. And we need to know the actual time."

"*We?*" said Catalina, disingenuously. "You mean I'm allowed along?"

Maguire discussed the uncertainties and risks Barbara would face in joining the search for the Landing site. She countered each potential problem he raised with her basic I'm-a-big-girl-now argument. He finally ended by saying, with mock gravity, "If you come, you have to have given your prior informed consent."

Barbara replied without hesitation, "Dr. Maguire, you couldn't keep me away with a crowbar." She gave him a brief, friendly hug. "Then, I'm in?"

Maguire smiled. "You're in."

Katoya's daughter's sister-in-law agreed to keep Catalina's car safe, in exchange for the use of it once a week to do shopping at the big trading post at Second Mesa. Maguire and Catalina transferred her luggage to Maguire's Pathfinder. Then they headed south on Arizona State Highway 87 to Winslow, Arizona, where it intersected with Interstate 40.

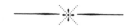

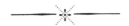

Chapter 4

CATALINA and Maguire were sitting in a corner booth in Muchacho Jaime's Cafe. They were its only customers this hot mid-afternoon. Its adobe walls were hung with brilliantly-colored serapes and two dramatic black-velvet paintings, one of a bullfighter, and another of a partially-draped maiden about to be sacrificed on a stone altar by an Aztec priest. Maguire had told Barbara that Muchacho Jaime served the best Mexican food in Winslow. The idea of a mid-afternoon stop for a snack had appealed to them. The break would also give Maguire an opportunity to clear his answering machine messages from his office in Chatsworth, California.

After the waitress took their orders, he excused himself and went to the pay phone. He passed a man with short brown hair, who was coming into the dining area. The man seated himself at a booth near theirs, opened up his newspaper, and held it up in front of him to read.

Among the several messages on Maguire's answering machine was one which caught his particular interest. It was a call from Don Cortlan. Maguire had met Cortlan at the 1992 MIT Abduction Study Conference. Cortlan had accosted him after Maguire had delivered a presentation about his experiencer research. Cortlan had requested a copy of his paper, "A Psychiatric Anthropological Study of Extraterrestrial Encounter Experiencers." Cortlan had identified himself as a free-lance reporter and stringer for the *Baltimore Sun*. He had conducted a lengthy interview with Maguire about his findings from his work with experiencers. When the interview was never published, Maguire had not thought too much about it, figuring that some editor had a poor impression of the whole extraterrestrial subject. But afterwards he noticed that Cortlan hardly ever seemed to appear in print. Furthermore, Maguire wondered how Cortlan could afford the Jaguar he drove, and the finest imported Danish aqvavit that was Cortlan's customary drink. Free-lance reporters who don't get published don't usually make big money. Maguire had heard a rumor about Cortlan at the MIT Conference — that he had come into a sizable inheritance, and actually didn't need to work. There had also been another rumor, that Cortlan had CIA connections. After the Conference Maguire had learned the truth of the second rumor.

Over the years since that conference, Cortlan had pursued frequent phone contact with Maguire, despite the anthropologist's initial lack of interest in cultivating a relationship. During these conversations, Cortlan always exhibited great interest in Maguire's work, wanting to keep abreast of what Maguire was finding out about extraterrestrials from his work with experiencers. During this odd, series of contacts, Cortlan also gave Maguire unsolicited leaks about UFO and extraterrestrial information from his intelligence contacts. The reporter seemed to want to help Maguire by furnishing reports and leaks about behind-the-scenes activity by those maintaining the UFO Cover-Up, as well as about UFO investigators' progress in exposing UFO reality.

Cortlan had told Maguire that his source for the leaks was an official within the CIA. What he did not tell Maguire was that his source was Roderick Birdsall, Chief of Special Projects within CIA's Intelligence Directorate. Nor did he tell Maguire that he did not have to pump Birdsall for the information. Rather it was that Birdsall who took the initiative in contacting Cortlan, feeding him selected information, and telling him precisely what he could and could not share. And certainly Cortlan did not tell Maguire that Birdsall was a member of the JANUS UFO-control group, because Cortlan himself did not know that fact. Maguire had never been able to figure which side Cortlan was on. His best guess was that Cortlan might be playing both sides of the street. Maguire made a mental note to call Don Cortlan before Barbara and he left Muchacho Jaime's.

He sat down next to Barbara just as the waitress was coming with their fajitas and limonadas. Down at the end of the bar at one end of the dining room, the TV programming switched to a special announcement. The announcer spoke with a dramatic tone.

"Tonight, at 8:00 p.m. on KSWL, don't miss a special documentary on space aliens visiting the Earth. This program, 'Alien Visitors,' will be brought to you by the Boeing Corporation, a leading pioneer in aviation and aerospace technology. During this exciting program, you will see actual close-up film footage of a UFO hovering low over the runway of a Southwest military installation!" The TV picture cut away to a brief filmed segment of a not-too-distant, structured UFO craft above a desert runway near a cluster of parked F-117A Stealth fighters.

"You will see an actual photograph of an extraterrestrial walking near a landed flying saucer!" The TV picture switched to a quick glimpse of a 4-foot-tall humanoid extraterrestrial with immense dark eyes, the hull of his disc-shaped craft in the background. "This startling photograph was not taken by a civilian. It was released by the U.S. Air Force in response to a court order under the Freedom of Information Act.

"Tonight you will also see experts interviewed about the avalanche of widespread, professionally documented cases of extraterrestrials visiting ordinary citizens." The screen switched to a picture of a distinguished-looking middle-aged man being interviewed, identified by caption as a "psychologist and alien-encounter expert." The psychologist was saying, "The extraterrestrials are here. Numerous professional colleagues of mine draw the same conclusions. We estimate that, taking just the U.S. into account, hundreds of people are contacted each day and night." The screen changed to a still photo of a large oval-eyed, flat-featured extraterrestrial face, with announcer voice-over. "This is an actual alien intelligent being, one of many visiting Earth on a regular basis! Yes, alien beings are beckoning mankind to join the galactic community. You and your family should be sure to watch this vitally important program! Tell your friends to watch, too. Remember the time, tonight at 8:00 o'clock, right here on KWSL-TV. Don't miss it!

"And Boeing Corporation wants you to remember that, now more than ever, America needs Space Station Alpha built without any further Congressional delay. Let your elected Representatives know that, in the era of extraterrestrial contacts, America needs a permanent space presence. Boeing: meeting America's future — now more than ever — in space!"

Maguire and Catalina stared at the TV set speechless, their forks frozen in mid-air as they gaped in astonishment.

"My God!" Maguire exclaimed, "did you just hear what they said?"

"I *never* thought I would hear those kinds of things on a regular television program!" Catalina responded. "Rog, does this mean that the Government is about to come out with an announcement?"

"I don't think so," Maguire replied with a cautious tone, "at least not yet. What I *do* think is that this program is a kind of test marketing by the 'friendlies' within the government, the ones who are willing to release UFO information. I think they're just trying to gauge how people will react to a no-holds-barred kind of presentation of extraterrestrial reality. But, imagine! A big prestigious defense contractor like Boeing, putting their corporate reputation on the line, to sponsor a documentary about extraterrestrials visiting the Earth! And they didn't say maybe or mince any words, either, just the ETs are here. There it is, get used to it."

Catalina leaned forward and spoke more in a more confidential tone. "You know, I got an intuitive flash while that announcement was on. I got the feeling that the ETs are mentally pushing the government to get people ready for open contact. Wow! Now this really gives me an even stronger desire to find out about the ET landing."

"Yeah, I'm feeling the same thing — a real push to get clear information about the Landing, Barbara. We need more than ever to nail down the timing of that. By the way, in my phone messages I had one from an acquaintance of mine asking to give him a call. He often has good information on UFO stuff. So, if you'll excuse me, I'll return his phone call while you finish your fajita."

Maguire went to the pay phone and placed a call to Don Cortlan. Cortlan, it turned out, was in, and eager to talk about some important news developments. Nevertheless, his voice maintained its usual dry, pedantic style.

"Hi, Rog." Don Cortlan immediately shared his first bit of news. "Have you heard that the Congressional Committee on Science, Space, and Technology is supposed to be holding hearings within the next couple of months? I hear that the subject will be UFO crashes in the 1940's."

"Really? That's a *most* interesting development. Do you mean that the Committee will dig into what happened to that saucer from the crash in 1947?" Maguire asked.

"Oh, I don't know that they'll get into that one directly," Cortlan replied. "More like, the Committee will call on the Air Force generals who were involved back in the '40's, and ask them under oath to reveal what actually went on. They'll let the Generals establish where the trail will lead from there. I hear that the Committee Chairman, Congressman Stevens, got steaming mad when he asked the Secretary of Defense for UFO information, and all he was given was a 30-year-old copy of Project Blue Book. A person in his office staff said that you could hear Stevens four offices down, when he opened that package from the Air Force."

"Don, I haven't heard anything about Congressional hearings. So, are you saying that the Committee is going to give those Generals congressional immunity from their National Security oaths, so that they can tell everything?" Maguire asked, hardly containing his excitement.

"That is supposedly what's being worked on," Cortlan answered. "The rumor is that Congressman Stevens is going to hold up NASA's budget in his committee as hostage, to force the Administration to agree to make the Generals testify about Roswell and some other saucer retrievals. Once the President blinks, then Congressman Stevens is going to call congressional hearings. His chief of staff says he's sure that Stevens has the committee votes to grant congressional immunity to the Generals."

"Don, you're really producing today," Maguire said, pumping up his source's ego. "Do you have any other interesting tidbits you can tell?"

"I was saving the biggest news for last," Cortlan responded. "But first, do the words 'Project Epiphany' mean anything to you? Have you heard anything about it?"

"No, I haven't," Maguire replied. "Should I?"

"Not necessarily. But I'll tell you this, Roger, it's the biggest thing on the horizon, according to my source, who is very, very close to the center of it."

"Okay, okay," Maguire said, slightly annoyed at having Cortlan tantalize him by drawing the news out. "Spill it. What *is* Project Epiphany?"

"Hold onto your chair," Cortlan replied, with dramatic flair. "This Project Epiphany is supposed to be an effort by a group of a few internationally known UFO researchers and a few highly placed governmental officials to make pre-planned official contact with the aliens. This group will be a contact team, acting as representatives of Earth. My source said that they will be seeking to have ongoing dialogue with the 'Visitors,' and to make that dialogue public as they go."

"Wait a minute!" Maguire exclaimed. "Do you mean to tell me that a group of civilians is going to meet with the ETs directly, and aren't they going to involve the official government in it?"

"Yes and no," Cortlan answered. "This group is not the government, but they *will* have several governmental types in the group. You know, somebody representing the executive branch or the military, and someone from the U.N., according to what I've heard. But the other members of this contact group will be civilians from various countries who have been deeply involved in investigating alien contacts."

"Now, Don, I gotta know. Did you get this information from your ole buddy Rod Birdsall at CIA?"

"No, no, Roger," Cortlan protested, "Not at all. This came from a totally separate source. A really interesting guy. A former Navy pilot, who has worked for practically every intelligence agency there is: Defense Intelligence Agency, Army Intelligence, the Defense Nuclear Agency, NSA, DoD's Advanced Research Projects Agency, Naval Intelligence, you name it. But the last few years, he's been talking and acting really metaphysical.

Word has it that he got into metaphysics while he was studying paranormal phenomena at Stanford Research Institute. He was under a National Security Agency contract back then. But it seems like he really got the bug. Now he has been using parapsychology to try to influence how things happen."

"You're going to tell me this guy's name, of course?" Maguire said in a mock-sweet tone.

"Sure," Cortlan dead-panned. "Commander Jacques Stone. Or Dr. Jacques Stone, as he is more properly known these days,"

"And how does this Dr. Stone know about Project Epiphany?" Maguire asked.

"Well, what I've heard is that he *is* one of the contact team of Project Epiphany," Cortlan said. "But that's only a rumor. Stone certainly isn't saying that. In fact, when I called him, he was evasive about who was in the Project, and acted as if he had no real knowlege about who the people who were. But this other source I have, sorry, I can't name him, he says that Jacques is right smack in the middle of the Project."

"Don, where can I find Dr. Stone?"

"That's a good question," Cortlan replied. "The guy is always on the go."

"Well, can you at least tell me where he lives."

"Sure, Roger. He lives in a little town called Mount Carmel. It's in Maryland, about 20 miles due east of Fort Meade," Cortlan said slowly, dropping the installation's name with teasingly droll humor.

"What!?" Maguire exclaimed. "You mean he lives practically in the back yard of National Security Agency headquarters?"

"Easy," Cortlan said, a smile in his voice. "Nothing to worry about. He's retired from the spook life. Besides, he'd rather chase poltergeists, anyway."

"One more thing, Don. Do you know what the timetable of this Project Epiphany group is? When they plan to make contact?"

"That's not easy to say. I don't have anything definite on that from my source. I got the general impression that it was pretty soon. In the next year, maybe. Say, why don't you talk to Dr. Stone yourself? Maybe you'll have more luck than I did. Well, I gotta get off here. Gotta get my kid to his riding lessons."

"Thanks for all the information, Don. I really appreciate it."

"Don't mention it." Cortlan started to get off the phone, then stopped himself. "Say, I forgot one more thing. Kinda important, too. Besides the Project Epiphany group, there's supposed to be another group trying to make contact with the aliens. This other group is supposed to be made up of people who have links to MJ-12. They're supposed to have some pretty heavy people in their group, important, highly-influential people. The word is that these people intend to be the *only* group present at the alien public landing. They want to have the power that comes with that. I heard about all this from Jacques. He didn't sound too happy about it either."

"Wait a minute," Maguire interrupted. "Does this other group have a name?"

"Not that I've heard of," Cortlan replied. "Well, excuse me, now, Roger. I absolutely have to get going."

Maguire hung up the receiver and stood there stunned. Cortlan had just laid bombshell after bombshell on him. Congressional UFO hearings. A civilian ET-contact effort called Project Epiphany. A rival group of heavies, name unknown, membership unknown, trying to secure exclusive presence at the landing for dark motives. Maguire's own plan to be present at the ET landing had just became immensely more complicated.

He came back to the table and shared with Barbara the news that Cortlan had given him. Catalina was excited to hear that there were finally going to be public Congressional hearings on UFOs. Maguire also told her about the Project Epiphany contact group, and asked her quick reaction from the standpoint of her psychic intuition.

"I don't know, Rog. I get pretty good initial feelings about this Project Epiphany. They seem to be a group with good intentions. But there's something I'm feeling that I can't quite put my finger on. A sense of danger, I guess is what I'm picking up. I'd have to take some more time to look at this Project

Epiphany more closely. I need to get a clearer idea of what I'm picking up."

Maguire then told her about the rival group of "heavies" and their plan to monopolize public ET contact.

"Oh, wow!" Catalina exclaimed. "I get a real bad feeling about those people! I get this tingle all over, what I call my super-danger feeling. I get it whenever I run across danger-ous or really bad people. And it's coming through loud and clear! We've really got to be on the watch-out for those people."

"But how can we do that?" Maguire said. "We don't even know who they are!"

"I don't know. But I'll tell you this: if we get close to one of them, I have a feeling I'd pick upon the danger signal with-out a doubt. It's *that* strong."

"At any rate, my thought is that we would do well to learn as much as we can about this Project Epiphany group," Maguire said. "They seem to have the kind of people that could actually pull off a public ET encounter."

"But how do we know that the ETs are going to pay any attention to the Project Epiphany group?" Catalina asked.

"We can't be sure," Maguire answered. "But if we can learn what they're up to, it could increase our chances of being at the right place at the right time. Barbara, I think it's time for us to pay a little visit to this Dr. Jacques Stone. Don Cortlan said that he knew something about Project Epiphany, and might actually be one of the members."

"Count me in," Catalina said enthusiastically. "Where does he live?"

"It's a ways from here," Maguire answered. "Maryland."

"Ouch! That's quite a drive," Catalina said, her enthusi-asm dipping as she anticipated the weariness. Then she brightened. "Say! As long as we're headed east, we've got to go right through upper New Mexico, right?"

"Yeah. Why?"

"Well, we want to get clearer about the ET landing, don't we?"

"Yes."

"I get some of my clearest psychic viewing when I spend

some time in a sacred energy space. And one of my favorite energy spaces is right near where we met."

"You mean Chaco Canyon?" Maguire asked.

"Yes. Specifically, the great kiva at Casa Rinconada. I go there when I've got something super-important to pick up on. I always do some of my clearest 'remote viewing,' as you call it, there."

Maguire was familiar with this enormous round, red rock ceremonial chamber, built halfway into the ground. It had three ceremonial altars in the middle, and a seating bench built into the wall all the way around. The 800-year-old Anasazi religious structure was now roofless and dramatically open to the New Mexico sky. During his few visits to Casa Rinconada, while he was doing contract archaeological surveying at Chaco, he had to admit that he had been impressed by some indefinable feeling there. "Okay, Barbara. That sounds like a plan. It's not that far off I-40 after we pass Gallup. If we get going, we can get there tonight."

After Maguire and Catalina left Muchacho Jaime's, the man sitting behind his newspaper two booths down folded his paper and went to his car. Zeta Three pulled a radio microphone out from under his dashboard and made a full report to Major Eberhardt on "Fellow Traveler's" and Catalina's conversation, plans, and travel destinations.

The summer desert air was at its coolest. The dim light of false dawn reached gently into Maguire's tent. He awoke and sat up in his sleeping bag. Rubbing the sleep out of his eyes, he looked out the tent door towards Catalina's tent, and noticed that she wasn't in it. They had gotten into the campground at Chaco Canyon after dark last night. Maguire was tired from the long drive and had not heard Catalina rise. Where was she, he wondered, and what was she up to? On a hunch, he got dressed, and headed his car over towards Casa Rinconada. The first rays of the shimmering edge of the rising sun had crested the canyon rim. No one else was stirring in the entire Park. He savored the rich silence, broken only by the gritty crunch of his hiking boots as he walked up the sandy footpath from the parking turnout. As he approached the edge of the sunken Anasazi structure, he looked down into the kiva and spotted Catalina. She was seated on the sandy floor in the middle, sitting cross-legged facing east, with her upturned palms resting on her knees and her eyes closed, deeply focused inwardly. She had a thin Navajo blanket with bold geometric patterns in faded hues wrapped around her over her nightgown. He was about to turn away so as not to disturb her, when Catalina opened her eyes and looked up in his direction.

"I'll be finishing up in a couple of minutes, Rog. I'll meet you down at the car," she said.

As Catalina approached the car, Maguire noticed a gentle radiant glow to her expression.

"So, how long were you down in there, Barbara?"

"I'm not sure. About a hour, I suppose," she replied.

"You were remote-viewing the ET landing?"

"Yes. I got some clear impressions, too," Catalina answered. "I knew I would here at this kiva. It's really powerful."

"So, are you going to tell me about what you saw, or would you rather do that over breakfast?" Maguire asked.

"Well, I *did* get kind of chilled, walking over to the kiva, and then sitting still on that cold floor for a hour."

"I'll build a fire just as soon as we get back to our campsite," Maguire offered. "You can warm up while I fix breakfast. Then we can talk. By the way, how come you didn't change into your warm day clothes before you went on your hike to the kiva?"

"I wanted to keep as little between me and the surrounding environment as possible," she answered. "Heavy street clothes seem to get in the way. But this thin old Indian blanket doesn't seem to interfere with the subtle energies I wanted to tune into. And it kept me somewhat warm. Actually, if it were warmer and I were in a more isolated place, I'd do my visioning work without clothes. I do my very best deep work in total contact with the environment. That way there's *no* interference. It's an old Indian way that was passed down to me."

"Whatever works," Maguire said, nonchalantly. "Let's get you back to camp and that campfire."

Catalina lifted her cup of steaming coffee in a salute gesture to Maguire. "Umm, that warmth is just what I needed."

Maguire was kneeling by the fire, stirring some salsa into a frying pan with scrambled eggs in it. "Barbara, you're in for a treat. This morning's menu item is my breakfast specialty, an old 'Mexican' recipe I call *huevos chingados,*" he said with a quiet smile.

"Gee," Catalina said, "I haven't heard of that before. But it does smell good. I'll be ready for some when it's done."

Over breakfast Catalina told Maguire what had come to her during her visioning at Casa Rinconada. After going into altered consciousness for a while, she had perceived in her mother's album a picture of a great-uncle who, she was told, had been a revered Ojibwa medicine man. After being in respectful silence for a while with the Indian, she put out a question to him about who he was. The figure spoke in her mind by way of response. He showed her a picture of himself as a younger man bent over Catalina's mother when she was much younger. Catalina saw him using an eagle's wing to fan the smoke from a bundle of smoldering sage all up and down over her mother's body, as she lay on a blanket looking pale and delirious. Catalina flashed on an old memory of her mother telling about how she had almost died from influenza when she was twelve, and how her uncle had done a curing ceremony after the white doctor had told her mother's parents that nothing further could be done to cure the illness. Catalina remembered her mother's voice getting very quiet, as she told Catalina that the next day her fever broke, and she was well by sundown.

Catalina was encouraged to know that this figure was her great-uncle. She respectfully asked this "grandfather" if he would tell her what the ancient traditions could say about the ET landing. The shaman uncle made a gesture with his hands, and she got a mental picture of the rolling fields of clover that she had seen before in her "dream." She then "saw" the desert antelope bending down to drink from a shallow natural well, which she had also seen previously in her "dream." Next she was shown a scene of a shiny metallic disc circling above a low range of desert mountains below leaden skies filled with dark low clouds. The long angled rays of the sun in the west broke through a hole in the cloud cover and illuminated a small patch of land below a particular peak in the range. The picture "zoomed in," and Catalina could see the details of the mountain peak right under the spacecraft. She made a mental note of the way the individual ridges and slopes lay on this particular peak, so that she could recognize it if she saw it again. She could see a swirl of large snowflakes falling onto the stately limbs of the saguaro cactus, the faded pods of the yucca plants, and the other desert plants around. But there was no significant accumulation of snow on the ground. Then this picture dissolved, and the image of the "grandfather" came back into her mind's eye. Catalina heard an old resonant male voice in her head, saying with serious yet warm tones that she should pay close attention to what she had been shown. She had important work to accomplish before her next birthday. Catalina started to ask her great-uncle about what she had been shown, but his image slowly faded away from her.

"So, that's what I got, Rog." Catalina set down her coffee cup by the fire, and poured herself another cup from a blackened metal pot resting on some coals.

"*Real* interesting, Barbara. It looks like you got some more confirmation of the location of the landing. Furthermore, we now know that the landing site is on the *west* side of the Animas Mountains."

"How do we know that?"

"Because of the slanting light you saw shining on the mountainside. Slanting afternoon light only falls on the west side. And, now, with your memory of what that specific peak looks like, and with our information from Timothy Katoya that the site is where the Continental Divide meets the U.S.-Mexican border, it looks like we'll be able to locate the precise peak that is above the landing site. That's *great* information!"

"But, Roger, what about the time of the landing? My great-uncle only showed me that it will be in the afternoon. But that could be any day."

"You have gotten more information than that," Maguire responded with enthusiasm. "You said that you saw snow starting to fall on the cactus, but that there was none on the ground. I take it you mean not even any snow in the crevices and shadows?"

"That's right," Catalina replied.

"That says to me that you were looking at the first snow-fall of winter. The winter freezes and snows had not come yet to knock the pods off the yucca or accumulate on the ground. First snowfall puts the Landing in early Winter. That narrows down the time frame considerably."

"But, Rog, that doesn't tell us what year," Catalina rejoined, and then stopped herself. "Wait! My great-uncle said that I had important work to accomplish before my next birthday. Meeting the ETs is certainly very important work. And my next birthday is in this year. December 22 to be exact. Do you suppose...?"

"...that what he said means that the Landing will happen in early Winter *this* year?" Maguire finished her question. "That's what it sounds like to me. Which means we've got a lot to do before then. We'd better pack up, hit the road, and see if we can connect up with this Dr. Stone."

Stopping at an Albuquerque gas station, Maguire made a phone call to Mount Carmel, Maryland. To his pleasant surprise, Dr. Stone answered the phone personally. Maguire dropped Don Cortlan's name as the person who had referred him to Dr. Stone, and told him his reason for wanting to come talk with him. Dr. Stone turned out to be charming and cordial on the phone, and graciously invited Maguire to come to his house for a chat. Maguire and Stone agreed to meet in four days.

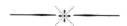

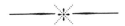

Chapter 5

THE peaceful green countryside rolling by along the Spellman Expressway was a welcome change from the traffic snarls of the Capital. A quarter hour ago, Catalina and Maguire had left Washington, D.C. behind and headed east. It felt good to get out into the Maryland country. As they were driving by the Patuxent Wildlife Research Center portion of the Expressway, Catalina spotted a doe and her fawn half-hidden back in among the trees, nibbling on a green shrub.

This had been Catalina's first trip to the South and to Washington, D.C. After leaving Albuquerque, they had taken I-40 east through Amarillo and Oklahoma City, then on up to Durham. At Durham they turned north on I-85 to Richmond, the old Confederate Capitol, then headed up I-95 into Washington, D.C. Now, after three days of long driving, Maguire and Catalina taking turns at the wheel, they were only 30 miles from their goal of Mt. Carmel, Maryland.

A few minutes later, Maguire came upon the exit for State Highway 32. He exited onto the Highway 32 expressway, and headed east across the Fort George Meade Reservation. Fifteen seconds later, a late-model white Ford sedan with Virginia license plates also exited onto Highway 32 eastbound. Dressed in the stylishly casual white suit and fedora of a Southern gentleman and wearing designer sunglasses, Captain José DiGiorgio drove precisely fifteen seconds behind Maguire and Catalina, keeping them in view from a safe distance.

A huge old Army installation, the Fort Meade Reservation stretched for five miles. Although it was still the headquarters for the Army Signal Corps, Fort Meade's largest and most famous tenant was the National Security Agency. As they drove deeper into the Military Reservation, they spotted the NSA's tan, nine-story central building, surrounded by a three-story, A-shaped green building. The entire NSA complex was surrounded by a ten-foot-high Cyclone fence topped with multiple rows of barbed wire. Inside this fence was a second fence, consisting of five strands of high-voltage wires attached to wooden posts at regular intervals. Behind this was a third tall Cyclone fence. Armed guards, with attack dogs pulling at their leashes, were visible patrolling inside the perimeter of the third fence. The roof of the main building was thick with various antennas, including two enormous radar domes shaped like giant golf balls, parabolic microwave dishes, and a huge white satellite dish.

"Brrrr!" Catalina exclaimed to Maguire, "that place gives me the creeps. I'm getting terrible vibes around here. What *is* that?"

"Well, I'm not surprised. To tell the truth, it kinda gives me the willies, too. *That* is the National Security Agency, the Defense Department's 'CIA'. It's ten times bigger than the CIA, and is probably the agency containing the folks most involved in controlling UFO information. But a number of us researchers think that there is yet another agency even more secret."

"You're not going to detour to that Headquarters building, are you?" Catalina asked worriedly, as they approached the entrance road turnoff.

"Not on your life," Maguire replied. "The only reason we're cutting through this military reservation at all is because it's the shortest route out to the coast and Mt. Carmel. Dr. Stone is expecting us to get there today, and I want to get us there as early as possible."

They soon connected up with Interstate 97. Seven miles later down the Interstate, they exited onto State Highway 100, and finally onto Highway 177 for their last six miles into Mount Carmel.

The warm afternoon had turned humid along the Maryland coast. The blue-gray sky was billowing up with white and gray strato-cumulus clouds, signaling the possibility of rain. Jacques Stone's home lay two miles southwest of Mt.

Carmel, on the water's edge where the Magothy River forms an inlet of Chesapeake Bay. The road changed from blacktop to gravel as it ran through lush woods. Only a few scattered houses were visible along the road. Where the road dead-ended on the bay, they found Commander Stone's house. As they pulled into the lush gravel driveway leading up to an attractive Cape Cod-style house, a golden retriever came out and barked a friendly greeting. A few moments later, a white-haired woman in her sixties, wearing a spotless white apron over a floral-print house dress, appeared on the porch. Several seconds later she was joined by a tall, distinguished-looking gentleman with ruddy complexion and a mane of snowy-white hair, dressed in neatly pressed shirt and slacks. The couple peered at the parked Pathfinder, and gave a friendly wave as Maguire and Catalina got out.

"Dr. Maguire, I presume?" the white-maned gentleman said, smiling and extending his hand.

"Dr. Stone? It's a pleasure to meet you," Maguire replied.

"And this must be Barbara," Stone said, turning to beam at her. Mrs. Stone smiled courteously at both the guests.

"Hello, Dr. and Mrs. Stone," Catalina replied.

"Oh, please, we're just Jacques and Lucy," Dr. Stone said modestly.

"And just call me Roger."

"Come in," Lucy said. "Can I get you folks some lemonade?"

"Sounds great," Catalina answered, with Maguire nodding in agreement.

As they entered the house, a late-model Ford sedan slowed to a stop a quarter-mile down the road. After surveilling the Stone house through his binoculars, José DiGiorgio set up a small parabolic acoustical antenna on the car's roof. After sweeping the house with an infrared scanner and determining that the targets of investigation were in the study, DiGiorgio directed an invisible-wavelength laser beam at the study window, and put on what appeared to be small Walkman-like earphones. He listened as the conversations in the study created the faintest vibrations against the window pane. These in turn were transmitted back by the laser beam to DiGiorgio's surveillance equipment.

After settling down the guests with some drinks in Jacques's walnut-paneled study, Lucy Stone excused herself and left. Jacques sat in a leather reclining chair, the wall behind him a floor-to-ceiling bookcase crammed with books. Maguire noticed that many of the titles were on metaphysical topics, although there were also numerous books on physics and UFOs. He also noted several framed old photos of Navy fighter planes, no doubt mementos of Stone's days as a Navy pilot. After getting acquainted, Maguire steered the conversation around to what brought them there.

"Dr. Stone, excuse me, Jacques, I've been talking with Don Cortlan," Maguire began. He noticed that Stone's pleasant set to his face twitched almost imperceptibly when Cortlan's name came up.

"Oh, yes, Don Cortlan," Stone replied. "He does seem to get around a lot," he added noncommittally.

"Don said that you might be able to help us with some information," Maguire continued. "But first let me tell you why we're here."

He decided to trust Stone and tell him about his quest to be at the first public extraterrestrial landing. Maguire also told him about the paranormal information sources which prompted his search, because of Stone's reputation of being well acquainted with metaphysical realities. He figured that a man with Stone's background could be immensely helpful if he chose to be. And if Stone turned out untrustworthy, there was not a great loss, because the group that conducted the Cover-Up would probably find out about his mission soon enough anyway, Maguire reasoned. So he proceeded to tell Stone about the cumulative information he had obtained from his research with experiencers, which pointed to a major extraterrestrial landing, one which would involve official extraterrestrial ambassadors meeting with representatives of Earth. He related to Stone the growing sense of mission Barbara and he had felt to be present for that Landing. To his surprise, Stone nodded understandingly, and with just a hint of a smile.

Catalina chimed in with her account of how she had been directed by various psychic indications to join up with Maguire in this quest. The three of them became relaxed, and spent some time in getting better acquainted. The Stones invited Maguire and Catalina to stay for dinner and visit some more.

Adjourning to the handsome formal dining room, they shared anecdotes about UFO experiences over dinner, and exchanged opinions on various UFO investigators and spokespersons. Maguire was struck by Stone's broad-mindedness and his metaphysical perspective on extraterrestrial visitation. Maguire thought to himself that he'd have to broaden his preconceptions about at least some older military men.

After dinner, Maguire, Catalina and Jacques Stone sat once again in Stone's study and traded views on where each thought the extraterrestrial phenomenon was heading. Lucy Stone had excused herself to watch her television shows. At a pause in the conversation, Maguire decided to get to his main reason for the visit.

"Jacques, maybe this is the time to bring up the matter of Project Epiphany," Maguire said. He noticed a crinkling around Stone's eyes as he mentioned the Project. Stone said nothing in response, so Maguire filled in the awkward silence. "Don Cortlan says you know something about the Project. In fact, I don't want to be disingenuous, Jacques; he suggested that you are a participant in the Project."

"And what do you know about this Project?" Stone inquired, skillfully deflecting the question about his own participation.

Maguire let the side-stepping go for the moment, figuring he could take it up later. "Project Epiphany is supposed to involve a few well-known UFO researchers and certain people who worked in the government. They are reported to be planning to form a contact team, and to be at the first public ET landing as representatives of Earth."

"Well, I have heard of such an effort," Stone said, with a candor which encouraged Maguire. "But it has not yet come together."

"Well, how much can you say about the Project's progress so far?" Maguire asked.

"To be candid, I've checked up on you, Roger," Stone confessed. "The word I have received is that you are honorable, highly knowledgeable and a truthful individual, and that you present your findings publicly in a forthright manner, which some call reckless, and others call courageous. So let's have an understanding here. I am willing to say a few things, *if* you and I have an understanding that what I will say about the Project will be used by you with *great* discretion. Your friend Barbara needs to make the same agreement if she is to stay in the room."

"You have my word, sir," Maguire replied.

"And I, too, promise to be very discreet about what you tell us about Project Epiphany," Catalina said.

"Very well, then," Stone continued. "The Project began in late 1995. A prominent researcher into Visitor contacts, Dr. Robert Bowen, put out a call to fellow specialists and to knowledgeable leaders selected worldwide, to help form a contact team to meet the extraterrestrials. You know Dr. Bowen?"

"Oh, yes," Maguire responded. "He's that noted psychologist who has written some pretty amazing articles on UFOs, ETs, and the Cover-Up."

"That's the man," Stone continued. "Roughly twenty persons from around the world responded to his invitation to plan for a Contact Team. The members were from various constituencies: governmental, geographical, scientific, religious, military, and of course ethnic. They held their first meeting at a remote location in the Nevada desert, and made the decision to proceed with identifying those persons who would be invited to serve as Earth's representation team. It was at that meeting that they named their effort Project Epiphany."

"Are there any women among them?" Catalina asked.

"Oh, yes", Stone replied. "Let's see. Unless I miscount, I believe there are five women in the group."

"Can you tell me who they are?" she asked.

"There's Sister Lisieux; you know, the French nun who created a band of religious sisters to minister to the poorest of the poor in the Third World?"

"Oh, yes, she's famous," Catalina said. "And the others?"

"Let's see. The South American representative, from Brazil, Alberta de Oliveira, a UFO investigator. There's Dr. Leena

Virtanen, the Visitors contacts researcher. She's Surgeon-General of Norway. And Dr. Ivana Kheraskov, the Russian cosmonaut, who has reported multiple UFO contacts in orbit. And Claudia Hill, the UFO investigator from Zimbabwe, who has published articles on numerous UFO contacts in Africa."

"It is encouraging to hear that there are some women in this group," Catalina said. "That's so rare in UFO leadership circles."

"Yes," Stone replied dryly.

"Jacques, would you say who the rest of this group are?" Maguire asked.

"The Project has received tentative commitments to participate from U.N. Secretary Kalim Salaam, and from former U.S. President Earl James. I understand that the Nepalese Lama is pretty firm that he will participate. The rest have made firm commitments to the Project. Those would be Timothy Katoya, a Hopi Elder ..."

"Katoya?" Maguire interrupted. "Really?"

"Yes. Why? Do you know him?" Stone queried, looking closely at Maguire.

"Yes, as a matter of fact, I do know him a bit," Maguire replied. Inwardly he was thinking to himself: why that little devil, Timothy. He certainly knows how to keep a secret. Imagine Tim letting me go on and on about trying to find the Landing, and here he's part of Project Epiphany. But Maguire said nothing to Stone about how close his friendship with the Hopi Elder was. Maguire wanted to preserve an independent source of information about the Project, in case he needed it.

Stone went on to name the rest of the Project's male members. "The others are Donald Cameron, perhaps the best-known UFOlogist in Australia. There's Professor Yat-sen Yuan, who heads a UFO investigation society in Beijing. And Karl von Reuter, a German anthropologist who publishes UFO reports. You've heard of him, I'm sure."

"Oh, yes," Maguire replied. "I've heard him lecture several times. He has those fabulously sharp, detailed pictures of saucers photographed over Europe."

Stone continued, "Then, there's Gilbert Murray; he heads

the British Close Encounters Society. And Manuel Gutierrez, the Mexican television producer, who has made many UFO documentaries and has over 300 videotapes of UFOs. Of course, Dr. Ian McCormack, the Princeton psychiatry professor who researches ET abductions."

"Yes," Maguire interjected, "I've met Dr. McCormack. He's very impressive, and unusually open to spiritual and metaphysical matters for a psychiatrist."

"Indeed," Stone said, wryly. "Did you know that he used to be a materialistic atheist? And then there's Dr. Leonard Spruance, the psychology professor who retired from the University of Idaho to study ET contactees. And Dr. Stewart Golden, the Jewish imam." Stone interjected the last epithet with just a touch of sardonic humor. "He's a physician from Knoxville who heads an organization dedicated to putting out friendly signals to UFOs, trying to get them to make an appearance."

"Oh, you mean ISFEC, the Interstellar Friendship and Exchange Committee," Catalina said. "I've heard Dr. Golden lecture about that up in Colorado where I'm from."

"He gets around," Stone replied noncommittally. "And, of course, Dr. Robert Bowen, who founded the Project. And then there's Dr. Brent O'Hara, the astronaut from Hawaii who lectures about UFO reality.

"But it's Dr. O'Hara's lectures about New Physics and free energy sources that make certain people in the energy industries anxious to silence him," Maguire commented. "That's one topic that may be more *verboten* than discussing UFOs. Anyway, O'Hara sure has guts."

Stone ignored the comment and finished naming the Project's members. "The Project wanted to include one or two current high-ranking military officers, but it was felt that they were all compromised by their National Security Act obligations and couldn't participate. So the group decided to include two retired officers. Those were Air Force Colonel Duane Warwick, who formerly commanded the Blue Light units in the Interior Zone, excuse me, the continental U.S. I must say, Warwick is one of the most metaphysically-minded members of the Project. And Army Major Roscoe Dent, who formerly served as Chief of Intelligence to SEATO. He was in charge of Intelligence during that retrieval of a saucer downed in the Gulf of Tonkin."

"Excuse me, Jacques, but what are Blue Light units?" Catalina asked.

"Blue Light units are secret compartments within the Air Force. Their task is to pounce upon downed UFOs, secure the area around them, and retrieve objects and personnel, dead or alive, while keeping all civilians away from the site," Stone replied with characteristic precision.

"I have a question, too, Jacques," Maguire broke in. "I never heard about a UFO going down in the Gulf of Tonkin. Was that during the Vietnam War?"

"Yes it was," Stone responded. "In fact, you could say it started the American entry into the War. You remember the Potrero?"

Maguire's jaw dropped. He recalled the stories about an American Navy ship patrolling in international waters that was boarded and taken over by North Vietnamese military. "You mean that that Navy spy ship was tracking a UFO in the Gulf of Tonkin?"

"More than tracking it," Stone replied. "They had seen the UFO moving in and out of the skies over Haiphong two nights in a row. It had been circling over the Potrero, too, as the Navy ship was eavesdropping on Viet Cong radio transmissions. The Potrero finally got orders to use an early version of a high-voltage directed-energy weapon on the UFO. They managed to disable its guidance system, and the UFO went down. But the Potrero's energy weapon put out so much power that it lit up the North Vietnamese radar screens like a Christmas tree. The North Vietnamese sent out a naval squadron and captured the Potrero in North Vietnamese territorial waters. And the rest, as they say, is history."

Maguire and Catalina remembered that when the Potrero was captured, and the Vietnamese refused to return it, the U.S. Congress, after a classified briefing, became inflamed and passed a War Resolution. Maguire could not be sure whether Stone was feeding him some disinformation, or leaking one of the most amazing untold incidents of the UFO Cover-Up. He decided to go back to the issue of the Project's membership.

"Have you named all the members of the Project?" In a flash of boldness, Maguire added, "Haven't you left someone out?" He was determined to flush out Stone.

"I've named everyone I know," Stone replied somewhat tartly. He was annoyed at having this newly-met guest pressing him on such delicate matters.

Maguire decided to get to the point. "How about you, Jacques? Aren't you a member of Project Epiphany?"

Stone shifted uneasily in his leather chair, and then turned back to fix his gaze straight at Maguire. "I am not a member. The role I play is that of an interface. I interface between the members and those I know in certain circles whom the Project members want to get messages to, or to obtain information from. I find that that is the role in which I am most comfortable. The Project members find such services useful." Stone's modesty was unbecoming to his connections. He didn't mention it, but Maguire had heard that those "certain circles" Stone had access to included Congress, the Joint Chiefs of Staff, the U.N. and the White House.

Catalina had been taking careful notes as Stone spoke. She had taken down every name in Project Epiphany. She marveled at the Project's international assemblage of brains, power, and prominence. She decided that she would have to compare impressions with Maguire privately later.

"Jacques, I know it's getting late," Maguire said. "But I'd like to ask you about what you think the timetable is for the public extraterrestrial landing? Do the Project members have a date?"

"There is some variation of opinion about the date. Some think the Landing will happen later next year. And a few even think it's two or more years off. But the majority think it will happen sooner, possibly before year's end. No one has a precise date. We, ah, the Project feels that the Visitors will give us a signal as to the precise time. The Project members have agreed to assemble on short notice when we learn the precise time."

Maguire decided to go for broke. "And the place?"

"Again there is some division of opinion," Stone replied. "The consensus is the Southwest. Of course, that is a very big place. But again, the feeling in the group is that the Visitors will give some membe ...." Stone started to say something more, but caught himself.

Maguire sensed an opportunity and pressed in. "And what is your sense of where the Landing will take place, Jacques?"

"I believe it will occur not very far from where the first saucer was retrieved in the early Forties by the U.S. military, in the desert area of Chihuahua State, Mexico near the U.S. border. Anyway, that is the impression I get from my meditations on the subject," he said quietly. Stone carefully downplayed his use of clairvoyance.

"Chihuahua State. That borders New Mexico and Texas."

Maguire figured that it was only fair, after pumping this gentleman for information, to offer a little back in return. "Jacques, I have received information from a Native American source, that the Landing will occur along where the Continental Divide crosses the Mexican border." Maguire decided not to name Katoya as his source."That information places the Landing as being near the New Mexico town of Cloverdale. How does that fit with your information?"

Stone was noncommittal. "That sounds as plausible as anything, but I really am not in a position to confirm a location. Like everyone else I will just have to wait for more information. By the way, what kind of Native American source did you use?" He eyed Maguire carefully.

Maguire matched the caginess Stone had been resorting to with some of his own. "It was an older man, who is well acquainted with the ancient Native American prophecies."

Stone's old intelligence training told him that Maguire was fending off any precise information about his source, so Stone gave up probing for now. "I see," he responded, resigned that he would get no more on this source.

Catalina changed the subject. "Roger and I have received a clear indication from psychic messages that we are supposed to be at the ET landing."

Stone perked up when Catalina mentioned the psychic source of her information. "So, you practice clairvoyance?" he asked, with deliberately disarming nonchalance.

His studied casual tone made her nervous. "I do a number of psychic things, including clairvoyance. But what I was about to ask you was if Roger and I could participate with the Project Epiphany group when they go to meet with the extraterrestrials at the Landing?"

Stone immediately got an uncomfortable, almost irritated look. He glanced first at Maguire and then at Catalina, and answered. "I don't know how to say this as gracefully as I would wish, but the membership of Project Epiphany is closed. As you can appreciate, we, ah, the Project has enormous security and secrecy problems. Everyone involved has already decided that they are doing so at the possible risk of their lives. The Project has had a number of planning meetings, and matters are at an advanced stage. The selection of who would be in the Project was made very carefully over time. The members chose whom they wanted a while ago. There is neither the inclination nor the possibility on their part to consider adding anyone else at this late stage in the process."

What Catalina referred to as her Chippewa Temper flared at the rebuff she felt she had been shown. "So you're telling me, 'Sorry. You're too late. You'll just have to wait for the next cosmic event.'" Catalina was bristling with angry disappointment. "What about what I was shown in vision, about Roger and I being at the Landing? Are you and the Project members just going to blow that psychic information off?"

Maguire jumped in to try to head Catalina off from moving any farther down the warpath. "Barbara, if Jacques says the Project doesn't want us, we'll just have to go our own way."

Stone jumped in, somewhat uneasy at the angry reaction to his comments. "Please, Barbara, understand that it is nothing personal. The Project has just got no room for change at this point."

Catalina was not mollified. "Well, I think that the Project

can just go . . ." She stopped short as she noticed Maguire shooting her the sharpest and darkest look she had ever seen him give.

Stone continued. "There is one more thing. there is a considerable element of danger for anyone participating in Project Epiphany. I have learned that within the organization which operates the UFO Cover-Up, there is a small secret group who also plan to be at the extraterrestrials' public landing. But this group's motives are the worst: power, greed, deception, and aggression. I believe that I may know one of the members of this secret group, if my source is right. He is an evil and very dangerous man. Such a group would stop at nothing, even deadly force, to eliminate any competition to their exclusive presence at the Landing. So you see, that is an additional reason why our Project Epiphany group cannot have anyone else come in."

"Does this other group have a name?" Maguire asked.

"I'm not sure," Stone responded. "My source said they use code names for their group and the members. He's not sure what the current code name is."

"Well, Jacques, you've been a gracious host, and we appreciate everything that you have been kind enough to share with us," Maguire said, not wanting to wear his host out. "It *is* getting late and..."

Maguire stopped in mid-sentence, as they all heard Lucy Stone shriek loudly from the living room, "Jacques!! Come here at once!"

Stone bolted from his leather chair towards the living room, followed a moment later by his concerned guests.

Lucy Stone was ashen and pointing towards the television set, which was tuned to CNN news. "Something terrible has happened! There's been a terrific earthquake in California. They interrupted the program I had on. The announcer says that they're going to go live with a report from the area."

"Large earthquakes are not that unusual in California," Maguire said. "I grew up there. I've lived through some pretty good ones."

"Not like this!" Mrs. Stone said tartly, annoyed at being thought overreactive. "They said this one was a 9.8 magnitude earthquake!"

"Wow!" Maguire replied. "That really *is* a big one!"

"The announcer said that it is the biggest one in the continental United States," Mrs. Stone replied.

On screen, CNN news anchor Natalie Allen was speaking. "We've just established satellite link-up with Station KLCN in El Centro, California, near the epicenter of this disastrous earthquake. We take you now to El Centro."

The TV screen switched to an announcer standing next to a TV remote broadcast truck parked outside the crumbled remains of a television station building. "This is Mike Ramirez speaking to you live from outside the offices of Station KLCN in El Centro, California. Half an hour ago, Southern California experienced the largest earthquake in modern times! The temblor has been given an initial magnitude of 9.8 by the Caltech seismology office! The quake's epicenter is estimated to be twenty miles east of the border town of Calexico, roughly halfway between Calexico and Yuma, Arizona.

"Initial mobile reports from sheriff's officers suggest that this was a violent thrust fault-type quake, with some sections of land shoved up in a few areas, and huge sections sunken down in most other areas of the region, in some places as much as a hundred feet down. F-16 reconnaissance aircraft dispatched from Coronado Naval Air Station, San Diego and F-18s from Luke Air Force Base, Phoenix have flown over the area and report incredible devastation. The towns of Calexico and Mexicali are totally destroyed and leveled. Extremely heavy damage has been sustained here in El Centro, in other Imperial County cities, and in Yuma, Arizona. Of the few buildings in the county not leveled by the earthquake, most are on fire. The fires were caused by ruptured gas and electric lines. All the roads are closed in and out of Imperial County here, including Interstates 8 and 10, as well as the roads around Yuma and the area of Mexico near the border. Huge cracks have appeared in many highways, and great sections of roadbed have sunk and buckled.

All bridges in the county have either been destroyed or have been declared unsafe by the authorities.

"Two dams on the Colorado River near us, Laguna Dam and Imperial Dam, have failed. Their reservoirs are emptying as I speak, causing catastrophic flooding. It is expected that there will be a great loss of life downstream from the dams. Upstream, Parker Dam has huge cracks. It is leaking seriously, and engineers expect it to fail before midnight. Farther up, there are cracks in Davis Dam, but we have no word yet on whether it too will fail, or how soon. The huge Hoover Dam, also known as Boulder Dam, is holding at this hour, but engineers are concerned about the pounding on the dam caused by the shock waves repeatedly pushing the waters of 110-mile-long Lake Mead against the Dam with terrific hydraulic force, weakening it.

"The Office of Emergency Services has issued a tsunami warning for a possibly huge tidal wave to roll up from the Gulf of California. As many people around here know, there are extreme tides normally at the mouth of the Colorado River 75 miles south of here, because of the extremely long, narrow shape of the Gulf of California. High tide levels of three feet at the mouth of the Gulf translate into thirty-foot high tide surges where the Colorado meets the top of the Gulf. The timing could not be worse for this tidal wave warning, since it is now high tide. Oceanographic seismic experts at OES predict that a rolling tsunami caused by the earthquake is heading north from the lower part of the Gulf of California, and, when it arrives at the Colorado River, it will produce a tidal wave as high as a fifteen-story building!

"There has been an incredibly huge sinking of the land mass around El Centro and Yuma, and south to the Gulf of California. Because of the land subsidence and the high tides, Navy pilot observers are reporting that sea water from the Gulf of California is beginning to roll up into the Colorado River basin. They also report that a huge opening in the earth about 30 miles southeast of Calexico is pouring out lava, and is apparently the start of a volcano. Another ominous report, this one from Air Force pilots, says that as a result of the shifting and sinking of land, the Colorado River has changed its course. The Colorado has begun to flow west, along a route that roughly parallels the All-American Canal. On its present course, a geology professor at Imperial Valley College estimates that the Colorado River will soon flow into the Salton Sea, an enormous inland lake formed the last time the Colorado River overflowed its boundaries during an historic flood a century ago. With us now is that Geology Professor, Henry Schielmann, to speak to us about these extraordinary events.

"Professor Schielmann, what are we to understand from reports that the Colorado River is rolling toward El Centro?"

"Mike, there are not words to do justice to what this means," Professor Schielmann said. "I have looked at the fragmentary reports that are available, and I have talked with the people at the State Office of Emergency Services in Sacramento about the situation. Basically, the situation seems to be this. This monumental earthquake has drastically lowered land levels between Imperial County and the Gulf. In addition, in broad areas of the county, excessive drawing off of ground water by wells has lowered the water table over a hundred feet, and created huge underground empty chambers. The tremendous shaking has caused these underground chambers to cave in. As a result of these factors, the elevation of much of Imperial County has been lowered below sea level by the earthquake and resulting collapse of land. And, as you know, Mike, about one-fifth of the county already lay below sea level even before the earthquake."

Professor Schielmann pointed at a large map of southeastern California displayed on the side of the mobile TV transmission van. "Besides this tremendous earthquake, now we have two new dangerous developments. The Colorado River has rerouted, and is heading for El Centro and the Salton Sea. At the same time the Gulf of California is extending northward, as sea water rolls over area that used to be above sea level. And that's not counting the predicted tidal wave which you just reported. Mike, I'm afraid my prediction to your viewers will be the same grim one I just gave the

Office of Emergency Services. Over the next several hours, sea water from the Gulf of California will spread across the border and into our area. It will eventually cover half of Imperial county and as far as 40 miles into Riverside County. With the rerouted Colorado River adding its water, I fear the submerging of land might extend almost to Palm Springs."

The announcer interrupted the professor. "Dr. Schielmann, thank you for your information on these developments, but I have to interrupt you. I have just been handed a bulletin that a 150-foot-high tidal wave has been spotted at the mouth of the Colorado River and is rolling upstream. And now we have been directed to break in with an emergency announcement from the State Disaster Office."

The television picture switched from the El Centro newscaster to a square-jawed figure in a khaki military uniform.

"This is Commander Phil Murray of the State Office of Emergency Services. All citizens of Imperial and Riverside County, please pay attention! The Governor has declared a State of Emergency, because of massive earthquake damage, dam failures, fires, loss of life, disruption of communications, major flooding, tidal wave, destruction of highways, and the advancing of the Sea of Cortez towards Imperial County. The Governor has also declared Martial Law in the affected counties. The Office of Emergency Services, under authority of the Governor, is ordering immediate evacuation of all low-lying areas of Imperial and Riverside Counties. This includes the communities of Blythe, Winterhaven, Calexico, El Centro, the Salton Sea area, Coachella, Indio and surrounding areas. Residents of Palm Springs and Rancho Mirage are placed on alert, and asked to monitor the radio or TV for further bulletins. Emergency evacuation and shelter centers have been established at the Marine Corps Recruit Depot in San Diego, and at Twenty-nine Palms Marine Corps Base in San Bernardino County. Low-lying residents are urged not to take any time to pack possessions, but to evacuate immediately. Residents in the affected areas are asked to follow the directions of either local authorities or of military units which are being flown in by helicopter. Please stay tuned for further bulletins."

The TV set then switched to an aerial view of massive flooding of the cities of Yuma and Winterhaven by the dam breaks. Other scenes of those few parts of the towns not under water showed buildings and homes which lay in ruins from the earthquake or on fire.

"My God!" Maguire exclaimed, expressing the sentiments of the other three gathered around the television.

"Earth changes," Catalina added softly in an awe-struck voice.

"What's that?" Lucy Stone asked. "What do you mean, Earth changes?"

Catalina proceeded to explain to her that "Earth changes" referred to the numerous predictions by psychics and experiencers of a near-future series of catastrophic geophysical, ecological and sociopolitical upheavals. These were events which the extraterrestrials had shown experiencers were coming, which often coincided with independent predictions of the same kinds of events made by clairvoyant psychics, as well as with the forecasts of certain scientists whose cautionary findings were seldom carried by the mainstream press.

Jacques Stone turned to Maguire. "Leave it to the Government to announce in one breath that all highways are shut, and in the next breath to order everyone to evacuate out of the county. Now tell me, how in blazes is a citizen supposed to follow that order?" He shook his head in disgust. "By the way, Roger, do you have any family down in that area?"

Maguire assured him that he did not, and that his Chatsworth office was over 200 miles northwest of the epicenter. Privately, he was worried that an earthquake of 9.8 magnitude might have done some damage to his office even at that distance, but did not want to worry his host. Mrs. Stone turned off the TV, unwilling to view any more of the horrible destruction. The four discussed the earthquake and the larger theme of predicted Earth changes for a while. Catalina shared her opinion that this quake was a major indication that the Earth changes scenario had begun in earnest. Jacques Stone expressed his cautious agreement with her analysis. He probed further about what she had learned using her psychic abilities. Lucy Stone then broke in to suggest that Catalina and Maguire stay overnight, because of the lateness of the hour. The two weary travelers agreed. After bidding good-night to Jacques Stone, they were shown by Lucy to spare bedrooms in the back of the house. Both bedrooms had a striking view of the bay, which shimmered in the dark in the reflected light of an almost quarter-moon.

When night fell, AFOSI Captain DiGiorgio had switched from his civilian summer whites to a charcoal gray-and-black camouflage jumpsuit and face mask. When the conversation in the Stone study wound down to an end, DiGiorgio moved up near to the house, using the cover of low shrubbery and scattered trees between the house and the bay. He aimed his hand-held acoustic pick-up equipment first at Maguire's bedroom window. And then, when Maguire went out to the bathroom, DiGiorgio aimed it through the open blinds of Catalina's room. DiGiorgio focused his binoculars on the raven-haired woman unbuttoning her blouse and whispered to himself, "C'mon, Mama, show us your chi-chis."

Catalina left her blinds open as she got ready for bed, in order to enjoy the moonlight on the bay backing up against this secluded estate. Way off in the distance she could hear the intermittent ding of a channel marker buoy. The night was soft, humid and warm. As she was removing her bra, she noticed out of the corner of her eye a dark figure move slightly next to a tree outside her window. She quickly pulled on a T-shirt and yelled for Maguire. He quickly hurried to her door just as she was opening it.

"Roger, there's a man outside my window, dressed all in black, looking in at me."

Maguire told her to stay put and raced out the back door to the yard. He spotted the dark figure running in a low crouch back towards the road. In the distance Maguire noticed that the figure was heading for a white car parked down the road, which Maguire now realized had not moved since afternoon.

DiGiorgio desperately raced towards his car while carrying an armload of compromising surveillance gear. Abandoning his low-profile slouch, he ran fully upright down the road. A fist-sized rock in the dark almost tripped him. He momentarily lost his balance and his acoustic pick-up unit slipped from his arms. He stooped down to pick it up quickly, and straightened back up into a full run after the briefest of pauses. He was within fifty yards of his car when Maguire came from behind and, in a flying tackle around DiGiorgio's knees, sent him sprawling into the gravel roadbed. DiGiorgio wheeled around on the ground and planted a combat boot hard into the bridge of Maguire's nose. As Maguire groaned and rolled backward, DiGiorgio reached into his military vest, pulled out a small aerosol canister, and directed a narrow stream of spray at Maguire's face. A strange pungent orange-blossom mist surrounded Maguire, and he instantly slumped to the ground unconscious. DiGiorgio was angry at being tackled, his face and hands smarting from gravel scrapes. He kicked the motionless figure on the ground in the back. "Fucking subversive *chusma*! You're lucky I don't end one National Security risk right now with my K-bar," DiGiorgio said, patting the knife in his belt. He strode quickly the remaining distance to his car, and sped off.

Jacques Stone was out of bed seconds after Catalina cried out. He saw Maguire rushing out the back door, with Catalina yelling after him not to take any chances. Stone hit the speed-dial button on his phone, preset for 911. He identified himself as Commander Stone and asked the operator for emergency police response.

Within a minute a patrol car from the Mount Carmel Police Department was racing south, closely followed by an Anne Arundel County Sheriff's unit.

DiGiorgio had his Ford floored as he sped up the gravel road off the peninsula and towards Mount Carmel. Up ahead in the distance he spotted the red and blue flashing lights of the two oncoming police cars. "Shit!" he exclaimed and slowed his pace to the legal speed limit, hoping they were on some other call. That hope evaporated as he saw the Mount Carmel car brake and skid sideways to a stop, forming a roadblock. The sheriff's car pulled along side the other unit, and both lawmen stood in their doorways, revolvers drawn and aimed at him. DiGiorgio pulled to a stop in front of the roadblock and sat behind the wheel. The Mount Carmel officer strode up and shone a flashlight in the driver's window at a sullen man in a black jumpsuit, his face mask resting on the seat. DiGiorgio's hands were carefully resting on the steering wheel in plain sight.

"Officer, if you'll permit me, I have some special identification in my wallet to show you," DiGiorgio said evenly.

"Okay, fella, but move your hand real slow," the Mount Carmel cop drawled back, revolver pressed against DiGiorgio's left temple, hammer cocked.

DiGiorgio pulled out his wallet and flashed the badge and identification card of "Alfonso Aguilar" of the Defense Intelligence Agency. The cop's eyes widened. DiGiorgio said, "Now, officer, if you're satisfied, I'm on very urgent National Security business. So kindly get your unit outa my goddamn way. I'm in a big hurry."

The Mount Carmel cop made a face, walked back to his car, waving off the Sheriff, then backed his car off the road. DiGiorgio gunned his engine and took off, leaving dust and flying gravel in his wake. The Mount Carmel officer pulled out a pack of Kools and extended it to the deputy, who took one. "You know, Roscoe, those Intelligence boys are just about the most arrogant bastards you run across in this work."

The deputy exhaled a plume of smoke and grinned. "Yeah, Granville, you got that right." He nodded his head in the direction of the car speeding away. "Y' know goddam well that that sonofabitch was the one who was playing Peeping Tom in the Commander's bedroom window. Ain't nobody else out on this lonely road this time of night. Tell you what. The goddam pervert better learn how to do an intelligence stake-out with his zipper shut."

The Mount Carmel cop doubled over laughing, tears in his eyes. The deputy joined in, chuckling at his own humor.

Lifting himself slightly, Maguire slowly opened his eyes, trying to focus. He shook his head trying to drive out the grogginess. The faces of Catalina and the Stones loomed above him peering down worriedly. He looked around feeling disoriented and noticed that he was on the Stones' living room sofa. "How did I get here? The last thing I remember, I was chasing that guy in black." He touched his hand to his nose and winced. "Ouch! And I remember something about getting kicked in the face. Umm, that smarts."

"Barbara, Lucy and I carried you back here," Jacques Stone replied. "Lucy called a doctor. Dr. Raleigh will be here right away."

"I don't need a doctor, Jacques," Maguire said. He started to raise himself up, and then, feeling light-headed, collapsed back on the sofa.

"Roger, don't be a hero," Catalina said. "That creep sprayed you with some chemical. I was behind you a ways, but I could see the mist. It left a strong odor on you for a few minutes afterwards, too. You don't know what was in that stuff. You better take it easy."

Jacques Stone chimed in. "When I was in the employ of the Agency back in the Sixties, they had a knock-out spray device that was the size of a lipstick. But it could put down a 300-lb. man in one second." Changing the subject, Stone observed, "That man was no ordinary Peeping Tom. He wore professional low-visibility clothes. And then there's that knock-out spray. It looks like you, Dr. Maguire, and your lovely friend Barbara have become the focus of some high-level attention. No doubt due to your efforts to be at the Visitors' public Landing. Permit me to suggest that in the future you exercise a high degree of caution and circumspection in your efforts and communications."

Dr. Gisela Raleigh had Maguire follow her right index finger, as she repeatedly drew it back and forth from his face to hers, and then passed it to the left and to the right. Maguire noticed her lovely hazel eyes as he tried to follow the focal point, which shimmered before his eyes. Dr. Raleigh noted the residual dilation in his pupils, and that his reflexes were slowed, but pronounced him basically healthy. She confided to Maguire that his symptoms were consistent with exposure to a combination of hallucinogenic, narcotic, and neurotransmitter-interference agents, but made the prognosis that he should be fine by morning. When Maguire warily inquired where she had acquired such familiarity with antipersonnel substances, she reacted with a blush. After a moment's hesitation, Dr. Raleigh acknowledged that she had served a brief rotation at Fort Detrick, Maryland, the Army's biological weapons laboratory, as part of her required government service to pay back her Uniformed Public

Health Services medical scholarship. She added that she hated every minute of it.

The next morning, over his third cup of coffee, Maguire assured Catalina and the Stones that he felt as good as new. During breakfast the four shared sections of the *Baltimore Sun.* It featured page after page of headline stories and photos of the monumental earthquake and inundation tragedy in California. The front page featured a heart-breaking photo of a father, up to his shoulders in floodwaters, reaching his pre-school daughter up over his head to a Sheriff's deputy in a sling lowered from a rescue helicopter hovering overhead. The photo caption said that a couple seconds later, the father was swept away by the water and presumed drowned.

As Maguire and Catalina loaded the Pathfinder for departure, Jacques Stone drew Maguire aside and told him that because he liked and trusted him, off the record he would keep Maguire informed about the plans of Project Epiphany. Stone said that he hoped Maguire understood that he was not in a position to extend an invitation to join with the Project in meeting the Extraterrestrials. Maguire thanked him for the courtesy of being kept informed and privately welcomed the trust of this key player.

The sun was brightly shining in an almost cloudless sky as Maguire and Catalina took off up the road toward the mainland. Lucy and Jacques Stone stood in the driveway waving good-bye. None of the four bothered to take any particular notice of a single-engine olive-drab Cessna, which puttered along lazily several thousand feet overhead. The pilot looked down at the departing Pathfinder and got on his radio. "Zeta One, this is Zeta Five. We have Fellow Traveler in sight departing northward toward Mount Carmel."

Chapter 6

ABOUT 15 minutes down the road from Mount Carmel at the town of Southgate, Maguire pulled off the road to a Howard Johnson's to clear his phone messages. He was relieved to find out that the California temblor had not hurt his answering machine. It contained two messages. The first was from Timothy Katoya. In Katoya's typically laconic, understated way, the message said to give him a call when Maguire had time. Since Katoya had never phoned Maguire before, Maguire knew it had to be important. The second message was from Don Cortlan saying that he had important news to share. Hanging up the receiver, Maguire recalled that Cortlan lived only about 40 miles away, in Greenbelt Park, MD. Maguire immediately returned both calls.

Timothy Katoya did not have a phone, but used the phone of his neighbor, Dolores Kokopilmana for the few times a year he had use for one. Maguire dialed Mrs. Kokopilmana, who was at home. She immediately sent her daughter next door to fetch Elder Katoya to come to the phone.

"How is the *bahana* with the bandanna?" Katoya teased, referring to the sweatband Maguire had often worn while working on the reservation.

"Fine, Tim. I hope my call finds you in good health," Maguire replied. "I got your phone message. Something is happening?"

Katoya's voice dropped to a serious tone. "Roger, I had a Dream last night. In it, Spirit told me something about you, and about some important things which are coming up. It is important that you hear these things personally, as soon as you can."

"And I assume that you can't tell me these things over the phone," Maguire said, knowing the answer.

"It is not wise to do so, Roger. You have many 'friends,' and they could be listening," Katoya said cryptically. "When do you think that you could come over here?"

"I'll start out tomorrow, but I'm in Maryland, so it'll take us at least four days," Maguire answered.

"Us?" Katoya questioned. "Have you gotten married?" he asked mostly in jest, but curious nonetheless.

"No, but I've got a new friend who is accompanying me on this search. She's a good person. She's part Ojibwa, by the way."

"But is her heart red?" Katoya asked, using the phrase for a person whose lifestyle is consistent with Native American teachings.

"Yes."

"Well, then, she is welcome, too," the Hopi Elder said. "Come as soon as you can."

"We'll be out there as soon as we can drive it, Timothy. I look forward to talking with you. Say, what do you make of that gigantic earthquake in California?"

Katoya's reply sounded grave. "Very bad. I was down in the kiva when it happened. Spirit showed me that this is just the wake-up call. Many more serious things will be happening soon. We'll talk more when you get here."

Maguire hung up, then dialed Don Cortlan's number. His luck was good this morning. Cortlan was home, too. "Don, this is Roger Maguire. I'm in Southgate, Maryland. You called. What's up?"

"Rog, thanks for getting back to me. By the way, what brings you to Maryland?"

"I paid a visit to Dr. Jacques Stone, as you suggested," Maguire replied. "He certainly was informative, quite forthcoming on the Project Epiphany group. He didn't know the name for that renegade group though, the one that's trying to horn in on the Visitors' landing and keep everyone else away."

"Funny you should mention them. I've gotten some fresh information from an intelligence source. But actually, for both our sakes, it's better if I don't have to give you this info over the phone. Since you're already here in Maryland, why don't you come down to my place in Greenbelt Park, and we can talk in person. Given the investigation that you're into, I think that the sooner you have this information, the better."

"Sure," Maguire replied, "that is, if you don't mind some company. I have a new research associate who has joined me for my search. But you needn't be concerned about her. She can be very discreet."

"Well, that wouldn't be my first choice of how to do it," Cortlan said. Maguire let Cortlan's prolonged pause of resistance draw out awkwardly without saying anything. Finally Cortlan continued. "I guess it's okay if you bring her along."

Over coffee inside the Howard Johnson's cafe, Maguire told Catalina about Katoya's and Cortlan's intriguing statements and their invitations to come visit. Catalina readily agreed that they should immediately proceed to pay these two a call.

Don Cortlan's home was a mini-estate on the outskirts of Greenbelt Park. It was a modern three-bedroom home situated on a small wooded knoll, surrounded by five acres of green meadows. In front of the garage, a restored classic 1968 Jaguar was parked.

Don Cortlan was a short, wiry, nervous man in his late thirties, with blond hair trimmed in a conservative cut. He showed Catalina and Maguire to his living room and offered them drinks from the adjacent full bar, although it was not yet noon. They settled into comfortable chairs with their Perriers, while Cortlan poured himself a double aquavit on the rocks. Maguire surmised from Cortlan's florid complexion that the drink in Cortlan's hand was not his first today.

Maguire gave Cortlan a brief history of how Catalina and he met. Then Cortlan and Maguire caught each other up on developments in their lives. By then it was noon, and Cortlan invited them to stay for some sandwiches. Over lunch, they exchanged UFO information and the latest rumors. After lunch, Cortlan got down to the business he had phoned about.

"Roger, there is some sensitive information I have gotten in the last week," Cortlan began. "I knew it was related to what you're doing with your search for the alien public landing. My information has to do with a secret group that is made up of people within the UFO Cover-Up organization."

"And they plan to be at the extraterrestrial public landing," Maguire added. "And to try to keep anyone else from being there."

"Where did *you* hear that?" Cortlan's tone was shocked surprise.

Maguire identified this information as just received from Jacques Stone, and that it seemed to back up Cortlan's earlier tip.

"Whew!" Cortlan whistled. "So Jacques has gotten the same report, eh? I didn't think that *that* information had gotten around."

Catalina joined in the conversation. "Jacques Stone briefed us on it."

"And did he tell you that they are planning a diversion exercise?"

"Damn! No!" Maguire exclaimed, caught off guard by this additional revelation of Cortlan's.

"What diversion exercise?" Catalina asked.

Cortlan sat up in his easy chair, rotated the ice cubes in his drink with a gentle clinking, and paused dramatically. He was enjoying having some exclusive information that even the great Jacques Stone didn't have. "This group is planning to stage a fake alien public landing in the very near future." He paused to let the bombshell sink in.

"Why?" Maguire asked.

"It will be a disinformation operation. As I understand it, this secret group wants to have the power that comes with being the only ones to negotiate with the aliens. Since this group cannot control when and where the aliens will emerge, the group is going to stage their own fake alien landing. They will be there waiting, to make sure that they control the outcome, as far as the public's perception is concerned."

Catalina commented in a serious tone. "That group is going to bring terrible karma down on their heads, if they try to exploit humanity by imitating the extraterrestrials and then setting themselves up as ambassadors."

"Bad karma? What else is new in clandestine operations?" Cortlan rejoined sarcastically.

"Don, when and where will this happen?" Maguire asked.

"It's supposed to happen around the beginning of September," Cortlan replied. "According to my source, it's supposed to take place near the Newport News-Norfolk, Virginia area. Specifically, in a field near the NASA Visitors Center at Langley Air Force Base."

"That way they can be sure of lots of spectators, but at a distance, since they can control access as to who gets onto the base, and how close the spectators can get to their 'UFO'," Maguire observed wryly. "You gotta hand it to those boys; they have got it set up very neatly." He sat back in his chair, took a drink of his mineral water, and weighed the implications.

"Do you know what their UFO will look like?" Catalina asked.

Cortlan made a flattened semi-circular motion with his right hand. "They're supposed to be using a model with the classic flying saucer disc shape. It'll have some lights on it, because they'll do the landing in the dark. Nothing too big or exotic in the way of a craft."

Maguire jumped back into the conversation. "Don, who is behind this? Who is this rogue group?"

"Well, now, that's the big question, isn't it," Cortlan replied. "My source said that they were named after some Roman god of new beginnings. This god was supposed to have a head with two faces, facing backwards and forwards."

"Janus!" Maguire exclaimed. "That's the Roman god you're speaking of. So the group's code name is JANUS?"

"I don't know. I was just given the hint about its being some Roman god of beginnings. But you seem to know who that is."

"Janus has two faces. For a group that plans a deception on a cosmic scale, that's very appropriate," Maguire said with ironic double entendre. "And do you know who *any* of the JANUS group members are?"

Cortlan chuckled at Maguire's pun in a half-hearted sort of way. "Well, I have to assume that my source is connected to this, JANUS as you call it, group. Because if they're half as secretive as he says they are, how else would he know so much about them?" Cortlan paused and coughed nervously, realizing that he might have already said too much. "Now, Roger, I hope you will be discreet with any use of this information."

Maguire brushed off his request. "Don, you didn't say anything at the beginning about this information's being off the record. This false alien landing is potentially the greatest deception in the history of the human race, and probably the most dangerous one. You better *believe* that I'm going to get this information out where it can do some good, so people can react appropriately."

Cortlan blanched white as a sheet and sputtered. "Roger, if you broadcast that widely, my source will know it was me and will refuse to talk to me any more."

Maguire studied Cortlan carefully. He noted that Cortlan was way too nervous to be just protesting the risk of having an informant dry up on him. "Your source is CIA, isn't it? In fact, I bet it's Rod Birdsall. His name has certainly been associated with enough UFO information 'leaks.' Are you afraid Rod will have you 'terminated' for this leak?"

"No, it would never come to anything like that," Cortlan answered. "But if it gets back to him that I talked, he'll . . . ah, be through with me."

"What you mean is that your under-the-table contract as a CIA 'asset' will be all through," Maguire said in firm voice with a tone of conviction, partly addressing his long-standing suspicion about Cortlan, partly bluffing him in hopes of forcing an admission.

"You know the drill, Roger," Cortlan replied, halfway regaining his composure. "I can neither confirm nor deny any connection with the Company. But I'm *asking* you not to spread that item."

"Sorry, Don," Maguire replied with a dour expression. He looked Cortlan squarely in the eye. "The stakes are too big here. This false landing could place some very bad people into positions of global power. There are overriding ethical considerations here, Don. The protection of global society from manipulation by this JANUS group is slightly more important than your Agency contract," he said with biting sarcasm.

"Rog's right," Catalina chimed in. "It would be a catastrophe if people got the idea that these dangerous JANUS people were officially approved by the ETs as Earth's representatives."

Cortlan attempted one more time to get Maguire to agree to silence, by promising to reveal the location of secret U.S. underground UFO installations in exchange. Maguire turned the offer down. When Cortlan saw that he was getting nowhere, his tone turned curt. "Well, I see that we have nothing else to discuss. So, since I am very busy, we can call it a day. I'll see you to the door."

"No need to, Don. We'll let ourselves out. Thanks for your hospitality."

"Yes, it was nice meeting you," Catalina said, somewhat lamely.

Maguire added, "As much as I can, I'll try to protect you from being identified, when I notify the UFO community about JANUS's fake alien landing."

Cortlan was not mollified. "Thank you so much," he replied, his voice dripping with sarcasm.

Maguire and Catalina exited to their car, and headed for Interstate 295 leading into Washington, D.C.

"Whew! That was tense," Catalina commented. "I'm glad to be out of there."

"Yeah. You never know with Don where he is on an issue. He takes this posture of Mr. UFOlogist. You don't want to alienate his Intelligence buddies, either. He'd like to have it both ways, but that's not in the cards when you deal with a matter of massive global deception. I think things are at the point where, more than ever before, it's time everybody chose up which side they're on."

"Amen, brother," Catalina said cheerfully, deciding to lighten up the tone. "So, Rog, why don't you pull over for a moment?"

Maguire obligingly pulled over to the gravel shoulder of Greenbelt Road. As the car stopped, Catalina leaned over and put her arms around him in a big hug. "Rog, I'm so proud of you. You're so daring, looking for the ET Landing. And you don't compromise on your principles. That meeting with Don just showed me that. I'm so glad you're having me along on this journey. I wouldn't trade being here for the world." She pressed her cheek against his. "I just had to tell you that." She released him and sat up straight. "I hope you don't think I'm too fresh, you know, hugging you like that."

"Oh, I don't shock too easily," Maguire replied, then went on, with characteristically mischievous deadpan humor. "Once, when I was doing field studies in a remote Inuit village, out of Umiot, Alaska, the chief offered to have his 20-year-old daughter share my bed during my stay, to keep me warm. Local custom. But I said no. So, compared to that, a friendly hug is no big deal." Maguire looked at the nonplussed expression on Catalina's face and then burst out laughing. Catalina was caught off-guard, at first confused, then peeved at being tricked by his over-the-top humor. Finally she joined in Maguire's contagious good-natured laughter. "You got me that time," she giggled.

Maguire became serious. "Actually, your hug felt good. I've grown to like you a lot, Barbara. I'm glad you're along. I just wanted to say that."

Catalina smiled in acknowledgment. After a moment she looked ahead down the Interstate and asked "Say, Dr. Maguire, are we heading for the Hopi reservation now?"

"Yep. But first I need to stop at the Library of Congress. I want to use an internet access terminal there to post the news about this rogue JANUS group and their fake alien landing scheme on the world-wide internet."

"Why?"

"Because the newspapers won't handle this story. The internet is the best way to spread the word to key UFOlogists everywhere in the U.S. and around the world quickly," Maguire answered. "Post a message and fifteen minutes later, it's delivered. Those key UFO investigators who read it will pass it on, and it'll get to the media that way, through key news source tips. Besides, UFO experts are the ones who would react first to such an attempted hoax. Once I've briefed them, JANUS's fake landing is going to be scoffed out of existence. The media would turn to UFO experts for their opinions of such an 'alien landing', and the UFO experts will all label the 'landing' as fake and disinformation."

"Won't that put you in danger with the JANUS group?" Catalina asked. "They're going to be really mad at you when the exposure gets traced back to you. And you heard Dr. Stone say that they are dangerous and powerful."

"You sound like my mother used to. 'Roger, put on your raincoat. Those clouds look like it's going to rain,'" Maguire said, teasing her.

"Damn it, Roger Maguire, I love you! I'm not going to have you killed by some fascist jerks." Catalina quickly cupped her hand to her mouth, not believing what she had just let slip out. A tear started to run down her cheek and she clenched her hands in quiet frustration, humiliated at having blurted out like a schoolgirl.

Maguire decided it was wiser to pretend he didn't hear her love statement. "Barbara, believe me, JANUS is not going to liquidate me for posting that warning on the internet. If they did, such an action would just tell everyone what I said was the truth."

"But they could get at you in other terrible ways."

"This fake alien landing is too important, more important than my skin. It has to be exposed. I just *can't* stay silent. Anyway, this whole UFO and ET investigation business has its risks."

Catalina was not pacified. "But not like the risk of taking on *that* kind of a powerful group."

"I have to take that chance, Barbara, don't you see? If you want to bail out, I won't blame you. Being around me could certainly bring some danger to you as well. Exposing the fake landing will increase that risk. I know that. And I care about you. I wouldn't want you to be harmed. I mean it. Give some careful thought as to whether you should leave now. I'll understand."

Catalina sat there a while in silence, frowning and dabbing at her eyes, as the Pathfinder sped down Interstate 295 into Washington, D.C.. Finally she said, "All right, Roger, I guess you know what you have to do. I'm still with you, danger or not. I'll just have to pray a lot more that Spirit keeps protection around us."

Maguire turned to her, smiled, and said playfully, "I'm counting on that. You know, you're better to have around than a lucky rabbit's foot."

Catalina, by now onto his teasing, gave him a playful punch on the arm, and finally managed a gallant smile.

An Air Force courier in dress blues hurried down cool underground corridors a hundred feet beneath the desert floor near Albuquerque. Overhead, the headquarters building of Sandia National Laboratories stood shimmering from the 105-degree heat still lingering in the autumn twilight from a week-long heat wave. Magnetic-induction plasma lighting panels in the subterranean corridor ceiling cast a yellowish-white light on the six-feet-thick walls, which were painted an off-white. The walls were bare except for stenciled alphanumeric direction signs. The courier turned into Room Z-1, the underground office of the Director of the PANDORA Unit. He strode up to the figure seated at the desk, and saluted. "Urgent satellite transmission for the Colonel, *Sir*!"

Jack Partridge dismissed the courier and opened the sealed packet, marked "Classified - ATS/Special Access - PANDORA One - J -Eyes Only." He looked at the transmission text and angrily snubbed out his cigarillo into the almost full ashtray. "Damn!" he muttered. The message was from "Roderick Birdsall, Chief of Special Projects, Directorate of Operations, CIA." But Partridge knew that this was not a CIA message. The letter "J" quietly embedded in the security classification text meant that this message was restricted to one of nine people: a message from JANUS.

Birdsall's message to Partridge told of getting a phone call from a source whom Birdsall self-protectingly identified only as "an informant" (actually Don Cortlan). The message said that the "informant" had reported to Birdsall that Roger Maguire had become aware of JANUS's plan to stage a fake alien landing. Furthermore, this Maguire had learned of the location and the approximate time the staged "landing" was planned for, less than two weeks away. Since the informant did not identify Maguire's source for these facts, that issue was not addressed in Birdsall's message to Partridge. The message pointed out to Partridge that it was extremely dangerous having a person like Dr. Roger Maguire in possession of JANUS's plan, and that the situation required immediate remediation. Birdsall ended his message with his customarily blunt language. "Jack, since you're Director of the PANDORA Unit, you have access to the exotic resources this situation requires. I think it's time our Dr. Maguire ended his UFOlogical career unobtrusively and permanently. It must look natural. Kindly notify me when you have accomplished your task."

Partridge set the message down and stopped to reflect. Maguire had to be eliminated and fast. Maguire's profile noted that he was an active participant on UFO-oriented internet Echos. All JANUS needed was to have that guy put JANUS's mock alien landing on the internet and we're done, the Colonel mused. He considered his options from the advanced technologies the PANDORA unit had at its disposal. An argon laser would be instantaneously lethal, but would leave tell-tale burn marks. Partridge toyed with the idea of doing it anyway and planting the story that aliens zapped Maguire. But then he decided that was too implausible, and would only raise more questions. Using a very strong isotropic energy-field radiator device would certainly fry the bastard, Partridge thought, but again the high-tech body damage would lead to unwelcome questions. He considered using extreme low frequency sound generation to disorient Maguire while he was driving, to induce a fatal crash. Difficult to set up, but possible. Partridge mentally checked that one off into the possibilities column. A concentrated electromagnetic-pulse generator could stop Maguire's heart, but might damage other organs and cause unwelcome questions at an autopsy. Likewise, Partridge ruled out a high-powered microwave emitter, since it created an indiscriminate frying of all the "target's" organs. Projecting an oncoming hologram in front of Maguire's car to force him off a mountainous road was an uncertain method. These damned abductees have been exposed to such exotic alien technologies during their abductions, Partridge mused, that he could not be sure Maguire would be spooked enough and overreact to a mere hologram. Beta-wave incapacitators worked fine, but mostly were useful for mental disorientation. JANUS wanted Maguire dead, not dazed.

The Colonel then considered the "soft" technologies on the "mental" side of PANDORA's armamentarium. His lab had made a special adaptation of a psychotronic weapon originally designed by Hungarian Intelligence. It could induce extreme suicidal impulses in a properly suggestible subject. However, Partridge was not sure that someone with Maguire's background would be sufficiently suggestible, since Maguire's dossier said that he had taken coursework in psychiatric anthropology. Besides, mental telepathic-control technology was so iffy. It depended so much on the parapsychological skills of the individual controller in mentally suggesting fatal behavior, and on the "target" person's ability to resist such suggestions. Maguire's parapsychological abilities were an unknown. The Colonel considered remote-viewing. It could be useful in locating where Maguire would be in the near future, for example, to plan an ambush, but did not in itself have lethal effects.

That left parapsychological-force attack. This was a technique which had been developed in a cruder form by some shamans and witch doctors many centuries ago. It involved carefully concentrating the life-force energy of the attacker and directing it psychically against the targeted individual. Such psychic force could adversely affect the target's thoughts and feelings, or even shut down their body systems and cause death. Yes! Here was the technique best suited to JANUS's assignment of inducing an unobtrusive, natural-seeming death. Colonel Partridge considered himself quite an adept at psychic killing. He remembered once having been invited to Lawrence Livermore National Laboratory, when Henri Fournier ran the Special Projects Department. In several extremely classified experiments in an experimental center there, Partridge had succeeded in cutting off the air supply of a young lab assistant volunteer "target." While Partridge stopped after a couple minutes, and the young man did not die, Partridge later heard that the unfortunate fellow suffered lasting brain damage. Other practitioners of the dark arts in the PANDORA unit had succeeded in creating epilepsy and even a fatal heart attack in several subjects. Partridge settled on lethal psychic attack as his weapon of choice in carrying out JANUS's death sentence on Maguire.

The Colonel realized that it was imperative to have current information on his "target's" whereabouts. He dialed Major Bryce Eberhardt's pager number and punched in the terse message: "urgent." When Eberhardt failed to return his page within five minutes, the Colonel rang Eberhardt's headquarters and demanded to know from the AFOSI Officer of the Day where Eberhardt was. The O.D. told him that the Major was out.

Partridge dealt with that response with customary directness. "God damn it, sergeant, I *know* he's out! I've been paging him on an urgent basis for five solid minutes. Tell me something I don't know. Where the hell is he?"

The O.D. tried to avoid giving a direct answer. "Sir, I can have one of the staff find him, and have him get on the phone with you shortly."

Partridge sensed he was being given the dodge. "Sergeant,

I didn't ask you for a search and rescue mission. I want to know where the Major is. Let me make it simple for you. Tell me his location, Sergeant! This is a direct order!"

The O.D. paused. Then reluctantly, in a subdued voice, he replied, "The Major told me not to disturb him. But since you're ordering me, and you're a Colonel, I can tell you that he's at the Nuts & Bolts downtown. Do you know that place, sir? Corner of Wyoming Boulevard and Indian School Road?"

Partridge indeed knew of the Nuts & Bolts. It was a quietly notorious leather bar that catered to a motley clientele of drugstore bikers, young macho airmen from the nearby Air Force Base, and the discreetly open members of Albuquerque's gay leather community. Partridge was taken back momentarily at the idea of a career officer frequenting a dive like the Nuts & Bolts. But then he decided that the best way to get hold of Eberhardt quickly was to go down there himself.

The Nuts & Bolts was busy and raucous. Neon lighting garishly illuminated the faux weathered-bunkhouse decor. Given the place's reputation, Partridge was not surprised to spot two MPs idling against the back wall, observing the patrons. A thick haze of cigarette smoke hung in the air, adding unintended atmosphere for the blaring redneck ballads sung by a truly mediocre country-western trio.

Partridge spotted Eberhardt down at the corner end of the bar. Eberhardt was in uniform but wearing polished black cowboy boots. In his left hand he was holding a cigarette holder at a rakish angle, as he leaned over too close to the young airman on the next stool. The airman was nervously laughing at something the Major had said. Eberhardt kept his gaze fixed on the airman's face, as he reached over and placed his right hand on the boy's knee. Partridge moved up behind Eberhardt. With his practiced eye the Colonel noticed the full ashtray and the Major's slouch on his barstool, sure indicators of too many hours of hard drinking.

The young airman noticed the Colonel's approach, and straightened up on his barstool as an automatic reflex. Eberhardt didn't notice Partridge. He was busy pulling a little baggie out of his inside jacket pocket which contained a white powder. Major Eberhardt dangled it in front of the airman, while his eyes were dreamily fixed on the 18-year-old. The airman's extremely uncomfortable expression finally registered through Eberhardt's alcoholic haze. He turned around unsteadily on his stool to see what the airman was looking at out of the corner of his eye.

Partridge wasted no time. "Airman, get out of here." The cherub-faced boy hastily got up and left. The Colonel turned to Eberhardt. "Bryce, I'm ashamed of you. I've never had a faggot under my command before. And a coke-head to boot."

Eberhardt was too drunk to measure his words. "Well, you *do* now, Jack. And your precious unit has harbored this fag for the past three years."

"Bryce, you stupid drunk fucker, let me give you a little free advice. Stop trolling for airmen half your age. I've got another bit of brilliant advice for you, too, jerk-off. Put in for a transfer as soon as you sober up in the morning. The sooner you're out of my command, the better. Now that we've got that cleared up, you sorry-ass queen, why the *fuck* didn't you answer my page?"

Eberhardt's answer was spoken in a tone of defiant sassiness. "Gee, Jack, it's my day off and I had my pager turned off."

"People under my command don't take days off!" Partridge roared into the Major's ear, then lowered his voice to avoid having what he was going to say next overheard. "Now, listen up, fruitcake. I need to get information on 'Fellow Traveler's' present location. It's time that his life on this earth was concluded by an 'executive action.' Now do you, or that burrito-bandit Captain of yours, just happen to know where he is?"

Eberhardt lurched back on his stool at Partridge's sarcastic blast, then tried to focus on what the Colonel was saying. Eberhardt put on a too-nice expression, replying with sing-song sweetness, "Gee, Jack, I'll just dial up José and see what I can find out. By the way, dearie, did I ever tell you you've got the greatest gluteals?"

Partridge saw red and exploded. He swung and planted a right cross punch on Eberhardt's jaw. "Goddamn queer!"

The Major slumped off the stool to the floor. The two M.P.'s who had been standing against the back wall raced up and helped Major Eberhardt to his feet. Before the M.P.'s escorted him off, Eberhardt pressed his face close to Partridge's and snarled, "Fuck you, Jackie boy. Go find Maguire yourself."

Roderick Birdsall sat in his corner office on the fifth floor of the new wing at Langley. A Lucky Strike held between his right thumb and index finger trailed a column of smoke as he gazed out over the Potomac. In the distance was the leafy green canopy of trees stretching towards Bethesda. Birdsall hated loose ends. And this matter of Roger Maguire acquiring intimate intelligence on the future plans of JANUS was most decidedly a *very* bad case of loose ends. It had not been pleasant calling Partridge to tell him what he needed to know in order to have Maguire terminated. In so doing, Birdsall had had to reveal that the information about the mock alien landing had gotten outside JANUS. So far, the finger of accusation had not pointed to him. It was Birdsall's aim to see that it never did. So far, only *he* knew that it was Cortlan who had snitched on Maguire. Birdsall knew that it was his own incautious gossiping with Cortlan, during one of their cozy excursions on Birdsall's launch up the Potomac when both men had had too much to drink, that had been the source of the leak outside the protective circle of JANUS. Birdsall understood well what would be the consequences for him, if his JANUS mates were to discover that he had been indiscreet. Luckily the problem was quite easily solvable, Birdsall reflected. The Dark Colonel was about to take care of Maguire. And that left Cortlan as the only tie back to him in spycraft. And Birdsall understood spycraft very well. He put out his half-smoked cigarette, picked up the phone, and dialed the Assistant Deputy Director of Operations for Special Projects.

Don Cortlan was in a rotten mood as he pulled away from his house and headed up Highway 295 towards the *Baltimore Sun* newspaper office. He was way behind with the story copy he had promised for tomorrow's edition. His talk with Maguire and Catalina, and the foul mood he was in after they left, had taken up most of the day. When he had finally decided to warn Birdsall about what Maguire knew, Cortlan was at first relieved that Birdsall had not directly accused him of being the source of the leak. But then he realized that he didn't have to. From the dark tone in Birdsall's voice, Cortlan knew that he knew, and that he knew that Cortlan knew he knew. When Birdsall hung up, Cortlan felt that the best thing that could happen would be that he would never hear from Birdsall again. Cortlan was also thinking of the other unsavory possibilities as he drove up the Parkway. Just as he passed by NASA's Goddard Space Flight Center, a Maryland state trooper vehicle pulled into his lane about 100 yards behind him. Shit, Cortlan thought, what this day doesn't need is a traffic ticket on top of everything else. He carefully slowed to 55, but the trooper remained exactly the same distance behind him. As he approached the Highway 197 exit to the Patuxent Wildlife Research Center, the trooper turned his emergency lights on, and pulled up behind Cortlan's car. Over the patrol car's loudspeaker the trooper told him to take the exit onto Highway 197. After Cortlan complied, the trooper directed him to drive south, and continued to follow him. Cortlan wondered at this strange approach to giving a speeding ticket. A little over a mile down 197, the trooper told Cortlan to pull over onto a dirt road on the right. As he did so, Cortlan noticed that there was another man in the front seat of the patrol car. The other man did not have a police uniform on, but wore a gray suit.

The Trooper barked through the patrol car speaker.

Cortlan emerged from his car and stood by the open door. The trooper swung him around and cuffed him roughly from behind.

"Officer, I can explain. I'm a reporter for the *Baltimore Sun* and I was just ..."

"Shut up, asshole," the trooper snarled, and shoved him up against the car. "I don't give a good god-damn who you are."

Cortlan noticed the man in the gray suit approaching with a large bandanna in his hand. In a swift motion, the man placed the bandanna over Cortlan's face and held it there while Cortlan struggled, trying to breathe. As Cortlan's limp body fell to the ground, the man opened Cortlan's mouth and placed a drop from an eyedropper in the back of his throat. The man waited a minute, then felt the carotid artery along Cortlan's throat for a pulse. Detecting none, he nodded to the trooper, who released the handcuffs, and placed Cortlan's body in the position it would be in if Cortlan had stopped his car and started to get out while having a heart attack. Then the trooper and the gray suit got back in the state patrol car, backed out onto the highway, and headed back towards the Interstate.

Chapter 7

TIMOTHY Katoya sat on a sun-bleached wooden rocking chair in the hard clay yard in front of his home. He put his hand over his eyes and squinted at something approaching in the late-afternoon sunlight. It was the familiar shape of Maguire's Pathfinder heading down the dirt road towards his house.

His gnarled bronze face crinkled with a smile as he rose with a wave of his hand to greet his guests. Besides a greeting, Katoya's smile was an inward recognition of this latest reaffirmation of the Kachinas' reliability. Last night he had had another vision Dream in which Saquasohuh, the Blue Star Kachina, came down from a far-off star, one which the Bahana astronomers have not yet found. Saquasohuh had enormous dark eyes and a blue four-pointed star painted on his flat face. The Blue Star Kachina had told Katoya that Maguire and his woman companion would arrive today, and that it was most important not to forget to tell them everything which Saquasohuh had shown Katoya during a previous vision Dream. Katoya still was in awe of that Dream. It had shown him many events which indicated that the end times which the old prophecies had talked about were near.

Katoya came up to Maguire and Barbara and reached out his hand in greeting. "How is my favorite paleface?" Katoya asked with good-natured teasing.

"I'm fine, grandfather. Barbara and I are a little worn out from the drive from Maryland."

"I'm thirsty," Catalina chimed in. "Can I have a glass of water, Timothy?"

Katoya waved towards his open front door. "Help yourself, but don't drink too much. And don't eat anything. We are going to have a sweat lodge ceremony before we have dinner tonight. You'll need to keep a pretty empty stomach."

Katoya got his guests settled with beverages. Then he

told them that Spirit had directed him that they should all purify themselves in the sweat lodge, before he shared his Dream visions with them. Maguire had participated in this pan-tribal sacred ceremony a number of times, as part of his participatory study of Native American culture. Catalina knew a bit about the sweat lodge ceremony from the Ojibwa traditional teachings she had been given growing up, but had not actually been in one before.

Katoya explained that the *inipi* ceremony was conducted in a small, 12-foot-diameter, dome-shaped structure, made of saplings and branches woven together and covered with blankets. Inside there was total darkness, as in a mother's womb, which is what the lodge symbolizes. The participants sat around a central pit into which football-size, glowing red-hot stones were placed. The stones were sprinkled with sage and cedar, and then water was poured over them. The resultant aromatic steam was hotter than any *bahana* sauna, and was considered to have curative as well as purifying powers. There would be four "rounds," with intermissions during which the blanket over the door was thrown back and cool air allowed to come into the lodge for a while. During each round, there were special prayers and Indian religious songs. Katoya explained that if everyone brought a pure heart into the lodge, and if the spirits willed it, that participants could have visions which provided guidance or sacred contact.

Katoya added that they would be joined by three other people in this late afternoon sweat lodge, the chief of his clan, the Snake Clan, the *kikmongwi*, traditional village leader of Hotevilla, and her twelve-year-old daughter who was preparing for her coming-of-age ceremony to take place later this Fall. He expressed satisfaction at the gender balance, three of each.

A band of gray clouds to the west of Hotevilla suggested the uncertain possibility of rain. The clouds blocked the rays from the lowering sun and cooled the wind blowing across Hopiland. Six figures stood outside a four-foot-high sweat lodge, situated near the base of a seldom-used cliff trail leading up to Hotevilla village. Tending the fire nearby was the designated Fire Man, Katoya's grandson.

At the direction of Katoya, the six stripped. Each was smudged with cedar smoke in sacred preparation for the sweat lodge ceremony. Then, one by one, they entered the lodge through its low doorway on their hands and knees, as a humble ritual gesture of reentering the womb. The six took a position around the circular wall. Katoya took a stone pipe with a long carved wooden stem, lit it, and prayed to Sotuqnang-u, the Sky deity above, to Masao, the Earth deity below, and to the spirits of the four directions. As he did so, he blew a puff of smoke from the sacred herb-tobacco mixture in each direction. Then he passed the pipe around the circle, so that each participant could pray, then draw and exhale some smoke, sending their prayers skyward. Then at Katoya's direction, the Fire Man brought in four large super-heated stones, each carried in on the tines of a pitchfork. Katoya pulled the blanket across the doorway, sealing out the fading light of sunset. He sprinkled cedar and sage on the sizzling rocks, and then ladled some water onto them from a bucket by his side. Fiery aromatic steam enveloped the sweat lodge as he began a spiritual chant in Hopi. The other Indians present and Maguire joined in a Hopi song to Eototo, the Kachina chief, to bless them. Catalina hummed along in a pure high voice.

After about ten minutes into the third round, Katoya's voice rang out in the darkness of the lodge. "Ho, Saquasohuh! Welcome! We are honored." Maguire strained in the dark to try to make out the figure of the Blue Star Kachina which Katoya was obviously seeing. Maguire noticed that, instead of the pitch blackness that there normally is inside the lodge, there was an irregular patch of ill-defined light above the rocks, which were no longer glowing. But he saw nothing that looked particularly like a kachina. He made a mental note to check with Barbara after the sweat lodge to see if she psychically saw anything inside.

In the clear starry night outside the sweat lodge, the remains of the fire were being stirred by the Fire Man. The six sweat lodge participants were huddled around the mound of fierce orange-red coals for warmth against the chill. The six were back in their day clothes, trying to ward off the nighttime breeze. Catalina told the others that she had psychically seen a tall Indian woman in the lodge during the third round. The woman was wearing a buckskin shirt, a Hopi sash and a fox skin, along with a reddish-brown cloth kilt and belt. Her body was painted black, with white shoulders and forearms. She wore a white case mask, on which were painted a moon and three four-pointed stars painted a rich blue. Katoya nodded in recognition. He told her that he had seen the same figure. He added that this same Blue Star Kachina had told him in the sweat lodge that after the ceremony, both Maguire and Catalina should be given the information which had been previously shown to Katoya in vision. Katoya stood up to deliver that message.

"Hear now the message of Saquasohuh," the Elder said. "The world we are living in — Indian and non-Indian — is not the first era of human civilization. There have been three previous such eras. In each of the three eras, humans turned away from spiritual principles and their world was destroyed. The First World was destroyed by sinking of land, what the *Bahanas* would call major earthquakes. The Second World was destroyed by freezing, what *Bahanas* call the great Ice Age. The Third World reached a level of high technology, far in advance of what is currently known. But because they pursued only material things and ridiculed spiritual principles, that world was destroyed by a Great Flood, which many nations still recall in their ancient writings.

"The Fourth World is where we now live. But humans have taken the world that the Great Spirit told us to take care of and have put it in terrible shape. Humans poison their own food, water and air with pollution. Many, including children, are left to starve. In many places wars are still being fought. Greed and concern for material things are common diseases. Many original native people are landless, homeless, starving and have no medical help.

"The Hopi were told in prophecy that humans would develop many powerful technologies that would be abused. We were foretold about the First World War, and a Second World War, which ended when the predicted gourd of ashes — what you call the atomic bomb — twice fell from the sky with great destruction, destroying thousands. The Hopi believe that the Persian Gulf War was the beginning of World

War Three. But it was stopped in time and the worst weapons of destruction were not used."

"My God!" Maguire exclaimed, "the Persian War could have been the End?" He shook his head and sighed, "We came so close."

"There is more, my friend," Katoya said. "We are seeing increasing floods, more damaging hurricanes, violent hailstorms, climate changes, and great earthquakes, as our prophecies said would come. Even the birds and animals are giving us warning by the strange changes in their behavior, such as the beaching of whales. If humans do not wake up to these warnings, the great purification will come to destroy this world, just as the previous worlds were destroyed. This is now the time to weigh the choices for our future. If the nations of this Earth create another great war, the Hopi have been told that we humans will burn ourselves to death with ashes. World War III will be started by those people who first received the light of intelligent culture in the old countries."

"Timothy, do you mean the Near East or Asia?" Catalina asked.

"That is what the Elders believe Saquasohuh meant."

"Will it affect us?" Catalina inquired.

"The United States will be destroyed, both the land and the population, by atomic bombs and radioactivity. Only the Hopis and their homeland will be preserved as an oasis to which refugees will flee. The Four Corners area of the Hopi is that spiritual center. Within it, the prophecies say, is a sacred site, which will have a special purpose in the future for mankind's survival."

"Timothy, what about fallout shelters?" Maguire asked. "The Federal Emergency Management Agency has created huge secure underground bunkers where the elite can escape to."

Katoya shook his head emphatically. "Bomb shelters are a fallacy. It is only materialistic people who seek to make shelters. Those who are at peace in their hearts already are in the great shelter of life. There is no shelter for evil. The war will be a 'spiritual' conflict fought over material concerns. But these material concerns will be destroyed by spiritual beings."

"Does 'spiritual beings' refer to the ET Visitors coming?" Catalina asked.

"The Earth will go through a great shaking; bombs will go off. We need to pray," Katoya continued. "The Star People will come; countless people will come. They will remain to create one world and one nation under one power, that of the Creator. That time of the Fifth World is not far off. It will come when the Blue Star Kachina dances in the village plaza. Hear the message of Saquasohuh! The emergence to the future Fifth World is at hand. In fact, it has already begun. You can read the signs in the earth itself. Plant forms from the previous worlds are beginning to spring up. New stars are being seeded. It is the humble people who will seed the Fifth World, which is emerging."

"Is this all predestined?" Maguire asked. "Is there any way things can change?"

"The prophecy says that there are two paths. The first path follows technology which is separated from natural and spiritual laws. That path leads to chaos. The second path is the one which proceeds in harmony with natural law. If humans return to spiritual harmony and live from their hearts, we can experience a paradise in this world. We have a choice. If we continue on the first path, we will come to destruction."

"How can we recognize who the people are who will seed the Fifth World?" Catalina inquired.

Katoya answered her question with a question. "Who in this world can speak for nature and the spiritual energy that creates and flows through all life? In every continent there are human beings who have not separated themselves from the land and from nature. It is through their voices that Nature can speak."

Katoya sat down and gazed at the glowing embers of the fire. The clan chief, the kikmongwi, her daughter and Katoya's grandson stood up and said their good-nights to Katoya and the *Bahanas*. Then they excused themselves to begin the trek up the cliff trail to their homes on the mesa. As they began the climb up the trail by starlight, no one gave particular notice to the sound of a twig snapping in a mesquite thicket near the cliff. All Hopi know that many animals move about at night.

After they left, Maguire and Catalina sat close to Katoya by the fire. Katoya told them that he had a further message for them obtained from his vision with the Blue Star Kachina. "There are two more things which Saquasohuh said. These are for your ears alone. The first one concerns the Star People. They will be coming down in what you *Bahanas* call a flying saucer. They will make a landing and have an official meeting with representatives of Earth. It is important for the right kind of people to be there."

"Timothy, there is a small group of world-famous UFO researchers and a few government, religious and military officials, who are planning to be at that Landing and represent the Earth," Maguire asked. "These people call themselves Project Epiphany. Are they the right kind of people to be representing all humanity?"

"Saquasohuh has shown me the group which you speak of. Some of them will be at there when the Star People arrive; some will not. The Star People will see that they get sorted out before the time."

"Why won't some be there?" Maguire asked.

"Not all of them have the commitment or the right intentions for being there," Katoya replied. "A few are looking for power or fame. The Star People will not permit this meeting to be manipulated for individual selfish purposes. Others will be led astray, because they do not make the Star People the most important thing. This coming meeting will be a public service of the highest kind, for both Star Nations and the human race.

"There is another group which is trying to be at the meeting between Star People and humans," Maguire interrupted.

Katoya responded, "This group is very bad. Only one of them will be at the Landing, and it will not be because he is good. It is just the Great Spirit's way to bring good out of an evil situation. Saquasohuh showed me a vision that is associated with this bad group. A man stands in a doorway, but he can't decide whether to go through or turn back."

"That fits the name I believe this other group is called, JANUS," Maguire said.

"What about us?" Catalina joined in. "I was shown a vision of Roger and me at the Landing, too. Did Saquasohuh show you anything about that?"

The Hopi Elder frowned slightly. "I was shown that you two are *supposed* to be there when the Star People arrive. But powerful forces want to block your path. It will be very dangerous and it will not be easy."

"You mentioned that there was something else Saquasohuh showed you," Maguire said.

"Yes. The official meeting between the Star People and the humans is near. Because of that, Saquasohuh showed me that it is time to call a gathering of all the Keepers of the Star Nation altars from many tribes from all over North, Central and South America. I have been shown that certain *Bahana* experts on the Star People should also be invited to this gathering. The purpose will be to share what has been kept secret up until now, that the Star People have been visiting the indigenous peoples all over this hemisphere for countless generations. They have taught us and healed our sick sometimes. All the secret knowledge about the Star People must come out in the open at this meeting. And the *Bahana* experts must share everything that they know with us. When everyone has contributed their knowledge, we can complete the hoop of knowledge about the Star Nations. Then we will have complete understanding. That is the time that such information can be shared with the whole world.

"This is a spiritual undertaking. It will take place in late September, after the time of our sacred Snake Dance ceremony. This gathering will take place underground in our Great Kiva. This will be the first time that white people have been allowed in the kiva. But because Saquasohuh has shown me this is what must happen, white people will be allowed." He looked up at Maguire. "You are invited, Roger."

"I am honored, grandfather."

"Timothy, may I come, too?" Catalina asked.

"Since you have been directed by Spirit to be with Roger wherever he goes, it will be all right." Katoya added as an afterthought, "Even though you will be the first woman to ever enter our kiva." He then added, "One more thing you should

know, Roger and Barbara. You are being followed by someone. He works for that bad group you call JANUS. I am going to ask the Kachinas to place special protection around
you now, so that it will be difficult for them to follow you.
But still, be careful."

"And now, my friends, I have passed on everything that
Saquasohuh showed me. I am tired. Tonight I will sleep in
the sweat lodge and pary and ask the spirit's help for you.
You two can find some beds in my house."

Maguire and Catalina said goodnight to Timothy and
started up the cliff trail. As they proceeded, they could hear
the low voice of Katoya in the lodge, praying in Hopi. After
they reached the halfway point, a dark figure stepped out
from behind a mesquite thicket, and began stealthily ascending the narrow trail a little ways behind them. The obscure
figure reached thirty feet up the steep trail, when he stepped
on a large loose rock in the path. It slipped sideways and
over the edge. In the darkness the figure lost his balance,
and went tumbling down the steep rocky slope to the desert
floor. He landed with his right ankle underneath him. "Ow,
goddamn-it!" José DiGiorgio groaned aloud.

He lay there holding his severely sprained ankle gingerly,
quietly cursing in Spanish. As shock set in, he reached into a
utility pack on his belt and extracted a syringe and a small
bottle. The Lidocaine soon began to numb his ankle.
DiGiorgio got on the radio to his controller. "Zeta One, this
is Zeta Four. I fell off a trail in the dark while following 'Fellow Traveler' towards Hotevilla. It feels like I've broken my
ankle. I can't continue surveillance."

Major Bryce Eberhardt was sitting at his desk at AFOSI
Headquarters with a hangover, waiting for the aspirin he
had taken to start to take effect. He held an ice-pack to his
swollen jaw, still throbbing from Partridge's right cross. The
MPs who had politely escorted him from the Nuts and Bolts
back to his office on base had just left. Eberhardt noticed a
light flashing, It was a waiting phone message from Colonel
Partridge. The answering machine played back the Colonel's
voice, apologizing for getting physical and asking him to

forget about putting in for a transfer. Eberhardt accepted the news that he was still in Partridge's command without enthusiasm. It meant his record would not show a forced reassignment, but he was not mollified. He figured that the Colonel was basically just covering himself after the altercation against a charge of conduct unbecoming an officer. Eberhardt mused over how he could get back at Partridge for humiliating him in the Nuts and Bolts saloon. After Eberhardt pulled rank on the two MPs who brought him back, he was fairly confident that that they had been sufficiently intimidated that they would not spread stories. But getting even with Partridge would be more difficult to accomplish. Eberhardt had begun to fantasize about tricking Partridge into showing up at a certain gay gym, where a couple of Eberhardt's overdeveloped buddies would forcibly teach the Colonel the finer points of Greek love. DiGiorgio's call interrupted his reverie, and it did not bring good news.

"Zeta Four, I've reached the conclusion that you're a klutz," Eberhardt shouted into the phone, irritation making his voice rise. "No, let me be more forthright. You're a fucking moron! First you let yourself almost get captured by your surveillance target in Maryland. Then you let yourself get ID-ed by some cops, who put you at the scene of that stakeout. Now you lose your target because you're too incompetent to walk up a trail and chew gum at the same time. Zeta Four, I'm pulling you off the case. Get your ass back here. I'm going to reassign you to the Judge Advocate General's Office. You're too goddamn stupid to do intelligence work. Maybe the Judge Advocate's office can keep you busy filing papers. You *do* know the alphabet, don't you?"

DiGiorgio was rattled by the outburst. First rage rose within him. It was quickly followed by fear at what being cashiered out of the JANUS Unit might mean for his career. But he controlled himself and tried to sound professional. "Sir, who will take over surveillance on Magui-, I mean, 'Fellow Traveler'?"

"Not that it's any of your damn business, Zeta Four, but

I'm going to send in Zeta Two. Now get off that reservation before you get yourself spotted and identified. I want you to drive back to Albuquerque nonstop. You got that? I don't want any more screw-ups with you. You can save those for the Judge Advocate. He's such a pompous ass that he probably won't notice how incompetent you are."

Eberhardt clicked off his radio without waiting for DiGiorgio's reply and slammed it down into its cradle. He remembered that Zeta Two was currently writing up a report from his last operation. It had been a nasty assignment. Zeta Two had been borrowed by the National Reconnaissance Organization to take out an elderly and kind Ohio UFO investigator, who had recently retired from working as an Air Force counter-intelligence officer. This "target" had published too many accurate and widely read reports on UFO crash retrievals conducted by the military. Zeta Two's trained specialty was to induce deaths which seemed completely natural. Zeta Two saw to it that the elderly UFO investigator's demise appeared to be a natural heart attack. Eberhardt recalled the motto posted over Zeta Two's cubicle, "You tag 'em; I bag 'em." He reached for his phone and paged Zeta Two to come to his office.

Air Force Master Sergeant Timmy O'Connell sat back on the sofa in his mother's living room, balancing a second serving of pie on his lap, while pretending to listen attentively to her story about her trip with her lady friends to the Santa Fe Opera House. A short, chunky man in his early thirties with brown hair slicked back into a pompadour, O'Connell was attired in the dress-casual style he affected as his cover. His movements were quick, with the nervous energy of a bantam rooster both looking for and afraid of a fight. His characteristic half-smile, half-sneer expression masked a deep sadistic streak, which frequently found its outlet in his special assignments. Although he disliked the nickname Timmy, which his mother still used, he kept it because it had always served to tempt various brash individuals to make fun of him. That gave O'Connell the excuse he needed to attack them back. When he was younger, those attacks had been physical and brutal. More recently, his retaliations took the form of vicious dirty tricks, which he enjoyed even more.

O'Connell nominally worked at Kirtland in Air Force Intelligence under Major Eberhardt, whom he considered a fool. O'Connell enjoyed manipulating the Major. He got great satisfaction from getting Eberhardt to assign him to the dirty-trick jobs and making the Major think it was his own idea. But AFOSI was a cover for what O'Connell considered his real assignment: frequent "black" jobs for the National Reconnaissance Organization.

The National Reconnaissance Organization was an agency unknown to most even within intelligence circles. Anyone who heard something about it tended to confuse it with its "cover" namesake, the National Reconnaissance Office. The National Reconnaissance Office (NRO-1) was the covert bureau whose existence had been recently declassified. Its mission was collecting information from a global network of spy satellites. The National Reconnaissance Organization (NRO-2) was a military/intelligence instrumentality of JANUS. It conducted their surveillance, interdiction and capture of UFOs and their extraterrestrial occupants for intelligence purposes. The National Reconnaissance Organization also surveilled and interacted with civilians who had had extraterrestrial contacts. NRO-2 conducted civilian kidnappings, using mind control techniques, coercive drugging, and psychological warfare assaults disguised as "alien abductions," to debrief and reprogram civilians who had previously undergone genuine extraterrestrial contact. O'Connell particularly enjoyed working on the pseudo-alien abductions. He took his turn at the gang rapes of the generally attractive kidnapped young women, who were then hypnotized to believe that they had been assaulted by aliens. None on the assault teams gave much thought to why he always used an object instead of his penis to rape the women.

O'Connell enjoyed even more the "wet jobs" which occasionally came his way, such as the liquidation of that snooping Ohio UFO investigator. He smirked, recalling the elderly man's last expression as the man realized that the cigarette O'Connell had offered him contained something which was slowing his heart down dangerously.

His mother broke into his reverie. "Timmy, you haven't been paying a *bit* of attention to what I've been telling you about 'The Magic Flute'," she complained. "What's the matter? Don't you *care* about Mozart? What kind of a boy have I raised? *Really*, Timmy, sometimes I don't know what's gotten into you any more. Ready for another piece of your mother's special boysenberry pie that you always love to have me make?"

"No, thanks, mom. I'm really getting kind of full."

"Now, Timmy, what's *wrong* with you? Where's my boy with the big appetite? Your father, God rest his soul, could always put away *three* pieces of my pie. Aren't you the man your father was? Of course he *was* getting a little plump before he died." The mother tittered with a self-absorbed grin. "But it wasn't my pie. He just didn't work it off like he should have. Certainly not in bed." The mother tittered again at her naughty allusion.

Normally, O'Connell would not have welcomed Eberhardt's paging him at night when he was off-duty. But his overbearing mother was starting to grate on his nerves. He was finding it hard to maintain the dutiful frozen smile he affected with her. Ever since she had recently moved across Albuquerque to a house two blocks away from his apartment, he was finding it more difficult to turn down her almost daily dinner invitations.

"Oops, mom, there goes my pager. It's the Major. It's gotta be something urgent. I gotta go."

"Now, Timmy, are you sure you just didn't have some guy page you, so you wouldn't have to spend the evening with your poor widow mother, like a dutiful single son should?"

O'Connell grabbed his coat, gave his mother a hurried peck, and headed for the door. He didn't appreciate that "single" jab of hers. He worried nervously whether his mother had somehow learned about his impotency problems.

Jack Partridge sat back in the swivel chair of his PANDORA

Unit office, and took a long drag on his cigarillo. It had been smart to bury the hatchet with Eberhardt. Things were becoming unraveled enough about the real extraterrestrial landing and JANUS's fake landing, now that Maguire was sticking his nose into these matters. Partridge didn't need the headache of having to break in a new supervisor, too. Later on he could still have the queer reassigned, he mused. After giving Eberhardt an insincere apology for decking him, and then asking the Major to stay on, Partridge had emphasized to him the vital importance of putting his best man on the surveillance of Maguire. Partridge had pointed out to Eberhardt that he needed to have the exact coordinates of Maguire's location, so that he could target him with directed lethal psychic energy.

Eberhardt had responded to Colonel Partridge that O'Connell was his best surveillance man, and that O'Connell had just gotten freed up after finishing a National Reconnaissance Organization job. Partridge agreed with his choice. O'Connell was thorough and had a zero miss record. Furthermore, in the off-chance that Partridge's lethal psychic attack was not successful, O'Connell could be counted on to see to it that Maguire met a swift end by more conventional means. Partridge reflected that everything was going perfectly. He'd get a good night's sleep tonight, and tomorrow he'd have O'Connell feed him Maguire's location. And then Maguire wouldn't know what hit him.

On the top floor of the Senate Office Building, Senator John Knapp turned away from his office window. A light mist partially obscured his dramatic view of the Capitol Dome and the Lincoln Memorial. He sat down at his desk to begin the work day. As was his usual routine, he began going over the intelligence summaries provided to his office at 7:00 a.m. sharp each morning by courier from Langley. As he started into the folder, his chief administrative aide came in with his morning coffee and a sheaf of printouts.

"Senator, I think you'd better take a look at these. There's something mighty strange going on. I downloaded these printouts from the internet last night. This stuff is all over all the Echos and web sites."

"What have you got there, Chris?" the Senator asked, taking a sip of coffee. He adjusted his glasses, and he began to glance through the printouts.

"Sir, the internet is buzzing with reports of a secret group which is planning to stage a fake landing of 'aliens' within the next two weeks. The original source of these internet reports seems to be a Dr. Roger Maguire, a UFO researcher. Maguire's informing everybody that the fake landing is scheduled to take place near Norfolk, Virginia, at the NASA Visitor's Center on Langley Air Force Base. The people on the internet are in an uproar over this fake alien landing, especially the people who follow UFO developments. They're ridiculing anyone who would attempt such a hoax as being pathetic. They're really up in arms about this secret group behind the fake landing. They say it's obvious the group has some government insiders in it, because of the site being Langley Air Force Base and the NASA Center there. And they say that this Dr. Maguire has identified the group's name. He says it's JANUS."

Senator Knapp's coffee cup slipped out of his hand and cascaded all over the CIA briefing folder. His aide offered to clean up the mess, but the Senator barked at him to leave him alone and get out. Knapp got on his encrypted phone and hurriedly placed a call to Henri Fournier.

Fournier took the Senator's call, turned pale, and then became livid at the news. "John, this is extremely serious." The octogenarian head of JANUS did not speak in his usual measured manner. "Our chief strategy to preempt the aliens has just been sent down a shithole."

The Senator could tell that Fournier was even more upset than he thought he would be. Knapp had never heard the academic Fournier slip into profanity before. "Henri, what do we do now?" Knapp asked.

"We need to canvass the Group and devise a response to this development. We can't let some busybody UFOlogist upset our plans at this late date. But there's an even more ominous aspect to this news, John. We have a leak within our group.

That cannot and will not be tolerated. I have a fairly certain idea about which one of us is the source of this leak. Now tell me, John, who has the loose mouth in our Group?"

The Senator paused for a moment to reflect, secretly glad that Fournier was confiding his suspicions to him. At least he didn't have to worry that Fournier might think that *he* was the leak. "Do you mean Rod Birdsall, Henri? He certainly plays fast and loose with the UFO intelligence that his CIA picks up."

"Precisely," Fournier said in an even and deadly tone that Knapp had never heard him use before. "I'm going to contact Admiral Clannon. I think he has the connections to take care of our problem in a sanitary and untraceable fashion. It's really too bad. Birdsall was really pleasant enough, even an amusing sort of chap. But you know the saying, Senator, 'Loose lips sink ships.' John, expect a conference call from my office tomorrow on your secure phone. I'll be putting together a caucus of JANUS members first thing tomorrow morning. We'll need to devise an alternative to our 'alien landing.' All of us, that is, except Rod."

"You mean Rod won't be informed about the conference call?" Knapp asked.

"John, what I mean is that Birdsall won't be around tomorrow morning, unless Admiral Clannon has lost his touch, which I doubt."

Senator Knapp shuddered. He knew when he joined with JANUS that he was playing with the big boys. But Fournier's unhesitating ruthlessness was not what he expected as the kind of treatment that would be meted out to members of the inner circle.

The late summer light was fading into dusk, as Roderick Birdsall steered his yacht up the river from the Potomac Boat Club. The steward at the Club had brought a chilled bottle of their finest champagne on board as he requested. Birdsall did not have his family along for this particular moonlight cruise. He needed time alone to think. Don Cortlan was dead. The report said a heart attack, but Birdsall didn't believe it. Cortlan's death had the look of a professional hit job. It was so good that it could have only been done by people with access to restricted assets. He steered his yacht to the right as he approached a small island in the river, After he straightened out in the right channel, Birdsall poured himself a glass of champagne and continued his analysis of the situation.

Why was Cortlan killed? Had he talked indiscreetly? That must be it. Birdsall could think of no other reason why Cortlan would earn a professional hit job. What could it be that Cortlan had leaked? Birdsall mused a few minutes, then the terrible answer came to him. Cortlan had turned around and leaked to somebody else what Birdsall had confided to him about JANUS's plans for a pseudo-alien landing! The fact that Cortlan had been killed for that leak indicated that the hit had to have come from JANUS. If JANUS knew that Cortlan had leaked their plans, they certainly had the intelligence capabilities to find out who within JANUS had been leaking information to Cortlan. That meant that someone in JANUS knew, or would soon know, that Rod Birdsall was the leak! That meant that he could now be a target at any moment. His only hope was to get out of town and disappear fast, maybe for the duration.

Birdsall noted his bearings and began to swing the boat around to head back to the Boat Club docks. As he swung around, he noticed with irony that the shoreline on the left bank of the Potomac was a stretch of the George Washington Parkway directly in front of CIA Headquarters. He lifted his champagne glass in a mock salute to his employer. He completed his turnaround and opened up the throttle. The crescendoing noise from the yacht's powerful twin Mercury engines was blotted out by the roar of a gigantic explosion, as the yacht was enveloped in a massive reddish-orange fireball.

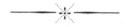

Chapter 8

A SMALL dark-colored Cessna crossed the boundary of the Hopi Reservation. The pilot, Zeta Five, peered through his night vision glasses at the terrain in the darkness below. The plane circled once around the broad valley of Polacca Wash east of First Mesa. Then the Cessna set down on an unlit desert landing strip near the base of the towering sandstone mesa and disgorged its sole passenger. Air force Master Sergeant Timmy O'Connell, wearing a charcoal gray shirt, blue jeans, and sneakers, emerged from the still-idling plane and walked over to a waiting Bureau of Indian Affairs car. As he opened the car door, the Cessna taxied back onto the runway and immediately began accelerating for take-off.

O'Connell drove west to Hotevilla. He parked near the small village's water tower and walked over to the yard behind the house of Timothy Katoya's neighbor. After satisfying himself that Maguire's vehicle was parked in front of Katoya's house, he stealthily climbed up onto the neighbor's roof and set up surveillance.

On the pale yellow desert floor far below the vertical edge of the Hotevilla mesa, Timothy Katoya sat inside the sweat lodge praying. As he continued to pray, an extremely unusual fog bank, coupled with a very low band of cumulus clouds, began to billow up to the west. As Katoya continued praying, the unseasonable weather front began to advance steadily towards Hotevilla.

The Virginia early morning air was damp and cool. Henri Fournier gave his car keys to the military valet in front of the Pentagon's main entrance and took an elevator down to the Pentagon basement. He strode over to the Science and Technology Advisor's Office across from the entrance to the Joint Chiefs of Staff complex. His watch showed 07:59 when the phone rang with the conference call operator.

"Dr. Fournier, I have all your parties connected: Dr. Nathaniel Brown, Dr. Hubert Tarnsworth, General Robert Lazarus, Dr. Morris Solomon, Senator John Knapp, Admiral Jordan Clannon and Colonel Jack Partridge. Go ahead, please, sir."

"Hello, everyone," Fournier began.

"Hey, Henri, where's Rod Birdsall?" General Lazarus asked.

"General, Rod was involved in an unfortunate and tragic accident last night." Fournier's reply was intoned with feigned concern. "The fuel tanks on his yacht blew up while he was boating on the Potomac. He will be missed, of course." No one but Fournier noticed when Admiral Clannon gave a quick slight cough. The news took a moment to sink in with the rest of the JANUS group. An awkward silence fell. Each of the members made a quick calculation of what this obvious assassination could mean, particularly because Fournier had not made any mention of an outsider threat. Each of them came to the silent conclusion that Birdsall had been terminated for cause. But since Fournier was not volunteering an explanation, everyone else was too intimidated to ask why.

Fournier broke the uncomfortable silence and got straight to the point of the conference call. "Gentlemen, as you might have surmised from this hastily set-up phone conference, we have a serious problem. I'll get right to the point. An outsider, a noted UFO researcher, has learned of our planned 'alien' landing. Furthermore, this individual, a Dr. Roger Maguire, has splashed the news of our landing's date and location all over the worldwide internet. And as if that weren't enough, gentlemen," Fournier continued, his voice rising in anger, "he has included in his news release the name of our group, JANUS!"

"That's terrible!" Nathaniel Brown exclaimed. "What do we do now?"

"The problem has several aspects, as I see it," Fournier replied. "The first aspect is putting a muzzle on Maguire."

"I'm already taking care of that problem," Colonel Partridge said. "I have constant surveillance on him, and within the next day or two, Dr. Maguire will experience an unfortunate medical condition which will prove fatal."

"His demise will be timely if accomplished sooner rather than later," Fournier said. "That man has already caused us a great deal of trouble. We cannot afford to give him the leisure to do anything more."

"Consider it taken care of," Partridge said. "One more thing, what about that woman who regularly travels with Maguire? Her name is Barbara Catalina. She's a psychic, by the way."

"If she's traveling with Maguire, then she knows too much," Fournier answered. "She needs to be taken out of the picture as well."

"Then I have National Security clearance for two 'executive actions'?" the Colonel persisted.

"Yes, Jack," Fournier replied in an exasperated tone. "I guess dear old Harry Truman's National Security Directive creating our predecessor agency is good for two more eliminations. Are you the man for the job?" he asked with an implied taunt.

"I *said* I was taking care of it," Partridge said, an edge in his voice. The Colonel did not like people questioning his ability to take decisive action. But when Fournier responded with dark silence, he quickly shut up.

"Even with Maguire out of the way, the situation has other aspects which need attention," Fournier continued. "Our 'Alien Landing' plan needs to be aborted. *And* we have the matter of JANUS's existence being exposed, as well as our name."

Hubert Tarnsworth of EG&G spoke up in response. "Gentlemen, I have a proposal for an alternative landing site. As you know, EG&G operates a super-secure site at a remote corner of the Nevada Test Range. It doesn't appear even on Pentagon maps. We could arrange to have our 'alien landing' there. We would totally control the site. No one could get in. We could remotely televise to the world the scenario we want without any interference. We would, of course, also need to pick a different date from the one this Maguire announced. And thus, since our 'landing' will take place at quite a different place and date, Maguire becomes discredited, and we still pull off our preemptive strategy against the aliens."

"That's great, Hubert," General Robert Lazarus shot back in a sarcastic tone. "You want us to pull off an alien landing at Area 51, the worst kept secret in modern intelligence history. Every goddamn yahoo with a television set has heard about that base and its reputation for UFO testing and government saucers. No, Hubert, your 'super-secret' Groom Lake Air Force Station is the *last* place in hell where we should stage an 'alien landing'."

"Robert's right, Hubert," Senator Knapp said. "Your ideas about a substitute secure site and a different date are good ones. But your Area 51 proposal is absolutely out of the question."

"I suppose you've got a better idea," Tarnsworth countered petulantly.

"Well, *I* do," General Lazarus said. "The Defense Department has a low-profile military reservation, which is larger and more secret than the entire Nevada Test Site and Nellis Air Force Range combined. It has all the security and logistical back-up that we'll need. It's not been associated with UFOs, and it is remote. I propose we use that New Mexico reservation for our rescheduled 'alien landing'."

"You would be referring to the White Sands 'Missile' Range, General?" Admiral Jordan Clannon asked.

"Precisely, Admiral," Lazarus replied. "More specifically, gentlemen, I propose we hold the 'alien landing' at a secure NASA complex deep in the center of the Range, called Space Harbor. We can clear the aerospace contractors out of there for a few days on some pretext, and bang, we have it all to ourselves. I also propose that we defer the landing slightly, just enough to make Maguire wrong. Of course, we retain the elements of our plan involving the 'aliens' acting up and shooting one of our men. We need that to have a basis to stir up the public to demand a military response against them."

"I have a suggestion," Colonel Partridge interjected. "Let's move the date to September 15th. People are back from summer vacation and their kids have gone back to school. Everyone's settled down and we can have their undivided attention. We can't delay this thing too long. The Cover-Up won't hold much longer. So, as I mentioned earlier, my PANDORA Unit will bring in one of our mock-up saucers, along with our specially-outfitted 'aliens', for that night landing on the 15th. It's much safer using a suspended mock-up saucer than to try to use one of our real ARV anti-gravity craft. Our pilots have not yet developed smooth control of the gravity-wave vectoring. Hanging a mock-up saucer from a silenced chopper is much more reliable, and will make for a much smoother landing."

"Jack's got some good points," Morris Solomon agreed. "Mid-September sounds good to me. Having PANDORA provide the saucer special effects makes sense. And I like General Lazarus's points about White Sands Missile Range as our replacement site. I move we go with those plans."

Henri Fournier jumped into the discussion. "Just a minute. That proposal takes care of a substitute 'alien landing.' But what do we do about the internet exposé of JANUS that our meddlesome Dr. Maguire has done to the world?"

"Simple," Colonel Partridge responded. "I'll have my PANDORA unit use good old psychological warfare disinformation techniques. We can utilize reliable NSA assets to 'leak' JANUS's existence to the public through easily discredited 'sources,' such as the more far-out UFO publications and the tabloids. We'll covertly provide both scant evidence of, and greater evidence against, JANUS's existence. That should leave everybody confused and slow to believe *any* reports. Meanwhile, we call on some of our well-known UFO investigator assets to debunk Maguire for us, arms-length of course. People like that Connecticut sculptor who hypnotizes abductees. What's his name?"

"You mean Boyd Hazzard?" Admiral Clennon said helpfully.

"That's the guy. And we can have that social studies professor from Trenton State University, the guy who did some quiet UFO research for CIA a while back, join in the debunking."

"You mean Dr. Jake Davis?" Clennon responded again.

"Yes," Partridge said. "We can use people like that to discredit this Maguire to the public as a nobody, while we keep them at arm's length. There's no reason they need to know about our ultimate goals. Most of the public will be put too off-balance by our disinformation campaign to know what to think. Even the UFO die-hards will be lulled off-guard by these respectable-front assets."

"Brilliant, Jack!" Henri Fournier enthused. "I say, go to it." Fournier polled the group. Consensus was rapidly reached on the replacement landing site and date, and on having ambiguous disinformation leaked out about JANUS's existence. "Then it's settled, gentlemen," Fournier said. "In a few days you will all be flown to White Sands. There we will meet the incoming 'alien' landing party as Earth's representatives whom they have designated to meet with them. You see, gentlemen, our patient planning is finally coming to fruition."

As Timothy Katoya walked through the front door of his house, Roger Maguire awoke. The first light of dawn afforded faint backlighting of Katoya. Shaking off sleep, Maguire sat up on the couch. "Timothy, have you been down praying in the sweat lodge all night?"

"Yes," the Hopi Elder replied. "And it is a good thing I did. Sotuqnang-u, the spirit of the sky and clouds, came to me. He showed me that you and Barbara are in great danger. You are being followed here by people who want to kill you. But I prayed, and Sotuqnang-u told me he is bringing in low clouds and fog for your protection. He will make you invisible. You and Barbara must leave quickly under Sotuqnang-u's protection."

While Catalina and Maguire hastily packed, Katoya fixed them a Hopi "instant breakfast" of *pinole*, parched corn powder, stirred into orange juice. While they drank this breakfast drink, Katoya stepped outside. He walked around to the back of Maguire's car and crawled underneath the back bumper. There he spotted a tiny metallic-gray box attached to the left leaf springs. He got out his pocket knife, and pried it loose. Then he stood up, raised his eyes to the sky, and prayed, "Thank you, Patusung-ala." The Spirits of the Four Directions had indeed provided him with a most helpful vision in the sweat lodge. Katoya carried the tiny box over to his outdoor beehive oven and tossed it into the flames. The tracking monitor inside O'Connell's parked car suddenly lost transponder signal.

After bidding quick but warm good-byes to Katoya, Maguire and Catalina drove out of Hotevilla onto Highway 264 and headed east towards Interstate 40. Their destination, Norfolk, Virginia, to intercept JANUS's fake landing.

Timmy O'Connell waited until Maguire's Pathfinder disappeared in the dust, then climbed down off the neighbor's roof and quickly strode to his car. As he swung out onto Highway 264, he noticed that dark clouds had now lowered to ground level on the 5700-foot-elevation mesa. The weather had formed a thick fog which his headlights could not penetrate. Frustrated, he reluctantly pulled off onto a sandy highway shoulder and radioed Major Eberhardt.

"Zeta One, this is Zeta Two. 'Fellow Traveler' and his lady friend are headed east on 264 towards Window Rock. But the weather has closed in and I can't follow them."

Bryce Eberhardt exploded on the radio. "What do you mean you can't follow them?"

"I mean it's zero-zero visibility here, Major," O'Connell said. "I can't see my front bumper."

"Zeta Two, continual surveillance of 'Fellow Traveler' is a top national security priority." Eberhardt's voice calmed to a steely edge. "You follow him no matter what the visibility is, do you hear me? That is a direct order, Sergeant! I'm going to have Zeta Five go airborne to track him from the air as well. You must not let him elude surveillance, got that, you gutless wonder? Now get going!"

O'Connell thought about protesting one more time, then reluctantly signed off. He pulled his car out onto 264, and began a cautious descent at 10 miles per hour down the cliff side road from Third Mesa. As he reached the bottom, he crept around a curve to a straight-away stretch, where the road had been recently resurfaced and there was no center line. Desperately trying to determine if he was in the right lane, O'Connell stuck his head out the window, cursing the fog. As he crept forward, two bright lights suddenly loomed up in his windshield. O'Connell pulled his head back in just in time to see the chrome grill of a Mack semi-truck behind the two headlight beams. He started to scream when his car crumpled, its full gas tank exploding in a huge fireball.

Zeta Five straightened his Piper Cherokee into a heading of 270 degrees, and looked ahead at the weather front over Window Rock. An immense, unseasonal squall and fog bank was blowing in from the west. It extended from one end of the horizon to the other, and from ground level to thirty-thousand feet altitude. He flew to the leading edge of the storm, then got on the radio to Major Eberhardt.

"Zeta One, Zeta Five here. I've got zero-ceiling up ahead. There's no way I can do surveillance on 'Fellow Traveler.' Shall I turn it around?"

Eberhardt weighed the idea of ordering him to fly on instruments into the raging squall. But even the PANDORA plane lacked the exotic imaging equipment to pick Maguire's vehicle out in fog and cloud-cover. Eberhardt also reflected on the call he had just received a few minutes earlier from the Chief of the Bureau of Indian Affairs Hopi Agency Police. The Chief had reported finding the burned-out wreckage of a BIA vehicle which had been checked out to O'Connell. Eberhardt gave consideration to the fact that it would not look good on his record to have ordered two men to their deaths in impenetrable weather the same day. He also realized that Jack Partridge was going to have his hide for letting Maguire elude surveillance. He hesitated some moments, then reluctantly answered Zeta Five. "Okay, turn it around and come back here. I'll ask the New Mexico State Police to keep a lookout for him at the state line at Window Rock."

Thirty miles east of the Hopi Reservation, Maguire and Catalina had stopped in Ganado for gas and coffee. The small cafe next to the gas station had only a handful of customers besides them, all Indians. Catalina pointed at the *Arizona Republic* headline article she had been reading.

"Rog, look at this! The World Health Organization is reporting a worldwide outbreak of a new strain of killer virus. It's called Pneumonic Hemorrhagic Fever, PHF. They say it appears to be a mutation, or possibly a cross between Ebola virus and influenza."

"Cross?" Maguire asked. "Do they think that somebody actually put that strain together?"

"They don't elaborate," Catalina replied. "They say it's

been reported in at least 18 different countries so far, including the United States, and appears to be spreading out of control. This strain is airborne, meaning that all an infected person has to do is breathe in your vicinity, and you'll get a dose. They say there is no cure for PHF, and all the antibiotics we have don't affect it at all. The World Health Organization calls it a pandemic, and says that airline travelers who aren't showing symptoms yet are spreading it everywhere. They estimate that deaths will hit thirty million next month worldwide, and keep on escalating."

"That's terrible," Maguire responded. "It reminds me of that old movie, 'The Andromeda Strain'. In fact it sounds like the kind of thing that the Hopi Prophecies were talking about."

"Looks to me like the world is headed for some grim days ahead, before everything finally balances out," Catalina replied.

"This killer virus pandemic is going to destabilize societies around the world," Maguire said. "It certainly does look as though we're heading into the end times those Hopi prophecies predicted. We're sure going to need any help the ETs can give us."

Maguire excused himself and went to the pay phone to clear his messages, while Catalina finished her coffee. One message in particular caught his attention. It was from Norbert Collier, an experiencer who had sought his advice about his extraterrestrial encounters. Collier was a former highly placed officer in Naval Intelligence, operating under cover as a modest Navy Chief. Collier had hinted at knowing some high people in Washington. He was also was an adept at clairvoyance, an art he once suggested had gotten him advanced rapidly in the intelligence service. Maguire returned his call.

"Dr. Maguire, what a pleasure to hear your voice again."

"Norbert, it's been a while since we've talked. I guess that something's up, huh?"

"Indeed it is, Doctor. I saw your posting on the internet about this secret JANUS group that's trying to stage a fake alien landing and position themselves as spokesmen for the Earth. A sensitive source of mine, I think you know what I mean, has informed me that the JANUS group has changed the plans from what you publicized. Also, I want to tell you that you were in my dreams the last two nights. I took that as a sign from the 'higher powers' that I should pass on this information to you. Do you want me to tell you over the phone?"

"I'm willing to risk that, Norbert," Maguire said. "Your information sounds urgent and sensitive. I'm at a pay phone. Just keep it brief, and then I'll get far away from this phone booth before any eavesdroppers can send anyone here. I'll just have to hope that the same 'higher powers' that gave you your message will give me the necessary protection. They seem to have done so in the past. So, let's hear the news."

"It's your risk. My phone is untraceable at my end. Anyway, this is what I just heard from a very highly placed source in Washington," Collier said. "The JANUS group has picked a new time and place for the fake alien landing you warned everyone about."

"Oh, yeah?" Maguire reacted. "Tell me more."

Collier continued, "The new location is the White Sands Missile Range in New Mexico. You know the place?"

"Oh, yes," Maguire replied. "I've driven near there before."

"Well then, you know how huge it is. The actual 'alien landing' site is supposed to be at Space Harbor, 40 miles into the Range, northeast of Las Cruces."

"O.K. I've been by the entrance road to Johnson Space Center on U.S. 70. But that's only supposed to be six miles in."

"That's the right road, but not the right place," Collier replied. "Johnson Space Center is just the place where all the aerospace contractors have their offices on the Range. The 'alien landing' will actually take place another 35 miles out, at Space Harbor, a secret aerospace installation. The date has been switched, too. It will now be September 15th."

"I really appreciate this information, Norbert, more than I can express." Maguire's warm voice conveyed his gratitude. "You're a really valuable ally in this business of trying to get to the bottom of the Cover-Up. But I guess you already know that."

"No problem, doctor. Glad to be of some assistance. I'm

happy for any small thing I can do to take those JANUS cowboys out of action. You go get 'em, tiger."

"I roger that, Norbert. My research partner and I are going to switch our destination to White Sands right now. Again, I can't thank you enough, my friend."

"Only doing my governmental duty," Collier chuckled. "Which is more than I can say for those JANUS renegades. And by the way, Doctor, 'may the Force be with you'."

Maguire cracked up laughing, then regained his composure. "O.K., Norbert, thanks. And don't forget to Fed Ex me my light saber."

"You got it," Collier chuckled. "Hey, I gotta get off here. My wife is calling me. I'll be talking to you."

Back in the vehicle, Maguire told Catalina what his Washington contact had told him about the new landing site and date.

Catalina started folding up the map of Virginia. "Looks like we're changing our destination, huh? Never gets dull around you, Rog, does it?"

Instead of entering northern New Mexico via Window Rock as previously planned, they started immediately heading southeast on US 180, which would have them making a southern entrance into New Mexico. Proceeding southward to I-10, they would then head east to Las Cruces and the entrance road to White Sands Space Harbor.

The unseasonable fog lifted as they headed south through the sagebrush desert, but the storm clouds hung low overhead. As they approached the foothills of the White Mountains, they broke out from under the storm front into bright autumn sunlight. As she rode along, Catalina had been using her psychic abilities to tune into their situation. As the sunlight began streaming through the Pathfinder's windshield, she came out of her psychic altered state and declared to Maguire that they were now safe. The ones following them had lost the trail. A few miles later they came into Springerville, a town on the northern edge of the central Arizona uplands. They decided to stop at a small restaurant to get lunch and celebrate eluding their pursuers.

Catalina waited until the waitress had brought lunch, before moving the conversation over to a subject which had been much on her mind.

"Roger, I want to ask you where it is between you and me."

Maguire looked up quickly from his plate, startled. "I wasn't expecting that kind of question. Are you asking if I'm satisfied with having you along in the search for the ET landing?" he asked, knowing very well that she probably had another level of relationship in mind.

"Roger, I think you know what I'm driving at," Catalina said tartly. "Here we've spent weeks together, day and night, traveling back and forth across the country in your car. We've camped out in the desert in sleeping bags, done everything but shower together, and yet you haven't made a pass at me once. What's the matter? I'm not your type?" she asked petulantly.

Maguire stared at her searchingly for some moments, and then his desert-tanned face broke into a tiny smile. "Barbara, I respect you. And I respect the reason you joined up with me, to be present at the ET landing. I'm not the kind of guy to get into sexual harassment just because the person working with me is female."

Catalina's face scrunched up into a frown. "Roger, it's not sexual harassment to appreciate a woman. It's not harassment to like somebody."

"These days I guess I'm not sure what is kosher behavior between the sexes anymore, Barbara. If you're asking if I like you, the answer is yes."

Catalina's frown turned to a look of irritation. "Roger Maguire, what am I going to do with you? I've already figured out all by myself that you like me, thank you very much. I'm asking about something more."

Maguire put on his best John Wayne accent to respond. "Ah, gee, ma'am, ya sure do know how to put a fella on the spot. Ah don't rightly know how to find the words ta answer ya."

Catalina picked up a utensil and waved it in front of Maguire's face. "Rog, if you don't stop using humor to dodge me and hide what your feelings are, I'm going to brain you with this spoon!"

Maguire dropped his grin. He looked into her eyes with calm searching intensity, saying nothing for a long time.

Catalina broke away from his stare and looked down at

her plate, a tear running down her cheek. "I guess I've made a fool of myself, pushing the issue like this. It's all right if you don't feel for me the way I feel for you. I'm a big girl. I can take it." She reached into her purse, grabbed a tissue, and began to dab her eyes. "Excuse me." She got up and fled toward the ladies' room.

When she emerged from the restroom a few minutes later, Maguire was standing in the corridor waiting for her. He crooked his finger in a beckoning gesture, saying nothing. Catalina stood next to him, her face inches from his. She noticed the gentle kindness in his eyes, and how the skin around his eyes crinkled up as part of his warm expression. Her face came up and forward, and her full lips met his. Maguire reached his arms around her and drew her to him. He felt the softness of her full breasts as she pressed herself against him. She felt the wonderful strength of his arms, the warmth of his chest, and how surprisingly soft his cheek felt next to hers. They stood entwined in a silent, soft embrace for two full minutes. Finally, Catalina let go and said, "Whew! I've got to catch my breath. You sure do know how to sweep a girl off her feet, Roger."

Maguire got out a handkerchief and rubbed his glasses. "Barbara, you're a pretty intense person yourself. Look. You've steamed up my glasses."

She noticed that he was grinning that dynamite, white-toothed grin of his. She had come to treasure it dearly. She laughed and gave him another passionate kiss. "How's that? Are your glasses melting yet?"

"I could give you a detailed answer, but not in this restaurant," he replied with a mischievous wink.

"Roger, I love you. Do you love me?"

"You'll get your answer this afternoon, Barbara. I promise. You won't be able to mistake my intentions."

Catalina was intrigued by his mysterious answer. "Well, I guess I can wait until afternoon, after waiting weeks to find out."

"You've been hoping this would come up for weeks?" Maguire asked.

Catalina twirled her finger around her right temple. "Silly boy. You men take forever to get it, don't you?"

"Oh, it's not that I'm so dense. There's a story that it's time

I told you. It's about my past. I'll tell it while we drive. After you hear it, I think you'll understand better why I go slow in revealing my feelings."

As they emerged from the restaurant, a Caucasian homeless man was sitting near the entrance begging, while coughing up bloody mucus into a rag he was holding. He was using his other hand to dab at blood trickling down from a tear duct.

"My God, he's got internal bleeding," Catalina said.

"He doesn't look as though he has tuberculosis. I wonder if he's got that hantavirus that's been showing up on the Navajo Reservation. It's different from the original strain of hantavirus from Korea. The Navajo kind affects the lungs, but this guy doesn't live on the reservation."

"Whatever he's got, he's in terrible condition," Catalina said. She leaned over towards the transient and said, "I'm Barbara. What's your name?"

The transient looked up at her and replied, "Shep Gorton, m'am."

"How are you doing, Shep?" she asked.

The sick man looked up at her briefly again, saying nothing as he continued coughing up blood-tinged mucus.

Catalina turned back to Maguire and said, "I'm going back inside and call 911."

As the ambulance pulled up, two Emergency Medical Technicians emerged. They were wearing total protective biohazard suits and gloves. They immediately placed a medical mask over the transient's nose and mouth. When Maguire asked the EMTs why they were using extreme protection, they told him that the symptoms Catalina had described on the phone meant the transient probably had the new killer virus, PHF. The EMTs questioned Maguire and Catalina about how close they had been to the homeless man. Finally they were satisfied when the couple said that they had kept adequate distance. When Catalina asked what would have happened if she had gotten any closer to the transient, the EMTs told her that she and Maguire would have been placed in federal quarantine, under a brand-new unpublicized order from the Surgeon-General. Out of curiosity, Maguire asked the EMTs what would have happened if they would then have tried to evade quarantine. The older EMT looked at his partner and grinned. He answered that they would have had to call the Sheriff to pursue them. He added that use of deadly force was authorized to enforce a quarantine on anyone exposed to PHF.

As they resumed their drive towards White Sands, Catalina spoke up. "You said you had a story to tell. You said it had something to do with why you're slow to show your feelings."

"Yes, although it's not much of a story. I was teaching and doing research at the University of New Mexico in Albuquerque. I had a woman graduate student named Deanna assigned to me as a research assistant. She developed a crush on me while working on a research project. The feeling was not mutual. It would have been out of line anyway. Then, when her assistantship year was up, she applied for another assistantship year with me, but was turned down by the department. Then she went to the Dean and filed sexual harassment charges against me, claiming that I was all over her and had propositioned her. None of that was true, of course. She was just operating out of spite, because she felt I was the one behind her not getting another year's assistantship. That wasn't it; the school just had budget limits. But she went to the student newspaper and raised such a stink with her false charges about me, that the cowardly dean caved in to her phony pressure tactics. It cost me my teaching job." He sighed and looked down at the floorboard. "I haven't taught college since."

"Oh, Roger, I'm sorry," Catalina said. "That must have been awful. Now I understand why you have kept your feelings so out of sight. I'm sorry for getting after you back in the restaurant."

Maguire reverted to his best John Wayne accent. "No harm, ma'am. It's just a flesh wound."

They both broke out laughing, then Catalina placed her arm around his shoulders and gave him a squeeze.

Forty miles south of Springerville, they passed twin signs saying "Leaving Arizona" and "Welcome to New Mexico, Land of Enchantment." As Catalina drove through the mountains of the Gila National Forest, Maguire pulled out the map.

"Barb, about an hour up ahead is San Francisco Hot Springs. It's a great natural hot spring next to a river. Would you like to stop and soak a while?"

"That sounds great, Roger. My shoulder muscles are getting a little stiff from driving. I could stand to loosen up. But I didn't pack a swimsuit."

"No problem. Usually any people around the Springs are fine if you want to skinny-dip."

"Are you going to, Roger? I don't want to be the only one."

"Skinny-dip?" he smiled. "That's the *only* way to enjoy a natural hot spring."

A mile south of Pleasanton, they pulled off onto a Forest Service dirt road on the right, and traveled a mile and a half down to a sandy parking area next to the San Francisco River. They walked over to a nearby misty shallow pool. It was large enough to hold a dozen people, but this afternoon there was no one else around. Catalina put her hand into the clear water and gushed, "Oh, Roger, this water is wonderful! It must be a hundred degrees."

They undressed and slid into the clear blue-green waters of the pool. At 4600 feet altitude, the late afternoon air was cool enough that a layer of steam hovered above the waters, its vaporous whiteness a visible contrast to the shadows thrown by nearby juniper trees. The low sun was filtering through the tree branches. The multiple-layered gurgles of the adjacent river created an ambience of sensuous sounds. Occasional calls of blue jays echoed cheerfully through the stand of junipers. As the water's heat soaked into the pair, Catalina sank into a languorous mood.

"Rog, I could stay in here for a long time. Let's make this our stop for the day, and camp overnight, ok?"

"That's fine with me. We still have a couple days before JANUS's fake landing at Space Harbor. We've got the time. *And* I still didn't give you the answer I promised you in the restaurant."

"You mean about what your true feelings are?' Catalina asked. "I think I know now."

"No, you don't," Maguire replied. "Come here."

Catalina slid herself over next to Maguire, who was lying on his back in the waters and resting his head on a stone ledge. He held her in a prolonged embrace. Some moments later he rolled her over on top of him, and kissed her passionately. His hands gently massaged her hair and the silken skin of her back and buttocks. Catalina kissed him back intensely. Tousling his hair, she ran a hand slowly down his side. After a few minutes, they rolled over on their sides facing each other in the warm water, and ran their hands lovingly all over each other's bodies. Taking their time, they luxuriated in leisurely foreplay. Her passion mounting, Catalina reached down, grasped his already stiffened member, and began slowly massaging it.

Maguire gazed at her with a smile and asked, "Do you want to?"

Catalina gazed back with a passionate grin. "Silly boy!" She rolled him onto his back and straddled him. Raising herself up, she gradually impaled herself on his erection, drawing herself down over him slowly, deliciously, until he was deep within her. She pumped her hips up and down slowly and rhythmically, biting her lower lip at the intensity of the sensations. "Oh, Rog, you feel so good!" Her eyes glazed with sweet pleasure. "I could ride you forever."

Maguire reached up with his hands and massaged her ample breasts as she rocked up and down. Their eyes locked in a shared gaze of helpless pleasure.

The sun was now near the horizon, and the sky was deep violet color. The few cumulus clouds in the sky radiated a brilliant magenta hue. The steam from the pool partially obscured the undulating figures. Finally, as he felt her muscles deep inside involuntarily clenching him, Maguire pulled her face down to his and gave her a prolonged kiss. She panted, moaned, pulled back to breathe and then climaxed. As her first orgasm peak was followed by another, he felt his own climax rise and explode within her. He gasped with passionate release. Thoroughly spent, they both rolled over and lay side by side in the warm pool for a long time, holding hands and looking up at the first stars to emerge in the canopy overhead.

Finally Catalina spoke up. "My dreams have come true, Roger."

"Mine, too, Barbara." He leaned over and gave her another kiss.

Chapter 9

AFTER a soak in the hot spring the next morning, Maguire and Catalina headed southeast towards Silver City. Plans called for a stop for breakfast before proceeding to White Sands Missile Range. Noticing the car clock reaching 9 a.m., Catalina pushed the radio scan button to find the hourly headline news. An ABC radio announcer was speaking. "We switch you now to Washington, and Sam Donaldson at the White House."

"Sam Donaldson here. In a few moments the President will be making what the White House has billed as an extremely important and historic announcement. No advance copy of the President's remarks has been made available to the press. This is a very unusual level of secrecy, without precedent in my years of covering Washington. An additional indication that this is a very serious announcement is the unusual arrangement the White House made yesterday. Besides having the American networks present, the White House asked CNN to reserve this time for worldwide live broadcast of the President's remarks. Yet another indication of the serious nature of events is the presence here of U.N. Secretary-General Kalim Salaam, Vice-President Gordon Alexander, the House Majority Leader, the entire Cabinet, the Joint Chiefs of Staff, the Director of the CIA, the National Security Council, and the Rev. Billy Graham. We have heard that the . . . ah, excuse me, . . . Ladies and Gentlemen, the President has just entered. We will now be hearing from the President of the United States, Jeffrey Williams."

The President had a serious tone, his usual boyish exuberance absent.

"Good morning, my fellow citizens of America, and all you other citizens of the Earth. Today I bring before you a momentous announcement, one with profound implications for our society, our world, and our children. During the past several weeks, I have been conferring with the heads of major coun-

tries, heads of major scientific bodies, the Director of the World
Council of Churches, His Holiness the Pope, the Dalai Lama,
and other world leaders. *All,* every one, felt that it was appropriate to make this announcement now.

"Fellow citizens of the Earth, we are not alone. Recently
I had startling evidence presented to me by the Joint Chiefs
of Staff. The evidence came from an extremely secret military storage facility which has been recently discovered and
was previously unknown to the Secretary of Defense and
the Joint Chiefs. This secret facility contained irrefutable evidence that in 1947, an aerial vehicle from elsewhere in space
crashed in the desert of New Mexico. I have now gone to
that facility and seen the evidence for myself. That evidence
includes the crashed wreckage of that UFO, as well as the
remains of four humanoid extraterrestrials aboard that craft
who died in the crash. In addition, this secret military storage
facility contains motion picture film taken of a fifth extraterrestrial who survived the crash, and who was secretly held in cap-
tivity at this facility for several years by an unauthorized military intelligence unit. That extraterrestrial later died.

"Furthermore, we have also recovered, from that facility,
evidence that a UFO landed at Holloman Air Force Base near
Alamogordo, New Mexico. Motion picture film was found,
which showed the landing and a secret meeting taking place
between the extraterrestrials from that craft and certain military officers. Those American officers were part of that unauthorized military-intelligence unit which has kept these
matters secret. Those officers apparently represented themselves to the extraterrestrials as speaking for the Government,
which, I can assure you, they did not.

"In view of that newly discovered evidence, the Joint
Chiefs have recommended, and I have accepted their rec-
ommendation, that the classified studies the military has been
conducting of UFOs be now made public, so that the whole
world can share in the information which has been gathered
to date. I wish to emphasize that there is no indication of a
threat to national or world security from these extraterres-

trial Visitors. All of the studies have reached the same conclusion, that the Visitors come here in peace. These studies indicate that multiple races of extraterrestrials are present in our atmosphere, and that on occasion they briefly land on Earth and sometimes interact with human individuals here. Contrary to some of the imaginative stories you may have seen on television, our governmental studies indicate that there is no record of any deliberate unprovoked attack on humans by these Visitors. Indeed, existing studies suggest that the Visitors have shown restraint, even when subjected to hostilities from humans. These UFO studies also indicate that the Visitors have expressed interest in interacting with humans in a more formal and open way. I have also consulted with John Draper, the Director of Central Intelligence, who has agreed to immediately make available all existing UFO studies performed by the intelligence agencies as well.

"In view of this recently discovered information, I have consulted with U.N. Secretary-General Salaam, here present. I have offered him the full cooperation of the United States in any initiative which the United Nations may undertake to reach out to the Visitors, and to establish formal and ongoing relations in peace. It is my firm conviction that we must never hesitate to reach out to strangers with the hand of peace and friendship, and to seek constructive discussions. Secretary-General Salaam has informed me that the United Nations will immediately create a Blue Ribbon panel of experts, who will study the issue of establishing formal communication and contact with the space Visitors, and who will then make their recommendations.

"Let me emphasize to you that we have much more to learn about the extraterrestrials. Available reports indicate that these individuals often look quite different than humans do. And yet, in every instance, they are conscious, intelligent life forms. As such, they deserve the same respect that we accord any person. Some people may find their appearance strange, even frightening. But let me point out that differences of origin, skin color or race must never be the basis for hostile action, whether it be between humans of different ethnic groups, or between human beings and the space Visitors.

"I am today issuing a Presidential Order that any physical

attack on an extraterrestrial will be treated as a federal offense. It will be investigated by the FBI, and prosecuted under existing statutes relating to crimes against persons.

"I have also conferred with the Attorney General, the National Security Council, and the Secretary of Defense concerning the renegade military-intelligence organization which has been conducting this unauthorized cover-up of UFO evidence. We have indications that they are still operating. The evidence which that group has kept buried all these years should never have been kept from the President and the people. No person is above the Constitution or the law. Let me assure you of this: we will go after them with every resource, make them account for their every action, and bring them to justice.

"This news of visitation by extraterrestrial civilizations is truly a breakthrough in our history, an event of cosmic proportions. Let us all summon up what is the best within each one of us, and face this new and potentially rewarding challenge with the hope, the courage, and the resolve which have always characterized the people of America, and indeed all people of goodwill on Earth.

"I know that there are many questions which could be asked at this time, but I am not going to take questions now. Tomorrow noon there will be a joint press conference. There, the Secretary of State, the Secretary of Defense, the Chairman of the Joint Chiefs of Staff, the Chairman of the National Security Council, the CIA Director, and the Director of the National Academy of Sciences will be present to provide additional information and to take questions from reporters.

"In the meantime, let us all engage in some thoughtful reflection and prayer, that we bring our best selves and our best ideas to address this new phase of our history. The people of America and of the world have faced every challenge before, and have prevailed. At this new threshold in our history, we can do no less. And we *will* do no less.

"Thank you. Good day, and may God bless you all."

The voice of Sam Donaldson came back on the radio. "Well, there you have it. The President has just made the most astounding announcement, perhaps, in history. We are being visited by intelligent life from elsewhere in space. There are so many unanswered questions now as. . . ."

Catalina shut off the radio and sat there in stunned silence. Maguire spotted a turnout, quickly pulled off the highway and parked. For a minute he was too shocked to trust himself driving. After allowing the news to soak in for a few moments, he pounded the steering wheel with his fist and whooped. "He did it! The President finally broke loose with the news. *That* took guts, even if we did have to wait a long time for this announcement."

"Rog, it's simply astounding! The secret is finally out in the open!" She paused, then added, "But how do you think this will affect JANUS's plans for a fake landing?"

"If they're smart, they will abort their plan and scrap their 'landing.' If they're desperate, which I suspect they are — after all, the Cover-Up is just about destroyed now — JANUS will hurry up and try to pull it off anyway."

"Would they be that foolish?" Catalina asked.

"The business they've been in has been taking foolish chances for a long time, ever since they started operating outside the constitutional chain of command. My bet is they do go ahead with their 'landing'."

"Well in that case, Rog, we should make it our business to be there, don't you think?" Catalina flashed a conspiratorial smile.

Maguire reached over and turned the ignition back on. "Funny you should mention that. White Sands is just where I was headed," he grinned, winking at Catalina.

Leaving Las Cruces, Maguire and Catalina headed east on U.S. 70. In five miles they saw the sign: "NASA — Lyndon B. Johnson Space Center." Maguire made a left turn onto a two-lane side road which bore no name. Two miles down the road, they came up to a sentry gate. A crewcut civilian-contractor security guard was standing in front of the barrier. Maguire thought fast. The University of California, where he had worked as an instructor, also operated Los Alamos Laboratory for the Department of Energy. He guessed that Los Alamos personnel would have regular business at Space Harbor. He quickly got out his U.C. employee photo badge and clamped it on his shirt, before the security guard walked up to their vehicle with deliberate casualness. Maguire gave the guard a story about being hired as a contract archeologist to survey some Indian burial site for an environmental impact report. He explained that this was required before building a new test facility on the range. Maguire made an excuse for the lack of a WSMR bumper sticker on his vehicle by saying that his regular car broke down, and he had to borrow his uncle's vehicle at the last minute. He explained Catalina's presence by saying that she was his field assistant, and that her photo badge was late in arriving from the University. The guard said he'd have to make a call, and walked back to the sentry station. Maguire and Catalina started to hope that he was buying their story, until the security guard reemerged with a serious expression. The guard started walking towards them while talking into a walkie-talkie. He was followed by a second grim sentry, who was carrying an M-16 over his shoulder. Maguire cranked the steering wheel all the way to the left. Tires spinning on the sandy asphalt, he made a U-turn, and sped back the direction they had come.

It was clear that penetrating White Sands Missile Range the forty miles to Space Harbor was not going to work. Guile had failed. They certainly could not hike that distance across the endless desert sands.

As they drove back towards Las Cruces, they developed an alternative plan. The technique which had worked the first time to force JANUS to abandon their "alien landing" at Norfolk could work again. They drove to University Park just south of Las Cruces. At the New Mexico State University campus, Maguire used the library's internet access to again put on the worldwide internet warning notices about the new place and new date of JANUS's fake landing.

They decided to stay in Las Cruces until after the fake landing, in order to assess its impact. As the rosy twilight faded, Maguire and Catalina for the first time rented a single room with only one bed. Maguire carried Catalina over the threshold, before playfully plopping her on the bed. Catalina giggled, and remarked that she almost felt like a bride again. She pulled him down beside her, and reached over for the remote, to switch off the TV news that he had turned on.

By mid-morning the next day there was a feeling of excitement and tension in the air around Las Cruces. Contractors and workers who normally would have been out on the
Range were milling idly around town. Rumors were flying
around. The President was flying in to announce huge lay-
offs. A secret new aerospace plane was going to be unveiled.
There had been a nuclear accident underground on the
Range, with release of radiation topside.

On the otherwise deserted road to Space Harbor, there
was no one to notice a caravan of white unmarked trucks
driving in. Nor were there any unauthorized eyes to see,
when a chartered Lear 35-passenger jet touched down at the
Space Harbor airstrip, and the remaining members of JANUS,
all but Colonel Partridge, emerged. Jack Partridge had explained
his absence as unavoidably necessary. He had to be at Gray
Air Force Base near El Paso, to personally supervise the
PANDORA Unit's off-site preparations of its "saucer" and
"aliens" for JANUS's fake alien landing that night. The other
seven JANUS members were whisked to VIP quarters at
Space City, there to await nightfall and their "alien landing"
rendezvous.

The late September northwest wind that swept across the
nighttime desert was chill. In the cloudless ink-black sky,
myriad stars twinkled furiously. The seven JANUS members
were standing in their long overcoats at the edge of the airstrip tarmac, huddled against the cold wind. The landing
area was brightly illuminated by banks of military light-all
units lining the airstrip. Spaced every twenty meters around
the landing zone were red-bereted Special Forces commandos of the Air Force's secret Blue Light unit, their MP-5
submachine guns held in the at-ease position. PANDORA
photographic intelligence specialists were perched on an elevated platform near the tarmac. Their tripod-mounted television and video cameras were turned on and aimed at the
landing zone. Besides those cameras recording this event on
tape for later broadcast, one of the cameras was sending live
feed to the local ABC network station in Las Cruces.

JANUS's plan included a two-part publicity strategy. One

part involved control and limited access to the event. This was to be accomplished by letting only one station, the local ABC affiliate, carry the landing live, and with only an hour's notice, not enough time to allow word of the event to spread to other stations. Such a precaution would not permit opportunity for swarms of reporters and TV cameramen to gather and demand that they also be allowed to cover the landing. The local ABC station would of course then later refeed the landing to the entire ABC network afterwards. In the unlikely event that anything went wrong, it was easier to cut the one local feed than many.

The second part of JANUS's publicity plan had been to build citizen interest. This was accomplished by beginning at noon to circulate the rumor throughout Las Cruces that an alien landing was to take place at White Sands this evening. Since the citizens could not get on the Range, they would be sure to be watching the television coverage when that was announced later.

At Gray Air Force Base, one hour's flying time to the southeast, a pilot wearing a night-vision helmet moved his throttle from idle to take-off speed. As Colonel Partridge gave the hand-signal to proceed, the dark, specially-modified, totally-silenced helicopter rose slowly into the air. Suspended underneath the heavy-lift chopper was a mock-up aluminum "saucer" on a 150-meter cable, its perimeter lights extinguished until its approach to the landing site.

Inside the "saucer" four thin dwarfish men sat facing each other in the cramped crew section. They wore light-gray latex body suits and large head pieces with huge dark slanted-eye coverings. Their arms were costumed in prosthetic limb-extensions which ended in three long fingers, to look like stereotypic "Gray"-type extraterrestrials. The "alien" leader was conducting last-minute checks on the tiny two-way radios fitted inside against the larynx portion of their suits. These covert radios allowed the "aliens" to appear to be communicating telepathically and silently with each other, and also with the secretly wired members of JANUS.

The helicopter's progress was slowed considerably, as

sudden gusts of wind caused the saucer to oscillate like a pendulum at the end of the towing cable. The chopper pilot turned to his copilot and cursed Colonel Partridge. "That god-damn arrogant jackass is going to get us all killed. The loadmaster *told* him that if the wind got above 25 knots, the mission should be scrubbed. Look at that windspeed indicator! Some of those gusts are hitting thirty-five knots or better. But no, the Colonel says we gotta go, no matter what. This is the date it was set, he says, and this is the date it's gonna happen. Fuck him, I say!"

The copilot gave him thumb's up sign. "Yeah. You don't see that chicken shit up here trying to fly this thing in this wind with that unstable payload underneath."

"I'll tell you what," the pilot rejoined. "If that saucer starts to swing out of control, I'm releasing the tow cable, and those 'aliens' in that saucer can take their chances. Be damned if I'm gonna go down for some fool Halloween stunt."

"Yeah, you got that right," the copilot chuckled.

Major Bryce Eberhardt was disturbed by the report he had received over AFOSI's encrypted teletype. This latest report bothered him more than the news he had received earlier, when the New Mexico state troopers had informed him that they never did see Maguire drive across the border from Arizona. When Eberhardt had phoned Partridge with the news of Maguire's and Catalina's slipping away from surveillance, Partridge had given him just as long and vicious a chewing-out as he had feared he would. The Colonel had raged for an entire day, placing five separate phone calls to bawl him out repeatedly. Partridge called him every demeaning name in the book, and demanded repeatedly that he do something about finding Maguire. In response Eberhardt had quickly dispatched an entire intelligence unit to comb Arizona and New Mexico for Maguire, but so far they had come up empty.

But this latest report Eberhardt had received added a new and more ominous light to things. The report indicated that Colonel Partridge had secretly rescinded an assignment which Eberhardt had made. Eberhardt had ordered Captain José DiGiorgio to be assigned to clerical duties at the Judge Advocate's Office at Kirtland AFB. Instead, Partridge had reas-

signed DiGiorgio to Elmendorf AFB, Alaska at the beginning
of September. Suspicious of this maneuver, Major Eberhardt
put a call in to an old classmate who worked within AFOSI at
Elmendorf, to give him the run-down on DiGiorgio's assignments. After the Elmendorf contact had checked some files, he
told Eberhardt that Colonel Partridge had exerted unusual influence, and had had DiGiorgio assigned to duty as a reconnaissance pilot. This assignment was unusual, because
DiGiorgio had been trained only briefly on jet trainers in Texas
under excellent weather conditions. Furthermore, DiGiorgio's
training had been years ago, when he first entered the Air Force,
before being reassigned to Intelligence. DiGiorgio's first assignment since arriving at Elmendorf had been to fly a reconnaissance bomber out into the Gulf of Alaska past the tip of the
Aleutian Islands during a powerful winter storm. Somehow,
DiGiorgio had managed to get the reconnaissance bomber airborne and on course out over the Aleutian archipelago. The
AFOSI report in front of Eberhardt said that DiGiorgio's plane
had encountered a gale on this initial reconnaissance flight, and
had struck a mountain during poor visibility conditions.

Major Eberhardt had seen this kind of suicidal assignment
administered before. But he was troubled by the questions it
raised. Why would Partridge want DiGiorgio dead? True, the
guy was a bumbler, but that hardly called for his demise.
DiGiorgio had been closely connected with the surveillance of
Roger Maguire before being pulled off and sent to Alaska. Was
Colonel Partridge so paranoid about the PANDORA Unit's secrecy that he couldn't allow any former members to survive?
Or was it Maguire who was the fatal connection? Eberhardt
wasn't sure, but he was starting to consider that his own longevity might be in peril with a man like Jack Partridge calling
the shots.

The Major placed a call on his secure phone to Ed Sodoma.
Eduardo Sodoma was a private contract operative he had used
for extremely sensitive missions before. Of medium build,
swarthy and muscular, Sodoma's well-sculpted body and
tight buttocks had not escaped the Major's eye. Eberhardt
fantasized more than once about a night with Sodoma.

The nickname "Sewer" had been quietly placed on Sodoma by his fellow intelligence operatives during his years of working out of the CIA Station in Belo Horizante, Brazil under the cover occupation of a catechist. The "Sewer" sobriquet stuck because of persistent rumors around the Station of Sodoma's predilection for taking young handsome altar boys into his home for "catechism lessons" which included pederasty. After Sodoma had "retired" from the Company, he moved into doing private contract "dirty jobs." He had an earned reputation as being clever and meticulous, as well as vicious and ruthless. Sodoma was also known to be willing to do anything for a buck. But when Eberhardt told him that his surveillance target was Colonel Partridge, Sodoma doubled his usual price. Eberhardt, feeling that he was in no position to haggle, quickly agreed.

Word-of-mouth announcement of the upcoming alien landing at White Sands had been racing like wildfire through Las Cruces all afternoon. Interest in UFOs had already been pushed to a fever pitch by the noontime televised Washington press conference on UFOs. The Conference had featured the Secretaries of State and of Defense, the Joint Chiefs of Staff Chairman, the Chairman of the National Security Council, the CIA Director, and the Director of the National Academy of Sciences. These key officials had presented an hour-and-a-half briefing on the basics of what the Government knew about UFOs, and had taken questions from reporters for another hour.

Their presentations provided background facts about UFO presence dating back to at least 1947. The Secretary of Defense displayed photographs of the "Roswell" saucer crash debris and film clips of the extraterrestrial corpses. The CIA Director read from a classified study, which described the various extraterrestrial races visiting Earth, and showed artist drawings of each type. The Chairman of the Joint Chiefs of Staff narrated a brief film documentary of a UFO landing at Holloman Air Force Base in 1964. The film showed several ETs emerging and communicating briefly with a group of military officers. The National Academy of Sciences Director presented alien autopsy reports and scientific analyses, which concluded that the extraterrestrials far exceeded humans in intelligence, longevity and health. The Chairman of the National Security Council outlined the consensus overview of alien contact which had been developed and shared by all NATO and SEATO member nations, and which concurred with USSR data recently released by the Commonwealth of Independent States. That consensus view was that the extraterrestrials were not a military threat, were here for peaceful contact purposes, and were enormously advanced beyond Western science and technology. The press conference concluded with the Secretary of State reiterating the President's point that the matter would be taken up by U.N. Secretary-General Salaam with the General Assembly and the Security Council by week's end. The Secretary of State expressed assurances that the United States would cooperate fully with U.N. recommendations and initiatives to reach out to the Visitors and establish formal relations. Reporters' questions, which mostly were based on curiosity about the Visitors, were answered by the government officials in a straightforward way. More than one official echoed what the Secretary of Defense said at the end of his remarks. "We don't know everything, and have a lot more yet to learn."

By mid-afternoon, Las Cruces was abuzz. The rumor going around was that one of the local television stations would be permitted to televise the landing. This was reportedly scheduled to happen that evening at 9 o'clock. By late afternoon, Las Cruces residents were channel-surfing, trying to find out which station was covering the landing. Around 8 o'clock, the local ABC outlet started flashing announcements that it would start covering the alien landing from Space Harbor by live broadcast just before 9 p.m.

Catalina and Maguire sat in their motel room watching the local TV station's pre-coverage of the alien landing. Maguire had set up a rented VCR to record the landing, which was supposed to have happened at nine. It was now nine-thirty, and the JANUS members were looking visibly fidgety on the television screen. Finally at 9:45, the TV camera panned around to the southeast horizon, where a bright light a thousand feet above the desert floor slowly resolved into a highly-illuminated disc. As the JANUS saucer drew closer to the landing pad, most of the light-alls were shut off. The saucer's black towing cable hanging from the black helicopter above remained unseen. The few remaining light-all beams were aimed at the ground, leaving a small pool of light in the middle of the landing zone. Television cameras zoomed in tightly on the approaching saucer, its aluminized skin brightly lit with a row of white lights glowing around its edge. From the underside of the saucer, a broad beam of extremely intense greenish-white light shone down on the landing zone. Maguire noticed that the saucer was oscillating back and forth in the wind. The silent stealthy tow helicopter quickly rested the saucer gently on the landing pad and hovered silently overhead, towing cable still connected and unseen by the Space Harbor TV cameras.

After a dramatic wait, a hatch opened in the side of the PANDORA saucer. Four thin, dwarfish "aliens" stepped out onto the tarmac. The glare of the light-alls reflected off the aliens' enormous shiny black eye-pieces. At a signal from their captain, the Blue Light commandos formed a large circle around the landing zone. The well-choreographed landing event began to unfold.

Lieutenant Gaylord Littey was at a position in the Blue Light cordon nearest the saucer's door. He was beginning to sweat and tremble. His mind was flashing back to a crashed UFO retrieval operation he had taken part in two years earlier in Puerto Rico. He had led the entrance team into that saucer. The first one inside, Lieutenant Littey's eyes had just been adjusting to the dim interior when he had seen a Gray alien in a corner moving towards him. Littey had instantly laid down a deadly stream of automatic weapon fire. It was only when he had drawn closer to the dead alien that he noticed that both the alien's arms had been broken by the crash. Now here at Space Harbor, watching as these four spindly aliens advanced from their craft, a sense of déjà vu and raw fear gripped the Lieutenant. Ignoring previous briefing orders, he nervously switched his MP-5 weapon to the fully-automatic setting.

The "alien leader" took a step forward into the glare of the Space Harbor TV cameras, and raised his three-fingered prosthetic hand in a gesture of greeting. The seven JANUS representatives started to step forward in response. They were waved back by the Blue Light unit captain. The other troops raised their submachine guns and pointed them at the "aliens," appearing fully ready for any trouble. The "alien leader" walked over to the Blue Light captain, and began gesticulating animatedly. Meanwhile, another alien, who had remained back near the saucer door, surreptitiously drew an object from his belt. Watching the television picture, Maguire thought it looked like one of those phasers from Star Trek. A Blue Light master sergeant, who at an earlier secret briefing had been designated the one to challenge the "aliens," and who was the only one who had been issued blanks instead of live ammunition, stepped forward. He crouched in a firing position, his MP-5 trained on the alien who had the "ray gun." As planned, the "alien" pointed his weapon at the sergeant. An intense red laser light beam shot out and hit the crouching sergeant, who groaned loudly and clutched his chest. A puff of smoke rose from a small canister concealed inside his jumpsuit, as the sergeant crumpled to the ground. At this point Henri Fournier began to step forward towards the "alien leader," making peace gestures in accordance with the carefully-crafted script.

Lieutenant Littey panicked at the flash of the laser light beam. He froze for an instant, caught up in a flashback to the earlier saucer retrieval. Then he opened fire on the alien holding the laser. He followed with sweeping fire, taking out the alien next to the fallen one as well.

Pandemonium broke out. Henri Fournier waved his hands furiously, yelling, "Stop! Stop!" The two surviving "aliens" sprinted back into the saucer, not stopping to shut the door. They screamed into their radio to the chopper pilot overhead to lift them off. Unnerved and confused, several other Blue Light commandos began shooting at the saucer as it slowly began to rise. The Blue Light captain took out his 9mm sidearm and shot Lieutenant Littey dead, while at the same time yelling repeatedly at his men, "Cease fire! Cease fire!"

All of the JANUS group except Henri Fournier had retreated back to the reviewing stand and were cowering behind its protective wall. Someone switched all the light-all units back on. With that intense lighting, television viewers could easily see the now-visible black cable leading up from the rising saucer, as well as the helicopter it was attached to. Fournier quickly strode over to the television platform. He tried to yell up to the technicians to turn their cameras off, but the wind and gunfire drowned out his orders. A sudden extra-strong gust of wind came up, causing the saucer to swing back and forth in a much wider arc than before, dangerously destabilizing the helicopter. The "aliens" inside the saucer, nervous at the sound of bullets hitting the saucer's hull, were screaming at the chopper pilot to rise faster. Meanwhile they hurriedly tore off their alien headpieces and limb extension prostheses.

Another very strong gust of desert wind struck the saucer and chopper. The helicopter was now gyrating and yawing precariously, swung around by its oscillating cargo of saucer, and losing altitude. The pilot yelled an order to the copilot, who nodded and pulled the towing cable release. The helicopter lurched drunkenly, then recovered, as the saucer separated. Slowly gaining altitude, the helicopter headed southeast on a course back to Gray Air Force Base.

The JANUS saucer had detached at one end of its wild arc, then tilted over and plummeted towards the ground. The six cowering JANUS members looked up in horror as the falling saucer blotted out the sky overhead. From beside the television platform, Henri Fournier watched in shock as the doomed saucer hit the reviewing stand where the other JANUS members were crouched. The impact hurled one of the "aliens" out the open hatchway, where he lay slumped on top of the wreckage of the reviewing stand. With his alien disguise gone, it was obvious on camera that he had been only a costumed human. Fournier turned around, walked over and unplugged the main power lead to the television cameras. Then he stood in grim defeated silence, his shoulders slumped.

Back at the motel in Las Cruces, Maguire and Catalina stared at the television screen as it suddenly went black. They turned and looked at each other in amazement.

"Holy shit!" Maguire exclaimed. "Talk about the Twilight of the Gods!"

"More than twilight, Roger; it looks as if night has fallen for JANUS," Catalina said with a wry expression. "And they're not Gods, either. We hoped that somehos their fake alien landing wouldn't fool people, but *this*! Wow! They must have had some pretty heavy karma stored up to come to such an awful ending."

Maguire nodded soberly. "Well, I wouldn't call it an ending quite yet. I did notice that Henri Fournier is still alive. And I didn't see Colonel Partridge around anywhere at the landing site. But still, JANUS's back has pretty much been broken, what with most of their group dead, and this horrible fiasco that got televised."

Catalina sighed. "I do feel sorry for all the people who lost their lives, even if they were scoundrels. Why is it that some people have to be so hard-headed?"

"I don't know. But don't forget, it was JANUS who set up all that fake landing technology. And they had millions of dollars available to do it safely. Which reminds me, I need to put in a call to a friend in the media, excuse me. I want to make sure that this local station's broadcast of the JANUS landing fiasco makes it onto the ABC network. My media friend can arrange to have a videotape sent by digital transmission to ABC headquarters, New York. *That* will spike JANUS's disinformation effort but good! When the Space Harbor footage goes on worldwide news, Fournier and Partridge aren't going to be able to peddle a Hubble Space Telescope photo and have anyone believe it's real."

"What do you want to do now?" Catalina asked.

"How about we stay here in Las Cruces another day and catch up on some overdue rest?"

"Sounds good to me," Catalina said. "I could use a little time anyway to come down from all of this." She paused and looked up at him brightly. "And after we catch our breath from this landing mess and you contact your media friend, a little later tonight I have some plans for you."

"Gee, are you suggesting that I get into some, ahem, undercover work?" Maguire asked, winking.

"Hey, you're pretty bright for a Ph.D.," she laughed.

Chapter 10

THE brilliant late-afternoon sun on this cloudless mid-September day made the Hopi elder squint. Timothy Katoya handed a piece of paper to the teenage boy standing in front of him. "Hurry, Chosovi. Run up to the general store and make a phone call for me. I must get this message to my *Bahana* friend as soon as possible. He must know what Spirit has shown me." The lad took the piece of paper and set off at a lope toward the store.

Two hundred fifty miles to the southeast, in the underground Albuquerque headquarters of the PANDORA Unit, Henri Fournier sat in Colonel Partridge's office. He was staring at a large television screen. Jack Partridge sat behind his desk, his gaze also fixed upon the screen. Fournier and Partridge had been going over video tape of the "alien landing" fiasco all day. Fournier had decided that the only way JANUS could retain its credibility was if the alien landing was made to disappear.

Partridge had quickly issued orders for the entire landing site to be secured, cleared and sanitized. The deceased JANUS members were whisked away under tight security to El Paso to a military morgue at Fort Bliss Military Reservation. The crumpled JANUS saucer and the reviewing stand wreckage were taken to a secure dump site deep inside the White Sands Missile Range. There they were bulldozed under several tons of sand. The Blue Light unit and helicopter pilots were each given death threats against talking. Each man was then given immediate transfer orders to a different Air Force base. Partridge had assured Fournier that he had gotten to the management of the local ABC television station, and that no personnel there would talk. He reassured Fournier that the videotape of the disastrous "alien landing" would not be transmitted to the network, because, in fact, the Colonel had personally confiscated the station's master tape.

As the six o'clock national news came on, both men tensed. They were waiting to be sure that the news broadcast contained no mention of Space Harbor. Their eyes widened when a large photo blow-up of the White Sands Missile Range loomed up in display behind the ABC anchor.

"Good evening. This is Peter Jennings with ABC News. Topping tonight's stories is incredible film out of New Mexico, backing an even more incredible story. We have to advise viewers that the film you are about to see contains graphic scenes of death.

"Last night, a shadowy group with links to the UFO Cover-Up attempted to stage a hoaxed alien saucer landing at the White Sands Missile Range in southeastern New Mexico. ABC News has managed to obtain videotape of this landing from a private citizen, who made a personal video-tape of the local televised coverage of the landing by ABC's affiliate in Las Cruces. Our Las Cruces affiliate's station manager, Foster Grimes, confirmed that they had broadcast the landing, but told us that the station's master videotape of the fake landing has somehow mysteriously disappeared.

"According to reliable sources, the shadowy group behind this hoax is called JANUS. JANUS is reportedly a secretive group of defense industry officials, military and intelligence officers and one United States senator who have been conducting a UFO cover-up. The purpose of their hoax was reportedly to convince the world that the aliens had chosen them to be the official representatives for Earth."

The television picture switched to a shot of a lighted desert landing area, with voice-over by announcer Jennings.

"In the dramatic nighttime footage being shown now, you can see JANUS's saucer coming in for a landing. Now watch for a door in the side of the saucer to open. Notice that in a moment, men dressed as aliens come out. Next you can see that there was apparently some confusion. Gunfire breaks out. To the right of your screen you can see two of the so-called aliens being shot and falling to the ground. In this next section of film, you can see the fake saucer start to rise. Now, if you look closely above the saucer, you can see that it is being lifted by a black towing cable attached to a dark helicopter overhead. Next, notice that apparently a strong gust of wind came up and destabilized the towing arrangement. In these next frames you can see that the saucer, now a reported 500 feet in the air, detaches from the cable. You can see it falling to the ground, incredibly hitting the reviewing stand where the JANUS group was gathered. In the next scene, that body in a gray jumpsuit which you see on the lower part of your screen, had fallen out of the saucer, and is one of the humans who had been costumed as an alien.

"Our sources tell us that among the JANUS casualties were a major division director within AT&T-Bell Labs; a physicist who worked for EG&G, a black-budget defense contractor; an Air Force Major General; the chief consultant to the Federal Reserve Board; a retired admiral who worked for Batelle Memorial Institute, a classified research company; and the senior United States Senator from Georgia, John Knapp.

"Sources indicate that two members of JANUS are still alive." A picture of Fournier flashed on the screen. "One, a Dr. Henri Fournier, is a top officer with BDM, a defense contract company. He is shown in this picture from last night's videotape, standing near the television platform at Space Harbor."

The screen switched to a photograph of Colonel Partridge.

"Our sources tell us that the other JANUS member is an Army Colonel assigned to military intelligence, Jack Partridge. Earlier in the day, ABC News provided a copy of this film and story to the White House. Presidential spokesman Mitchell Moore announced this afternoon that the President had directed FBI Director Reid Linker to personally supervise an immediate investigation into what Moore characterized as an 'apparent act of treason by JANUS.' This afternoon, a task force of 250 FBI agents fanned out over New Mexico and elsewhere to apprehend Fournier and Partridge on suspicion of sedition and treason. We will bring you more on this incredible late-breaking story as soon as further details become available.

"Elsewhere in the news, the World Health Organization

reported a sharp increase this month in reported cases of Pneumonic Hemorrhagic Fever. The epidemic has now reached into every country of the. . . ."

Partridge clicked off the television, and slowly exhaled a long sigh. Across the room the glass which Fournier had been holding fell to the floor, cracking and sending ice cubes and scotch flying in all directions. Partridge turned away from the screen and looked at the octogenarian leader of JANUS. Fournier's face was pale and his eyes fixed. His hand clenched and then went limp. The silver-haired physicist slumped over and slowly rolled out of his chair onto the maroon carpet.

"Oh my God!" Partridge exclaimed. "Not another body. Shit!" Partridge rushed over to Fournier and felt his carotid artery for a pulse. Finding none, the Colonel buzzed for Major Eberhardt. Eberhardt quickly sent for a special squad to dispose of the corpse. Partridge then rang the Joint Chiefs of Staff complex and notified Fournier's confidential secretary to route all future JANUS messages to him as its only surviving member.

As the squad left to transfer Fournier's body to the same Fort Bliss Army morgue where the other JANUS corpses had been secreted, Partridge sat and considered his situation. He was now the head and sole member of JANUS's leadership. JANUS's assets were too valuable to walk away from. The advanced extraterrestrial technology, the large database about alien messages and methods of contact, the exotic set of weapons systems including HARDON in place at classified ground locations and in orbit, the substantial secret security forces, and the infiltrative network with compartments within conventional military and intelligence agencies, all of these could continue to provide wealth, power and influence if kept under his control.

Yet there were definitely major down-side factors now to continuing to operate JANUS. Much of the networking which had made JANUS powerful was done through the other JANUS members. And they were now all dead. JANUS's grand plan to take power through manipulation of society by the "alien landing" was a spectacular failure. Partridge still believed that he could order the HARDON system to be fired without Tarnsworth or General Lazarus around, but he was not sufficiently briefed on its operation to be sure he would know how to use it effectively. Besides, invading aliens, if indeed invasion was their plan, were not his chief concern now. His immediate problem was that the FBI was hunting him. With Rod Birdsall dead, Partridge was not confident that he could contain the FBI search. Especially not with the FBI Director taking personal charge of the manhunt. Also, with all the other members of the leadership dead, Partridge was not sure whether the JANUS chain-of-command structure would stay loyal to him, especially after this nationwide television exposé. If anyone along the chain "turned," Partridge was as good as jailed. Neither could he just walk away from JANUS. All the intelligence personnel and security forces would not just peacefully accept losing very well-paying jobs. Someone, probably more than one, would talk, if they were removed from the payroll. No, like it or not, he would just have to continue steering the JANUS organization. But the Colonel decided that the only group he could really trust was his PANDORA Unit, which he had long since formed into his own praetorian guard. He regretted not having gotten rid of Major Eberhardt long ago, but now was not the time to have to break in someone new. Like it or not, he would have to rely on Eberhardt's assistance and loyalty for a while longer.

Partridge next considered his action options. Technically he was no longer under orders to kill Maguire. Rod Birdsall, who had given the order, was dead, as were the rest of JANUS. Hungry for influence, the Colonel now wanted more than ever to intercept the real extraterrestrial landing. There was where real power lay now. And if the aliens showed any signs of presenting a challenge to the status quo, he would activate the HARDON system, and deny them access to Earth's atmosphere. That would give him power, too, as a grateful Earth recognized that it was he who had saved them. Partridge felt equally sure that Maguire would lead him to the real extraterrestrial landing. Signal intelligence from Jacques Stone's house during the meeting between Maguire and Stone indicated that there was a select group which was preparing to meet the extraterrestrial landing. Their code name had been identified as Project Epiphany. Since JANUS had not been able to penetrate and control this contact team, Maguire could likely be a way to link up with them. Maguire's instincts so far seemed to be unerring in positioning himself to be at the real Landing. Besides, Partridge thought, I might as well get some benefit out of the bastard before I eliminate him. And Maguire's female companion, Catalina, he reminded himself, was another loose end that needed to be disposed of at the same time.

Catalina got up, shut off the television in their motel room, and turned to Maguire. "You know, Rog, this JANUS thing becomes more incredible each day. First they manage to kill almost all of their own leadership in the midst of horribly botching that hoaxed landing. Then, all of that mess gets on television and makes them the laughing stock of the country. Next, their two surviving leaders go on the FBI's most wanted list. You know, if they hadn't tried doing something so awful, I'd actually be starting to feel sorry for them by now."

"Save your sympathy, Barbara. What's left of JANUS is still a dangerous organization. But the FBI can take care of them. We've got another agenda."

"You mean going to Timothy Katoya's gathering of Star Nation shamans?"

"Right," Maguire replied. "And knowing the fluidity of Native American time, I'd better find some way to contact Timothy and see if the date of the gathering is still the same." Maguire picked up the room phone to check his office answering machine messages. There were two messages. One was from Jacques Stone, saying to call him because he had some "timely" news. And Maguire was pleasantly surprised that the other message was from Timothy Katoya, although the voice relaying the message was the Hopi teenager Chosovi.

The message said that Katoya had had another Dream.

In it Saquasohuh, the Blue Star Kachina, indicated that the dates of the Star Nation convocation should be September 22-27. Katoya's message added that Maguire and Catalina should come two days early before the convocation, to participate in a purifying ceremony. And the message carried a warning that someone who wanted them dead was going to be following them.

Maguire was startled at the last part of the message. He had expected that sooner or later his pursuers — JANUS, if that's who it was — would find his trail again. But Timothy had said that some pursuers wanted "them" dead. That meant Barbara as well. He frowned as he thought about this latest news. Barbara was clearly in danger. Should he tell her and worry her, or spare her the worrying? No, she needed to know. She needed to be alert. Maguire attempted to return Jacques Stone's call, but got no answer.

He shared with Catalina Katoya's message. After taking a long breath, Maguire added the part about both of them being followed by someone who wanted them dead. "I hate to be the bearer of bad news, but you should know that now you, too, are on someone's hit list. Probably JANUS's. Timothy was quite firm about that in his phone message. I'm sorry, Barbara. This is undoubtedly because of your association with me."

"I'm a big girl, Rog. I chose to come along with you. You warned me a long time ago about the danger. I can handle it. Besides, I've fallen madly in love with you, you big handsome lunk." Catalina flashed a radiant, loving smile. "If I have to go down, I hope it's in your arms."

Maguire's voice was choked with emotion. Such total sacrificial love he had not known before. He reached over to give her a hug. "Barbara, I'll do everything I can to protect you. I promise. I love you so much."

Catalina raised her face to his, stared lovingly into his eyes, then reached her lips to his. They melted into a prolonged kiss.

Colonel Partridge sat alone in his PANDORA office, the lights rheostated down to only the faintest of a dim glow. His eyes were closed and his brow crinkled with concentration. Partridge prided himself on being an advanced master of the psychic art of Remote Viewing, and this morning he was employing it on his most important target yet: the location of Roger Maguire. A photograph of Maguire, extracted from his NSA intelligence jacket, sat propped up on Partridge's desk as a target focus. As Partridge focused his inner mind's attention on Maguire's physical location, the image came up of a city limit sign. As the Colonel concentrated, he made out the city's name. Las Cruces. As he continuied his remote viewing, an image developed of a four-wheel-drive vehicle passing the city limit sign. It was headed in the outbound direction. As Partridge focused in on the vehicle, the image was interrupted by a stronger overlay image. A giant Thunderbird glowered with dark menacing clouds in the background. The Thunderbird's clouds emitted strokes of forked lightning. Partridge tried to push aside the distracting image and resume focusing on the vehicle, but the Thunderbird image stubbornly persisted, dominating his psychic view. Finally he gave up in disgust. He grabbed the phone and ordered a long-range stealth helicopter readied for immediate take-off. *At least I know Maguire is headed out of Las Cruces,* he thought to himself. *And I just bet I know where he's going.*

Partridge had previously received a briefing from Captain DiGiorgio about Katoya's call for a gathering of medicine men from all over the hemisphere. They were to meet on the Hopi Reservation in late September to exchange oral traditions about the returning extraterrestrials. He knew Maguire wouldn't miss such a gathering. Partridge no longer trusted Major Eberhardt and what was left of the Zeta Team to do surveillance on Maguire. They had failed too often. In fact, Partridge suspected that the reason they kept failing was that somebody's psychic forces were being used to protect Maguire. *Well, two can play that game,* Partridge thought, *and I play it as well as the best.*

The elevator doors opened up onto the ground level lobby of Sandia National Laboratories headquarters. Dressed in his Army Colonel's uniform, Partridge stepped out the front door into a blue government car, which hurriedly whisked him the two miles to a waiting helicopter at Kirtland Air Force Base. When his car pulled away from SNL headquarters, Partridge did not notice Ed Sodoma's vehicle pull out from down the street and follow him from a discreet distance behind.

The car radio in the Pathfinder was tuned to the hourly network news. Maguire's ears perked up when the announcement came on about the death of Henri Fournier, whom the announcer described as a top consultant to the Joint Chiefs of Staff, with a distinguished career as a defense industry physicist before ending up on the FBI's most-wanted list. They were just passing through Truth Or Consequences on the interstate when Catalina sat up with a start. "What's up?" he asked her.

"Oh, Rog, I just got a mental image of a portly man with brown receding hair and eyes like a ferret. Ooh, he gives me the creeps! He's not very far away from us, and he's looking for us."

"You know, Barbara, the person you're describing sounds like that picture of Colonel Partridge that they showed on ABC."

"Let me concentrate. Uh, oh! He's up above us and ahead of us a little ways. He's headed our way."

"That means he's in some search plane. We've got to get off this interstate." Maguire quickly checked the map, and pulled off at the Highway 25 exit. "Barbara, bear with me on this. We've gotta shake the Colonel. We're going to go to Hopiland over some back roads, a lot of them dirt. We'll head north on New Mexico 52 to Datil, west to Quemado, up New Mexico 36 to the Zuni Reservation, west from there to U.S. 191, and then north to the Hopi Reservation. Some of it's bumpy, so hold on to your hat."

"I'm not wearing a hat. But I'm cinching my seatbelt tighter. You know those male drivers," Catalina grinned.

Maguire pressed the accelerator towards the floor as they sped west from the interstate.

A dull-black helicopter sped southbound high over the Rio Grande River that ran parallel to I-25. Colonel Partridge nudged the pilot, as they passed over Elephant Butte Reservoir. "Pull closer to the interstate. I want to be able to spot Maguire's car."

Zeta Five obligingly steered the chopper over to a position above the interstate. In a couple minutes they passed over the Highway 52 exit, but did not see Maguire's vehicle. It was now out of sight, well to the west of I-25 among the winding canyons.

Twenty-five miles down the rural highway, Maguire spotted a narrow sandstone side canyon lined with tamarisk trees. He pulled the Pathfinder deep into the ¡ side canyon and parked under a canopy of trees. "We'll stay here until dark," he said. "If we travel only at night, it'll make us that much harder to spot."

"Sounds good to me, Rog," Catalina answered. "Besides, it's kinda cozy here underneath the trees. And no one can see us this far up the canyon." She laid out her sleeping bag on the canyon's sand floor and started to undress. "You'd better get some rest, too, Rog. You've been going at quite a pace, and we've got a long night drive ahead of us."

Maguire unrolled his sleeping bag and placed it next to Catalina's, who was now sitting in her underwear on top of her bag. "I'll be happy to get some rest, but how can I with such a gorgeous woman sitting there in her lingerie?"

"You certainly know how to flatter a woman, Dr. Maguire," Catalina said with a sly grin, as she slipped into her bag and closed her eyes. "Nighty night. I'll see if I get any useful premonitions for us while I'm asleep."

"Happy 'remote-viewing'," Maguire answered, as he slid into his sleeping bag. "Oh, by the way, did I tell you this was the prime season for rattlesnakes?" He made a hiss and reached over and gave Catalina a playful pinch on the rump through her bag.

Catalina lifted visibly off the ground, then turned over and shot Maguire a mock-severe stare. "Watch out, buddy, or I'll psychically get you in a tender and very vulnerable body part while you're asleep."

"OK, OK, I surrender. I know when I'm out-gunned, so to speak."

Catalina grinned and replied in her best cowboy drawl, "Smile when you say that, pardner."

The Great Kiva of the Hopi had been a closely guarded secret. No White man had ever before learned of its existence. It had been reserved for very special events. Five centuries ago this very large, round, sunken religious ceremonial chamber had been dug out of the sandstone atop First Mesa. The chamber lay underneath the Hopi village of Walpi, the oldest continually inhabited village in North America. Anthropologists who had surveyed the kivas of Walpi from the outside had not realized that what they had assumed were three kivas was actually one large room.

On a stone bench that went all the way around the circular walls of the Great Kiva, forty men and women sat surrounding the speaker in the center. Half of them had the lined and deeply-tanned features and shamanic regalia of medicine men. They came from all over the hemisphere: Winnebego, Iroquois, Ojibwa, Lakota, Dakota, Nakota, Cherokee, Choctaw, Hopi, Mescalero Apache, Mayan, Aztec and Incan, all keepers of traditional knowledge about the Star People. The other half were non-Indian specialists on extraterrestrials: researcher professionals with doctorates, lay investigators, a famous author, a retired Air Force Colonel, two retired intelligence officers, several psychics, two channelers of extraterrestrial messages, and an observer from the United Nations.

Two days before the convocation, Maguire and Catalina had participated in sweat lodges led by Katoya as purification in preparation for the gathering. During long, hot hours inside the sweat lodge, they joined in Hopi and other tribal songs and chants. Several people, including Catalina, had visions, but Maguire saw nothing unusual. Finally, the purification rituals completed, Katoya pronounced everything ready.

On the beginning day of the convocation, the first speaker was Anpo Wie, a senior medicine person of the Lakota (Sioux) whose non-Indian name was George Morning Star. He told about being visited by extraterrestrials while he was in isolation on a *hanbleceya*, Vision Quest. Morning Star described how a concave disk set down near him while he was praying on Bear Butte. Short people had came out of the saucer who could read his mind. The medicine man found out that he could read their minds, too. He told the gathering that "we have UFO-people landing on my reservation all the time." He told about joking with the Star People and about their mentally laughing back. He stated that human scientists have lost the ancient wisdom. "They have to see everything with their naked eye, so they shoot down a UFO to see what it is made of, and how it was shaped and formed. But their intention was wrong, so they have been misled." He said that they even have scientists who are hired to cover up the truth about UFOs. The medicine man said that the leader of the Star People was dead serious and never blinked his eyes. This made the medicine man get a spooky feeling and his skin covered with goose bumps. He said that he felt that the extraterrestrial could see right through him. When he looked into the Star Person's eyes, he felt he could see through them and into the whole universe. He was shown jets flying in formation and tanks moving across the land. Then there was a bright light, and the jets were gone, and the tanks sizzled and bubbled. He said to the assembled people that it will be impossible for our military power to challenge the Star Nations. He finished by saying that Lakota means "peace," and this is why the Star Nations are coming. "Countless people are coming: to visit peaceful persons, to urge peace around the world, no more war on other people, no more war on th e four-legged and two-legged nations [animals and birds], no more war on the land [ecological destruction], no more war against other peoples' cultures, but instead to live in harmony with the Earth." When George Morning Star finished, the other medicine people gave shouts of approval. The non-Indians present gave his speech a standing ovation.

During the first four and a half days of the convocation, many medicine persons had shared their tribes' lore about the Star Visitors. From northern tribes living near the Arctic Circle to the native peoples of the Peruvian Andes to the South, some general themes emerged. The Star Nations have visited since time immemorial. They have brought sacred teachings, which have provided the foundations of basic culture, spirituality, primitive medicine and metaphysics. The Star People came in friendship, but with serious teachings about the right way to live. And again and again, the medicine people stated that the Star People would return at a pivotal point in human history. That time was imminent.

The Anglo experts also took their turns in presenting. They shared information about the extraterrestrials which they gained from interviewing experiencers, and in some cases, from being experiencers themselves. Because the non-Indian speakers came from cultures which had not had a tradition of extraterrestrial intervention, their talks tended to focus more on changes in awareness and transformations of perspective which resulted from extraterrestrial contact. They, too, generally found such contacts to be beneficial and growthful, although among the speakers were a couple of investigators who described the Visitors according to the stereotype of the "Evil Alien."

It was late afternoon, the fifth day of the convocation of Star Nation Altar Keepers. It was Timothy Katoya's turn to speak. The Hopi Elder stood up and walked to the center of the kiva. He was a striking figure, with his bright red bandanna sweatband, shirt of vibrant purple, shamanic necklace, long breechclout, leggings and moccasins. Katoya recited the Hopi Prophecies one by one, as he had done for Maguire and Catalina earlier in the summer. They foretold major events which he said were about to unfold. His face became more grave, as he talked about the coming day when the Hopi abandon their faith and all their ceremonialism for a while. He paused, tears rolling down his leathern cheeks. His voice grew stronger as he went on, foretelling that World War III will start soon, and that atomic bombs will harm land

and people, even in the United States. At that Prophecy, a noticeable stiffening and chill went around the room. He added that "the War will be over spiritual disagreements." He spoke then of "an intervention by spiritual beings, who would stop the War, and remain on earth to create one world, one nation, operating under a spiritual power."

Katoya went on to say, "That time is not far off. It will be when Saquasohuh, the Blue Star Kachina, dances in a Hopi village plaza. She represents a shining bluish celestial object, which has been far away and invisible, which will now be making its appearance."

Catalina leaned over to Maguire and whispered, "My God, Roger! Can he be referring to the Hale-Bopp comet?"

Maguire shrugged his shoulders, and they both turned back to listen to Timothy.

Katoya talked about it being time for all humanity to leave the Fourth World, the Hopi term for the current historical time, and to emerge into a Fifth World. "This time of emergence has already begun. The humble and little people of the Earth, the truly wise ones, are already starting to make this transition. Our Star Brothers and Sisters, whom the Hopi have remembered as the Kachinas, are helping us make this emergence."

He stopped suddenly, and stared at the wall behind the *sipapu*, the traditional hole in the floor of kivas which reminds the Hopi of the place of their emergence from previous worlds. All eyes in the room turned to look at what he was staring at. The wall started to shimmer. First a long, thin gray arm, then a spindly leg, and then the entire body of a tall, large-headed extraterrestrial with enormous black slanted eyes emerged through the wall. The extraterrestrial's skin was a pale bluish-ashen color. She wore the embroidered white ceremonial robe of a Kachina Maiden. The extraterrestrial stood next to the *sipapu* a moment, then walked over and stood facing Katoya . He had to look up to face this almost seven-foot-tall figure. There was not a sound in the kiva, as forty people held their breath awestruck.

Then Catalina leaned over and whispered to Maguire, "The ET is communicating mentally with Katoya."

Maguire whispered back, "You're picking it up telepathically?" Catalina nodded.

Katoya indeed began gesturing, as he silently responded to Saquasohuh.

Catalina again whispered to Maguire, "Now she's telling him that the Emergence to the Fifth World has begun, and some other stuff."

After a minute, Katoya turned to the assembled gathering with a stunned expression on his face and said, "This is Saquasohuh, whom the Hopi call the Blue Star Kachina. She said that the Lakota people know her best as White Buffalo Calf Woman. She has told me that she and her people are glad that we have gathered here to share information about the Star People. She has some things to say to all of us, and is asking me to pass on her thoughts to you out loud."

The gathered medicine people and Anglo experts started to buzz with excited comments. After some moments Katoya held his hand up for silence.

"She says that her people will make a major landing in a huge ship in two months," the Hopi Elder continued. "It will be at the time of the Full Moon, during the time which the *bahana* call November. She says that three people in this room already know the general location of the Landing. Those people are the *bahana* anthropologist Roger Maguire, his research companion Barbara Catalina, and myself. This is so."

The eyes of everyone in the room turned to Catalina and Maguire, who ignored their stares, and then back to Katoya. He looked up to the extraterrestrial for a minute, then faced the group and went on.

"She says that a small group of UFO researchers and government officials plan to be at the landing of the Star Nations. She has directed me to reveal to you that I am part of that group. That group call themselves Project Epiphany. Saquasohuh says that Project Epiphany needs much prayer from the Native Elders gathered here. The prayer is needed so that the Project Epiphany people will truly be ready for the Star Nations Landing. She also says that the Project needs to add to their group someone from the Lakota Nation, and that those of you who are here should choose that person."

Katoya's voice quavered with emotion as he went on. "Everyone needs to prepare for this Landing. The Star Nations want this Landing to be the thing which causes everyone in the world to be aware of their presence. Saquasohuh says that the public awareness about the Star People which will result from this Landing is very important. Everyone in the world must have a chance to decide whether to accept the Star People as friends or not. This decision will have very serious results, either way, as we are all moving into the time of major changes on the Earth. Those who accept the Star People as friends will have their help. Those who do not will have to cope with the Earth's changes without their help. Saquasohuh says that it is very important that all of us here figure out a way to let the whole world know that the Star People are coming, starting with their landing in two months. She says that this is the main reason we were all moved to come together for this gathering, so that we could hear this message, and pass it on." Katoya paused.

The Blue-Star Kachina turned and faced the assembled gathering. Each person now heard in their own head a distinct, sweet but strong, feminine voice speaking aloud to each in their own language.

"Keepers of the Star Nation Altars! We the Star Nations salute you for keeping alive the memory and the knowledge of our earlier visits with you. Now we ask that you take on a new task, to let all the peoples of the world know about our return very soon, and to tell them what kind of people we are. Let them know that we bring beneficial messages for the good of all.

"And you non-Indian people, who have studied us well, we salute you too! Work together with our Native brothers and sisters in spreading the word that we are returning. Many among you already know why we are returning. Let the whole world know.

"Thank you all for listening to our message. Now I must go. My ship is waiting, and enemy humans are closing in on it."

With that, she walked back to the wall behind the *sipapu*. The wall shimmered again, as she walked into and through the wall. Some of the group sat there stunned, while others, including Maguire and Catalina, clambered up the crude wooden ladders to the entranceways in the ceiling. On the kiva roof they stood watching, as the Blue-Star Kachina extraterrestrial rose up in a bluish-white beam of light to a 40-meter-wide saucer hovering silently overhead. Then they turned around to face a deafening noise out of the southwest. Three Air Force F-111 fighters, dispatched from Luke Air Force Base, Phoenix, screamed in low to engage the saucer. Saquasohuh had just entered the saucer, when the lead F-111 launched an air-to-air missile at it. A second before impact time, the saucer rose suddenly from 30 feet altitude to 30,000 feet, then hovered motionless. As the missile whistled by and exploded harmlessly against a nearby ridge, the lead F-111 roared past low overhead, followed a few seconds later by the second and third fighters. Now a mile and a half to the northeast, the F-111s turned around and began to climb vertically with their afterburners on, trying to catch up to the high-altitude saucer. As they closed in on it, the UFO suddenly zipped off to the west, moving from straight overhead to past the San Francisco Peaks on the horizon, a distance of seventy miles in one second. Hopelessly outmaneuvered, the F-111s turned southwest to return to base.

After the convocation finally reassembled back down in the Great Kiva, the group discussed the tasks which the extraterrestrial Saquasohuh had given them. The Native Americans talked over who should be the Lakota representative, and then unanimously voted for George Morning Star as the Lakota to be recommended as an additional member of Project Epiphany. Timothy Katoya volunteered to contact the Project Epiphany leadership and inform them that the extraterrestrials wanted a Lakota representative added to the Project, and that the Star Nation convocation had selected George Morning Star.

Their next order of business was to get word out to the world that the Star People were coming in two months. An Anglo psychologist present got out a calendar, and calculated that the Full Moon landing date mentioned by the Blue Star Kachina coincided with November 25th. Since CNN had already been scheduled to televise the closing summary session of the Star Nation convocation the next afternoon, the group decided to devote most of the closing session to announcing to a world television audience the message from the Star Nations about their public landing in two months.

On Thursday afternoon, the Lakota and the Hopi medicine men, George Morning Star and Timothy Katoya, stood in full shamanic regalia in the center of the Great Kiva. They were illuminated by the glare of CNN television cameras. Morning Star briefly summarized the various Native American traditions of extraterrestrial contacts for centuries past, which had just been shared at the Star Nation convocation. Katoya told of the prophecies many tribes shared, which foretold geophysical, ecological and man-made cataclysms soon to envelop the Earth. The Hopi Elder related how an extraterrestrial had come into their gathering to pass on an urgent message to the world. Katoya announced that the Star Nations would do a public landing within two months, and that the extraterrestrial wanted everyone to decide whether they would accept the Star Nations as friends or not. Katoya talked about the Star Nations' teachings, the healings, and the spiritual information which they had shared with the Native Americans, and which had enriched their lives.

The CNN cameras zoomed in as Morning Star stepped forward and made concluding remarks. "The Indian people whom you call the Sioux have been friends with these Star People since earliest times. It would be well if the *wasicu*, the White man, develops friendship with them, too. But everyone must make their own decision. We have told you what we know. It is true. May the Great Spirit guide your hearts. *Mitakuye oyasin*."

Chapter 11

For the past three days, the Hopi Reservation had been mobbed by reporters and camera crews from around the world. They had sought interviews with Katoya, Morning Star, and anyone else associated with the Star Nation convocation, trying to extract every detail about the extraterrestrial's appearance, her message, the Air Force attack, and the UFO's escape. Finally at the end of the third day, the reporters and the satellite trucks went away. Desert calm returned to the Hopi mesas , serene in their lofty isolation sixty miles from the nearest city.

Maguire and Catalina huddled by the fireplace in Timothy Katoya's living room. At almost 6000 feet elevation, the nighttime chill penetrated the stone walls. Katoya walked in, having just finished an evening meditation which he did daily inside the kiva of his Snake Clan. He pulled up a chair by the fire and sat facing them.

"Grandfather, We have some questions for you," Maguire began. "Yesterday I returned a phone call from Jacques Stone and talked to him. Jacques was set to pass on to me some more information about Project Epiphany's plans to be at the ET landing. But when he heard that I was staying with you, and that you had been instructed by Saquasohuh to openly declare your membership in Project Epiphany, he said that there was no point to his passing anything on. He said I could get the information directly from you. Now I know you've been busy with the press and TV media the past few days, but I've got some questions I'd like to ask you."

"I know," Katoya replied. "I could feel your questions for me forming while I was in the kiva."

Catalina spoke up. "We want to know about Project Epiphany's plans for the ET Landing. What can you tell us?"

Katoya stared at the fire, and then said, "First, tell me what you already know."

"Well, we certainly know the date, right out of the Blue Star Kachina's own mouth. Or mind, I should say," Maguire replied. "It'll be at the Full Moon, November 25."

"And we know the location pretty well, from what we discussed with you earlier, Timothy, and what we put together on our own," Catalina added. "It'll be on the west side of the Animas Mountains, southeast of Cloverdale, New Mexico. I was shown that the time will be in the afternoon. Oh, and it'll be lightly snowing."

"Well, you two *bahanas* seem to know just about everything already," Katoya said with a mischievous grin, testing them.

"Oh, we've still got a few questions," Maguire responded smoothly.

"And please don't call me a *bahana*," Catalina added tartly. "I'm part Ojibwa tribe."

Katoya was put on the defensive. He adopted a placating tone. "No offense intended, Barbara. Now, let me see if I can be of some help to you two. What are your questions?"

"Why do the people in Project Epiphany want to be at the ET Landing?" Catalina asked.

"The reasons are as many as the people involved," Katoya replied. "For many in our group maybe the biggest reason is that it is a great honor to meet with the Star People and represent all humans. And, of course, people in the Project are curious about what the Star People will have to say."

"OK, fair enough," Maguire said. "But what authority do they have to represent all the people of the Earth?"

"Project Epiphany has no formal authority," Katoya replied. "Earlier they met and tried to get the United Nations to undertake meeting with the Star Nations. But in the end, the U.N. would not get involved. As a matter of fact, Dr. Bowen told me that U.N. Secretary Salaam has just bowed out as a personal member of Project Epiphany. 'Too politically explosive' was his excuse. Luckily for the Project, his wife, Leila, doesn't care about the politics, but is fascinated by the 'ETs'. So she is replacing him on the team. I will give a more complete answer to your first question, Roger, Project Epiphany is going to be at the Landing for two reasons. First, because no one else has organized an international group, a group which could represent the Earth the Star People are going to land on. Don't worry about a — what is the *bahana* word? — a power grab, that's it. The Project Epiphany people have all taken a pledge to work only for the good of the planet."

"But how are the people of the Project going to find out where the ET Landing is?" Maguire asked.

"Simple," Katoya answered with a smile. "You and Barbara already told them where it would be. You told them through me, of course. When you figured out that the location was southeast of Cloverdale, I passed that word on to Dr. Robert Bowen, and he passed it on to the others in the Project. Same thing with the date. After Saquasohuh told us it was during the Full Moon in November, I passed that information on to the Project people as well. They will be there waiting when the Star Nations land."

"Who else knows of the location besides Project Epiphany and us?" Maguire asked.

"No one that I know of," Katoya replied. "All the people in the Project are pledged to keep such information secret."

"Is there any way we can join up with them around the time of the Landing?" Catalina asked.

Katoya looked into the glowing fire for a minute, then said, "I do not have the power to let you join with the Project."

"Look, Timothy," Maguire said emphatically, "you're supposed to be my friend. And we know when and where the Landing is going to be. Do you mean to sit here and tell us that the Project people will gather near the same location where we're going to be, and they'll just exclude us? This is the most important event in history!"

Katoya looked uncomfortable at the upset in Maguire's face and voice. "I understand your wishes, but I cannot make a decision for the group." The Hopi Elder paused, and then added, "If you and Barbara are at the Landing area, all I can say is that I will put in a good word with you with the Project Contact Team. After that, it will be out of all of our hands. The Star People are going to interact with whom they want to. That is their way."

Maguire, now calmer, said quietly, "I know. I know."

Catalina gave him a look of sympathetic understanding, "Roger, that's probably as far as we can take it for now. I'm heading for bed. And I'm going to ask my higher powers to give me some guidance about the Landing. Maybe something will come to me during the night. Good night, everyone."

At the Bureau of Indian Affairs Hopi Agency office at Keams Canyon, Police Chief Claude Rohona picked up the phone and dialed the back-line number for PANDORA Unit headquarters. Colonel Partridge picked up the phone on the second ring.

"Chief Rohona here, Colonel. I've got an update report for you. It's been hell trying to locate the people you asked about. There have been hundreds of white New Age types hanging around that Star Nations conference. Then, when the national press and TV got wind of the alien that supposedly appeared at the conference, it went crazy around here. People pouring in from everywhere." Chief Rohona attempted a little Native American humor. "You know how it is, Colonel. All you whites look alike to a poor Indian like me."

Colonel Partridge did not laugh.

Faced with dead silence at the other end of the phone, Chief Rohona quickly went on. "Anyway, my men finally located those suspects that you sent me photos of, Maguire and that female with him. They don't appear to be armed. I've got Sergeant Nayatewa tailing them now. But once they leave the Hopi Reservation jurisdiction, we can't follow them. You know how it is. I just gotta say, Colonel, they look pretty tame. They sure don't look like serious national security risks."

Colonel Partridge's frustration found an outlet. "Captain, when I want an opinion about national security matters from some two-bit lawman stuck on some goddamn reservation, I'll ask for it. I've already made clear to you that surveilling them is top priority under special federal authorization. You savvy, Tonto?"

Chief Rohona bristled at the racist blast from Partridge, but he had learned before not to give grief to intelligence officers. There had been several tales around the police training academy he had attended about how nasty intelligence types can get when rubbed the wrong way. "Yes, I understand, Colonel. You want them tailed right up to the edge of the Reservation?"

"Better than that, Chief. I want a report when it looks like they're headed off the Reservation. And if I don't arrive in time to relieve your man before they cross the boundary, he keeps on trailing them, no matter how far off the Reservation he gets. You got that, Captain?"

"But Colonel, I'm already short of men. I can't afford to have Sergeant Nayatewa gone."

Partridge's tone got cold and dark. "Chief, you want to see your damn BIA police budget lose much wampum real fast? Don't give me grief over this."

"Yes, sir." Chief Rohona spoke in a cowed tone. "I'll make sure the Sergeant stays right on their tail."

"I'm glad that we understand each other, Chief. Keep me posted."

Partridge was not inclined to take any more chances with Maguire and Catalina eluding him. With the rest of the JANUS leadership wiped out, intelligence information was not so reliable now. He felt sure that Maguire would lead him to the extraterrestrial landing. He still wanted Maguire dead eventually, and was still fairly sure that at short range he could kill him psychically. But now Partridge was not so concerned about making Maguire's death looking natural. When the time was right, if necessary he could shoot Maguire, and that female with him, too. But first he wanted to give Maguire the opportunity to lead him to the Landing.

Catalina took the turn-off from Arizona Highway 264 onto Indian Highway 2, heading south towards Interstate 40. She was telling Maguire about a disturbing vision that came to her during the night. She had seen Maguire and herself standing at the foot of a low mountain range among some patches of cholla cactus with clumps of snow on them. A huge cylindrical UFO was lowering out of the sky, when suddenly brilliant green laser beams came up from two different locations on the ground and struck the UFO. Her vision of a military attack on the descending UFO only reinforced what Katoya had told them earlier, that they would be in great danger if they tried to be at the Star Nations landing. They discussed the risks as she drove along. Both decided that they were still committed to their efforts to be at the extraterrestrial landing.

They also decided that, since the Landing was over a month away, and since it presented unknown risks, that they should take some time to visit their children, in case it might be for the last time. Maguire had not seen Melissa since early June, when she had moved to San Luis Obispo to start a summer job, before beginning college as a freshman there this fall at Cal Poly University. Catalina had not visited her son, Jason, an apprentice graphic artist in Denver, since early July when she had joined up with Maguire.

They shared with each other their secret thoughts that if their attempt to be at the extraterrestrial landing proved fatal, they wanted one last chance to spend time with their respective eighteen-year-olds. And, in any case, they both wanted to have their kids meet their respective new love partner.

The decision was made to go to California first. Maguire wanted to stop by his office in Chatsworth and check his mail. Then their plan was to drive north to San Luis Obispo, so that Catalina could meet Melissa. After that, they would go east to Denver, so that Maguire could meet Jason.

As they crossed the boundary of the Hopi Reservation, passing a sign saying "Welcome to Navajo Nation," Maguire looked in the right side mirror. He quickly told Catalina to speed up. She accelerated the Pathfinder to seventy-five. Maguire looked around and noted that the Hopi BIA police vehicle, which had been following them a half-mile behind, also speeded up to seventy-five, but still kept the same distance behind. "We've got a tail, Barbara. That Hopi cop car is out of its jurisdiction now, but he's still coming. And he isn't red-lighting us, even though we're breaking the speed law. He must be working with JANUS, at least with what's left of it."

"Well, with Fournier and the others dead, that leaves only Colonel Partridge."

"JANUS is still more than the Colonel. There's got to be a lot of other lower level personnel around. We'd better stay sharp and cautious."

"Jeez, back at Chaco Canyon, I thought I was taking up with Indiana Jones," Catalina said with a tight-lipped smile. "Looks like I'm in with James Bond instead."

Maguire gave her a wry grin back.

At a rest stop on I-40 east of Kingman, Catalina pulled over to have Maguire take a turn driving. A mile back, they had noticed the Hopi BIA police car stop and turn around, apparently headed back to the reservation. Maguire got behind the wheel, pulled out into westbound traffic, and headed towards Los Angeles and his Chatsworth office. Neither Catalina nor he noticed a single-engine white Cessna, which was approaching at 5000 feet altitude from behind them. As the plane closed in on the Pathfinder, Zeta Five, the pilot, looked down and pointed towards the ground. "Colonel, there they are."

"OK, Miller, just ease off your airspeed, stay behind, and keep 'em in sight," Partridge replied.

"Roger that, Colonel."

Two miles east, and an additional 4000 feet above the Cessna, a Beechcraft Bonanza, painted sky-camouflage colors, purred along. The signal on Ed Sodoma's locator screen was crisp and clear. The special transponder he had secretly attached to Partridge's plane was working perfectly. Sodoma flashed tobacco-yellowed teeth, permitting himself a rare smile.

Darkness was falling over California. The last light of day played faintly along the tops of the forested ridges of the San Gabriel Mountains east of Los Angeles. Maguire turned on his headlights and speeded up slightly, as he crested Soledad Pass and began the descent down Highway 14 towards the San Fernando Valley. With any luck, he thought, we can reach my office in Chatsworth in an hour, and get some sleep in the office annex bedroom. Catalina turned on the car radio to listen to some music. A song by The Eagles was playing. She started singing along with it softly. When the song finished, the announcer interrupted in an urgent tone of voice.

"This is a bulletin which has just come in over the wire service. There has been a series of tremendous earthquakes which have rocked the islands of Japan. Associated with the quakes was a spectacular eruption of Mount Fujiyama, which is currently hurtling fiery lava high into the day time sky. Scattered reports indicate that other dormant volcanoes in Japan have also erupted. Initial estimates by the Earthquake Center at Caltech puts the largest of the Japanese quakes, centered 100 miles southwest of Tokyo, at an unbelievable 10.4 magnitude! Emergency tidal wave warnings have been posted for all of Japan, for the western Pacific from the Kamchatka Peninsula to the Philippines, and for the eastern Pacific from the Aleutians down the entire American West Coast all the way to Peru. These tidal waves are predicted to be the most dangerous in history. All citizens are advised to evacuate all low-lying coastal areas within five miles of the ocean and below 300 feet elevation. All citizens are warned to stay away from anywhere near the Pacific coast.

"The report of destruction of major Japanese cities is incredible. The capital city of Tokyo is in ruins. Skyscrapers have toppled everywhere. Roads and rail lines are fractured, and thousands of fires have been caused by ruptured gas lines. The nearby port city of Yokohama has sunk fifty feet, and was leveled by an immediate hundred-foot-high tidal wave that pushed two miles inland. Similar scenes of devastation come from fragmentary reports out of Kyoto, Osaka, Kobe and elsewhere. Estimates of casualties are not available, but one government official, who asked not to be identified, said they would be lucky if the fatalities were fewer than one million. He would not even estimate the number of injured. Five of Japan's plutonium-reactor power plants, located near major cities, have lost their reactor controls, and are in the process of undergoing melt-down. Japanese authorities fear that these reactors could soon go critical and create radioactive explosions. Prime Minister Sukenori Ishii has declared martial law. Government troops are being stationed to maintain order in the cities, but they are encountering widespread panic.

"The tremendous force of the quakes could be felt as far away as Seoul, Korea and in Vladivostok, Russia. And in Hawaii, U.S. Geological Survey volcanologists report that swarms of moderate earthquakes are occurring around the major Island chain volcanoes, Mauna Kea, Mauna Loa and Haleakala. All three are showing signs of nearing eruption. And on the U.S. mainland, Mount Rainier, a dormant volcano near Seattle, has begun to vent clouds of steam. Venting activity has also been reported at Long Valley, a long-dormant volcanic area next to Mammoth Lakes, California. President Williams has ordered U.S. troops in Okinawa and the Philippines to begin immediate airlifts of food, medical supplies and other emergency assistance to Japan, as soon as the Japanese authorities can make temporary repairs to airport runways, which have been buckled by the quakes. We will bring you more updates as details become available."

Catalina turned to Maguire, a shocked look on her face. "Roger, *that's* eerie. I had this vision come to me earlier today about giant earthquakes, but I didn't know what time period was being referred to. Oh, those poor people in Japan. How awful!"

Maguire shook his head sympathetically. "Yeah, first the bottom part of California goes into the drink. Then that killer Pneumonic Hemorrhagic Fever starts sweeping the world. Now a major portion of Japan gets leveled, and the Ring of Fire volcanoes around the Pacific have started going off. All in all, I'd say that the 'earth changes' that the ETs have been predicting are upon us."

"Is your office in Chatsworth in any danger?"

"You mean from volcanoes or tidal waves? No; there aren't any volcanoes around. And Chatsworth is roughly about 600 feet above sea level. So you can sleep safely tonight."

"That's good." Catalina yawned. "I'm tired. You must be too, dear. I hope we're almost there."

As soon as Maguire pulled into the parking slot by his office, he knew something was wrong. The main overhead light in his office, which he always turned off before leaving, was on. He told Catalina to stay in the car while he checked out inside. He noted worriedly that the front door was unlocked, though he always locked the deadbolt. Stepping inside, he could see furniture in disarray, and his anthropology research papers strewn all over the office floor. He looked over his files quickly. The lock on his extraterrestrial research file drawer had been clumsily picked, so that his own key hardly fit in the lock any more. When he finally got the drawer open, Maguire noted that his files were missing. He stepped into the doorway to the annex, and saw more furnishings thrown around in there, in a deliberate effort to be as destructive as possible. A creaking sound on the floorboard in the main office made Maguire swing around, right fist clenched, ready for the intruder. Catalina jumped back as he wheeled around.

"I thought I told you to stay in the car," Maguire said, with a mixture of annoyance and protectiveness. "There could have been someone in here."

"But you were taking too long. I knew there was a problem."

"But what if there were some bad guys in here? You could have gotten hurt."

"And so could you," Catalina retorted. "I'm not going to leave you to the bad guys and hide in the car."

"Oh, a women's libber, huh?" Maguire said, pulling her to him and smiling, as her face drew near to his.

"I'm a big girl. And I'm not going to have you face risks alone, because I love you. So you might as well get used to it, Roger." Catalina's mouth reached up to his, and they joined in a prolonged kiss.

With the extraterrestrial landing still seven weeks away, Maguire and Catalina had the first block of unscheduled time in months. They decided to give themselves some vacation as they traveled to visit their children. They chose the scenic coastal route for the drive north from Chatsworth to San Luis Obispo. News on the radio had said that the severe tsunami alert, which had been generated by Japan's tremendous earthquakes yesterday, was declared over. Large devastating tidal waves had struck near Pusan Korea, Anchorage, Alaska, and at the northern-most tip of California at Crescent City. But the rest of the American Pacific Coast mercifully had suffered nothing worse than tides which were six feet higher than normal.

As they drove along, they tried to put thoughts of the office burglary behind them. The police had been of no help. Once the Sheriff's deputies learned that "nothing of value" had been taken, meaning "only" Maguire's UFO research papers, the cops treated the break-in as a case of juvenile vandalism. When Maguire mentioned the harassment he had previously experienced from goons working for the UFO Cover-Up, and that he suspected that intelligence operatives were involved in this break-in, the L.A. Sheriff's detective in charge smiled patronizingly and closed his notebook. He assured Maguire that the local patrol officer would keep an eye on his office for the next few days.

By noon, the sun had broken through the light coastal overcast north of Santa Barbara. Maguire pulled off Highway 101 a couple miles past Refugio State Beach. "Time for a break."

"I'm ready. It'll feel good to stretch." Catalina stepped out of the vehicle, and walked down a brushy path to the side of the bluff above the ocean. Maguire grabbed the day-pack and caught up with her. They descended a narrow trail down the face of the sandstone bluff to the pale yellow sand below. The tide was almost out. The rhythmic surf broke gently in turquoise one-foot waves. The sky was an unbroken cobalt blue. The almost empty beach stretched miles in both directions. Maguire spread out a blanket from the day-pack, and laid out a French baguette, cheddar cheese, and a couple of non-alcoholic beers. Catalina was watching a few students from nearby U.C. Santa Barbara tossing a Frisbee a hundred yards up the beach. As the Frisbee went back and forth, a brunette coed's collie dog was trying to jump up and intercept the Frisbee. Catalina noticed that the students were wearing only their tans.

"Great day to get some sun." Catalina said cheerfully, peeling off her shirt. She sat on the blanket, applying suntan lotion to her shoulders.

Maguire replied jokingly, "Now I understand that you New Age hippies believe that you can exist on pure sunlight alone, if you are spiritually evolved enough. But as for me, I still need lunch."

"There's plenty of time for lunch," she shot back with a grin. "What's the matter, Rog? I thought all you Californians practiced sun worship. Here, rub some of this sunscreen on my back, will you?"

After Maguire had anointed Catalina with SPF-15, and she had returned the favor, he laid on the sand, an ice-cold Clausthaler by his side. Eyes closed, he savored the sun's warmth and the gentle ocean breezes caressed his skin. Catalina lay on the blanket next to him. She reached her hand over to hold his.

"When's lunch?" she asked dreamily.

"Lunch can wait. I've got you, babe," he said, giving her hand a gentle squeeze. The gentle swish of the small waves washing up on the sand nearby exerted a hypnotic spell, pulling all the tension out of them, as they began to doze off.

The late afternoon sun was nearing the horizon when Maguire pulled out of a Lompoc gas station and back onto Highway One. Catalina awoke from a cat nap with a start.

"Roger, where are we?" she asked animatedly.

"Oh, just north of Lompoc. Why?"

"Is there some kind of a missile base near here?"

"Well, we're about seven miles from Vandenberg Air Force Base. That's where the military side of NASA does classified missile launches into space. That's also where they're rumored to be putting Star Wars weapon systems into orbit, and doing secret launches to the Moon. Why do you ask?"

"I just got this vision while I was dozing," she replied. "It was a huge spectacular missile launch. The missile was carrying some kind of space weapon that puts out the same kind of green beams that I saw in my last vision. You know, where they were coming up from the ground at the saucer that was trying to land?"

"My God!" Maguire exclaimed, "They're putting killer lasers in orbit? That's a violation of that treaty restricting space to peaceful uses!"

"I got this really strong message from my ET friend, Arica, that we should get near that place, that the launch is going to happen real soon."

"You mean at Vandenberg?"

"Yeah, that must be it," she replied. "It must be an Air Force Base, because I could see guys in blue uniforms walking around the missile before it was launched."

"We can get pretty close to the launch pads," Maguire said. "I know a little beachfront town that is right in the middle of Vandenberg. It's called Surf. It's got a civilian access road right through the Base, so that you can drive to Surf without the hassle of military gates. And I know a place at Surf where we can camp on the beach. We'd be only three miles from the Vandenberg launch complex. We'd be in a position to see any launches they do."

"Roger Maguire! Sometimes you *amaze* me. How do you know so much about secret military space bases? You sure you're not secretly an intelligence agent?"

"Aaagh!" Maguire croaked comically, grabbing his throat. "You said the 'I'-word. Actually, my secret is simple. It just takes ingenuity, lots of research, detailed maps, smart deductions, and patience."

"You left out chutzpa. And a bit of Coyote Spirit to help you do your sneaky penetrations of bases without getting caught."

"Well, Coyote *is* my totem animal," Maguire agreed cheerfully.

"You may *claim* that you're not in intelligence work," Catalina said with a smirk, "but I personally think you're a spy for the ET side."

"Ah, Roger that, Houston," Maguire replied, in his best NASA engineer-nerd voice.

It was after 2 a.m. The clear night sky was a carpet of millions of stars twinkling in the blackness. Catalina and Maguire were sleeping in the tent they had pitched behind some sand dunes north of Surf, near where the Santa Ynez River meets the ocean. The gentle sound of the distant surf beyond the dunes had long since lulled them to a deep sleep. Suddenly, a terrifically loud deep rumble shook the tent. A moment later, it was joined by a huge bright glow to the north which lit up the sky. Maguire quickly clambered out of the tent and stood outside, staring at the huge fireball that was slowly rising from the direction of the base. Catalina quickly joined him, rubbing her eyes at the brightness.

"They've launched the same rocket that I saw in my vision," Catalina exclaimed. "It looks just like it!"

"I checked the local paper over dinner. There was no launch scheduled," Maguire said. "But there it is. A secret launch."

"That rocket has that same odd-shaped package on its nose that I saw in vision. That must be the killer lasers."

"Look!" Maguire said excitedly, "there's something flying along the rocket at the same speed and direction. Geez! It's a UFO!" He pointed to a 100-meter-wide glowing amber disc that was pacing the ascending rocket from a distance of a quarter-mile away out to sea. The military rocket was now picking up speed as it climbed. From watching earlier space shuttle launches on television, Maguire estimated that this rocket was now at about five miles altitude out over the ocean. The rocket's glow was still visible, as was the glowing UFO. Suddenly a thin beam of red light shot out from the side of the disc. In a millisecond the rocket exploded into a huge ball of fire and white smoke.

"Wow!" Catalina shouted. "The saucer blew up the rocket!"

"Yeah, that's *one* illegal space weapon that's never going to make it into orbit. Looks like the ETs are helping the U.S. keep its treaty commitments," Maguire said with a wry smile. "Now I wonder if the military will get that message."

Catalina shook her head. "Vandenberg must have some heavy karma to pay off!"

On the drive to California Polytechnic State University at San Luis Obispo, Catalina asked Maguire more about his daughter Melissa and about his former wife. Maguire had not wanted to discuss Millie, and limited his description of her to a few remarks. Catalina did learn that Millie was a nurse's aide, and that she had been abused as a child. During the marriage she had become increasingly emotionally distant with both her husband and her daughter. As a result Maguire and she had grown apart. When Melissa was a junior in high school, he announced to Millie his decision to divorce and move out. Although he wanted Melissa to come live with him in Chatsworth, she was too attached to her friends and school life in Northridge to leave the family house. He had kept up weekly visitations with Melissa through high school, then less frequently as he started to accept out-of-state work contracts.

Melissa stood in the doorway of her freshman dorm room, smiling proudly at how neatly she had straightened it before her father's arrival. Catalina could see at once the family resemblance. Melissa was a tall, angular, pretty young woman who did not use makeup. Her straight brunette hair hung down below her shoulders. Her broad, open face relected her father's Celtic heritage. She was wearing a black wool sweater and a dark plaid skirt, and looked the quintessential college freshman. Maguire gave Melissa a big hug, then introduced her to Catalina. Melissa flashed a broad beaming smile and gave Catalina a warm handshake. Catalina smiled back and complimented Melissa on her outfit.

After getting acquainted, Melissa took them on a campus tour, proudly showing off the labs where she did her work for her Biology major. She went on to show them the other buildings where she studied and participated in campus life. Maguire smiled proudly at her mature competency when Melissa announced that she had already made arrangements for them to stay in the visiting parents' guest quarters on campus.

Over a celebratory dinner at the area's fanciest dinner establishment, Maguire and Catalina filled Melissa in on their past adventures. They outlined for her their plans for their upcoming trip to Denver, and their plans to be at the extra-terrestrial landing later this year. Catalina marveled at how matter-of-factly Melissa took all these UFO matters, but then remembered that after all, Melissa was her father's daughter. She acknowledged to herself a twinge of jealousy at how easily and naturally the warm and light-hearted conversation went between father and daughter. Yet she had to admit that Melissa had warmed up to her almost instantly. And she found herself taking a quick liking to this girl, who she hoped would be her future step-daughter.

As they ate and talked, none of the three particularly noticed a beefy, medium-build man in his early thirties, with reddish-blonde hair and a pock-marked face, seated alone at the next table. The man looked over in their direction from time to time. Robin "Ice" Miller, JANUS's Zeta Five, was wearing a "hearing aid" with a wire. He kept his briefcase on the table while he dined.

After dinner, the trio returned to campus. Melissa got them situated in their quarters, and then excused herself to do homework for tomorrow's classes. Maguire and Catalina discussed their travel plans for the next day, and then got ready for bed. Because it was not in the visible-light wave lengths, they did not notice an infrared laser beam listening device directed against their window by a figure standing in the shadows of a nearby tree.

After tracking Maguire across Arizona and Southern California by plane, Colonel Partridge had grown weary of the effort of day-to-day surveillance. Although he was unwilling to admit it, he had grown soft in his command position. Partridge did realize that, with his face shown on national television as an FBI fugitive, he could not afford to be out in public where he could be spotted. He reluctantly admitted to himself that he had better delegate the job of tracking Maguire. His pilot "Ice" Miller was trustworthy enough and a logical choice. Besides, Miller's face was unfamiliar to Maguire. As Partridge sat in his San Luis Obispo motel room, he listened with growing impatience to Miller's report on "Fellow Traveler's" conversations.

"Miller, you *sure* you got their travel plans straight?"

"Yeah. I got all their chatter on tape. There's no mistakes."

"Jesus!" Partridge exclaimed, "You mean Maguire and that bitch he travels with actually are going to do a major tour of sensitive installations over the next three weeks?"

"That's right, Colonel."

"I wish I could stay on their ass, but I can't. Now listen up, Ice. I'm counting on you big-time. You be on those two like flypaper. And no fuck-ups, like that bozo DiGiorgio did. And I want continual reports. You see anything that looks like a rendezvous with Project Epiphany members, you get me on the scrambled phone *immediately*. I am hereby authorizing you to use the Presidential National Emergency Network to reach me. The frequency is in your code book. Access Code Name is 'Imperial'; the PROWORD is 'Mena'."

"Gotcha," Miller replied

"Don't use it for anything but Maguire's contact with Project Epiphany. Any unauthorized use is subject to immediate trace and on-the-spot execution. We only get one chance to use that Network. As soon as we communicate, and keep it short, we both have to destroy our phones and immediately relocate. The Internal Security Agency that operates the Network will put satellite visual and ELINT surveillance on any unauthorized user in 30 seconds. So keep your report shorter than that. I can use my NSA authority to cancel the trace once. The ISA will take a few minutes to check out my authorization, before they find out it has been revoked and resume the trace. That'll buy us a little extra time to relocate. Any questions?"

"Yeah," Miller drawled, his thickening Alabama accent revealing his nervousness. "That female psychic that rides with 'Fellow Traveler'; we need a radio code-name for her."

"Simple." Partridge chortled at his own sardonic humor. "Let's call her 'Princess Leia.' Now get out of here, Miller, and stay on Maguire's tail, no matter what."

Using a set of National Reconnaissance Organization credentials saved for a special emergency that identified him as Air Force Lt. General James Pratt, Partridge commandeered a fully-armed, charcoal-black Apache helicopter with no insignia to be flown down from Fort Hunter Ligget Military Reservation.

A young hot-shot Army pilot landed the Apache on the helipad at Camp San Luis Obispo National Guard Reservation next to "General Pratt's" car. Stepping out, he saluted smartly and handed over the keys to the "General." Partridge dismissed him with an order to turn his car in to the motor pool.

Gaining altitude above the National Guard Reservation, Partridge pointed the Apache northeast. His destination would be the JANUS underground emergency "bolt hole" in Nevada, located in the side of Corey Peak, within the boundaries of a facility which the public knew as "Hawthorne Army Ammunition Depot." He smiled as he thought of what the public's reaction would be if they knew what that military reservation was really used for. Hawthorne was a good choice. The personnel there were under standing orders never to inquire about what took place at Corey Peak. He would be undisturbed in the palatial quarters JANUS had so foresightfully provided. Besides, Hawthorne had some no-questions-asked brothels. He was certain he could requisition a couple of young girls who would be willing, for the promise of big bucks, to put up with his rough sexual tastes. Those tastes ran to daddy-daughter games and involved severe discipline and bondage. Afterwards, he would of course make sure they kept silent. No use having a chance that one of them might recognize him later from some FBI wanted poster and start blabbing.

As he flew along, he was troubled by a flickering amber light on the Electronic Counter-Measures panel. Someone had a multi-band radar signal targeted on his Apache. Furthermore, if that was no equipment malfunction, the flickering indicator light meant that whoever was tracing him had the kind of state-of-the-art equipment which sent out a tracking signal only intermittently, and which jumped radar bands continually to avoid detection. He checked visually for his pursuer using the Apache's 360-degree telescopic periscope, but could see no one behind him.

Forty-five miles behind, Ed Sodoma flew a terrain-hugging course in a camouflaged Special Operations Cobra helicopter. It was equipped with classified anti-detection avionics. Sodoma had requisitioned the Cobra from Edwards Air Force Base, using NSA national security authorization which he had obtained through Major Eberhardt. Sodoma allowed himself a tight-lipped smile. He enjoyed these little games of cat-and-mouse almost as much as he enjoyed termination assignments.

With a national FBI manhunt targeting him, and someone doing high-tech tracking of him, Partridge started to panic. Security dictated that it definitely was time to tie up a few loose ends. He had eliminated Zeta Four in the Aleutians. Zeta Two had bought it on a Hopi highway in a head-on collision in the fog. But even without DiGiorgio and O'Connell, there were still too many people left within the PANDORA Unit who could learn about his location. Time to prune the vine. He needed Zeta Five to tail Maguire. But Zeta Three and Zeta Six were expendable, as was their controller, Zeta One. With Zeta Five taking care of surveilling Maguire, there was no reason not to tighten up security within the unit and dump some deadwood at the same time. The old rule he had learned at Camp Peary years ago still held true. Keep the number of people with a need-to-know to the absolute minimum. Partridge got on the encrypted MILSTAR satellite radio, and placed a call to Major Eberhardt. He had decided there was no time like the present. He knew that he could entice Eberhardt with an important assignment.

"Bryce, I've got a emergency situation up here in Nevada," he lied, urgency in his voice. "I need all PANDORA ops here *now!*"

Eberhardt had suspected that he was on Partridge's shit-list, since their altercation at the Nuts and Bolts saloon. He figured that for his career's sake, he'd better appear like a team player. The Major put on his best kiss-up voice and tried to sound concerned. "Gee, Colonel, what's the problem?"

"Project Epiphany is pulling a fast one. They're setting up to meet 'Charley' tonight! That's when the goddamn aliens are going to set their saucer down in the Smoke Creek Desert here. It's sixty miles north of Reno. We don't have much time to intercept and take control of the situation. Zeta Five is tied up. Bring Zeta Three and Zeta Six with you. Carry full weapons and night vision gear."

"Shall I use the Unit's Lear jet to get out there?"

"Too slow, Bryce. This situation requires you to get here immediately! Requisition an F-111 from Kirtland. You can squeeze Zeta Three and Six in the back seat. And fly that bird as fast as it goes all the way here."

"Yes, sir. Where do you want us to rendezvous with you, Colonel?"

"Bryce, listen. You'll be landing at a small desert airstrip about seven miles northwest of Pyramid Lake, near where two dirt roads intersect. You'll see it. There isn't much else out here."

"I hope I don't have to land that F-111 on some dirt strip. I'm rusty on dirt landings."

"The airstrip is hardened sand. But don't give me any grief about the runway, Bryce. It'll be OK. If you ding up the landing gear, the Air Force can always buy another F-111. This is an emergency, understand? And hurry!" Partridge decided to butter up Eberhardt with uncustomary courtesy to assure his unquestioning compliance. He added with fake earnestness, "Major, I'm counting on you."

Eberhardt was flattered. It was the first time Colonel Partridge had ever called him Major without being sarcastic. It had to be extremely important and urgent! Eberhardt got the Kirtland Air Police to send two police units out, red lights flashing, to fetch Zeta Three and Zeta Six from their homes and bring them down to Kirtland. By the time they arrived at the restricted tarmac, Eberhardt was already in the pilot's seat and warming up the sleek plane's engines. As soon as the other two were seated, Eberhardt took off immediately and turned on the F-111's afterburners. Leveling off at 50,000 feet, he set course due northwest.

Partridge refueled his Apache at Sierra Army Depot, northwest of Reno. Flashing the credentials of "Lt. General James Pratt, National Reconnaissance Organization," he ordered the Gatling gun pods on his Apache taken off and exchanged for a set of heat-seeking missiles. Then he headed east towards the desert landing strip.

As the deserted air strip came into view, Partridge maneuvered his chopper around to the west. He set the Apache down in a saddle between two ridge tops, next to some junipers which would mask his presence. Although difficult to spot, he had a commanding view of the airstrip. The sun was low on the horizon to his back. It would be in the eyes of anyone coming in from the southeast, the direction of approach from Kirtland. Eberhardt and the rest of the PANDORA crew would not notice him. He lit up a cigarillo and waited, blowing an occasional smoke ring.

As the F-111 did a first-inspection pass over the deserted sandy airstrip, Eberhardt shook his head. It was risky setting a heavy jet fighter down there. But the Colonel said it was urgent and top priority. He swung the fighter around and headed south to begin his final landing approach. In the back seat Zeta Three and Zeta Six grumbled about setting the jet down in such a godforsaken location. As he reached the southern end of the valley, he swung the F-111 around and pointed the nose towards the landing strip. He lowered his wing flaps and pulled back on the throttle, slowing down for the landing.

As Eberhardt began his descent, Partridge lifted off the ridge top, then swung his Apache in behind the distracted Eberhardt. The Colonel's targeting screen lit up with lock-on on the F-111. He depressed a button, firing a missile at the fighter's exhaust port.

Inside the F-111, the ECM control panel lit up as the lock-on was detected. Eberhardt's plane was almost landing, and dangerously near stalling speed. The Major quickly pulled back on the joy stick, trying to bring the jet up and turning to the right. Simultaneously, he pushed a button to eject decoy flares, in a desperate maneuver to evade the detected heat-seeking missile. The F-111 slowly began to lift and turn, but was flying too slow to sustain both lifting and turning maneuvers. The heat-seeking missile redirected towards a nearby flare and exploded. Its shrapnel sliced through the F-111's tail rudder. The jet yawed, then stalled, its tail lifting and swinging to the left. The F-111 rolled over, dropped towards the ground and exploded in a orange ball of flame.

Moments later Partridge flew over the burning wreckage to assure himself that no one had ejected or survived. Then he permitted himself a tight smile. "Adios, Eberhardt, Clarke and Preston. It's been interesting." Out of mock respect for his dead Unit on the ground, he swung the Apache around and did another fly-over, dipping his rotary wing back and forth in a macabre and sardonic version of the traditional air salute for dead aviators. Then, pointing his helicopter southeast, he headed over Pyramid Lake and on towards Hawthorne Army Ammunition Depot and the JANUS facility inside Corey Peak.

As Partridge disappeared over the lake, Ed Sodoma flew in low over the still-burning wreckage of the F-111. He had no idea of what possessed Partridge to shoot down an Air Force fighter. But after seeing the total destruction on the ground, Sodoma developed some further respect for the treachery of the man he was assigned to follow. He made a mental note to leave a little more airspace between Partridge's plane and his from now on. He did not want to become another missile target.

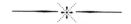

Chapter 12

THE Saturday evening air was chill in the outskirts of Chantilly, Virginia. The green woodsy charm of the suburban community was occasionally punctuated by the sound of an airplane taking off from Washington Dulles Airport four miles away. Parked cars lined the quiet street in both directions in front of a pale yellow two-story house. Down at the end of the block, a Fairfax County Public Utilities van was parked next to a pole. A lineman was perched up atop a utility pole next to a transformer, working on some electrical problem. In the back of the utility van, two men wearing headsets sat in front of an instrument panel. Atop the van's roof, an inconspicuous antenna was aimed at the yellow house down the block. One of the men was checking meter readings for maximum audio pickup. The men normally worked for the Defense Intelligence Agency, but were on temporary duty assignment to the NSA's Central Security Service.

Inside the house the twenty-two members of Project Epiphany were gathered in the large living room, chatting in small groups. After a while, a tall silver-haired, distinguished-looking man in his fifties stood up and cleared his throat. Dr. Robert Bowen raised his voice over the conversations in the room, and called the meeting to order.

"It is very good to see all of you here. I appreciate the distance each of you has come, and the effort to pull away from your busy schedules. As you know, we have several important decisions to make tonight. But first, since this is the first time we have had our entire membership at the same meeting, and since we have a proposed new member joining us for the first time tonight, let's have everyone introduce themselves. Say a word, too, about why you decided to be part of Project Epiphany.

"I'll start off. I'm of course Robert Bowen, a psychologist and researcher into extraterrestrial encounters. I convened Project Epiphany under inspiration from ET sources, to put together a Contact Team to represent the Earth when our extraterrestrial Visitors make their pre-announced landing later this Fall." Dr. Bowen turned to the tall, olive-skinned, distinguished-looking woman to his left and smiled. "Why don't you go next?"

"It is an honor to be here. I am Madame Leila Salaam, the wife of the United Nations Secretary-General. When my husband decided that he could not participate, I gladly accepted Dr. Bowen's invitation to serve in his place. My religion, Islam, honors the God who made many worlds. And, as a member of the United Nations staff, it is my privilege to represent the humanity-wide aspirations of that vital organization."

A middle-aged brunette wearing a tweed skirt and matching jacket spoke up next. "Hello, everyone. My, what adventuresome souls we all are. I'm Claudia Hill from Zimbabwe. I guess I was invited because I have written many news stories about UFO and ET sightings on the African continent. I'm thrilled to think that I'll be meeting people from another world at the forthcoming Landing."

An elderly man with splotchy pink complexion, freckles, graying hair and a pleasant expression spoke next. "I salute all of you far-sighted people who are gathered here today. I'm former President Earl James. The reason I decided to become a part of Project Epiphany was because of my longtime dedication to world peace. And we cannot have total peace without peaceful relations with our galactic neighbors as well."

A tall, gaunt, craggy middle-aged man with intense but kindly eyes stood up. "I am Dr. Ian McCormack. Although I have a reputation for knowing a great deal about aliens, I have never met one. But I would like to. I joined the Project because the official landing of beings from another world has profound implications for the expansion of human consciousness beyond the manifest physical world. It will necessitate changing how we perceive ourselves in the cosmic order."

Next to him a short, black-haired woman with Slavic features gave the group a smile. "It is a pleasure once again to be in America. I am Dr. Ivana Kheraskov, retired cosmonaut. I have lectured widely on UFO phenomena in the Russian Republic. It is an honor to represent my great nation."

To her left, a trim, well-tanned older man in an immaculate white suit sat ramrod-straight. He gave a beaming smile to the group and said, "I guess it's my turn. I'm *excited* to be here! I am Colonel Duane Warwick, United States Air Force, retired. These days I mostly study metaphysics. The reason I'm here is because we are dealing with cosmic consciousness. Ladies and gentlemen, these Visitors are here to usher in a new era of cosmic awareness. And we need to open our minds to the higher dimensions where they operate. I know *I'm* ready. How about you?"

A number of heads nodded in agreement. Next to him sat two short, older Native American men. The first one stood up with a serious expression and looked at the group for some moments. "My Indian name means Black Snake Of The West. I am called Timothy Katoya. I am a Hopi Elder, keeper and guardian of my people's prophecies about the Star People. Long ago, one of our prophecies said that the day would come when a Hopi Elder would meet the Blue Star Kachina, a being you call an extraterrestrial. At that meeting the Blue Star Kachina will remove the mask and let its actual appearance be known. That day is less than two months away. It was also prophesied that the *bahana*, the white people, would finally join with the red people in seeking the true way. The work that we are doing here is, I believe, a fulfillment of *that* prophecy."

"What my brother says is so," the other Native American elder said as he stood up. "My Native name is Anpo Wie. The *wasicu*, the white people, know me as George Morning Star. I am a spiritual leader of the Lakota, the people you call the Sioux. A sacred gathering of medicine people was held last month. There they decided that your group needed an additional Indian representative, and that I should come and join your group. So I am here, if you will accept me."

Dr. Bowen spoke up. "Having George Morning Star join the Project is the first item on our agenda. Let's finish introductions, and then we'll discuss that." He nodded to the tall, broad-shouldered Scandinavian woman next to Morning Star.

"I am Dr. Leena Virtanen, Surgeon-General of Norway. I am also a researcher into extraterrestrial contacts. I founded the first international organization for women experiencers, Daughters of the Cosmos. I am here because I love and respect my cosmic brothers and sisters, and wish to greet them on behalf of the peace-loving peoples of Scandinavia."

A lanky, balding man with horn-rimmed glasses and a bow tie spoke up. "I'm Dr. Leonard Spruance, a psychology professor. I work with people who have had encounters with the space Visitors. I'm here because my good friend, Dr. Bowen, invited me, and because I want to walk up to the beings from space and tell them, as we say in Idaho, 'Howdy!'"

As Spruance sat down, a medium-build man in a dapper suit and curly blond hair stood up to introduce himself. "As many of you know, I am Dr. Stewart Golden, a physician from Knoxville. I am also the Founding Director of ISFEC, the Interstellar Friendship and Exchange Committee. We have reached out successfully to the Visitors many times. I am confident that I can be of great assistance to this group." He stopped and nodded to the small, frail elderly woman to his left, who was wearing religious garb.

"Merci. My name is Sister Lisieux. I am a member of the religious order of the Servants of the Holy Spirit. We minister to the sickest and poorest of God's people. I was born in France, but am now living in Bangladesh. The reason I came here is so that I could ask our space brothers and sisters to help the suffering people on Earth. That is all. Thank you."

The next to introduce himself was a robust older African-American man, whose stiff posture hinted at his military career. "Hello, everyone!" He had long since learned the art of flashing a toothy smile while subtly scanning the room at the same time. "I'm Major Roscoe Dent, United States Army, retired after thirty years serving my country. I was the former Chief of Intelligence for the Southeast Asia Treaty Organization. I have been close enough to saucers to put my hand on them. I have also been that close to aliens. Unfortunately, they were all dead. I'm here because I'd like to meet some live ones face to face. I'm ashamed to say that, years ago, I was involved in some military actions the Army took against UFOs. I'm here, among other things, to apologize to the aliens for my behavior in the Armed Services. I'm also here to help create some friendly relationships with them."

"I guess I'm next," said a red-headed man in his early forties with a boyish face. "I'm Dr. Brent O'Hara. I used to teach physics at Cornell. Before that, I was an astronaut. I salute my cosmonaut colleague, Dr. Kheraskov. Now I am investigating the connections between zero point energy and universal consciousness. As for why I'm here, I recognize the ETs as fellow consciousness." He paused, then nodded to a distinguished-looking woman with Latin features and light brown skin sitting next to him.

"It is a pleasure to be in the company of such distinguished people. This is the first meeting I could attend. It is so far from Brazil, and I have a busy practice. I am Dr. Alberta de Oliveira, a psychotherapist and UFO investigator. It was an honor to be invited. I will help any way I can. Many of my patients have had UFO or encounter experiences."

A short, stocky, casually-dressed man with a cocky grin spoke up in an unmistakable accent next. "Hi, everybody. You probably expected me to say 'G'day, mates', but I don't say that sort of thing. My name is Donald Cameron, from Melbourne, Australia. I'm president of the Down Under UFO Society, DUFOS. It's my pleasure to represent the original continent, as we peoples from everywhere plan to gather and meet our Visitors." He turned to the slight, impeccably well-dressed Asian man next to him.

"Good evening. I am Professor Yet-Sen Yuah from Beijing, China. I am director of the All-China UFO Investigation Association. When Dr. Bowen invited me to this meeting, I was honored to come and represent my country."

To his left a mahogany-skinned man with a deeply lined face sat in monk robes. "Hello. I am Lama Dharam from the Kingdom of Nepal. I am pleased to be with this group, and to represent Buddhism, a faith which accepts many worlds and many lifetimes. As my Hopi brother Timothy knows, the ancient Buddhist scriptures share with the Hopi traditions some of the same teachings about the people from other worlds."

"It's good to be here with you fine people." The crisp British accent belonged to a dapper gentleman in his thirties. "I'm Gilbert Murray, president of the British Close Encounters Society. I decided to join this group, despite the risk I feel is entailed, because frankly, I want to be among the first humans to shake the hand of a person from another star system."

Next to him sat a swarthy man in his late twenties, wearing an expensive blue suit. "My name is Manuel Gutierrez. I am a TV producer in Mexico City. I made many programs about *ovnis*, excuse me, UFOs. Pardon my English. It is not too good. I am here to extend the love and open hearts of the Mexican people to our celestial visitors."

The last person to introduce himself was a beefy Germanic man with nervous gestures. "I am Karl von Reuter. I am an archeologist. I have made some very interesting finds of artifacts from ancient astronauts who visited German soil. Those artifacts establish, I believe, that the ancient Nordic runes are derived from the extraterrestrials' writing. I wish to meet these people who educated my ancestors."

Dr. Bowen brought up the first item of business: whether to accept the person sent by the Star Nations convocation of Native American medicine men. Timothy Katoya got up and told the group about how the extraterrestrial, Saquasohuh, came into the Great Kiva and told the convocation that they should send an additional Native American elder to Project Epiphany. When he finished speaking, the group promptly voted to have George Morning Star become a member of the Project.

The next order of business was to select the Contact Team, the actual band of individuals who would wait at the Landing site and meet the extraterrestrials as Earth's representatives. Dr. Bowen had imagined that everyone in the Project would want to be on the Contact team. That many people could be unwieldy, and yet he knew too that limiting people could hurt feelings. His worries turned out to have been misplaced.

He explained that Contact Team members needed to be prepared to be in the desert mountains southeast of Cloverdale, outdoors in potentially snowy winter weather. In order to prevent being blocked from getting to the landing site by snowed-in roads, the Contact Team would need to arrive and camp out early, while awaiting the extraterrestrial landing November 25th. Using a large map of New Mexico, he illustrated the remote and rugged location of Cloverdale.

Major Dent followed up the physical hardships advisement with a sobering briefing on the personal risk. In classic military briefing style, he ticked off the forms of opposition that the Contact Team was likely to face. The Contact Team could expect to encounter surveillance and harassment, if not outright obstruction, by JANUS's military assets. Major Dent noted that in the worst case scenario, they could encounter interdiction and kidnapping , or a full military assault on the Team, or be caught in hostile crossfire during an attack on the UFO and killed by "friendly" fire. His deep rumbling voice fit the somber scenario he painted.

When he finished, Dr. Bowen decided to start by asking which Project members were *not* prepared to serve on the Contact Team, in view of the physical hardships and the danger of being attacked. There was a long awkward silence. Then Professor Yat-sen Yuah raised his hand and explained that, as much as he wanted this extraterrestrial contact, a prudent man would not die for this experience, and therefore he did not wish to be on the Contact Team. After a few moments Claudia Hill spoke up and said that she too had not counted on the possibility of military attack, and so declined to serve on the Contact Team. Gilbert Murray echoed Hill's sentiments that the extraterrestrial meeting was not worth dying for. Donald Cameron spoke up next to say that he was not volunteering for the Contact Team either for the same reason. While Cameron was speaking, Dr. McCormack's pager went off and he left the room. Sister Lisieux expressed her feeling that ministering to the sickly poor was more important for her than personally meeting the extraterrestrials, and thus she would return to

Bangladesh. Alberta de Olivieira said that she could not spare the time away from her patients to serve on the Contact Team. Manuel Gutierrez noted that he was very busy with media productions, and the best way he could help the Project was by seeing that the Project's extraterrestrial contact was given wide television coverage in Mexico. Karl von Reuter told of how his grandfather had been shot by the Nazis, and that he had no interest in being caught in some military crossfire. He excused himself from the Team. Dr. Ian McCormack reentered the room and announced that the pager call had been from the President. He had been appointed chairman of a National Academy of Sciences task force which was being urgently convened to study the extraterrestrial phenomenon, and had to leave for Washington immediately. He apologized for not being available for the Contact Team and excused himself to catch a cab. Dr. Brent O'Hara somewhat apologetically explained t o the grou p that he had recently married, and therefore, in all fairness to his new bride, could not afford to place himself at risk of being killed.

Dr. Bowen then turned to the remaining Project Epiphany members. One by one they said they were prepared to join the Contact Team. After the last person confirmed his commitment, he noted that the Team would number twelve: Mme. Salaam, former President James, Lama Dharam, Dr. Virtanen, Dr. Kheraskov, Elders Katoya and Morning Star, Dr. Spruance, Dr. Golden, Colonel Warwick, Major Dent, and himself. The group then unanimously voted these twelve to be the Project Epiphany Contact Team.

Next Bowen gave each member of the Team some US Geological Survey maps of the approximate location of the Landing. The Contact Team agreed that they would meet at Lordsburg, New Mexico two days before the Landing, with everyone bringing supplies sufficient to camp out for several days. The Team would car-pool in four-wheel-drive vehicles the remaining seventy miles to Cloverdale, and then head out southeast cross-country to the base of the Animas Mountains. Major Dent advised the group to make sure they had a current will drawn up, and had made provision for dependents and any unfinished business before showing up.

Timothy Katoya raised his hand to request the floor. He explained to the group that Dr. Roger Maguire and his research assistant Barbara Catalina had asked to join up with the Contact Team. Katoya said that they were planning to be at the Landing site in any case. He explained that they were the source of the information he had given the Project about the location of the Landing, and that Catalina was an experiencer and psychic, one who had long had contacts by a Star Person, the same one who had told them where the extraterrestrial ambassadors would land. Katoya said that he favored having them join up with the Contact Team.

Discussion ensued, with it soon becoming obvious that the group was deeply divided on whether to allow Maguire and Catalina to join. Dr. Golden spoke for the opposition, noting that they had not been invited originally, had never been to planning meetings, and that it was too late for new-comers now. Others, led by Katoya, favored their joining because of their unique contributions. Because the Project could not come to agreement, Katoya was directed to tell Maguire and Catalina the answer was no. As the meeting broke up and people went to their cars, the Fairfax County Public Utilities van drove away from its telephone pole "repair job."

Ten miles from China Lake Naval Weapons Center, a sport utility vehicle was heading east on Highway 178 towards the main gate. Catalina's psychic radar told her Maguire was not just going to drive by this sensitive "black projects" base, but was intending to go inside.

"So, Rog, how do you plan to get by the sentries at the gate?"

"Mind reading again, Barb? I was just thinking about that. I guess I'll try the old Chaplain ploy. Since I'm a recovering Catholic, I think I can still remember how to do it."

Maguire stopped at a pay phone in Ridgecrest and made a call to the Catholic Church in town. That was followed by his second call, to the Catholic chaplain on base. Intrigued, Catalina stood at the doorway of the phone booth, listening in.

"Chaplain's Office, Father Clancy speaking."

"Yes, Father, I need to go to Confession right away. I've committed a mortal sin. I'm traveling long-distance on the road, and I don't want to take the chance of getting in a highway accident and going to hell."

"I understand, my son. But why don't you go to the Catholic Church in Ridgecrest? Navy chaplains are for Navy personnel."

"I tried them already, Father, but I was told that Father Mahony is away all day."

"Really? Well then, I guess I'll have to hear your Confession. I'll call the Marine sentry at the Main Gate to give you a pass. He can tell you how to get to the Chaplain's Office. We can't have a good Catholic lad going to hell, now, can we?" he chuckled paternally.

"Thank you, Father. I'll be right over."

"By the way, son, is there anyone else coming in with you?"

"Well, yes, Father, there's Barbara. She's the woman I committed the mortal sin with."

When she heard that line, Catalina scrunched up her face in an I'm-going-to-kill-you look. She whispered through clenched teeth, "Tell him I'm not Catholic. And I'm not confessing *anything*."

Maguire, hand over the mouth piece, had all he could do to keep from breaking out laughing.

"I'll tell the sentry to let both of you in," Father Mahony said. "Does she want to confess, too?"

"She's not Catholic, Father."

That's OK. I'll give her a little talk, so that you're not tempted any more."

"Gee, thanks, Father. I appreciate that."

Maguire was issued a pass by the young Marine sentry at China Lake's Main Gate. He drove to the Chaplain's office and made a quick if dubious Confession. He made an excuse for the still-nervous Catalina, who stayed out in the car. As he got back in the car, he said, "Mission accomplished. We're inside the Navy's top weapons and classified technology base, *and* we have a pass. Now let's look around a little."

"So, now that your soul is clean, you feel like taking some chances, huh?" Catalina said teasingly, no longer peeved.

"Chances means not planning ahead. I've planned ahead." Maguire pulled out a USGS map covering the area of China Lake Naval Weapons Center. "There's a mountain near the north end of the test range called Maturango Peak. A Navy source on the internet told me about UFO activity centered on that peak. Let's check it out."

"Then I'm going to place a protective shield of white light around this car and us. *Maybe* we won't get caught," Catalina said, looking doubtful.

Maguire took Tower Road north through desert scrub brush and sand to the junction with the upper Navy range. He turned onto Etcharren Valley Road and proceeded the rest of the thirty-five miles to Maturango Peak. The peak loomed above 7800 feet, the highest mountain around. A cluster of communications towers and radar domes was perched at its summit. The winter sun was already setting across the valley behind Coso Peak to the west. Maguire pulled off the main road onto a jeep trail that he had spotted on his map. About a mile up this trail, they came to a dead end, next to a sign which read Tennessee Spring.

"This'll be as good a place as any to do our saucer watch," Maguire said.

"Ah, Roger, one thing. Our gate pass is only good for today."

"Not to worry. We'll be out of here by midnight."

"It's when you say don't worry that I start to worry."

Twilight dimmed to night. Several hours of vigil passed. Feeling the need to take a break, Catalina walked a way down the jeep trail by herself in the moonlight to meditate. She stopped by a flat rock to sit. After a few minutes the hair of the back of her neck suddenly stood up. She felt a strange slight electric current pass through her body. It was an odd feeling, but one which she felt that she had experienced somewhere before. She turned around and saw a disc fifty yards to the north, hovering thirty feet above the ground. The disc glowed slightly, emitting a pale violet luminescence. Her heart was beating rapidly. The disc settled down to the desert floor and came to a rest. The glow around the disc subsided, and an opening appeared in the side of the craft. After a few moments a figure emerged. Catalina's jaw dropped open. It was Arica! The medium-height thin extraterrestrial raised one hand, palm outward, in a gesture of greeting. Catalina could see a faint smile on the lipless-slit of a mouth. She sensed the altered-consciousness feeling she always got at the initiation of telepathic mind-link.

"Hello, Barbara, our dear sister," Arica telepathed.

Catalina started to shout back an answer across the fifty yards separating Arica from her, but then decided to reply telepathically instead. "Arica, my cosmic sister, it's so *good* to see you. Can I come over there?"

"Not now. We came down briefly just to encourage you and your fine companion, Dr. Maguire. We want you to know that you two are on the right path. You will see me again."

"But Arica, when will I see you again? Do you mean during sleep?"

"No, you will see my ship again later. Tell Dr. Maguire that we will come when you get to the part of your itinerary which places you on Athabascan lands. He will see my craft, too. Now I must go. Already your military's radar has tracked my craft. Good-bye for now." The extraterrestrial turned around and reentered the craft. It immediately lifted to 300 feet altitude, then shot off on an upward diagonal track over the Sierras in three seconds.

Catalina ran all the way back to camp to tell Maguire the news. As she came running up, Maguire had a disgusted look on his face. He told her that he felt he had been given a bum tip about Maturango Peak, and that he had not seen any UFOs. Catalina could barely contain her smile as she spilled out her story of her encounter with Arica and the disc she had landed in.

While Maguire headed the Pathfinder back to China Lake's Main Gate, they discussed Arica's contact. Catalina filled him in on Arica's message of encouragement and her promise to meet again soon. As they reached the gate, the sentry relieved Maguire of their pass. Maguire explained to the guard that the long time they had spent on base was due to picking up a lot of trash around the Capehart enlisted personnel housing area, as an assigned act of penance after their Confessions. The sentry, a green recruit from rural Baptist Alabama, thought all Catholics were crazy. He accepted the explanation, noted their exit time as 23:11 hours, and waved them through.

At a motel in adjacent Ridgecrest, Catalina and Maguire planned the next leg of their trip.They would drive through Death Valley National Park into Nevada and on to the "non-existent"Groom Dry Lake Air Force Station. Groom Lake was better known as Area 51, the most classified base in the world, and reputed home to antigravity craft of both extraterrestrial and human manufacture.

Rotating a dial on the communications console of his Apache, Colonel Partridge set the microwave transmitter for the classified frequency setting of JANUS's Corey Peak complex.

"This is Colonel Partridge, Corey Peak. I'm approaching in a helo. Respond and confirm. "

"Major Arthur Tigard here, Colonel. We've been painting your chopper on radar from fifteen miles out. Glad you radioed us and identified yourself before you got much closer to our mountain, Colonel. Otherwise at two kilometers distance, we would have taken out your chopper with a SAM-missile. Standing orders, you know."

"Yeah, well, that's just swell, Tigard," Partridge said in a thoroughly nasty voice that dripped sarcasm. "Just open the goddamn doorway, if you would be so kind."

Part way up 10,000-foot Corey Peak, a camouflaged entrance way swung open. Partridge flew his helicopter through it to the landing strip inside. From fifteen miles away Ed Sodoma spotted the Corey Peak entrance through the magnification visor on his pilot's helmet. He locked the coordinates into his terrain-mapping computer, and set down his Cobra chopper across the valley on the shoulder of Mount Grant. Sodoma lit up a cigarette and blew a thin trail of smoke. He would just sit and outwait Partridge. He was unaware that the man who had hired and paid him to surveille Partridge, Major Eberhardt, lay dead in the rubble of the shot-down F-111. Since he had been paid in advance for the first three months of surveilling Partridge, Sodoma didn't know that he would never get an order to stop tracking the Colonel.

Inside the JANUS complex, Major Tigard hastened over to the just-landed Apache and ducked under the still-slowing rotor to greet Partridge. "Colonel Partridge, welcome to the Corey Peak complex."

"Swell to be here," Partridge deadpanned. "Say, Tigard, you know the cat houses in Hawthorne? Order me up a couple of young girls. They gotta be definitely under eighteen but older than eleven. And don't take all day."

The thirty-year-old Scotch glowed a deep amber among the ice cubes in Partridge's glass. A cigarillo sent up lazy smoke curls into the air of the complex's executive suite. Partridge didn't mind getting out of his recliner to answer the door, when he saw how pretty the two thin blonde girls were who were standing there. They had an innocent country farm-girl look, yet were neatly dressed in prep school uniforms and black patent leather shoes.

"Hi. I'm Dana and this is my younger sister, Carlene."

"How old are you girls?"

"I'm sixteen and Carlene is fourteen."

"Fourteen and a half," Carlene corrected proudly.

"Mister, this is the strangest place we've ever been," Dana said. "What is this called?"

"Never mind," Partridge replied. "That's not important."

Carlene cut in. "What's your name?"

"Just call me 'Daddy'," Partridge replied evenly. "I take it you girls know how to play some games?"

"Sure, mister, er, Daddy," Dana answered. "What'd you like to play tonight?"

"Why don't you girls undress, and you, Dana, tie your sister to the bedposts spread-eagle. We're going to play 'Sandwich.' Carlene will be on the bottom and you'll be on top."

"Oh yeah? And where will you be, ah, Daddy?" Carlene asked.

"Me? I'll be the meat in the middle of the sandwich," Partridge replied, smirking at his own raunchy humor. The girls giggled nervously. He walked over and got a riding crop out of his suitcase, mentally preparing for an exceptional evening of fun and games.

The clock in Major Tigard's room showed 02:19 hours. He couldn't believe that Colonel Partridge was summoning him at such an ungodly hour. He quickly dressed and hurried up to the executive suite. The door was ajar. He walked in. Although a seasoned combat veteran, Tigard was not prepared for what he saw. The 14-year-old was still tied to the bed, heavily bruised and lacerated, and not breathing. A riding crop was jammed up between her legs, and blood was all over the sheets. The 16-year-old lay lifeless on the floor, her purplish face distended, and blood covering her legs. A leather shoelace was tied tightly around her neck.

"Looks like we've got a bit of a mess here, Major," Partridge said dispassionately. "See that these bodies are disposed of at once, very discreetly. Make sure nothing ties them to this place. And get someone in here to change the sheets and clean this place up right away. I feel like getting some rest now." Partridge went over to his suite bar and poured himself another Scotch. He sat down in his recliner, lit up another cigarillo, and awaited housekeeping service.

After a simple country dinner at the UFO Diner in Rachel, Maguire and Catalina turned west on Nevada Highway 375 and drove toward Queen City Summit. At the western foot of the summit, they turned left and headed southbound on a broad, well-maintained dirt road, graded to federal standards.

"That's a give-away," Maguire said to Catalina, pointing at the first-class road. "When's the last time you saw a dirt road out in the middle of nowhere graded and maintained like *that*?"

"Now that you mention it, that's the only really smooth dirt road I've ever seen. Even the roads in the National Monuments look scruffier than that. Where does it go?"

"You know where," Maguire said in a conspiratorial tone.

"Roger, you mean we're going into Area 51?"

"Go to the head of the class."

"But that's off-limits. We'll be arrested, or worse."

"Well, Barb, you always say that you gotta trust that the Force will be with you. We're going to go in with lights out. If anybody comes, we'll turn around and beat it out of there.

If we get stopped, we'll just say we took a wrong turn and got lost. Of course, if you want to get out of the car here and wait for me, feel free."

"I'm not waiting here by myself! What if you don't come back? What if you get arrested or shot?" Catalina was silent for a few moments, then said glumly, "I guess I'll stick along."

In the dark, Catalina's mouth was set in a grim line. Maguire extinguished the headlights and drove the Pathfinder forward by starlight. About five miles down the road, they came to a small sign by the side of the road. It read "Range Hours: Monday-Friday, 0800–1800 hours." Strangely, there was no warning sign forbidding crossing into a military reservation. Maguire slowly advanced some more. An additional five miles down the road, they stopped as they saw a watch tower up ahead and to the left. They could make it out in the darkness by the one dim yellowish light on the its roof. Ahead to the right the terrain opened up into a large box canyon. They sat looking into the canyon, where an astonishing event was taking place. Five hundred feet above the desert floor a silent, wingless object was strobing off and on, alternately emitting a very bright bluish-white light for two seconds, and then going dark for two seconds. During the lighted phase, the object hovered motionless. When the strobe was off, the object "jumped" to its next position, then hovered there motionlessly while its glow came back on. The object's course was roughly a series of sequential triangles. The craft jumped to a different corner of the triangle during each light-off phase, in a sequence of forward, backward, up and down maneuvers. Each jump covered a distance of about 150 yards.

"Wow! Rog, what is that?" Catalina asked, entranced. "From a distance it looks like a firefly."

"I've seen them flying high around the airspace outside Area 51 before, and near the White Sands Missile Range too. But I've never seen one being test flown right near the ground, and never this close up. Must be some new pilot getting the hang of antigravity flying."

"It's neat! Want to take a ride in that one?" she teased.

"Yeah, right," Maguire dead panned. "Look, I'm getting nervous. For all we know, they could be detecting us in the dark right now with infrared sensors. We've seen what I came here hoping to check out. Frankly, we're in an area where they have authorization to shoot us. Let's get the hell out of here now."

"Why, I never thought I'd see the brave Dr. Maguire lose his nerve," Catalina crowed, secretly glad they were leaving.

"Ice" Miller had parked a quarter-mile behind the turn-off into the Range. When he saw that Maguire's Pathfinder did not emerge after ten minutes, he radioed Area 51 Security that an intrusion was in progress. Twenty minutes later, an EG&G security truck roared by him and turned onto the Queen City Summit entrance road to Area 51. The two contract security guards had almost made it to the Range boundary, when they saw a Pathfinder turning on its headlights as it approached them. The guards slowed down to a stop as the Pathfinder passed by. Maguire drove staring straight ahead. Catalina looked at the guards, illuminated in the headlights, and flashed them a sweet smile. The security guard driver reached out his open window and gave Maguire and Catalina the finger as they drove by.

"Gee, Rog, those big strong cops don't like us 'UFO nuts' getting too close to their secret range," Catalina said mischievously. Now that they were safely back on non-military lands, she relaxed and allowed herself some humor.

"No, they don't. But since we're on Bureau of Land Management land, there's not a damn thing they can do about it." Maguire let out a sigh, releasing his held-in tension. Checking in the rear-view mirror, he noticed that the security truck had turned around and was following them back out to the highway. It made no effort to catch up with them. "Looks like we made it."

"Rog, did you know there would be a government anti-gravity craft back in that canyon doing test flights?"

"Nope. I just had an intuition that that particular access road would be a good one to explore."

"You may call it intuition," Catalina said, "but I think you're getting psychic."

"Must have been around you too long," Maguire said with a chuckle. "That stuff is catching."

Thirty miles north of the New Mexico state line in Colorado, Catalina sat by herself in a back booth of an Alamosa coffee shop. Maguire had taken their vehicle to a gas station for servicing. She relished having some time alone to mentally go over the boggling adventures of the last few weeks. This was also a chance to bring her journal up to date.

The pages filled with enthusiastic jottings about this outdoors trip of a lifetime. After their exciting trip into Area 51, where they had spotted the U.S. "saucer" doing maneuvers, she made a glowing entry about beautiful southeastern Utah and Zion National Park. She described Zion as like a cross between the Grand Canyon and Yosemite. A verdant desert valley, watered by the Virgin River, Zion was flanked on both sides by dramatic sheer walls of crimson, bronze and cream stone, towering thousands of feet above them.

Her next entry recounted their hike through the Paria Canyon Wilderness in Arizona's northwestern Panhandle. There the 300-foot-high crimson sandstone walls of Buckskin Gulch narrowed so dramatically that in places they could touch both walls simultaneously. The next page of her journal recorded impressions of Betatakin Ruins, the 700-year-old Anasazi cliff dwellings village in Navajo National Monument, where she had felt a mysterious sense of ancient Native American presence. She enthused about Monument Valley, and the tour given by a Navajo Tribal Park guide which had allowed them to go back to places where unescorted tourists are not allowed. Maguire and she had visited dramatic yellowish-gold stone arches that spanned hundreds of feet, and wonderful hollowed-out stone amphitheaters where their voices echoed for a half-mile.

Another entry described their adventure approaching the Ute Mountain Tribal Park right after entering Colorado. As they had descended a long mountain grade leading towards tribal park headquarters at Chimney Rock, Maguire had pointed out to Catalina a brilliant light resting on the ground five miles ahead. Its intense shimmering stood out from the desert landscape despite the bright afternoon desert sun. Maguire had noted that the light was coming from a spot on a flat dirt side road less than 500 yards from U.S. 160. A few minutes later, as they reached the side road and looked down it, there was nothing there. She recalled their puzzlement, because there was no place that the lighted object could have hidden in the broad flat terrain, and there were no side roads off that dirt road. Catalina wrote down her impression that it was the return visit by Arica's craft as promised, signaling that she was escorting them from nearby.

The entry about their drive around Archuleta Mesa near Dulce, New Mexico was brief. She frankly had found the drive boring. She did note that Maguire seemed quite impressed with the one fancy "ranch" complex they found among the many impoverished ranches on the north side of the mountain. She had to admit that the four elevated guard towers on stilts in the pasture in front of the many large buildings on this "ranch" did not look right. Maguire had told her that this was rumored to be a surface entrance way to a former joint alien-human subterranean base. This base had supposedly been nuked by the military, after the aliens had not gone along with the military's direction of the facility. Catalina had then looked psychically inside the mountain and "seen" that there were indeed several levels which had been artificially excavated and then had later caved in due to some force.

Her last entry was about the previous night. They had camped at an 8000-foot-elevation campground overlooking Great Sand Dunes National Monument. She described the strange wonderful energy there. Their campsite was at the foot of the forested, 14,000-foot-high Sangre de Cristo Range to the east. To the west was a panorama of fifty-seven square miles of 800-foot-high sand dunes. Beyond the dunes stretched the sixty-mile-wide flat expanse of the San Luis Valley, headwaters of the Rio Grande River, with the San Juan Rockies as dramatic background. She put down her pen as Maguire approached her booth.

"Everything fine with the Pathfinder, dear?" Catalina asked.

"Oh, it's fine now. Just needed a tune-up and some new transmission fluid. But I think we've got a tail again. Some guy was in the gas station while I was gone, asking the mechanic about how long the repairs on my vehicle would take, and if I had mentioned where I was headed next."

"They never give up, do they?" Catalina responded in a frustrated tone.

"Where we're going next ought to get his attention."

"Where's that, Rog?"

"Cheyenne Mountain."

"What's there?"

"Oh, a huge underground military city carved out inside the mountain. It's where the North American Air Defense Command tracks everything moving in the atmosphere and space. A Pulitzer Prize-winning New York Times reporter wrote about how NORAD regularly has alerts there, when they spot UFOs coming in from space."

"And we're going to go there? Won't it be dangerous?" Catalina listened to herself, and decided that her fears about danger were getting old, even for her, and most probably for Roger as well. She decided to set protective white light around the two of them and lay her fears aside. "Forget my last comment, Rog." She reached over and gave his hand a squeeze.

———✴———

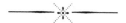

Chapter 13

IN A private conference room at the finest hotel in the prosperous Dutch city of Oosterbeek, Prince Heinrich Adler fidgeted impatiently in his chair. The prince was attired impeccably in a conservative dark blue pinstripe suit, white shirt and gray tie. The man he had summoned from America was late. The Prince did not take such royal affronts lightly. The crowned head of a thirty-miles-square European monarchy southeast of the Netherlands, and owner of 85% of his country's State Bank, Prince Adler was not used to having to wait for anyone. As the current chairman of the Bilderberg organization, he was used to the deference that came from global influence. Bilderberg was a clandestine group of powerful West European and North American multinational corporation executives and national political figures, who met regularly for transnational coordination and collective management of the world order. The Prince had reserved time this day, between chairing sessions of the Bilderberg Executive Committee, to meet urgently with this American. And now he was being kept waiting. Finally, a valet announced the arrival of the man he had been expecting. Colonel Jack Partridge strode in wearing civilian attire, red-faced from the exertion of hurrying.

"Good morning, your Highness," Partridge puffed, out of breath.

"Actually it's afternoon, Colonel. Our appointment was for eleven-thirty; it's now twelve-fifteen. You're late."

"I'm sorry, your Highness. I can explain. My flight from Heathrow was delayed. . . ."

"You can dispense with the excuses, Colonel," Prince Adler interrupted. "I am only interested in results, not excuses. Your delay has used up some of the time I had for this meeting, so I will get right down to the subject at hand. It has come to the attention of the Executive Committee that the JANUS organization's handling of our little UFO secret has gone very badly. In fact, intelligence I have received about JANUS, and not from you I regret to say, indicates that the JANUS organization leadership is all dead except for yourself. Isn't that true?" The Prince cast a baleful eye at Partridge.

The colonel's facial color went from florid to pale. "It is true, your Highness, that the rest of the JANUS leadership have met with unfortunate demises. But as for mishandling the secret of the upcoming alien landing, that secret is intact."

"Oh?" the Prince sounded unconvinced. "You mean that besides the Bilderberg Executive Committee and you, *only* the Project Epiphany group, an anthropologist named Maguire, and his female companion know? Is that it?" The Prince's voice had a distinctly unpleasant edge of sarcasm.

"Ah, well, that is to say, ah, . . . yes," Partridge responded lamely, unnerved by the Prince's flawless intelligence.

"I see. Well, now, Colonel, how is the Executive Committee going to be assured that these aliens and their pesky landing are not going to upset the customary order of international society and commerce? We can't have an unpredictable international group of people like Project Epiphany intercepting the Landing and presenting themselves for the aliens to dialogue with. Not to mention the additional messy detail presented by that Dr. Maguire and his companion being there also. No, Colonel, the situation is extremely untidy, and completely unacceptable. Not to mention that *you* should have brought all these matters to my attention yourself long ago."

"Your intelligence information is excellent," Partridge said, attempting to mollify the Prince. "I was intending to give your Highness a complete briefing in the very near future, but . . ."

Prince Adler cut him off. "Now, since our time is limited, let us focus on the critical situation at hand. We cannot afford to have outside meddlers negotiating and interfering with our exclusive control position vis-a-vis our coming Visitors. By the way, is that female alien you have been holding beneath Andrews Air Force Base still being cooperative?"

"The EBE has been giving us only minimal cooperation since she learned that representatives from the Inter-Stellar Federation will be landing November 25th."

"Have you determined why? And why haven't you informed me of this before?" the Prince asked heatedly, raising his voice.

"We're not sure why the EBE's not revealing much. Our analysts are divided. Some think that she has been feeding us disinformation, and she knows that the alien Federation representatives will soon be giving us correct information that will contradict what she has been telling us. Other analysts think that she sees no point in cooperating, now that her people are about to arrive and will insist on her being released to them. I was going to inform you of this, but I assumed that Henry Fournier would have briefed you. I've been very busy . . ."

"Busy?" The Prince cut him off with a withering look. "Too busy to keep your superior informed about vital information? Dr. Fournier has been dead for several days now. I need critical information on a continual and real-time basis. Since leadership fell to you by default after Dr. Fournier's death, it was your responsibility to provide me with information. It appears that we may not have the right man for the job at hand," he said darkly.

Partridge blanched. He knew that there was only one way that a person was relieved of assignment inside the Cover-Up leadership. That was by a death certificate. He recovered quickly. "Your Highness, I have already developed precautions to assure that the alien landing does not upset the, as you say, 'customary order of international society and commerce.' I have troops and weapons systems in New Mexico now adjacent to the Landing zone, ready to move into place. My forces will take out the Project Epiphany representatives, as well as that Maguire and his lady friend, when they approach. The troops are equipped with classified technology weapons of high-energy pulsed-microwave and argon laser types. The civilians' deaths will be blamed on the aliens. Then, when the alien ship is about to land, we will take it out with lasers and EMP weapons. Just to make sure that no untidy evidence remains after the aborted Landing, we will nuke the entire site with a small tactical weapon. We will blame that nuclear explosion on the alien ship's reactor blowing up from a malfunction. *That* should scare off the alien-lovers crowd. And it should keep the aliens from trying any more landings. For even extra insurance, after this operation is over, I will activate the HARDON upper-atmosphere high energy field to create a global electro-magnetic shield, which future alien craft will not be able to penetrate without being destroyed. That *will* keep the aliens at bay, and allow the customary order of life and business on Earth to continue."

For the first time in their conversation Prince Adler's face beamed. "Excellent, Colonel! Now tell me, is there any possibility of this plan not working? Any at all? Be frank with me."

"None, your Highness. We have field-tested all weapons systems. The anti-personnel weapons are guaranteed to generate an autopsy report of 'death by exotic means,' in other words, by alien weapons. And we have already destroyed one alien craft at high altitude with the HARDON system, so we know that works."

"Well, Colonel, your plan sounds very good. I will so inform the Executive Committee when we resume our meeting in a few minutes. Now, may I remind you, let there be no mistakes. The penalty for such would be your demise, extended over a number of days, and accomplished in most unpleasant ways."

"Yes, sir! er, your Highness! The operation will go off as we have discussed, without fail. You have my word on it."

"For your sake, I hope so." The Prince put on a formal smile. "Now, Colonel Partridge, if you'll excuse me. I must get back to the Executive Committee. So good of you to come over and join me for this discussion."

"My pleasure, your Majesty," Partridge replied with equal insincerity, bowing slightly.

The road up to Cheyenne Mountain was steep and very winding. One mile south of the Colorado Springs suburb of Broadmoor, Maguire and Catalina encountered a toll booth. Beyond the toll booth they began the last two miles of their drive up Cheyenne Mountain Highway to the mountain entrance of NORAD command center. They did not particularly notice a tan, late-model Ford pulling up to the toll booth as they left. "Ice" Miller got out, flashed NRO credentials at the toll-guard, and commandeered the phone in the toll booth.

Maguire had just finished navigating a particularly serpentine set of highway curves, when Catalina pointed out two cobalt-blue Air Force Police vehicles racing down the highway towards them. The lead USAF vehicle skidded to a stop sideways, blocking the highway. Maguire brought his Pathfinder to an abrupt halt next to it. The second vehicle screeched to a stop behind to the first. Four Air Police jumped out and pointed their M16s at the Pathfinder. An Air Force Captain emerged from the first vehicle and walked up to Maguire's side window.

Maguire rolled down the glass part-way. "What's the problem, Officer?"

Catalina turned towards the officer, a cheerful look fixed frozen on her face.

"Step out of the car," the captain barked.

"Beg your pardon? This is a public road," Maguire rejoined evenly. "What's the problem?"

"Step out of the car, sir," the captain repeated more firmly.

"And I said that you have no jurisdiction here, Officer. We're on a *state* highway. We paid our toll. So, what's the problem?"

The captain lifted his hand to signal to the other Air Police. They quickly advanced to take positions around the Pathfinder, automatic weapons trained on the two occupants. The captain opened Maguire's door. A burly sergeant reached in, pulled Maguire out forcibly, and slammed him up against the hood. Another airman opened Catalina's door and pulled her out by the wrist. Then he twisted her arm up behind her, while he wrapped his other arm across her throat and held her immobilized.

Spread face-down across the hood by two airmen, Maguire turned his head to the right and said, "Officer, this stop is illegal and outrageous. I demand you release us at once!"

"Shut up, Dr. Maguire," the captain replied coldly. "We're operating under authority of the National Security Act. You don't have to be on Air Force property. You were headed for Cheyenne Mountain?"

"Yes, we were," Maguire answered. "No law against that."

"You and Ms. Catalina have been determined by proper authority to be extreme national security risks. As such you have no 'right' to approach sensitive government installations." The captain turned to the man next to him. "Sergeant!"

The beefy sergeant came up behind Maguire and gave him a powerful punch to the right kidney. Maguire cried out from the pain. The sergeant followed with five more strong punches, until Maguire's knees buckled and he slid to the ground.

The captain leaned over the slumped Maguire and said, "Turn your vehicle around and get off this mountain at once. And don't ever approach here again. That goes for any other sensitive government installation, too. And, off the record, if I were you, Maguire, I'd leave the country. You're a marked man."

He gave Maguire a final kick in the ribs, and walked around to where Catalina was being held. "M'am, you're a very good-looking woman. A pretty woman like you can get in a whole lot of trouble sneaking around government installations. These bases have a lot of men who are starved for a little female contact, if you know what I mean, and I think you do. A lady could find herself compromised real fast if she's not careful." He leaned into her face. "You catch my drift?"

"I know one thing," Catalina said in a hoarse voice, still in a choke-hold, "you and your men are pigs and gutless cowards."

The captain grabbed her by the crotch and squeezed unmercifully hard. Catalina moaned involuntarily from the pain as his fingernails dug in.

"That's right," the captain said, "not taking a warning hurts real bad. And furthermore, it's going to get your boyfriend killed. Just think about that before you go smart-mouthing off any more."

Catalina glared at him, but said nothing more. The captain smirked triumphantly and walked back around to Maguire.

"Dr. Maguire, I'm sure we can be reasonable people. Here, let me help you up. Now, why don't you and your companion get back in your vehicle, turn around, and get the hell off of my mountain. Understand?" The captain gave a signal, and the airmen placed Maguire and Catalina back inside their vehicle.

As Maguire started to turn the Pathfinder around, he stuck his head out the window and said to the captain, "You're AFOSI, aren't you?"

The captain stared at him disdainfully and said, "That's right, Air Force Intelligence. And if *you* had any intelligence, you wouldn't have tried getting anywhere near NORAD, traitor."

Maguire shook his head in disgust. After determining that Catalina was all right, he headed back down the mountain highway.

"I have to apologize to you for getting you into that," Maguire said, looking over sympathetically towards Catalina.

"No need to apologize, Rog," Catalina replied in a husky voice, rubbing her throat. "*They* were the ones who were in the wrong. I'm basically all right."

"You *know* they were handing us bullshit about having the authority to stop us."

"Yeah, but the fact that they knew who we were tells me that we had better lay off visiting any more military bases."

"I suppose you're right. At least for the time being, I agree. We'll leave sensitive bases off our itinerary."

An hour north of Colorado Springs, they exited from I-25 in downtown Denver, and drove to Catalina's son's work place at Front Range Graphix. As Catalina and Maguire walked into his work-cubicle, Jason looked up from his work table with a surprised smile. "Hi, mom!"

Jason Catalina was a tall, thin, enthusiastic 18-year-old with an unruly mop of brown hair. Catalina gave him an extended hug, and said how much she had missed him. Then she introduced Jason to Maguire. When Maguire mentioned learning that Jason had recently started out in a new career as a graphic artist, Jason corrected him that he was a graphic *designer*. He proudly pulled out his portfolio, and showed them some examples of his graphic designs. Since it was practically quitting time, Maguire offered to take Jason and Catalina out to dinner.

Settled in at the restaurant, Jason proudly caught them up to date on developments in his life over the past few months. His mother in turn told Jason about all her adventures since meeting Roger. She told him that Maguire and she had developed a serious relationship, and that Jason should get used to the idea of Maguire's being a part of their lives from now on. Catalina gallantly tolerated Jason's "no duh!" response, as he pointed out to her that he was an adult and could see for himself how romantically bonded his mother was acting around her boyfriend. Jason, proud of his first apartment, insisted that they stay at his place while they were in Denver. Warming up to Maguire, he offered to show him some UFO hot-spots he had discovered. And since tomorrow night was Halloween, Jason told them of a "way cool Halloween party" happening the next night, which he recommended.

Intense ultraviolet lighting illuminated the dance floor of the Club Ravin. The spooky atmosphere was intermittently punctuated by super-bright flashes from banks of strobe lights. Jason was rocking in the middle of the crowded dance floor with a cute strawberry blonde courier he had met delivering graphics orders to his company.

As a dance tune ended, Catalina leaned over to Maguire, excused herself, and headed to the powder room. Maguire moved over to the sidelines of the dance floor to watch the people dancing, while he awaited Catalina's return. A strikingly beautiful woman in her late twenties, with strawberry-blonde ringlets and wearing a tight-fitting drop-dead-red dress with an incredibly short skirt, walked up to him and smiled.

"Hi, handsome. I couldn't help spotting you from across the room. My name is Donna. I'd like to get to know you. What's your name?"

"Roger," Maguire replied politely.

"Roger, you want to dance?" Donna said, flashing her most seductive smile.

"I'm waiting for my girlfriend to return from the ladies room."

"It won't hurt anything if we get a quick dance in while she's gone. By the way, I really like dancing close."

Donna drew herself up against him, pelvis thrust forward, and her large breasts crushed against his chest.

"Ah, look, Donna, I'm happy just taking a break here and waiting for my girlfriend. I'm really not interested in dancing with you."

"Well, why don't we go over to the bar and get a drink then, Roger? It'll be my treat. Small price to talk for a few minutes with a nice guy like you." Donna placed her hand on Maguire's rear and pressed him into her pelvis.

"Look, Donna, I said no," Maguire responded, moving back from her a bit. "I'm sure you can find someone here who is alone. A beautiful woman like you won't have any problem."

"But *you're* the only one I'm interested in," she cooed in an unmistakably flirtatious voice.

"Well, I'm already taken. No sale. Look, please don't bother me any more."

Donna turned contemptuous, a sneer on her face. "So, you're a faggot, eh, Maguire?" Then she cupped her hand to her mouth and hurried outside the Club. Out in back behind the Club Ravin, "Ice" Miller relieved Donna of the listening device she was wearing under her low-cut dress. As he fished the wire out of her brassiere, he copped a feel. Then he handed her three $20 bills.

"Hey! Where's the rest of my money?"

"Look, lady, the $300 was only if you got him away from the Club and had a little back-seat love-fest. Be glad you got anything at all, you loser."

"Fuck you," Donna responded, quickly tucking the twenties into her brassiere.

"And remember our little understanding, Donna. No talking. I've got people in this town. I hear you've been talking; you're going to have a very terrible accident. You got me?"

Donna's eyes widened with fear. She hurried away to her car.

As Catalina rejoined Maguire, she asked, "Who was that woman?"

"You mean the bimbo in the red dress?"

"Yes, her."

"She said her name was Donna. She was trying to get me to do the Lambada with her, I guess. Anyway, I think she was sent in to try to get between us."

"How do you know?"

"She slipped up. I only told her my first name, but when I gave her the brush-off, she called me by my last name."

"My God! Don't they *ever* give up?"

"You mean the 'Intelligence' Community? They won't give up until a generation after they've been disbanded. Sort of like old Civil War Southerners. They keep hoping that the South will rise again."

"Let's not stay up too late dancing. I want to get back to Boulder in the morning and see how it's doing."

Catalina's modest ranch-style house was located in downtown Boulder. It was a pale yellow with white shutters. While Maguire was unloading the Pathfinder, Catalina went to unlock the front door. She found it unlocked and let out a shout. "Rog, the house has been ransacked!"

Maguire rushed up to the front door and stepped inside. "Oh, no! Not your house, too. Damn those bastards!"

"And where is Pamela? She is supposed to be house-sitting for me. It doesn't look like she's been around for some time."

Maguire walked through the house quickly to make sure there was no intruder still inside. Catalina sat on an overturned recliner chair, holding a broken vase that Jason had made for her in high school ceramics class. She cried softly. After a few minutes, she regained her composure and placed a phone call to Pamela's mother, where she guessed that Pamela might be staying. The mother acknowledged that Pamela was there, but when Catalina asked to speak to

Pamela, the mother passed on Pamela's reply that she didn't want to speak with Catalina.

Catalina put down the phone and looked up at Maguire. "Roger, Pamela was one of my dearest friends. What could have gotten into her?"

"Oh, I imagine that the people who did this really got to her, too."

"How can people who do things like that sleep at night?"

"If they had a conscience, they'd have insomnia. But those dirty-tricks operatives don't lose any sleep. To them it's just a job." He put his arm around her to comfort her, and gave her a loving squeeze. "Take it easy, dear. I'll go out to the car, get my camera, and take some photographs for evidence. Then we'll call the police and your insurance agent and make the reports. I'm just glad you *weren't* here when they did this."

A couple of days later, with Jason helping out on the clean-up team, they had the house back together. New lamps and vases brightened the rooms. The insurance adjuster assured them that everything would be covered by her policy. Having learned about police indifference after Maguire's office break-in, Catalina did not even try to tell the Boulder police her belief that the ransacking of her house had been an intelligence operation. The Boulder police sergeant wrote it up as a burglary, even though nothing had been taken except the one UFO book she owned. The sergeant told her that when he had attempted to interview her former house-sitter, he had gotten nowhere. Pamela gave them a story about going back to her mother's for a night, and then after returning to Catalina's house, finding it ransacked. After that, Pamela had said that she was afraid to stay at the house any more. The policeman told Catalina "off the record" that he doubted Pamela's story, because of the bruises he had spotted on her cheek and arm and the shifty way she avoided eye contact. He promised Catalina that the Boulder Police would drive by her house more frequently during the next few weeks.

Catalina got her next-door neighbor to agree to keep

watch on the house. With things back to normal, she said a fond good-bye to Jason, promising to see him in four weeks, after the Landing was over. Then Catalina and Maguire set off to continue their travels toward the Landing site.

While still in the Denver area, Maguire could not pass up a chance to detour out to a notorious "black operations" site. Functioning under the name of Buckley Air National Guard Base, the site was southeast of Aurora, a Denver sub-urb. Catalina was in a good mood after getting her ransacked house all straightened out. She readily agreed to the detour, with the understanding they would not go onto the base.

They drove along Highway 30 around to the northeast corner of Buckley ANG Base. Maguire parked near the fence by a row of tall bushes that would mask their car. He got out his binoculars and swept the airfield. They were too preoc-cupied to pay any attention to a blue sedan which parked three-quarters of a mile back up the highway. A balding beefy man with a pock-marked face emerged from the car and went through the motions of changing a tire. Maguire was just about to give up his surveillance of the base, when he no-ticed a military truck towing a low-boy trailer. The trailer held a very large heavy object covered under a large blue tarpaulin. What drew Maguire's attention was that the truck was headed at high speed straight for the side of a large hill along the back side of the base. He called over to Catalina and gestured animatedly at the speeding truck.

"Look, Barbara!"

"What's up?"

"Either the airman driving that truck is on a suicide mis-sion, or we're about to see something unusual. Look how he's barreling towards the side of that hill."

"Oh my God, Rog, what *is* he doing?"

When the truck drew within a couple hundred yards of the side of the hill, a large camouflaged door rolled side-ways into the hillside. The truck-trailer combination rolled through the opening without stopping.

Barbara's eyes widened. "Wow! There's got to be some-thing *huge* inside that hill. What could be going on in there?"

"I don't know, but this sure is not just some Weekend Warriors airfield, I'll tell you that."

"Do other bases have underground, ah, ..."

"Facilities?" Maguire completed her question. "Yeah. A lot of them. Air bases like Edwards, Andrews, Nellis, Eglin and Cape Canaveral. Navy bases like China Lake that we were just at, and Fallon Naval Air Station, Nevada. Army bases like Fort Irwin."

"Why put things underground? I couldn't stand living underground. There'd be no sunlight down there."

"The military figures, 'Out of sight, out of mind.' If the public doesn't know about an installation, they can't ask any questions about it."

"But this is a democracy, Rog. We're supposed to know what our government is doing."

"Ah, yeah, right," Maguire replied, trying to control his contempt for the pervasive secrecy that had turned America into a National Security state. "If the military thought that you were safe to let know about things, they would have shown you. So, obviously you're a threat to the military," he said with a wry grin.

"Me?" Catalina looked askance. "I'm just a mother."

In the subdued lighting of the single-bed hospital room, the young nurse could see that her patient was in trouble. The semi-delirious middle-aged woman who was lying there continued to cough up blood. She had already gone through two boxes of tissues. The nurse handed her a fresh box of tissues, then went out to the nurses station to consult with her supervisor.

"Svetlana, our patient in Room Three is getting worse. Shouldn't you summon Dr. Karsavina?"

"*Nyet*. Dr. Karsavina said there is nothing more he can do."

"But surely we can't just let her die. Cosmonaut Kheraskov is a Hero of the Soviet Union!" the young nurse insisted.

"That she was. But now the Soviet Union is no more. And soon, too, I'm afraid, our brave cosmonaut Kheraskov will be no more. That damn American Pneumonic Hemorrhagic

Fever will kill us all before it's all over. Look at her. She looked fine when she came back from her trip to America. But then three days later, wham!"

"So, is it then that the PHF virus came from America?"

"That's the story I read in *Pravda* this week," the supervisor replied. "The news story came from a leak from the KGB."

"Poor Ivana, so brave! And she so admired the American astronauts. To think that she'll die from an American virus."

"It's a pity, to be sure. Dying all alone in a cosmonaut infirmary."

"She keeps talking half-delusional. Something about she won't be there to meet the star people. What could she mean?" the young nurse asked.

"Maybe she's referring to the graduating class of cosmonauts? Who knows? She's delirious, after all."

Leaving Denver behind, Maguire and Catalina headed south at a leisurely pace, gradually wending their way towards the extraterrestrial rendezvous below Cloverdale three weeks hence. After traveling down I-25 to Walsenburg, they crossed over the Sangre de Cristo Range to the beautiful, immense San Luis Valley, the largest alpine valley in the world. From there they followed the Rio Grande River in a southward course.

As they drove along, Catalina spoke to Maguire of her need to do a spiritual retreat before meeting with the extraterrestrial representatives. With all the excitement of the past weeks, she had not maintained enough time for meditation and spiritual renewal. She told Maguire of the wonderful shrine of Santuario de Chamayo, 25 miles north of Santa Fe. There was a timelessly old sacred spring there. In the early 1800s the Spanish friars had built a chapel next to it. But the fame of the healing powers of the earth around Chamayo had been established among the local Indian people long before the friars had come. It was there that Catalina said she could best renew herself mentally and spiritually. Maguire, responded that he, too, felt the need to recenter and balance himself metaphysically before the extraterrestrial Landing. They agreed to spend a few days at the sanctuary as a place of spiritual retreat. As they passed down through the Carson National Forest toward Chamayo, Catalina had Maguire stop the car, so that she could gather some supplies for cleansing and blessing ceremonies. While she gathered some mountain sage, Maguire harvested a few small aromatic cedar branches. Soon their car was filled with wonderful natural fragrances.

In the executive suite of the Corey Peak facility, Colonel Partridge leaned back in his swivel chair. A satisfied smile spread across his face as he read the intelligence teletype he had just been handed. He noted with satisfaction that the Special Operations "assets" within the JANUS organization still responded swiftly to his commands. The Colonel was gratified to know that being marked by the President as wanted by the FBI had not destroyed his command and control powers over JANUS. The teletype in front of him indicated that his order to create a destabilizing incident in Nepal had been carried out. An insurgent group of rebels had captured a strategic mountain above the capital and had begun shelling Kathmandu. The rebels had demanded the exile of the Buddhist Lama, after falsely accusing him of being a puppet of the Communist occupation regime in Tibet, and of trying to organize a Communist coup. The Nepal uprising should remove one more member of Project Epiphany from the equation, Partridge figured. Just as sure as PHF-laced airline food had taken care of Dr. Kheraskov.

At the Friends of Nepal headquarters in Santa Fe, Lama Dharam's face grew clouded. His host, the director, had just handed him an urgent situation report on his home country. According to the confidential dispatch, an insurgent group had emerged near the capital. It appeared to be made up of local malcontents, supplied and directed behind the scenes by mercenaries of some American intelligence agency. The Lama was requested to take a return flight home at once, since the government felt that a statement by him in person would quiet the rumors and fears that he had gone over to the enemy. The Lama crumpled up the dispatch. He had become as upset as his approach to enlightenment permitted him. It was clear that he was not going to be able to be present at the Landing to greet the Star Visitors. After a few moments of reflection, he consoled himself with the thought that other lifetimes provided further opportunities.

It was the fourth day of their fasting and meditation retreat at Chamayo. Catalina had just finished smudging Maguire with sage smoke as part of a Native American purification ritual. Deep in meditation, the two were seated quietly on the healing earth, next to a rocky depression in the ground where Chamayo Spring emerged during the rainy season. Their reverie was broken by the call of an old Indian woman.

"Hello."

Catalina looked up to see a wizened Pueblo woman in her eighties taking labored steps towards them. "Hello, grandmother." Catalina used the respectful Native American term for an older woman.

"My name is Iawala, Corn Medicine. I am from the Taos Pueblo. The spirits sent me here to find you."

Maguire looked up in surprise. He had never seen this woman before. And from the tone of Barbara's voice, he was sure she had not either. "Ho! grandmother, why did the spirits send you to us?"

"I had a vision last night that you two would be here. I was shown that I was to come to you and tell you to go to the place you know as Bandalier National Monument. In a ceremonial cave upon the cliffs above the canyon floor, there is a kiva. You are to go there and pray. The spirits want to show you something." The elderly woman smiled, showing a number of missing teeth. Then she turned around to leave.

"Grandmother Iawala," Catalina called, "wait. Can we give you a ride somewhere?"

"Oh, no. But thank you. My granddaughter is waiting for me outside the wall in her pickup truck."

"You mean you got a ride to come all the way from Taos to tell us this?" Maguire was impressed at her effort.

"That was all the spirits told me to tell you," Grandmother Iawala replied laconically. "So now I have done that.
I will be on my way. Good-bye."

"Good-bye, grandmother," Catalina and Maguire replied,
almost in chorus. Catalina added, "And thank you."

In the briefing room of JANUS's Corey Peak facility, four
men and two women sat around the table. The six were clean-
cut and wearing fashionable civilian attire. Their ages ranged
from mid-twenties to early thirties. An outsider might guess
that this was a group of young business professionals at a
sales briefing. Only a handful of people in the United States
knew that these were contract "assets" of the Defense Intelligence Agency, on temporary duty to the JANUS NSA com-
partment. Every one of the DIA people around the table was
a world-class expert remote-viewer, with a further special-
ization in psychokinesis. At the front of the room stood Jack
Partridge. He stubbed out his cigarillo, as a blonde in the
chair nearest him fanned away the smoke, and called the
session to order.

"Today our target is located in Panama City, Florida,
located between Pensacola and Tallahassee. He is an older
man, in his sixties, a retired Air Force Colonel. He is living in
a modest one-story house several blocks outside the fence of
Tyndall Air Force Base. He is at home this morning." Lifting
up a one-foot-square photograph of Colonel Duane Warwick,
Partridge continued. "This is your man. I am advised that he
has a slight heart flutter at times. This morning we are going
to concentrate on making his heart problems major. In fact,
catastrophic. This man is an extreme national security risk."
Partridge picked up and waved a fraudulent but convinc-
ing-looking document. "His elimination is sanctioned by a
special Presidential Emergency National Security Directive.
This Directive specifically names this unit, and grants Presidential amnesty to you all.

"Now, our procedure will go like this. We will first call
up this man's image, then travel to his presence." Partridge
next held up an enlarged drawing of the human heart. "Then,

on my signal, we will all target his aortic valve, to induce paralysis so that the valve will not open. We will maintain psychokinetic lock-on to his heart valve for over two minutes. That should be sufficient. At that point I will remote-view this man and determine that death has occurred. After I have made that determination, I will signal you all again, and you can stop psychokinetic lock-on. Are there any questions?"

Duane Warwick sat at the table in his study, sorting through the morning mail. A wave of dizziness passed over him, then subsided. A plain envelope which had Dr. Robert Bowen's return address on it caught his eye. He opened it and read the terse message enclosed. It read:

"Colonel Warwick, Greetings. Team will rendezvous at the Best Western Inn, Lordsburg, NM, Saturday, November 23 at 12 noon. You will check in under an assumed name. A block of rooms has already been reserved for our Team. Your room is reserved under "Henry Aldrich." Remember to bring complete supplies to be outdoors for three days. Please destroy this note after reading. In cosmic solidarity, Robert Bowen"

Warwick studied the note, then began to tear it up. As he started to do so, he felt a strange pressure in his chest. As he tried to stand up and reach for the phone, he paled. Massive dizziness overcame him and he slumped to the floor. After a couple of minutes, his clenched right hand trembled, then unclenched and hung limp.

Deep in Bandelier National Monument, the sloping walls of Frijoles Canyon had patches of snow where the tree shade provided shelter from the sun's melting rays. The bright green of the junipers and the glistening white of the snow contrasted with the soft creamy yellow color of the sandstone cliffs. Just before sunset, Maguire and Catalina had left their campsite and trekked down the dirt trail to the bottom of the canyon. From there, another trail led upstream towards the Ceremonial Cave which Grandmother Iawala had spoken of. Maguire had earlier conferred with the Head Ranger about doing "special research" at night at the Cave. Because he had identified himself as an anthropologist, the ranger had granted special permission to stay at the Cave after the monument trails closed at sunset.

In the fading twilight, they carefully clambered up the north canyon wall, using handholds etched out of the sandstone by the Anasazi 700 years earlier. Eighty feet up the sloping cliff, they reached the Ceremonial Cave. The fifty-foot-wide, forty-foot-deep cave had a floor of uneven sandstone. Near the cliff edge was the slightly raised, partially intact circular roof of a kiva. The upper portion of a crude wooden ladder was sticking out of a rectangular opening in the kiva's roof. Catalina lighted the sage bundle she had brought and performed a ceremonial smudging of the cave and the kiva. Then they both descended the ladder into the sunken, windowless kiva to meditate and wait.

After a couple of hours, the cold from the kiva's stone walls had penetrated through Catalina and Maguire's jackets. They were shivering in the darkness and Maguire was about to call it a night when suddenly Catalina sat bolt upright.

"Rog, I feel something."

A faint bluish-white glow began to form along the southern wall of the kiva. The glow grew stronger, then coalesced into a luminous figure of a translucent female in a diaphanous gown.

"It's Arica!" Catalina exclaimed.

The extraterrestrial stood in the middle of the kiva and smiled at the seated pair. They heard a gentle feminine voice telepathically in their heads. "Catalina and Roger, greetings."

Maguire blinked his eyes to make sure he wasn't hallucinating. When he saw Arica's glow reflected off Catalina in what would have otherwise been pitch blackness, he knew this was real.

"Hello, Arica," Catalina exclaimed.

Maguire telepathed to Arica a message of respectful recognition of her presence.

The extraterrestrial's face grew serious. "Notice carefully the things I have to show you. These will be important for you to accomplish before the Inter-Stellar Federation ambassadors arrive in a few of your days."

In their mind's eye, Arica mentally presented a picture of a large metallic disc lowering towards the ground above a gently sloping area of cactus. The site was next to the base of a low mountain range. A small group of seven men and women could be seen standing near a dry lake bed at the foot of the mountain. Suddenly, multiple laser beams shot at the small group. Catalina cringed as people cried out and fell over. Then green laser beams shot up towards the disc. After that, the picture sequence dissolved.

Next, the extraterrestrial showed them a very high mountain five miles southeast of Santa Fe. The mental picture zoomed in towards the snow-capped mountain and then inside. Catalina and Maguire were shown caverns inside the mountain, where they saw extraterrestrials living. On the west side of the mountain they were shown a camouflaged entrance to a tunnel leading to the caverns inside. Then the sequence stopped.

Next, Arica showed them a desert military reservation. Maguire recognized it as Sandia National Laboratories, on the southeast edge of Albuquerque. Then she shifted the scene to a National Forest lookout tower to the east of Sandia Military Reservation. Catalina and Maguire got the strong mental impression that they should go to that lookout tower.

Next the handsome, high-cheek-boned, ebony face of Roscoe Dent appeared in their mind's eye. Arica said: "This is Major Roscoe Dent. He lives in Oracle, Arizona. You must give him a warning to take to his Project Epiphany Contact Team mates. The warning is about the attack being planned for the Landing site. The attack will come from military forces." She then showed them the location of Dent's house, near where a gravel road ended at the mouth of a canyon. Next to the canyon's mouth, they could make out a sign, "Dead End — Kannally Wash Road." Arica told them, "A quarter mile up this canyon there is a small cross. It marks the spot where Major Dent's pet Labrador was buried after it was hit by a car. Remember that."

The luminous figure started to move back towards the kiva wall. "You must deal with all these situations in the few days before my people's ambassadors arrive. Hurry. There is not much time." Arica merged into the wall and disappeared.

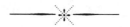

Chapter 14

A BLUE sedan had just crested a rise along a dirt road in the Santa Fe National Forest. From that vantage point the driver could see that the sport utility vehicle he had been following stopped a mile up ahead, at where the road dead-ended. The blue sedan quickly slowed down and pulled over behind a grove of junipers. His car now hidden, the driver got on the radio.

"Eagle One, this is Zeta Five. Do you copy?"

Inside the Corey Peak executive suite, the communications link was set to speaker-phone mode. Colonel Partridge remained in his recliner chair as he responded. "This is Eagle One. I copy you, Zeta Five."

"Eagle One, I have Fellow Traveler and Princess Leia in sight by binoculars. They have taken a Forest Service road to where it dead-ends against a mountain peak. The peak is about six miles southeast of Santa Fe. It's the tallest peak around except for one a mile north of it."

"Christ, Zeta Five! The mountain you're referring to is called Glorieta Baldy." Partridge's voice had a nervous tightness to it. "Goddamn-it! How did Maguire figure that one out?"

"Beg your pardon, sir?"

"Zeta Five, since you now have a need to know, I'm informing you that the mountain in front of you contains a colony of 'Visitors.' Somehow Fellow Traveler has learned about this. Maintain extremely rigorous surveillance on them. There's a camouflaged entrance into the mountain that's a few hundred yards in front of them. If they happen to find it, let me know at once. We will then have to take extreme measures."

As they stood in front of their vehicle facing the mountain, Catalina looked at Maguire. "What do we do now, Rog?"

"I don't know exactly. We've gotten this far. We're pretty sure it's the mountain that Arica showed us. She didn't indicate what we're supposed to do once we get here."

"How about I psychically view into the mountain and establish connection with the ETs inside?"

"Sounds good to me."

Catalina sat cross-legged on the earth facing the mountain, her eyes closed in concentration. After a few moments, a look of surprise crossed her face. She opened her eyes.

"Wow! I'm getting a strong response from a number of people inside there. They're tuning into me."

"So, we have the right mountain?"

"Oh, yes! There must be hundreds of ETs in there. They're actually quite happy that we've come. I told them that Arica sent us. They seem to be aware of who she is. They say she is an important representative from the Federation."

"Ask them what they would like us to do."

After a quiet pause, Catalina spoke up. "They would like us to come into the mountain. They want us to be very aware of them, before we go to meet the ET ambassadors from the Federation."

"Whoa! OK, then, find out how we gain entrance into the mountain."

"They're telling me that we need to walk about two hundred yards ahead. When we get near a place at the foot of the mountain where the vegetation has been cleared away, they will open up a concealed doorway there for us."

"OK. Tell them we're on our way."

"Ice" Miller set down his binoculars. He had advanced around his quarry's left flank, and was positioned between them and the mountain. When he saw them begin to approach the side of the mountain, he radioed Partridge. "Eagle One! Eagle One! They're advancing towards the entrance! What should I do?"

"Jesus, Miller," the Colonel exclaimed, breaking code, "shoot at them. Scare them off. If they keep on advancing, then shoot to kill."

"Am I cleared for 'executive action'?"

"Goddamn-it, Zeta Five, I'll take care of the paperwork later. Start shooting!"

"Ice" Miller hesitated. If he killed them and then later were caught, there was a good chance Partridge would deny knowing him. Miller could foresee having to take a murder rap without the immunity granted by a National Security Directive. Yet if he disobeyed the Colonel's order, he was as good as a dead man. "Damned if I do and damned if I don't," he muttered to himself. "About standard for one of these goddam FUBAR operations." He picked up his rifle and scoped in on Maguire and Catalina.

A .30 calibre round whined, ricocheting off a rocky out-cropping next to where Catalina was walking. A sharp stone fragment penetrated her upper arm. A fraction of a second later the crack of a rifle could be heard.

"Get down!" Maguire yelled, diving for the ground and pulling Catalina after him. He turned to see if she was all right and saw a patch of redness on her upper sleeve. "Oh, no! You're shot!"

Catalina put on a brave face and said, "Don't worry, dear. It's not very deep. But it sure is colorful."

Maguire rolled up her shirt sleeve and dabbed away the blood. He dug in with his fingernail and worked loose the stone shard. "Looks like it's a rock fragment, not a bullet."

"It still stings like crazy," Catalina replied gamely, wincing.

Maguire tore off a section of his tee-shirt and quickly made a field dressing for her wound. After he rolled her sleeve back down, he said, "Let's get out of here. We need to get you to a clinic where they can clean up that wound right." He led a roundabout path back to the car, staying behind trees and tall brush to avoid giving the sniper another clear shot at them. Once inside the Pathfinder, he had Catalina lie on the floor. Then he started the engine and floored the gas pedal, retracing their route back to Santa Fe and the nearest urgent care center.

"Ice" Miller lowered his binoculars and picked up his radio. "Eagle One, I think I winged Princess Leia. Doesn't look like it was a vital spot hit, though. They both high-tailed it back to their car and took off like a bat out of hell. I don't think they'll be back here."

"That's good, Zeta Five. Just keep track of them."

Miller grinned as Maguire and Catalina flew past his hiding spot, leaving a cloud of dust behind them. Using the dust cloud as cover, he pulled out a few moments later and followed behind.

Knoxville was experiencing an unusually heavy snow-storm. It was almost time to go home for the day. Dr. Stewart Golden stood looking out the office window of the Interstellar Friendship and Exchange Committee. He was marveling at the torrent of flakes coming down when the ring of the doorbell broke his reverie. At the door stood two well-dressed men in dark business suits, each carrying a briefcase. Dr. Golden invited them in, showed them to their chairs, and sat down. The shorter man sat, but the taller, middle-aged man remained standing. He flashed the credentials of the National Security Agency and spoke for them both.

"I'm Jonathan Gracie. I'm with the National Security Council. Dr. Golden, we come here on extremely urgent and vital business. May we speak in confidence?"

"Certainly."

"Dr. Golden, let me get straight to the point. We have been instructed by the White House to give you an important message. But first, may I have your promise that you will keep what I tell you absolutely confidential?"

Dr. Golden looked up at the NSA agent and said, "Of course, you can trust me. I'm a doctor. My whole career involves keeping people's confidences. But why do you wish to speak with *me?*"

"We're glad you can keep a secret. We've come to you because you are the head of ISFEC. The matter to be discussed involves the most sensitive National Security matters. I have been instructed to relay to you a message we have received from extraterrestrial sources over deep-space dishes in the last few days. It appears that the extraterrestrials are quite aware of the efforts which you and your ISFEC group have been making to reach out to them."

"They are?" Dr. Golden was flattered.

The NSA man continued. "As a result, they communicated to us through our government listening dishes several days ago. They've let us know that it is their intention to specify ISFEC as the group they want to meet with them and represent Earth when they conduct their formal ambassadorial Landing. That Landing will occur on November 24th at Holloman Air Force Base, Alamogordo, New Mexico. The National Security Council has pledged to the extraterrestrials to give their landing craft a full military jet escort, to assure that the extraterrestrials encounter no problems. We will, of course, provide full protective escort for you and those you select as your ISFEC contingent, as well."

"But I had understood that the extraterrestrials were landing the next day, November 25th, and that it was near the Animas Mountains."

"Oh, you mean that disinformation that the CIA fed to Project Epiphany?" The NSA man's voice dripped with patronizing disdain.

Dr. Golden's jaw dropped. "You know about Project Epiphany?"

"Dr. Golden, it's the National Security Council's job to keep apprised about many things."

"And the actual extraterrestrial Landing is going to be on the 24th, you say?"

"That's right."

And the ETs want me and my ISFEC group to be the welcoming group?"

"That's correct, Doctor. Because the extraterrestrials have identified you and your ISFEC group alone as the ones they want to have meet with their representatives, you have a 'need to know.' That is why the National Security Council is telling you the extraterrestrials' message. And that's why I'm letting you know that Project Epiphany is operating on the basis of CIA disinformation. But you can't let them know. Because of National Security considerations, I'm holding you to the confidentiality you promised when we began this conversation."

"Well, you can tell the President that I accept this great honor on behalf of the Interstellar Friendship and Exchange Committee. I will be greatly honored to represent all humanity. You can assure the National Security Council that I will make a full report of everything the extraterrestrials have to say."

The NSA man beamed a complacent smile and said nothing.

"So, then, I will contact my top ISFEC people right away, and have them all meet me at Holloman Air Force Base the day before the ET Landing. Will that arrangement be satisfactory, Mr. Gracie?"

"That will be perfectly fine, Doctor. Just give me the names, addresses and phone numbers of your ISFEC welcoming committee, so that we can have security clearance badges made up. We'll also arrange to have military escorts pick them up in time to arrive at Holloman by the 23rd."

"Of course, Mr. Gracie."

Dr. Golden handed over a list of the ISFEC officers' names, addresses and phone numbers to the NSA man. "Tell the President that ISFEC will conduct itself according to the highest standards of civilized behavior during the extraterrestrial meeting."

"I'll do that," the NSA man replied with a friendly smile, barely concealing his contempt for this man he considered a gullible fool. "Oh, by the way, just so you know. You and your team will be picked up by Air Force Security Service personnel. They'll be wearing civilian clothes and traveling in unmarked cars. For security purposes, of course."

"Of course," Dr. Golden echoed agreeably. "Thank you very much, gentlemen. You've made my dreams come true."

The younger man developed a coughing fit and pulled out his handkerchief in an effort to disguise his barely-contained laughter.

Outside in the car, Special Agent Jonathan Gracie contacted Corey Peak via MILSTAR satellite link-up. "Eagle One, the person you had us pay a visit to has accepted the 'special invitation' without a problem."

"Good job," Colonel Partridge responded, chuckling at how well his plan to deflect Dr. Golden from the Project Epiphany Contact Team had worked. "You know, there are no limits to the seductive power of being in a special position."

"That's right, Eagle One. That Dr. Golden was so flattered that I had to hurry up and get out of there. I'm sure that if I stayed much longer, he'd have offered to give me a blow job." Agent Gracie guffawed at his own crude humor.

Now that he had yet another success in his plan to dismember the Contact Team one by one, Colonel Partridge couldn't resist sharing his sadistic pleasure with Gracie. "Can you imagine Golden's face when he gets to Holloman, and he and his ISFEC group are taken down to Level Nine and are held there on fake treason charges, while the real Landing takes place a day later and 200 miles away?" Partridge laughed so hard that he dropped his radio microphone.

The sign next to the locked gate read: "Cibola National Forest, USFS. Tijeras Fire Lookout Tower. Elev. 8052. Gov't. personnel only allowed on the tower." Catalina and Maguire clambered through wide openings in the gate's metal bars and walked up to the tower. It was off-season for fires. No one was manning the lookout. They climbed up the stairs to the lookout deck with its commanding view. To the west they could see the vast stretches of Sandia Military Reservation's pale yellow sands tinted pink by the early morning sun. They huddled on the leeward side of the tower and pulled the hoods of their down jackets over their heads, trying to shut out the biting cold wind. Maguire occasionally swept the range with his binoculars.

After two hours of watching and waiting, he spotted an elliptical drone. It was flying at about 1000 feet altitude approaching Sandia's Coyote Canyon, site of classified Star Wars weapons tests. As the drone reached a position directly over Coyote Canyon, a brilliant green laser beam shot up from inside the canyon. As the beam struck, the drone exploded and fell out of the sky.

Catalina screamed, "That's the same kind of laser beam I saw in my vision about the ET-landing! And it's the same type that Arica showed us they would use to try to destroy the ETs' craft."

"It's clear now that the military actually have such a weapon. *And* they're practicing for the Landing."

"Rog, that gives me the chills."

"It's so stupid. The Defense Department's answer to extraterrestrial contact is to blow them out of the sky," Maguire said disgustedly. "Won't they ever grow up and stop playing Cowboys and Indians?"

Sojourner Dent's mahogany skin glistened in the noonday heat. Even in mid-November, the southern Arizona sun this cloudless day felt hot, as she worked in the garden behind her modest tract-house. She was working fresh loam into the sandy soil. She had finished one row and started on another, when the sound of an unfamiliar car engine made her look up. She turned towards the house and called out, "Roscoe. Someone's coming!"

A stocky muscular African-American man with graying hair stepped out the front door and squinted in the bright sunlight. Retired Army/SEATO Major Roscoe Dent shaded his eyes with his hand, peering at the friendly-looking white couple emerging from their vehicle.

"Major Roscoe Dent?"

"Yes."

"I'm Roger Maguire. I'm an anthropologist and researcher of extraterrestrial encounters."

"And I'm Barbara Catalina, a psychic. I'm Roger's research assistant."

Dent extended his hand. "Pleased to meet you." He gestured with his head to his wife standing at the edge of the garden. "That's Sojourner Dent, my wife. What brings you to our humble home?"

"You are a member of Project Epiphany, Major, are you not?"

"Just call me Roscoe." Dent paused and phrased his response carefully. "What makes you think I'm part of this Project Epiphany you mentioned?"

Catalina piped up. "Because Commander Jacques Stone said you were."

"I see," Dent replied noncommittally. "But what specifically brings you here?"

"An extraterrestrial ambassador who visited us recently instructed us to bring an urgent message to you," Catalina answered.

Dent's eyes widened. "What? Me?" Then he recovered his even composure and his manners. "Please come inside and make yourselves comfortable."

Once seated, Maguire and Catalina told him how Arica had contacted them at Bandelier Monument with a warning message. They passed on to him Arica's forewarning about the attack on the Project Epiphany Contact Team at the Landing site. Catalina added that Arica had said that Major Dent should be advised of this planned attack.

"With all due respect, Barbara and Roger, how do I know that you actually had a visit from an extraterrestrial? How do I know that you're telling me the truth?"

Maguire looked him squarely in the eye. "Roscoe, Arica showed us that a quarter mile up the canyon behind your home, there is a small cross marking the spot where your pet Labrador lies buried after it was hit by a car."

The soft drink Dent was holding slipped from his hand. Only his wife and he had known about that burial. As the truth of what they were telling him sank in, Dent reacted with visible alarm. "Good God, there *is* going to be an attack! I've got to get this message to our Project leader, Robert Bowen, right away! Everybody on the team must be warned!" Dent started to move towards the phone, then stopped himself. "Say, you know the Hopi elder Timothy Katoya, don't you?"

"Yes, we do," Maguire replied.

"Well, Katoya spoke up about you two at our Project Epiphany meeting a month ago. He was mentioning your request to join up with the Project's Contact Team at the ET Landing. Since I'm a stranger to you, and you know Timothy well, why did you bring this warning to me? Why not take it to Katoya?"

"We were just following Arica's orders." Catalina smiled. "You're an old soldier. You know how it is about following orders. And, if I can bring something else up, Roscoe, you've had a chance to meet us now. You can see that we're serious and not flakes. We'd like to ask you to persuade the Contact Team to let us join up with you."

"I'll see what I can do when I'm talking with the Project leader. I can't promise anything. Now, if you'll excuse me, I've got to make a vital telephone call to Dr. Bowen."

Sojourner Dent walked in from the kitchen. "I've got a big pot of stew ready. Please honor us by joining us for lunch."

Catalina and Maguire gratefully accepted their hospitality.

Former President Earl James was rummaging through his bedroom closet, trying to decide what kind of clothing he should pack for outdoors in the winter desert, while waiting for the Landing. He was considering a plaid wool shirt as one possibility when his wife came in to call him to the phone. James heard the voice of a young White House counselor. "Mr. Former President, this is the White House calling. Will you stay on the line while we connect you with the President?"

"Certainly. I'm always ready to talk with President Williams."

After a pause, a cheerful voice with a slight Southern accent came on the line. "Earl? This is Jeffrey Williams. How are you, sir?"

"I'm fine, Mr. President."

"Please, just call me Jeff. Say, Earl, I've got a terribly important request to make of you. It involves a matter of national and international security. I think you're the right man for the job, but it will be a challenging assignment." President Williams prided himself on being able to craft his message to match precisely the temperament and character of the person he was dealing with. In Earl James's case, the President knew that an appeal to selfless duty, mixed with prestige and flattery, was sure to work with the former President.

"Jeff, you know my track record when I was President. I never shirked the most difficult tasks. You can count on me for the assignment you have in mind. What is it you would like me to do?"

"You know those courtesy daily Presidential Briefing packets you get from CIA as past President? Did you happen to notice that a little over a month ago, I appointed Dr. Ian McCormack as chair of a National Academy of Sciences task force to study the extraterrestrial phenomenon?"

"I recall seeing something about that."

"Well, I put that Task Force on fast track because of the public announcement I made about extraterrestrial reality."

"Yes, I watched your announcement on TV, and thought it was courageous of you. I only wish that I could have made it during my presidency."

"Courageous, hell! I *had* to make that announcement, Earl. The night before, I had some damn alien in my bedroom in the middle of the night. The bastard like to scared me to *death*! Goddamn Secret Service never saw a thing. The alien told me that I had to make the announcement without any further delay, or else!"

"Or else what, Jeff?"

"The alien showed me a mental picture of that renegade military-intelligence unit, the one that's behind the unauthorized UFO Cover-Up. They were conducting a *coup d'etat*! The coup would have come after they had gotten themselves endorsed by the "aliens" in that phony alien landing of theirs at White Sands, the one they botched up and got a lot of their bigwigs killed at. The alien said that some of that group still are active, and that they're still planning a coup. Only this time it would happen after they intercept a real alien Landing that's happening soon and kill off any competition at the site."

"My God!" the former President said in a subdued tone. "Now I know the rest of *that* story."

"Anyway, Earl, back to why I called you. I wanted the U.N. to handle the world announcement of UFO reality that's supposed to be made. But Secretary-General Salaam, that gutless coward, hasn't followed up, after I dumped the alien problem on the U.N. during that speech two months ago. So, since the pressure from the media isn't letting up, I've had the National Academy of Sciences do a study on the aliens. The NAS Task Force has completed their findings within the urgent time-frame I gave Dr. McCormack. Their report is now ready to present. It'll describe the different races that are visiting, their agenda, how widespread their human contacts have been. The Report will also go into that woo-woo stuff: the consciousness changes the aliens want us to make, the inter-dimensional aspects of the phenomenon, the whole nine yards! It's going to be a doozey.

It's going to take a non-partisan, well-respected international figure to present it to the public. Earl, I need *you* to present it at a Washington press conference at the National Academy of Sciences just as soon as possible."

Earl James sucked in his breath. He saw his chances of being at the real extraterrestrial landing disappearing. But he had never been one to shirk his country's call. "Yes, Jeff, I'll do that. I can be ready in two days. You'll send me the NAS Report today and a prepared briefing speech, so I can start going over it?"

President Williams chuckled a bit self-consciously. "Actually, Earl, I *knew* I could count on you. Two federal couriers are already in the air on their way. They should be touching down in Macon within two hours. The press conference is set at the NAS Head-quarters for 10 a.m., Washington time, day after tomorrow. Earl, *do* sound reassuring when you're giving the briefing! I'm counting on you. Your country will be counting on you. The whole world will be counting on you. After you're done, come on up to the White House and we'll have a drink. We *should* see more of each other. Stay in touch now, Earl, y'hear?"

Earl James heard the click of the President hanging up. He sat on the bed, absorbing the hand which fate had dealt him.

Mrs. James took one look at her husband and said, "I can tell from your expression that that bastard Williams is using you again to do his dirty work for him, huh, honey?"

The former President replaced the now-useless wool shirt back on its hanger and said nothing.

The White House counselor who had placed the call to the former President placed another call from a secure phone in his briefcase. "Eagle One, this is Casa Blanca."

Colonel Partridge picked up his phone. "Eagle One here, Casa Blanca. How did it go?"

"Just great, sir. Former President James will indeed be up here in Washington at the NAS when the alien landing is hap-pening in New Mexico. And I got President Williams to think it was his own idea to have Earl James present the Report."

"Casa Blanca, you're a real asset to the cause."

"Glad to be of help, Colonel. Just keep me in mind for a good position when it's time for the power shift."

"Will do." Partridge hung up and sat back satisfied. "One more down," he said to no one in particular.

An hour out of Oracle, Maguire noticed that a blue sedan had been following his car since leaving the Dents' house. It was keeping exactly a mile behind. He turned to Catalina. "I think we've got a tail." He accelerated to 75 mph and watched as the distant sedan speeded up. Maguire pressed the accelerator down until he was going 95. Still the sedan kept up. He slowed down to the posted limit, and within seconds the sedan slowed and kept pace. When he reached the junction of Interstate 10 to Lordsburg and Interstate 19 to the Mexican border, Maguire took I-19. He proceeded at a leisurely pace until he saw the one-mile warning for the exit to the tiny hamlet of Sahuarita. He waited until a semi-truck was slowly passing another, creating a rolling block of both freeway lanes behind him and obscuring the blue sedan's view. He accelerated to top speed, then exited at the freeway exit, braking all the way down the off-ramp. He headed east from the freeway, barely slowing down as he passed through Sahuarita. Fourteen minutes later, he had covered the eighteen miles to reconnect with I-10 eastbound towards Lordsburg.

Catalina had been keeping watch out the rear window the whole ride. "I think we lost him, Roger. No sign of that blue car anywhere."

"Great! Whoever that was probably figured we were headed for Mexico." He pulled over by the on-ramp and said, "Your turn, Barb. I need a break." He grinned and added, "My nerves are shot. My driving back there scared even me."

She gave him a mischievous grin. "Your driving *always* scares me."

Catalina was enjoying her turn behind the wheel. They were passing through the scenic jumbled-boulder landscape of southeastern Arizona's Little Dragoon Mountains.

Maguire looked up from a map he was reading. "Another hour and we'll be at the New Mexico line. Fifteen minutes beyond there we'll be in Lordsburg. It isn't that big. We should be in a good position to spot the Project Epiphany Contact Team.

They'll *have* to pass through Lordsburg to get to the Landing site. That's the only road in."

"The Landing isn't until the day after tomorrow. Where are we going to stay tonight?"

"I saw a billboard back there that said the Best Western Inn in Lordsburg is the nicest motel in the area. Given how God-forsaken it looks up ahead, maybe it's the *only* motel in Lordsburg." He chuckled then looked at Catalina. Her mouth remained set. "Getting nervous, Barb?"

"A little. I feel as though we're heading into a combat zone. I don't want to be sliced in two by a laser. I want to live to see Jason get married, and have a chance to hold some grandchild on my knee."

"Time to call down that psychic protection you're so famous for," Maguire replied, with just a touch of gentle irony. "Look. I'm just as anxious as you are not to get killed. We'll take full precautions. We'll be near the Landing site two days early, so we can reconnoiter and see if any troops are around."

"Just the same, I'm getting a prickly feeling about what we're headed into. And that *bugs* me! I wanted to feel joyful about going to meet with Arica and her people. But I'm feeling afraid of attack."

"I know what you mean. It's those damn humans. They always seem able to mess up even the most transcendent event."

"Very funny, Doctor Maguire." Catalina's grim mouth yielded to the slightest hint of a smile.

When Catalina reached the state highway 339 turn-off, Maguire had her take the exit and head south towards Cloverdale. He wanted to reconnoiter the landing zone. A half-mile down 339, Catalina pulled off to the side and stopped for a restroom break and to switch drivers. As Maguire walked around to the driver's side, he spotted heavy traffic leaving the Interstate and headed his way. He quickly got behind the wheel and pretended to be dozing, peering out the window through barely open eyes. A convoy came roaring by, looking strangely out of place on this remote two-lane road that dead-ended near the Mexico border. Maguire counted three desert-camouflage humvees, followed by four white tractor-trailer trucks with "Science Applications International Corporation" stenciled on their doors. After these came two heavy lowboy trailer rigs, one carrying armored personnel carriers, and the other carrying a huge D-9 tractor with a desert camouflage paint job. Bringing up the rear of the convoy were five all-black Land Rovers with no insignia. Each Land Rover carried six heavily-armed men wearing all-black jumpsuits, black watch caps and camouflage face paint.

When Catalina returned to the car, Maguire said, "You missed the parade."

"I heard something while I was out there behind the bushes. What was it?"

"Well, the *good* news is we don't have to drive any farther. We've found JANUS's welcoming committee."

"What do you mean?"

"I mean the convoy that went past here appears to have enough special forces, equipment and firepower to take over a whole town."

"And I *know* you're going to tell me the *bad* news next."

"I just did."

The lobby of the Lordsburg Best Western Inn was almost empty, as Maguire and Catalina checked in. When the manager pointed out the way to their room, Maguire looked around and spotted a familiar deeply-tanned figure on an upstairs balcony, turning around and entering a room. Maguire and Catalina raced up the stairs, leaving their luggage next to the bewildered manager. They knocked on Katoya's door.

The Hopi elder opened the door with a blank expression. "Do I know you?"

Maguire was taken aback. Had JANUS gotten to Katoya too, so that he was pretending he didn't know them? Then he spotted the slight crinkle that formed around Katoya's eyes, whenever he was putting a fast one over on a *bahana*. "Grandfather, you old rascal. Always trying to see if we're awake."

The Hopi elder answered in movie-Indian pidgin English. "Many moons no see white eyes as ugly as you. And stray dog next to you heap ugly, too."

Catalina bristled until Maguire nudged her, then she broke into a smile. Katoya invited them inside.

"Grandfather, did you ask Dr. Bowen if we can join with the Contact Team?" Maguire asked.

"No, I did not. Roscoe Dent beat me to it. Dr. Bowen will ask the rest of the Team about it at a meeting tonight. You can come to the meeting as observers. You'll be the first thing we discuss."

"That's great," Catalina exclaimed. "And now we've got fresh news for the Team."

"Yes," Maguire chimed in, "a huge military contingent was headed out towards the Landing site about a half-hour ago. They looked heavily armed, and appeared to be hauling in some exotic large weapons."

Katoya frowned. "I will call Dr. Bowen. I'm sure he'll want to hear what you have learned."

Outside, the evening air was still and cool. Millions of stars twinkled brilliantly in the cloudless night sky. The mood in Robert Bowen's hotel room was a mixture of warmth and seriousness, as old friends greeted one another and discussed the upcoming extraterrestrial landing.

At precisely 8:30 p.m., Dr. Bowen called the Contact Team meeting to order. He introduced Maguire and Catalina as the first order of business. Timothy Katoya presented Maguire and Catalina's request to join up with the Contact Team. Katoya noted that Spirit had shown him in vision that they were to be at the Landing. Major Dent related how Maguire and Catalina had visited him previously to pass on Arica's warning. He turned to Catalina, who then shared with the group the details of her earlier psychic vision about the landing UFO coming under fire from laser beam weapons. She told about Arica's appearance at Bandelier, and the extraterrestrial's warning that not only would the UFO be shot at, but that the Team members would also come under fire.

Roscoe Dent made a motion. The vote was unanimous that they be allowed to join the Contact Team. Maguire followed up with a report of the heavily-armed military convoy he spotted earlier in the day, headed towards the landing zone. The mood in the room grew grim at this news.

Madame Salaam spoke up voicing the thoughts of many. "Dr. Bowen, is it sensible for us to go ahead with our plan to be at the Landing? It appears that we will almost certainly come under military attack."

Dr. Leonard Spruance spoke up. "I for one have been waiting for many years to meet again with our extraterrestrial cousins in the flesh. If I have to die doing that, well, I'm getting older now. At least I will die pursuing my life's work."

"Can I break in here?" Roscoe Dent stood up and faced the others. "This is as good a point as any to let you in on what I've been doing, since Dr. Maguire and Barbara paid me a visit two days ago with news about the attack. First, I informed Dr. Bowen, of course. Since then, I've been spending a lot of time on the phone, trying to reach trusted old friends in intelligence and Special Forces. I've been calling in every favor owed me by these old friends. Frankly, it's been hard for them to believe that an official extraterrestrial landing is happening. Then it's been even harder for them to believe that there is a rogue unit like JANUS, possessing Star Wars weapons no less, and which would fire on an extraterrestrial craft without Presidential authorization. Others felt that if some clandestine unit is going to fire on a UFO, then that unit must have secret Presidential authorization that I don't know about."

"Have you had any success in convincing anyone that the attack threat is real?" Dr. Bowen asked.

"Well, I think there may be one possibility," Dent replied. "I reached Admiral MacKenzie, who heads the Navy Seals Team Six program. I tried to do a lot of convincing. He sounded sympathetic, but he thought that the timetable for doing something by the day after tomorrow was unrealistic. Too much red tape. He said he'd try to do what he could. I'm afraid he's the only one I reached who even took me seriously."

"So, where does that leave us?" Dr. Virtanen asked.

"I'm afraid I can't tell you for sure. If Admiral MacKenzie can cut through the red tape, we may have some assistance. Otherwise, we're on our own."

"One thing we know for sure," Maguire said, "JANUS's troops are out there near the landing site, digging in with their weapons."

"Roscoe, have you got any ideas how we can get to the landing zone without getting shot?" Dr. Bowen asked.

"To the landing zone, no," Major Dent replied. "But I think we might be able to get as close as we can, and then hope that help arrives in time, so we can move in closer."

Major Dent outlined a strategy of stealthy approach the following night to a position a mile away from the landing site, which had some ground cover. After digging in, the Contact Team would need to stay in place until the extraterrestrial craft came. And then, if friendly forces arrived in time, the Team could approach the landing site under their protection.

Dent would head a small contingent to drive down in the morning to El Paso and buy desert-camo jumpsuits and face hoods for everyone. The suits would then be lined with sewn-in aluminum-foil, to hold in body heat and prevent detection by infrared scanners. He told them they wouldn't be able to use any heat near the landing zone, so they'd be eating cold MRE's, the modern field-rations. Lying still in the winter desert for 24-36 hours would be extremely difficult. And there would be no guarantee that, despite all these precautions, the JANUS troops might not find them anyway and kill them.

As Major Dent sat down, Dr. Bowen stood up. "So, on that cheery note, we need to know who is still willing to be on the Contact Team. I'm still committed. How about the rest of you? Let's go around the room. Mme. Salaam?"

"As the wife of the Secretary-General, I learned long ago that risk came with my position. I will go."

"Dr. Virtanen?"

"My ancestors were Vikings. I am not going to let some criminals in military uniforms keep me from meeting my cosmic brothers and sisters."

"Elder Katoya?"

"The Star Nations long ago foretold that they would return during a time of great human turmoil. I will be there when they land."

"Elder Morning Star?"

"The Lakota have generations of experience dealing with *wasicu* treachery. Star Nation medicine is stronger than a few paleface soldiers. I'm still on the Team, as I promised the medicine men who sent me."

"Dr. Spruance?"

"As I said earlier, at my age, death holds few terrors. I'm still committed to the Landing. Let's not forget that our ET friends will be aware that these JANUS troops are waiting."

"Major Dent?"

"Hell, pardon my French, ladies, I'm going!"

"Dr. Maguire?"

"Yes."

"Ms. Catalina?"

"I'm going. Can I say something else, Dr. Bowen?"

"Of course."

"I hope we can all join in prayer and meditation before we go out there. If we have spiritual power with us, we will be all right."

"My Ojibwa sister is correct," Katoya added. "Tomorrow I will conduct a sweat lodge ceremony with my brother, George Morning Star. It will be a time of fasting, meditation, personal sacrifice and prayer for protection. Everyone is welcome."

"There is great power in the Stone People Lodge," Morning Star added. "Tomorrow I will pray that Tunkashila, Grandfather, Maka Unce, Grandmother Earth, and the Thunder Beings come into the Lodge and bring protection for us."

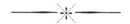

Chapter 15

THE camouflaged entrance door of JANUS's Corey Peak complex swung aside to reveal the inky blackness of night. A charcoal-black, unmarked Apache helicopter flew out the entrance way and headed southeast. After flying several hours and getting low on fuel, the chopper set down beside the refueling facility at Tucson's Davis-Monthan Air Force Base. Colonel Partridge flashed credentials at the airman in charge, identifying himself as "National Reconnaissance Organization/Air Force Lt. General James Pratt." Refueling completed and airborne again in minutes, Partridge pointed the Apache southeast towards Cloverdale and the extraterrestrial landing site. Far behind the Apache, a camouflaged Cobra helicopter kept pace from a safe distance. Ed Sodoma had no interest in being shot down, after seeing what Partridge had done to those poor fools in the F-111.

As the Apache flew over Cloverdale, the sun was just rising over the Animas Mountains. Within moments Partridge made radio contact with the JANUS Special Operations unit, which was at the foot of San Luis Pass, dug in around the dry lake bed. Partridge set the Apache down on the edge of the hard sand lake bed. There he was met by the Special Operations officer in charge, Major Ivan Lear.

In the national forest ten miles to the west, Ed Sodoma set his chopper down on the shoulder of a peak. There he knew he would have line-of-sight view of Colonel Partridge's helicopter.

Major Lear drove Partridge to the underground command bunker. Along the way, the Colonel grilled Lear on the state of preparations. The Major assured him that a roadblock had been thrown up at State Highway 338, so that no one could come into the landing zone. The dug-in and camouflaged electro-magnetic-pulse cannons and argon battle lasers were in strategic placement around the landing site. A concealed temporary bunker had been constructed underground to hold the troop cars. Special Forces troops ringed the landing site in foxholes. Each commando was covered under a tarpaulin topped with sand, so that only a short, sand-colored breathing tube showed above the desert surface. Each was linked by in-helmet radio to the underground command bunker. In the center of the dry lake bed landing zone lay a shallow-buried tactical neutron weapon. It was capable, if needed, of taking out every living life form in a one-mile radius. If other weapons only disabled the soon-to-land UFO, and the extraterrestrial emissaries inside decided to hole up and refuse to come out, the JANUS Special Operations unit could withdraw a safe distance away and eliminate those aliens. All the large vehicles had been driven out to remote Clanton Canyon, deep within nearby Coronado National Forest. The landing site now appeared to be just undisturbed desert.

When Major Lear had completed his run-down of completed preparations, Colonel Partridge grunted his approval. Then he told Lear to take his Apache and fly it from the landing site over to the canyon where the large vehicles were stored. With that, Partridge switched uniforms with the Major, relieved him of duty, and took over command of Operation Gray Matter.

Major Lear took off in Partridge's Apache and headed for the Clanton Canyon vehicle storage site. As the helicopter headed northwest, Ed Sodoma was confused. He had used the code-breaking radio in his Cobra to listen in on Partridge's radio conversation with the Special Operations commander. He knew that for Partridge to have left the safety of his Corey Peak stronghold, he must have considered the alien landing site a top priority mission. Why would Partridge leave so soon after arriving? As the Apache sped by to the north, Sodoma stopped puzzling and started up his Cobra to follow him.

After Major Lear steered the helicopter into the draw leading into winding Clanton Canyon, he lowered altitude and flew close to the canyon floor. Behind him Sodoma closed the distance separating the two helicopters to within a mile. Sodoma turned on his Cobra's ultrasonic tracking gear. He did not want to lose the Apache in the twists and turns of the canyon.

A control panel detection light in the Apache lit up, indicating to Major Lear that his helicopter was being tracked. The Major radioed a coded warning to the JANUS troops guarding the vehicle storage site in the canyon. Then he deliberately flew over and past the vehicle compound, and continued up the canyon. Hot in pursuit, Sodoma saw the vehicle compound coming up ahead too late. He desperately tried to stop and reverse his Cobra in the narrow canyon. As he did, two surface-to-air missiles streaked upward from the compound. Ed Sodoma's high-risk career ended, as his Cobra, enveloped in a ruddy orange fireball, fell from the sky.

At the landing zone bunker's communications station, Colonel Partridge barked into the microphone with accustomed authority. "Attention, all personnel! This is Colonel Partridge speaking. Major Lear has been relieved of command. I am now in charge of Operation Gray Matter's strike force. Sometime in the next 36 hours, 'Charlie' will be coming in from space and landing here. NRO will give us up to several minutes' warning of Charlie's approach. This is the first phase of Charlie's invasion of Earth. Understand, we have to stop him here, or the whole world will be lost. If you don't want your women and children to live under alien rule, here is where we stop the aliens. We are about to have the most serious enemy invasion in military history, starting here with a small scout party. We also have a group of human traitors coming to this site to *welcome* these alien invaders. These humans are a mix of foreigners and so-called Americans, who call themselves "Project Epiphany." Because it is too complicated to give their descriptions, you have standing orders to shoot *anybody* you see who is not in Special Operations uniform. Immediately shallow-bury any bodies. We need to keep the site sanitized and looking natural, so Charlie will fall into our trap. When he gets down within 500 meters of the Landing Zone, I will give the order to fire our EMP and laser weapons at his ship. After Charlie's ship falls on to the LZ, you will emerge from hiding and surround his spacecraft. If anyone emerges from Charlie's craft, shoot to kill. If no one comes out of his ship, I will order a boarding party to forcibly enter the ship and clean out any alien vermin inside. We have special Presidential National Security authorization to use deadly fire. You have blanket amnesty for any firing on non-combatants, aliens and civilians. Any questions?"

The communications link was silent except for the faint electronic hiss of background noise.

"Good. Then everybody lock and load. Charlie may try to fool us and come in early. You are all on red alert for the next 36 hours. Keep your radios on stand-by. And remember, your country is counting on you to exterminate this invading menace *and* the human traitors who are working with it. This is Colonel Partridge, signing off."

Earlier in the day, Roscoe Dent had done some research on the approach to the landing zone by chatting with a ranger at Coronado National Forest Headquarters. Dent learned that there was a military roadblock set up on the road, ten miles north of Cloverdale. The ranger said that she had been told that there was some kind of special training exercise going on that involved live ammunition fire, and that everyone, including forest rangers, was to stay out of the area until further notice.

When Dent thanked the ranger for the information, she turned towards him in a confidential whisper and said, "Frankly, Mr. Dent, the officer in charge of that military operation down there was a real jerk. He swore at my boss when he asked what they were doing, and told him to keep clear if he knew what was good for him."

Winter solstice was less than a month away. Night had fallen early in southwestern New Mexico. Fifty miles south of Lordsburg, the Contact Team's pair of four-wheel-drive vehicles left Highway 338 a little ways before the JANUS road block. The Team's drivers stopped, turned off their headlights, and put on war-surplus night vision goggles. Then they first headed west, then south, then east on a circuitous route of dirt roads and detours. They traveled around and below Cloverdale, carefully keeping their distance from the roadblock. Two hours later they arrived at a position up against the Animas Mountains, three miles south of the landing zone. The Team had agreed this was as close as they dared get to the LZ. Dark stratus clouds almost totally blocked the full moon. A bitter wind had sprung up. It was cold enough to snow.

Once the Team was in position, Katoya and Morning Star sent up prayers that the Star People would find them at this new location. Catalina sent out telepathic messages to Arica, advising her of the JANUS ambush, and mentally picturing for the extraterrestrials the Team's revised position.

The November night cold made the Team members shiver, as they dug into the ground to make entrenchments in which to hide. Flurries of snow flakes fell from the skies intermittently, creating a light dusting on the mesquite and cactus. Catalina and Maguire decided to make a common entrenchment. Catalina commented wryly to the others that her entombment might as well be romantic. When everyone's foxhole was completed, Roscoe Dent covered the roof of everyone else's position with sand. Then he slipped into his own entrenchment, reached out with one arm, and covered himself. The inky blackness of the sky outside matched the earthen darkness surrounding the Contact Team member, as each kept solitary vigil in anxious silence.

Fifty miles above the Earth, a shiny, 150-meter-wide metallic disc hovered above the point where Arizona, New Mexico, and the Mexican states of Sonora and Chihuahua came together. Staring at the disc's command center viewing screen were the representative from the Zeta systems, Arica, as well as the representatives from the Sirius and the Pleiades systems, and a non-corporeal luminous figure who was a member of the Interstellar Federation Council. These four were examining a detailed image of the terrain below. The image showed the Sonoran Desert landscape of the landing zone at the foot of the Animas Mountains illuminated by the midday sun.

"It is beautiful, is it not?" Arica commented telepathically. Then she added, "I have received information from my human contact, Barbara Catalina, that the Contact Team is in position south of the zone we had identified for the landing and meeting. Furthermore, she advised that a military group, not sanctioned by either their United States government nor their United Nations, is lying in ambush to attack us at the original landing site."

"Careful attention to various of our sensors makes it clear that extreme-voltage weapons are present on the ground," the Sirius representative telepathically replied dryly, nodding at a nearby instrument panel. "Further indication of human treachery is a sensor reading I see which is detecting ionizing radiation of the kind characteristic of one of their crude fusion weapons."

"It is hostility and duplicity such as that which make some of my people wonder whether these Earth persons *are* truly ready for interstellar contact," the Pleiades representative agreed.

They turned to the Federation representative, who paused some moments. Finally he commented. "All, even the renegade human soldiers lying in ambush for us, are children of the Supreme Source of consciousness. We must not let the evil doing of some humans become the occasion for us to ignore the fine development of many others. If a child is not allowed to fall, how will the child learn to walk? It is time for the Earth people to have an opportunity to decide about cosmic citizenship. We cannot put out an invitation to them to meet, and then withdraw it because of those few who are allowing fear and aggression to blind them. It is time to descend and honor our commitment to letting this stage of contact happen. Do you all agree?"

One by one, the other representatives telepathed their assent. The disc slipped down 50 miles through the atmosphere, then hovered at 5000 feet above the ground. The Sirius representative alerted the crew to set shielding against electromagnetic-pulse, laser, plasmoid, particle-beam, projectile and nuclear attacks. Appropriate neutralization counter-measures were authorized. Then the crew was ordered to descend the rest of the way.

A yellow Sonoran Desert scorpion was retreating from the noonday sunlight. Tail held high, it scuttled towards the cover formed under the curled edge of a tarpaulin flap, where the sand had been blown away by the intermittent strong gusts of wind. Underneath the tarp, Dr. Leena Virtanen lay hot and sweating. The sand edge around the tarp flap gave way. The arachnid slid down the edge of the entrenchment and dropped onto Dr. Virtanen's face.

With a shout she stood up, knocking the cover off her foxhole as she desperately brushed away the scorpion.

"Freeze!" A JANUS soldier on patrol leveled his automatic weapon at her. The commando radioed for back-up. Within minutes three carloads of Special Operations troops arrived and fanned out. Stabbing the ground with their bayonets, they quickly located the entrenchments where the other Contact Team members lay hidden. Reached by radio at his bunker, Colonel Partridge gave orders to tie the Team up, interrogate them, and then bring them in for later disposal. Partridge's attention had been divided. He had been focused on the printed message emitting from his de-encryption printer. The National Reconnaissance Organization was advising that an "anomalous target," NRO–speak for a UFO, had been spotted on their radars descending from space right over his location. They also advised that additional "targets" had been spotted thirty kilometers to the southwest and to the northwest. Partridge got on the com-link and barked an alert to all gunners and troops.

Out of a partial cloud cover of stratus threatening to snow, the huge metallic disc lowered to a height of 300 feet and hovered right over the middle of the dry lake bed landing zone.

Partridge bawled into the microphone, "Fire! Fire at will!"

Camouflage netting was ripped aside. Argon battle lasers shot murderous photon beams at the saucer. EMP cannons let loose with volleys of unbelievably powerful electromagnetic pulses. The disc became surrounded with a faint pastel-violet high-voltage plasma corona.

"The target is overloading, sir!" a jubilant EMP cannon gunner shouted over the radio to Partridge. "Just you wait. In a moment, their drive is going to fail and they'll drop like a rock! Eee-hah!"

The Colonel barked back, "Take no chances! Keep firing!"

The disc tilted slightly to one side. Then a brilliant white beam emitted towards the ground. An EMP cannon emplacement instantly vaporized. Other beams shot out of the disc, and vaporized the remaining laser and EMP cannon positions. Complete panic overtook the remaining landing site troops. They dropped their weapons and sprinted towards the safety of the underground command bunker.

Partridge snarled into the microphone. "Get back to your positions, you gutless cowards! Keep firing at them! Use grenade launchers, anything!" Ignoring his commands, the troops piled into the bunker and huddled under furniture for protection. Then the shiny disc rose slowly back into the sky in a stately withdrawal.

Three miles to the south, the JANUS patrol group had finished their field interrogation of the Contact Team. They were just finishing loading the prisoners into their vehicles, when one of the soldiers pointed towards the south and shouted. The other Special Operations troops looked up to see seven silent black Apache helicopters swooping over and down a nearby ridge, and fanning out to surround the JANUS troops. Dozens of Navy SEALS poured out of the choppers, wearing their trademark all-black jumpsuits with the Team Six insignia, body armor and watch caps. They sprinted to surround the JANUS patrol group, pointing their MP-5 machine guns at them. A burly man in a Navy admiral's uniform stepped down from the lead Apache. He stood and faced the JANUS troops and held up a document.

"I am Admiral Malcolm MacKenzie, United States Navy, here under special authorization from the Joint Chiefs of Staff. You are no longer under the authority of Colonel Partridge. You are all under arrest for violation of the National Security Act and other statutes. You will each be furnished with a defense lawyer pursuant to the Uniform Code of Military Justice. You are to surrender immediately. If you resist, or if you harm United Nations First Lady Salaam or any other of your prisoners, you will all be shot. Drop your weapons! NOW!"

The stunned JANUS troops stood motionless as statues. The SEALS fanned out behind every JANUS soldier, relieved each of his weapons, and handcuffed him. Other SEALS helped the Contact Team out of the vehicles and untied them. Then the Admiral commandeered one of the JANUS soldiers' radios.

"Colonel Partridge, this is Admiral Malcolm MacKenzie."
There was an excruciatingly long delay. Then a strangely calm voice come over the radio.

"Colonel Partridge here, Admiral."

"Colonel, SEALS Team Six has captured your troops at the Contact Team's position here. Another SEAL group has taken control of your forces in the canyon where your vehicles were stored. I am here by emergency authorization from the Joint Chiefs of Staff and the Director of Central Intelligence. You are under arrest by order of the JCS. You and your remaining men are to stack your weapons in one pile, line up at the edge of the dry lake and surrender. If you resist, I am authorized to use deadly force. We will be up to your position in our Apaches in two minutes. Colonel, do you surrender?"

"Surrender? Admiral, surrender is a military option I have never given consideration to in my entire military career. I'm hardly going to start now."

"Colonel, I *urge* you. Avoid unnecessary bloodshed. You and your men surrender *now*! Do I have your commitment to that?"

"Admiral, with all due respect, sir, fuck you!" With that Partridge reached over to an electronic assembly at his feet and punched in a code.

The SEALS, Contact Team and JANUS prisoners threw themselves to the ground as a blinding flash occurred three miles to the north. A half-second later, the flash was followed by a cataclysmic roar which shook the ground.

"My God!" Admiral MacKenzie muttered, "the fool went nuclear."

The Admiral ordered everyone into the helicopters for an immediate evacuation of the area. The extraterrestrial Landing, if it was still going to occur, was certainly not going to happen here. The seven Apaches proceeded upwind to the west for 12 miles, and set down safely behind the protective shield of the Guadalupe Mountains. Some SEALS quickly set up a temporary camp, while others ringed the area with patrols. The Contact Team gathered in the central bivouac area and began to unwind. Maguire walked over to connect with Catalina, whom he found crouched down a little ways away from the camp trying to tune in psychically to Arica.

One chopper with a volunteer crew headed back to do a stand-off reconnaissance of the nuclear-blasted original landing site. Admiral MacKenzie got on a radiation-shielded radio linked to the emergency MILSTAR communication system and notified the Chairman of the Joint Chiefs about the situation.

As he finished his report, Catalina walked up to him and said, "The extraterrestrial ship is coming, sir."

At almost the same moment a SEAL scout on a ridge above the camp shouted into his radio, "In-coming alien craft, Admiral."

A large stately disc descended from almost straight overhead to an elevation fifty feet above the ground. A faint, almost subaudible hum came from the underside of the ship. The SEAL scouts broke discipline to stand and gape at the enormous, 450-foot-wide saucer. Catalina placed her fingertips to her forehead as she received a telepathic message from Arica, inquiring if the Contact Team was ready. After checking with Dr. Bowen, she mentally replied that they were. The silvery craft then lowered the rest of the way to the ground.

Admiral MacKenzie ordered SEALS commandos back to full alert. He had them form a protective perimeter 200 meters out from the craft, facing outward, weapons ready. Inside the perimeter, the Contact Team, now expanded to nine including Maguire and Catalina, lined themselves up in a row facing the disc. The Team members tried to compose themselves as they waited for the extraterrestrials' next step.

After a minute, a doorway appeared in the side of the craft which was facing the Team. A ramp extended from the base of the doorway to the ground. The pale-skinned Arica walked slowly down the ramp and out into the afternoon sunlight of Earth. She looked diminutive next to the six-foot-tall Sirius systems ambassador who followed her down the ramp. The Sirian was an angular figure with greenish skin wearing a stately white robe. They both were dwarfed by the over seven-foot-tall Pleiades systems representative, a well-proportioned, muscular humanoid figure in a close-fitting blue tunic. Last to emerge was the Federation Council member, a short, rotund, luminous Buddha-like presence in a translucent white gown, who seemed to float down the ramp. At the foot of the ramp, the four extraterrestrial representatives arrayed themselves in a slight crescent facing the Contact Team.

The Pleiades representative raised his hand, palm outward, in a salutation gesture. Each of the Contact Team members heard in their head a resonant masculine voice with no discernible accent.

"We bid you greetings, citizen representatives of Earth. We are official representatives from a federation of inhabited star systems in this sector of the galaxy. To my left are the representatives from the Zeta and Sirius systems. To my right is the honorable Member of the Interstellar Federation Council, our supreme governing body."

Dr. Bowen took a small step forward. On behalf of the Team he audibly replied, "Welcome to Earth. We extend greetings to you on behalf of peace-loving peoples from around this planet. Please forgive the regrettable violence that occurred at the original landing site. Those renegades do not represent the vast majority of us Earth people."

"We are aware of that," the Pleiades representative responded telepathically. "Otherwise we would not have followed through with this landing and meeting. We have some important messages for you. We request that you pass these messages on to your world government."

Leila Salaam spoke up. "Do you mean the United Nations?"

"Whatever you Earth peoples consider your world government is what we mean," the Pleiades representative replied dryly.

A mature feminine voice entered the Contact Team's heads next. The Sirius representative held up all four long fingers of her left hand and three of the fingers of her right hand. "We have seven messages. You must listen carefully and remember them all.

"Your first message is that Earth is dying. The Terran ecology is in a state of middle-stage systemic collapse. It appears to many human scientists and government leaders that the situation is not too bad, but they are wrong. Over the next few years, if radical changes are not made in human practices harming the environment, there will be a cascading cumulative effect which will resemble what you humans might call an ecological meltdown. For example, the sea is losing its ability to sustain plankton, which form the basis for the oceanic food chain. The seasonal loss of radiation-shielding, which you call the Antarctic Ozone Hole, is actually occurring in several areas. These are growing in size continually. Eventually ultraviolet radiation will eliminate many food plants. All these catastrophes will result in numerous species die-offs, including even humans. Your agricultural soils in many areas are laden with chemicals which your scientists do not label toxic, but which are. These chemicals are creating many wasting illnesses and mutations. There are groups of Earth scientists who know all these things. If humans do not listen to their warnings, and to ours, then the human race will not survive.

"Your second message is that very serious hazardous events are going to occur over the next several years, starting this year. Earth will experience many earthquakes, escalating in severity to 9 and 10 on your magnitude scale and well beyond. There will be a widespread occurrence of old volcanoes erupting anew, and new ones forming where there were no volcanoes before. In many cases these earth movements will cause tidal waves of a size not seen before. There will also be subsidence of land masses in many places. In some cases, whole countries will disappear under the advancing sea. New human epidemic diseases of unprecedented virulence will emerge, taking many lives. AIDS and the recent outbreak of Pneumonic Hemorrhagic Fever are just beginning examples of this. The combined effect of the ecological damage and these cataclysms will cause great shifts in climates. Fertile lands will become desert. Heavy rainfall will occur where it never has before, and weather changes will become more extreme. These events will cause a significant proportion of the Earth's human population to die off. We are willing to help, but we have foreseen that many humans will fear or ignore us and thus reject our help."

The Sirius emissary held up three fingers. "The third message is that all humans need to attune to what you call metaphysical aspects of reality. A few examples. There are four dimensions of space-time which your conventional science currently accepts. It would be an improvement if you accepted even the twelve dimensions that a few of your advanced theoreticians have proposed, although there are more than twelve dimensions. You cannot understand us and our presence across hyper-dimensional space with your present crude attachment to only visible physical phenomena.

"Also, time, as your industrialized cultures understand it, is an illusion. Some members of our Federation live in what you would consider your past or your future time, yet they are available to make contact with you in the present.

"Another area which your materialistic cultures do not recognize is that thought is 'real.' Thought can cause things to happen. Thought helps create reality. If your world and ours are to truly meet, you must expand your understanding of reality in these and other areas."

The Contact Team members heard the resonant masculine voice of the Pleiades representative next. "Our fourth message deals with spirituality. What we have to say about this matter will be very difficult for many humans to accept. The Federation respects the spiritual strivings of most humans. However, many humans have allowed the structured forms of official religions to limit their understanding of true spirituality. Every conscious being in the Universe has a right to complete spiritual attainment. Because of this, we wish to share with you some of our spiritual understanding. What you call God is what we know as the Supreme Source of everything, and which is embedded in everything and in all processes. The closest human expression for this is 'truth-consciousness.' Truth-consciousness is everywhere. It is that which makes everything what it is, and integrates everything with everything else in the greater Whole. This truth-consciousness understands itself through the many levels of consciousness present in nature and underlying all reality. It extends from what you call inanimate objects to the most highly evolved sentient and intelligent beings, who no longer operate through a physical body. We respect the intelligent spark of this truth-consciousness in each human. It is that which makes us spiritual equals. And it is on *that* level of spiritual equality that we come here as your brothers and sisters, beings who share your respect for the divine.

"Our fifth message will be no surprise to some of your government officials and military leaders, but it will present some concern to certain fearful humans. Over the millennia, there have been limited contacts with humans by some extraterrestrials in order to obtain reproductive material. The purpose has been to help create hybrid individuals. There have been a number of important reasons for this, which we will not go into detail about now. Suffice to say that there are thousands of alternatively-developed persons whom you would call hybrids. Some are residing in ships out in space, or on our home planets. Several hundreds live on Earth, mostly in temporary underground shelter, awaiting the day when humans are prepared to accept extraterrestrial presence and make them welcome on the surface. Some other few hundreds are living and walking about in your midst, undetected because of their close resemblance to you. We wish to present a request to your Earth government soon to permit these resident hybrids to emerge from hiding and live among you as fellow citizens. In return we will be prepared to accept certain numbers of Earth volunteers to take up residence on our planets. In both these ways, our understanding of each other can increase. We ask that, as a token of good faith, the United States government release to us the extraterrestrial individual known to them as EBE, when the ambassadors land again on February 15."

A red-headed SEAL sentry who was scanning the skies to the south halted suddenly, and spoke into his shoulder-mounted radio an urgent message for Admiral MacKenzie. The Admiral was standing a discreet fifteen yards behind the Contact Team, carefully focusing his attention on the telepathic discussion. His voice-activated radio picked up the sentry's alert.

"Admiral, there are incoming aircraft from the south!"

MacKenzie sprinted up to the top of the slight rise where the sentry was standing over a portable radar screen. The screen was being fed images from a stand-off AWACS plane five miles up and twenty miles to the west.

"Look, Admiral! Two military jets coming in fast! They're about 120 kilometers to the south. AWACS computers make them out to be F-5s."

MacKenzie got on the com-link to the AWACS plane above, and requested identification of whose jets those were. Moments later the AWACS reported that radio contact had been established with the jets' lead pilot. The F-5s had been identified as Mexican Air Force. They had been sent out to investigate the nuclear explosion on the northern Mexico border. MacKenzie had the AWACS patch him through on an emergency channel to the Chairman of the Joint Chiefs of Staff. The Admiral urgently requested the JCS to contact the Mexican Air Force Secretary to call the fighters off in the interest of not creating an interstellar incident.

The F-5s had closed to within four miles of the landing site, when suddenly they veered off to the left. Completing their turns, the F-5s headed back south, kicking in their afterburners as they departed, sending the rumble of artificial thunder across the desert landscape.

The Pleiades representative glanced in the direction of the jet sound for a moment, then nodded to Arica. Her sweet feminine voice came across telepathically to the Team. "I will present the sixth message. It is my honor to inform you that the member worlds which make up the Interstellar Federation have decided to offer Earth membership in the Federation, that is, provided certain things happen. The Earth must be able to speak to the Federation with one voice. And your Earth government must make a formal request to receive member-planet status in the Federation. But there are preconditions to membership. The peoples of the Earth must renounce and destroy all their nuclear weapons. The Earth must have in place an effective global conflict-resolution mechanism, so that war is eliminated. The Earth government must guarantee the safety of all authorized extraterrestrial visitors to Earth. When these conditions are met, membership in the Interstellar Federation can occur.

"And now, the final message will be presented by the honorable Council Member of the Interstellar Federation."

The short, rotund luminous figure spoke up telepathically. "This seventh and last message must be passed on to all of the Earth's leaders. We, the official representatives of the Interstellar Federation, request that Earth's government designate its official ambassadors to meet with our ambassadors. We request that Earth's government arrange for television and radio broadcast of this meeting worldwide. At this meeting the Federation ambassadors will present the formal invitation to join the Federation and to initiate formal cultural exchange. They will also present our formal request for permission for the establishment of a surface colony for hybrids, and for a guarantee of safety for extraterrestrials visiting Earth. This will be Earth's opportunity to formally accept or reject contact with us. This meeting is scheduled for this coming February 15th. We will announce the location later. Make sure that Earth's leaders get this important message."

"Good heavens," Dr. Virtanen exclaimed in disbelief, "February 15th is only two-and-a-half months away. The U.N. will never get itself organized in that short a time."

Madame Salaam spoke up quickly, a defensive tone in her voice. "Esteemed representatives of other solar systems, I will personally bring your messages tomorrow to my husband, the United Nations Secretary-General. You can rest assured that I will *insist* that he take immediate action. I only hope that I don't forget anything of what you have said."

George Morning Star turned to Madame Salaam and said, "I can repeat all the Star Peoples' messages. I have memorized every word." He added with ironic apologeticness, "We Indians have to be able to do that when we don't know how to read too well."

Dr. Bowen took a step forward and responded to the extraterrestrial ambassadors' final message. "On behalf of the Earth I offer you and your Federation thanks for this opportunity to meet. I can assure you that every member of the Contact Team will exert maximum effort and pressure on our respective leaders to have formal representatives of Earth ready to meet with your ambassadors. We will also pass on your other messages to the world."

Arica bowed slightly and telepathed a reply. "All four of us are grateful for your kind attention and goodwill. We look forward to open and sustained contacts between our worlds. Meanwhile we will be overhead in orbit, watching Earth's progress in meeting the necessary preconditions for open contact. Farewell for now."

The four representatives turned around and went up the ramp into their silvery disc. A few moments later, it rose, shot up into the sky, and rapidly disappeared.

The Contact Team gathered in a small cluster, staring up

at the spot where the UFO disappeared. For a minute they were speechless. Each stood there processing what had just happened. Their reverie was broken by the approach of Admiral MacKenzie.

"I'm sorry to interrupt, ladies and gentlemen, but we need to get you out of here right now for your safety. We don't know whether all the JANUS forces have been captured. In addition, the President radioed me while you were finishing your talk with the alien representatives. He asks that you all come to Washington now. He wants to have you participate in a briefing for the National Security Council tomorrow morning. We will evacuate you out of here now in our helicopters to Holloman Air Force Base east of here. There you will board the Vice-President's plane, Air Force Two, and fly with fighter escort directly to Andrews Air Force Base, Maryland. Air Force Two will have phones on board, so that you can call your families and let them know where you are. At Andrews you will be put up overnight in VIP suites. In the morning you will be airlifted to the White House for the NSC briefing. Can the President count on all of you for cooperation?" Admiral MacKenzie looked in turn at each of them. "Is there anyone who doesn't wish to participate?"

Dr. Virtanen's hand shot up. "Admiral, if I participate in this briefing, will I get in trouble with my Norwegian government? Do you know, that there's a prohibition against a civilian representing her country to a foreign power?"

Admiral MacKenzie smiled. "I can assure you, Dr. Virtanen, that the White House will take care of getting the Norwegian government's approval for you to participate. Consider it done."

"Then count me in," she replied resolutely.

"And the rest of you?" the Admiral asked.

A chorus of affirmative responses came back.

"Fine. Then let's load into the helicopters and clear this area."

The Admiral signaled to the SEAL Team leader, who barked an order into his radio. Instantly the SEALS retreated backwards towards the Apaches in a constricting ring. As the Contact Team were escorted into the choppers by watchful commandos, the rotors on the seven Apaches started revolving. The remaining SEALs clambered aboard briskly. The squadron of Apache helicopters immediately lifted up into the azure New Mexico sky, which was now cloudless except for a few tufts of cirrus. The squadron headed north-northwest at a low elevation, keeping the protective ridges of the Peloncillo Mountains between them and the nuclear horror still roiling to the east.

Timothy Katoya stared out of the helicopter window at the mushroom cloud looming above the eastern ridgeline. He turned to George Morning Star in the seat next to him, and nodded his head toward the window. "The gourd of ashes has shattered and sent up a great cloud of dust into the sky, as was prophesied long ago."

Morning Star nodded. "The *wasicu* are very good at making things which destroy."

"George, I don't look forward to this meeting with the National Security Council tomorrow." Katoya's voice had a worried tone. "Those are the same kind of people who sent secret agents out to the reservation in the 1950s, and warned our clan leaders not to say anything to the whites about the kachinas who come down and visit us."

"Tim, those Washington agents came to the Lakota reservations, too," Morning Star replied. "Our medicine men humored them. We know that Wakan Tanka determines the time that is right for the whites to know about the Star Nations. Not Washington." He spat out the last two words.

Catalina leaned her head on Maguire's shoulder in the half-light at the back of the helicopter. She was emotionally exhausted from all the excitement of the extraterrestrial landing and the strain of almost being killed by the JANUS forces. But she could not sleep. The buzz of excited conversations of the other Contact Team members, and her own racing thoughts about the meeting with the extraterrestrials, precluded sleep. She looked up at Maguire, who was staring ahead deep in thought.

He sensed her looking at him, turned towards her, and smiled. "Care to share your thoughts?"

"Oh, I was thinking what a privilege it was to have met with four representatives from other star systems. And I never knew that Arica was such an important person within her society. When we've met her before, she was so humble that she never mentioned it. Rog, we're really blessed to have been there. What a truly extraordinary experience!"

"Yeah, I know what you mean. But I've been thinking about the huge responsibility of getting the ETs' messages out to the world. I don't have a lot of faith that our meeting with the National Security Council tomorrow will be much help. We're basically just giving them information. They've operated so long in a climate of UFO secrecy that I doubt they would have the guts to issue a press release."

"Don't worry, Rog. We've got a lot of dedicated people on the Contact Team. They're activists. And then there are the ETs. They're bound to open some doors for us." She gave him a wink.

Maguire's serious expression softened. "I suppose you're right." He glanced out the window. "Look, there's White Sands National Monument down there. That means we'll reach Holloman Air Force Base in five minutes. I hope that Air Force Two plane has recliner seats. I'm bushed. I could use some sleep between here and Washington."

"Poor dear. You didn't get much sleep last night, did you?"

"Nope. You know, Barb, people might think you and I were making whoopie because we shared that entrenchment near the Landing site. What a laugh. It was such a cramped hole. If we had tried to move around in there, the whole damn thing would have caved in on us."

Catalina laughed. "I'm *sure* I was going to get naked in a sand pit. Not likely! I might get sand in my, ah, well, never mind."

It was Maguire's turn to laugh.

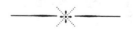

Chapter 16

The glass panels in the tower of the United Nations building glistened like so many mica chips in the brilliant morning sun. In an executive suite on the top floor, Secretary-General Kalim Salaam set the Interim Report he had been reading down on his desk. He dabbed his forehead with a handkerchief. The Special UN Study Committee on Extraterrestrial Contact he had created three months ago at the U.S. President's urging had very little to show for its four meetings.

At the first meeting in New York, there had been political in-fighting. The Russian delegate had insisted on being Committee Chairman. He complained that for too long the United States had been acting as the most important country, and that such was an insult to the prestige of the Commonwealth of Independent States. The French delegate had insisted that the Chairmanship rotate, so that France would not be slighted. The Chinese delegate had threatened to walk out if China did not chair at least one meeting.

Then there had been cultural conflicts at the second committee meeting in Cairo. The delegate from Iran had conducted a filibuster. Progress had been brought to a standstill while the delegate, a member of the Shia branch of Islam, repeated the Supreme Ayatollah's *fatwa*. That religious declaration had pronounced that the aliens were tricksters and *djin,* devils, who were sent to divert the Islamic faithful from the one true faith. The Iranian delegate had insisted that the Special Study Committee *not* deal with issues of welcoming and dialogue with the extraterrestrials. He threatened to continue his filibuster indefinitely unless the Committee substitute as its agenda "the problems and dangers posed by the alien *djin.*" The Secretary-General, a Sunni-branch Muslim, winced at the distorted picture of Islam presented by this Shiite delegate. Eventually the Committee members wearied of the filibuster and went home.

The third committee meeting in Moscow had been pick-
eted by numerous charismatic and fundamentalist Christian
organizations. They had characterized the Committee's purpose as "a sell-out to Satan." The fundamentalists had stormed
the building the Committee was meeting in. They overwhelmed
the police and violently disrupted the meeting, until Russian
Army reinforcements arrived and restored order. By that point
the Committee members were too shaken to continue, and the
chairman had to adjourn the meeting.

The fourth meeting in Beijing was sidetracked when the
heads of several international academic societies of the physical sciences had insisted on addressing the members. They argued that the "so-called extraterrestrial phenomenon" totally
lacked acceptance by "the mainstream scientific community."
The traditionalist academics had declared that "alleged space
aliens" represented poorly-understood natural phenomena, and
that the aliens' reported utterances were nonsense, which "totally contradicted the long-established physical laws of Science."
They argued that the Committee "should not return to the Dark
Ages" by seeking to enter into negotiations with "apparitions,"
which may represent "novel electromagnetic field effects."
Unsettled by these challenges from scientists, the Committee,
in disarray, had adjourned early.

The Secretary-General shook his head and pinched the
bridge of his nose. He could feel a headache coming on. How
could the United Nations ever be ready in time to meet the
extraterrestrial ambassadors, when even seasoned diplomats
could not rise above habitual human narrowness to address
this cosmic opportunity. Would the alien ambassadors have to
return to their council and report that the Earth had rejected
the offer of ongoing contact they had offered? He considered
the discouraging flow of events. Salaam reflected that his wife
might have been hoping for too much when she had come home
all enthusiastic from the extraterrestrial landing in New Mexico.
She had insisted that he push the Special Committee into rec-
ommending representatives for an official Earth ambassadorial team to meet with the extraterrestrials. Although the chairman had added the requested item to their agenda, the accursed
Committee seemed incapable of agreeing on anything. Worse,

the Committee's disarray had been featured in news magazines around the world. This had only increased the outbursts by the anti-alien extremists worldwide. Unaccustomed tears welled up in his eyes. The Secretary-General knew there was one option left for him to try next. Although it was a desperate move, he was not going to accept any more bitter failure. He was not about to have United Nations history record that Earth's opportunity to engage in constructive relationship with cosmic cultures was lost on *his* watch. Salaam's fist came flying down on his desk with resolve. As sure as Allah is the most holy, *this* Secretary-General was not going to be paralyzed into inaction.

The bright television spotlights felt too hot even in the underheated studio's chill on this foggy London winter morning. The smug BBC interview host, an attractive brunette in her mid-twenties, gazed with practiced disconnection at the panel, who were shifting restlessly as they awaited the on-the-air cue. Dr. Leena Virtanen leaned over to Catalina and Maguire and whispered a comment which made them smile. Dr. Leonard Spruance was chatting cheerfully with Major Roscoe Dent. A technician pointed at the program host and said, "Ten seconds to broadcast time."

The interviewer faced the camera, put on a smile, and awaited the countdown. "Good evening, ladies and gentlemen, I'm Leslie Lophtess. Tonight the BBC brings you a special live program featuring a panel discussion with five members of the Project Epiphany Contact Team. The Contact Team has been in the press lately as a result of their *claim* to have met with several extraterrestrial representatives in the American Southwest desert a month ago. These Team members have made additional extraordinary claims about some alien messages which they say the aliens gave them.

"With us tonight are Team members Dr. Leena Virtanen, Surgeon-General of Norway, Dr. Leonard Spruance, professor of psychology, retired U.S. Army Intelligence Major Roscoe Dent, Dr. Roger Maguire, an anthropologist, and Miss Barbara Catalina, his research assistant. These five are part of that nine-person Team who claim that they met with space aliens on November 25th.

"Let's start with Dr. Virtanen. Leena, why should people believe your Team's claim to have actually met with alien ambassadors?"

Dr. Virtanen sputtered. "Why *should* they believe? I'm the Surgeon-General of Norway. Why would I tell a lie? Are you saying that I would jeopardize my career by making up such a thing?"

The host retreated and switched to Dr. Spruance. "Leonard, you're a psychology professor. Your profession specializes in determining what's crazy and what's normal. Why shouldn't people think that *you've* lost your sanity, when you claim that you and your self-appointed group of civilians actually met with official ambassadors from outer space?"

Dr. Spruance paused, took off his horn-rimmed glasses and wiped them quickly. Then he replaced them and responded. "Well, Ms. Lophtess, it is true that people shouldn't believe *everything* they hear. But let's look at the evidence. First, we have a Team that is made up of some very credible people, including the wife of the UN Secretary-General."

"Let me interrupt you right there," the host said quickly. "If this meeting with important alien representatives actually did happen, why hasn't the UN done anything about it? The UN's Special Study Committee on Extraterrestrial Contact was set up after the U.S. President acknowledged that a UFO had crashed at Roswell, New Mexico, *not* as a result of your group's supposed encounter. Also, that same UN Committee hasn't made any statements about your supposed meeting with the alien ambassadors. If they don't believe you, why should we?"

"Can I break in here?" Maguire asked. "Ms. Lophtess . . ."

"Please! Just call me Leslie," the interviewer said with a stiff smile.

"Leslie, there's the matter of the nuclear explosion that was set off by a renegade group who were trying to intercept our meeting with the extraterrestrial representatives. The radiation from that explosion was measured around the world."

"Yes, Roger," the host replied with a patronizing tone. "So there was some radioactive fallout. But your government has explained that fallout as an 'unfortunate low-yield accident.'

I believe that was the term they've used. "But you're asking us to believe that a renegade military group stole a nuclear weapon, and then used it to blow themselves up? Really now, Roger, do you expect us to accept that explanation?"

Dr. Virtanen leaned over to Maguire and whispered, "We are being ambushed here. Where did they get this host from?"

"I'd like to say something here." Major Dent's deep booming voice made all heads turn to him. "Leslie, you seem to have forgotten that after our meeting with the extra-terrestrial representatives, the next day we met with the National Security Council. We briefed them on the messages from the Interstellar Federation."

"Well, I'm glad you brought that up," the interviewer responded. "Our program director has made repeated requests to the U.S. National Security Council, asking for the minutes of that supposed meeting, and have been told that their minutes are not available. We asked the NSC to tell us at least whether a meeting with the Contact Team took place on the day you say it did. We were told that they can neither confirm or deny whomever the NSC meets with. So, there doesn't seem to be any proof that your group actually did meet with the Security Council. It's just your word." The host sat back with a smug smile.

Catalina raised her hand tentatively. "Can I say something?"

"Sure," the interviewer replied snidely. "Go ahead. I understand that you're a psychic, so perhaps you can help us find the missing proof that your supposed alien meeting ever actually happened."

Catalina turned to Maguire and commented out loud, "Psychic? How does she know I'm a psychic? All I ever said in the warm-up interview before the program was that I was your research assistant."

The interviewer looked flustered and didn't reply.

Roscoe Dent leaned forward across the panel table and turned to face Catalina. "Perhaps I can help clear up that mystery, Barbara."

Dent turned to the interviewer and continued. "You see, Ms. Lophtess, when I learned that we were going to be on this interview program, I did some background investigation on you. It's some old training I got a long time ago, when I first started out in intelligence work. I've still got a few friends left in the trade. With their help I learned that you were recruited right out of college into MI-6, British intelligence. Your first assignment was to infiltrate the Labour Party. There you were to develop a 'close relationship' with one of their most prominent Parliament leaders, and, how can I say this delicately, 'compromise' this supposedly happily-married Member of Parliament. After that successful assignment, you were given the cover position of working for the BBC as a broadcast journalist, although you still receive special intelligence assignments from time to time. I wasn't prepared to bring all this up if you had conducted a fair interview."

Dent sat back in his chair and continued to fix Ms. Lophtess with an unwavering gaze. The interviewer look dumbfounded, her cheeks flushed a bright crimson.

"So *that's* how she knew I was a psychic!" Catalina was livid.

Dr. Virtanen stood up and said, "That does it! I've heard enough. This whole debunking interview is a spy organization set-up! I say we all get up and leave this place. This program is rigged." With that, she wheeled around and marched off the set.

The interviewer looked around helplessly. Roscoe Dent stood up next and followed Dr. Virtanen off the set, with Maguire and Catalina right behind him. The program director, seeing the program dissolving before his eyes, yelled to his crew, "Cut! Go to black!" All across the UK, television sets suddenly showed blank screens.

The ornately paneled executive conference room of the Mont d'Arbois Hotel in Megeve, France was warmed by the crackling fire in the brick hearth. Around a massive oaken table the Bilderberg Executive Committee, thirteen men in conservative dark business suits, sat oblivious of the raging snow-storm outside. The meeting had not been going well.

Prince Heinrich Adler pushed his high-backed chair away from the head of the table, stood up, and waved his finger scoldingly. "Gentlemen, let me take the Chairman's prerogative and be quite frank. All I have heard so far today is useless prattle and hand-wringing. The problem is simply stated. We have to stop that meddling Project Epiphany Contact Team from successfully persuading the UN to appoint representatives to meet with the aliens. Despite presumably having some of the finest minds in the world sitting around this table, no one has yet come up with an effective solution. Gentlemen, may I remind you that if the UN gets in the driver's seat with the aliens, we will have been circumvented. The power we have enjoyed will rapidly diminish, perhaps vanish. Is there no one here who can present a sensible solution?"

A dapper man with fading blond hair sitting near the foot of the table raised his hand. David Kline, Ph.D. was a board director of the Institute for Strategic and International Studies at Georgetown University. He was no stranger to thorny problems. "I think I have a suggestion."

"Yes?" Prince Adler peered down his glasses.

"The problem seems to be that these Contact Team people think that they can use their meeting with the aliens to influence world affairs, and yet never have to pay a price. I have a question for you. What if the price they had to pay was too high?"

"What do you mean?"

"What if one of their Team were to disappear, and the others were to get a message that they needed to stop trying to influence world reaction to alien contact if they wanted to see their comrade ever again?"

The portly vice-chairman of the Organization for Economic Cooperation and Development leaned forward in his chair. "Dr. Kline, what do you mean, 'disappear'?"

"Oh, I'm not talking about extreme measures. Just an enforced vacation, until we get past the date the aliens set for Earth to designate its ambassadors."

Prince Adler brightened. "Well, that's the first constructive suggestion I've heard today. Any others?"

The room fell silent.

"Well, then. It seems that it is time for a vote. All those in favor of Dr. Kline's suggested solution, indicate by aye."

A chorus of assents went up around the room.

"Those opposed, indicate by the same sign." The Prince paused. "There being none, I declare the motion passed. In the interest of preserving Executive Committee deniability, I will take the prerogative of meeting with Dr. Kline alone after we adjourn and working out the details of the solution, if that meets with Committee approval. Any objections?" The Prince peered around the room. "There being none, I will proceed as outlined. I will now entertain a motion of adjournment."

Although it was two days before Christmas, most of the nine members of the Contact Team were traveling around the U.S. and abroad. They were busily at their mission of trying to encourage groups and influential individuals to pressure the United Nations into designating ambassadors to meet with the extraterrestrials.

Barbara Catalina had decided to take a quick break and spend the last two days before Christmas with her son Jason, who had come home to Boulder for the holiday. She had seen Maguire off on his plane to California, where he was planning to connect with his daughter, Melissa, home from Cal Poly on Christmas break. Catalina and Jason had planned to go out to a shopping mall and do some late Christmas shopping. Jason was upstairs in the shower when Catalina heard the doorbell ring. At the front door were three men in trench coats. Despite the overcast day, they were wearing dark glasses. A muscular Germanic-looking man in front flashed credentials in front of Catalina. "Barbara Catalina?"

"Yes?"

"Karl Siemens, FBI. Come with us."

"Why? What am I supposed to have done?"

"We're not going to hold a discussion here. We'll talk downtown."

"Let me see some photo identification," Catalina said.

"OK, guys, let's get her to the car." Siemens placed a vise-like hand grip over her mouth as the other two "FBI" men quickly grabbed her and force-walked her to their car. Upstairs, Jason heard a shriek. He stepped out of the shower, threw a towel around himself, and hurried down the stairs. He arrived at the front door in time to see a late-model dark sedan speed away from the curb.

One hour later, each of the remaining eight members of

the Contact Team received an envelope by commercial courier. The envelope contained the identical message on ordinary typing paper with no letterhead or address. "A fellow member of your so-called Contact Team, Barbara Catalina, has been taken into custody. *You* will determine whether she reappears safely or not. The Contact Team must stop at once any effort to influence the United Nations concerning alien matters. If you ignore this warning, her life will be your responsibility. If you cooperate, she will be released unharmed on February 17. Do not tell anyone about this message."

When Maguire came back from his front door with the courier's message in his hand, Melissa knew from his stricken face that the news was bad. "They've kidnapped Catalina!" he groaned. "The dirty bastards! I never should have let her go off by herself. God, what animals! To kidnap someone practically on Christmas Eve!"

His daughter threw her arms around him in a compassionate hug. "It'll be all right, dad. You guys have gotten through so much already. There must be a higher power that will look out for her. She'll turn up OK. Just you wait and see."

Maguire looked up at Melissa, forcing a brave smile, and hoping she didn't notice tears forming.

Dr. Robert Bowen wasted no time after receiving his courier message. Within four hours he had arranged an emergency international telephone conference call for the rest of the Contact Team. The conference call discussion had been surprisingly short. Dr. Virtanen had summed up the feelings of the others when she acknowledged her sympathy for Catalina, but proposed that they redouble their efforts to get the UN to appoint ambassadors. She also proposed that each member quietly contact whomever they knew in law enforcement to pursue a search for Catalina. Maguire had agonized aloud about the risk to Catalina if the Team went ahead with their efforts. George Morning Star pointed out to him that proceeding as before is exactly what Catalina would have told the Team to do, if she had been there to speak. The other

Team members voiced their agreement. Maguire acknowledged Catalina's grit and courage, and quietly accepted what
Morning Star had said. The Lakota Elder also noted that there
was no guarantee that her captors would release her if the
Team complied. In the end, the Team agreed unanimously
on both proposals. Each then began to discreetly contact their
friends in law enforcement.

At the Pine Ridge Indian Reservation's Tribal Center, a
circle of Native American medicine people filled the modest
wooden meeting hall. Although the non-Indian world was
busy celebrating Christmas Day, the mood in this room was
serious. Spiritual leaders from many tribes had gathered together to hear in detail the messages which the Star Nations
had brought to the Contact Team. Timothy Katoya had just
finished his introduction of George Morning Star, and was
taking a seat at the rear of the hall. George Morning Star had
begun to speak when he was interrupted by shouting from
the middle of the group. A well-built Indian youth in his early
twenties stood up.

"I speak for the American Indian Movement. Morning
Star, you are a traitor to the traditional ways of the Lakota!
This message you say is from the aliens but it does not agree
with what I was taught about our origins. It is disrespectful to
White Buffalo Calf Woman to make her out to be some bug-
eyed alien instead of a beautiful example of Red womanhood!"

While this agitator had every eye in the room turned toward him, his accomplice, a young man with long braids,
stood up at the front near Morning Star. The young man
pretended to whisper something to him. When Morning Star
leaned over to hear better, the youth swiftly reached under
his shirt for a bowie knife. He sank it between Morning Star's
ribs, severing a lung artery. Morning Star crumpled to the
floor with a groan, blood pouring from his mouth. The
assassin whooped a war cry and ran out of the meeting room,
quickly followed by his agitator confederate. The others
present sat there shocked a few seconds. Quickly recovering, Katoya ran out the door after the young men, followed

by other elders, only to see a weathered pickup truck with no license plate speeding away down the highway.

The Potomac shoreline around the Pentagon was being pelted with a heavy New Year's Eve snowfall. Dr. Robert Bowen had plenty of time to think while the elevator made its descent far beneath the surface of the military headquarters building. On either side of him stood two Delta Force escorts at attention. Their faces were expressionless. Bowen had never known before that the Pentagon went twenty stories down. He was musing over the tragic news he had just received of George Morning Star's murder. It was no coincidence that during the Team's conference call, it was Morning Star who had been one of the most vocal in urging the Team to continue with its assigned activity. Whoever had kidnapped Catalina had undoubtedly been listening in. When her kidnapping had not stopped the Team, they calculated that murdering a Team member would be more persuasive.

Today's meeting was certainly a first for Bowen, a command performance before the Pentagon's top brass. The generals and admirals had requested a private briefing about what the extraterrestrial representatives had told the Team. Admiral MacKenzie had phoned Bowen from SEALS Headquarters, Coronado to personally transmit the Pentagon's request. Privately, the Admiral had cautioned Bowen that many of the brass were afraid of the extraterrestrials. Many top officers feared that the aliens' messages spelled a radically diminished role for the military in society. Bowen reflected that such a concern was undoubtedly realistic.

The elevator doors finally opened onto floor B-20. Bowen stepped out, flanked by the Delta Force soldiers. They escorted him to a large "secure room," shaped like a small amphitheater and shielded with lead and gold sheeting against any listening device. Inside sat more senior officers than Bowen had ever seen assembled before. A three-star Army General showed him to the podium and introduced him. Before him stretched a sea of grim older men in uniform.

Bowen began by recounting for the brass how Project

Epiphany had gotten involved with the extraterrestrial landing. He told of the efforts by JANUS to thwart the Contact Team and to disrupt the extraterrestrial landing. He presented the seven messages which the extraterrestrial representatives had given the Contact Team. At the end of his detailed presentation, the three-star general standing near him stepped back up to the podium and asked if there were any questions.

A Marine Corps Adjutant was the first on his feet. "Dr. Bowen, why does Project Epiphany trust what these aliens are telling us? We really don't know anything about these people. And they are very well armed."

Bowen gave the man a condensed history of extraterrestrial contact over the past 5000 years. He pointed out that their track record did not indicate conquest or deception. He stated that professional research to date had also shown that the extraterrestrials appear to give predictions which later come true.

A four-star Army General, whom Bowen was sure he had seen on television before, was the next with a question. "If the aliens mean us no harm, how is it that they warn us about upcoming disasters, but don't say that they'll do anything about stopping them?"

Bowen explained that many of the geophysical cataclysms predicted are the result of natural processes which it might be dangerous to interfere with. That trying to stop one eruption, for example, could cause built-up pressure to blow out elsewhere. He pointed out that the extraterrestrials *had* stated that they were prepared to assist with warnings, and even help with certain limited evacuations if asked.

An elderly man in an Air Force blue officer's uniform had his hand up next. "Frankly, Dr. Bowen, this talk about hybrids who look like humans gives me the willies. Our national security goes down the drain if we can't tell them from us. There's no way I can back the idea of giving these aliens a welcome and offering them protection to live among us. And what about alien disease?"

Bowen decided to take a bold approach. "The entire idea of security against an alien 'enemy' has to be given up. This meeting with cosmic civilizations is *not* a confrontation with an aggressor. You are our military leadership. You need to revise your thinking. We are dealing with a more civilized and more advanced set of civilizations than ourselves. In these meetings, *we* are the only potential aggressor. We have to abandon a military response to this historic event. Instead, we need to undertake a diplomatic response. And as for the risk of infection, the extraterrestrials take sophisticated measures to prevent cross-species contamination. There are no recorded cases of such infection from the tens of thousands of extraterrestrial encounters which have been reported."

A man in an admiral's uniform with a splotchy complexion asked the next question. "We in Naval Intelligence have studied the alien messages about metaphysics for some time. Is it your opinion that the alien metaphysics is so advanced and beyond us that it is unknowable?"

"That's a good question," Bowen replied. "If you want my opinion, based on research so far, I think their metaphysics is not that far advanced beyond the most sophisticated metaphysical systems we have on Earth."

"Follow-up question, Dr. Bowen," the admiral responded. "Please identify what you consider to be the most advanced metaphysical systems on Earth."

"In my opinion, if you integrated the core metaphysics of Native American teachings and of Taoism, what you would have is not that different from what the extraterrestrials present, just to give one example."

A man in an all-black jumpsuit and cap with no insignia stood up in the back row. "I have a question for you."

Bowen acknowledged him, then added, "Pardon me, sir. You don't have any insignia on, and I don't recognize your uniform as any I've ever seen before." A ripple of laughter went around the room.

The officer in black replied, "That's because my unit stays out of sight."

"What unit is that, sir?"

"Dr. Bowen, with all respect, you don't have a 'need to know'."

"Sir, every day the members of our Contact Team risk their lives to get out the messages we were entrusted with by the extraterrestrials. We never know when some fanatic is going to act out some paranoid or racist urge and blow one of us away. Already one of our team has been kidnapped, and another has been murdered. I came here at the request of you all. I am giving of my time to brief you on matters of cosmic significance. And now you're trying to give me that 'National Security secrecy' mumbo-jumbo. With all due respect, sir, I god-damned-well have a right to know whom I'm talking to."

Murmurs of agreement went around the room. Every head turned to see what the officer in black would say. "OK, you've made your point. I'm General Luther Schaukraupt, Intelligence Liaison between the National Reconnaissance Organization and the Air Force Space Command. Now, if I can ask my question. If the Earth is dying, as these aliens claim, why should we go through the bother of trying to deal with them when we're goners anyway, according to them?"

"The answer, General, is that the Earth doesn't have to die. They have said that our global ecology is in a middle-stage of system collapse. It's not in the final stage. By the way, that's essentially the same message we're getting from progressive Earth scientists as well. If the world acts together to reverse ecological damage, we can still save this planet."

"So then, what you're saying is that we don't need the aliens," General Schaukraupt responded craftily. "So why bother with them?"

"They can help us. Their scientific knowledge is more advanced. And they have had experience with many planets at various levels of ecological trouble. We'd be foolish to throw away an offer of technical assistance like that."

"Well, call me old-fashioned, but I just don't trust creatures who can fly circles around our most advanced aircraft, and have a track record of disabling nuclear missiles and our most advanced orbiting weapons systems." General Schaukraupt sat down with a sigh.

"The extraterrestrials want peace and a nuclear-free

planet," Bowen added. "They have made some demonstrations of firing in self-defense at times, it is true. That was to show us the foolishness of thinking that our advanced weapons would present any threat to them. The fact that they haven't taken advantage and attacked us after disabling our weapons tells us that we're not dealing with an aggressor."

There were murmurs of assent here and there from officers around the room. After a few moments a man in a pin-striped gray flannel suit stood up. "Dr. Bowen, you mentioned that one of your Contact Team has been kidnapped? Is anyone working on that?"

"You mean Barbara Catalina. We've informed the Boulder police, but frankly they don't have any leads about her captors."

"Maybe we can help," the suit replied. "I'm with the Central Intelligence Agency. We have a group of talented psychics who may be able to remote-view Ms. Catalina's location and determine where she is being held."

Admiral Malcolm MacKenzie was instantly on his feet. "If CIA can pin-point her location, my SEALS Team Six stands ready to assist."

Dr. Bowen's expression brightened. "If you two could do that, all of us on the Contact Team would owe you the greatest debt of gratitude!"

The cavernous General Assembly chamber of the United Nations was filled to overflowing. Television cameramen and reporters jostled with U.N. delegates trying to get to their seats. Never in their lives had most delegates experienced a Special Plenary Session of the United Nations. Such an extraordinary meeting, a joint session of the governing Security Council and the member states' General Assembly, was used to address the most unusual situations. Such a joint session was empowered to go beyond the UN's adopted Charter and even to amend it. Secretary-General Salaam had taken a lot of criticism from the Security Council members for creating a 'dangerous context.' The powerful nations were referring to the risk that a coalition of developing countries could amend the UN Charter and strip the wealthy nations of their chief mechanism of control, their majority on the Security Council. Salaam had resisted their criticisms, pointing out that today's agenda made the power struggles by the wealthy nations seem a petty and irrelevant matter by comparison.

The members of the Security Council sat in the center seats of the front row, a *realpolitik* concession to their power. In the back row sat the seven remaining members of the Contact Team. They were in attendance as the Secretary-General's special guests. When the last delegates got to their seats, the Secretary-General stepped to the dais and gaveled the Plenary Session to order. Rows of television cameras lined along the outer aisles swung around toward the dais. The delegates grew quiet.

Secretary-General Salaam began. "Good day, fellow members of the United Nations, and citizens of the world watching this Plenary Session today. Special greetings to those of you for whom today is the observance of Orthodox Christmas, and for others, the celebration of Epiphany.

"A Plenary Session of the United Nations is called for only the most extraordinary and weighty matters. Our agenda today *is* such a matter. I have called this Plenary Session so that all the representatives of the Earth, meeting together as close to equals as we humans have managed, can decide today the future course of the Earth. As has been widely reported in the media around the world, forty-two days ago a brave group of nine citizens met with representatives from other worlds. Project Epiphany, who set up this Contact Team, is a non-governmental international group whose mission is to respond to extraterrestrial outreach. The Contact Team's intentions were the most honorable, to take the initiative to reach out to our extraterrestrial visitors, while official bodies, including this one, I am sad to say, avoided the politically risky challenge of dealing with the extraterrestrial presence. For their courage the Contact Team have paid a heavy price. One of their members has been murdered. Another is being held hostage by those who would have prevented today's meeting from happening. By the way, the remaining members of the Contact Team are sitting with us today." The Secretary-General gestured toward the back row. Spirited applause broke out from many of the delegates.

"While some voices of dissension have criticized the Team, claiming that they have usurped UN prerogatives, I believe most delegates will be grateful that an international group, free of self-serving motives, was prepared and in place when the Interstellar Federation representatives landed. Proof of this group's integrity is that they immediately afterwards contacted me, and through me the United Nations, to bring the messages from the extraterrestrial representatives to us. This brave team, and the messages from the extraterrestrials which they brought, are the reasons I have decided to cut through the political and bureaucratic roadblocks all too common in our deliberations, and convene this extraordinary Plenary Session.

"Please permit me to be unusually frank. While I appreciate the efforts of its members, the Special UN Study Committee on Extraterrestrial Contact, which I established four months ago, has *not* achieved its mission. That Committee's top priority assignment was to select a truly representative group of ambassadors to speak for Earth, when the cosmic ambassadors land one month from now. We can wait no longer. I will appoint no more study committees. This chair will not recognize any motion to continue this discussion to another date. Before all the world watching us, I confront and challenge all of you, my dear brother and sister delegates, to decide on, and designate *today*, a group of twelve people to represent Earth at the historic cosmic meeting which will occur February 15th. Will you rise to this challenge? Or will you go home to your peoples after today's session, and admit that the noblest body ever assembled on Earth was impotent and ineffectual on the eve of the most important event in human history? The choice is in your hands, and it rests there *now!*" The Secretary-General paused and peered out over the Assembly chamber. The delegates were quiet, letting his words sunk in.

"In order to speed up the process of deliberation today, I am setting forth for your consideration a proposal to estab-

lish a UN Ambassadors Group to meet with the Interstellar
Federation ambassadors. Since we already have in the Contact Team a multi-nationality group who have demonstrated
their acceptability to the extraterrestrial ambassadors, I
propose that the UN Ambassadors Group be composed of
six members from the Contact Team, and in addition, six UN
delegates.

"From the Contact Team I propose that the following
serve: Dr. Robert Bowen, the founder of Project Epiphany,
Dr. Leena Virtanen of Norway, Elder Timothy Katoya of the
Hopi Tribe of Native Americans, Major Roscoe Dent, an African-American former officer of the Southeast Asia Treaty
Organization, the First Lady of the UN, my wife, Leila
Salaam of Tunisia, and Dr. Roger Maguire, who has taken
many risks to expose those who would seek to divert extraterrestrial contact to their own narrow selfish purposes. If
this is acceptable, then there remains for the Plenary Session
the task of designating the six delegates to serve on the UN
Ambassadors Group."

A hand shot up.

"The chair recognizes the delegate from India.

"Mr. Secretary, India moves that we accept your proposal,
with the addition that the six UN delegates shall be chosen
by lot here today."

Loud murmurs and informal discussions erupted across
the room. After allowing a couple minutes of discussion,
Salaam gaveled for order. Another hand was in the air. It
was the delegate from Ecuador, seconding the motion.
Secretary-General Salaam called for formal discussion.
Vigorous debate see-sawed for several hours between the
Secretary's proposal and several alternatives. Finally, a vote
was taken. The Secretary's proposal was adopted. A lottery
barrel, which Salaam had prearranged, was brought into the
chamber. A cynical delegate from Zaire commented to his
colleague from Zimbabwe, wondering how many slips of
paper had the name of the U.S. delegate on them.

The Secretary-General was about to begin the drawing
of lots when the back door of the Assembly chamber opened.
Two UN guards entered, escorting Admiral Malcolm

MacKenzie and the UN Under-Secretary. The Admiral and the Under-Secretary strode up to the dais and whispered to Salaam. Salaam's tense face broke into a broad smile. A few more moments of whispering, and his face grew serious again. The Under-Secretary and the Admiral stepped to the side, as Salaam turned to the assembled audience.

"Esteemed delegates, I ask your understanding that I interrupt these deliberations now to share with you important and timely news. The persons next to me are U.S. Admiral Malcolm MacKenzie, and, of course, our esteemed Under-Secretary. Admiral MacKenzie is in charge of the U.S.Navy's SEAL Team Six, an elite special operations unit. The Admiral has just informed me that the kidnapped member of the Contact Team, Barbara Catalina, has been located and rescued. She is here at the UN now to reunite with the rest of the Team."

Wild screaming and yelling broke out in the back row, as the exuberant Contact Team came up out of their seats. The two UN guards in the back exited momentarily and reappeared escorting Catalina in. Maguire, tears rolling down his cheeks, ran over to meet her. The other Team members swiftly followed, forming a circle around the joyous pair. All delegates' eyes were turned toward the exuberant and tumultuous scene in the back of the hall.

"Barbara," Maguire's voice was breaking, "I was so afraid I might never see you again alive."

Catalina gave him her widest grin. "Rog, my precious, precious love, don't cry. I'm unharmed, and it's all over."

As Maguire and Catalina embraced, the rest of the Team cheered, followed by loud cheers from the assembled delegates. Maguire looked Catalina straight in the eyes and whispered, "Will you marry me?"

It was Catalina's turned to cry. Dabbing at her tears away, she whispered back to him, "Of course, you silly. I want to spend the rest of this lifetime and more as your mate." Hearing the marriage proposal accepted, the rest of the Contact Team sent up a chorus of whoops. Maguire swept Catalina into an embrace again and gave her a lengthy kiss. As he did so, the chambers broke into thunderous extended applause.

After several minutes, the Secretary-General gaveled for order. "The remaining news I have received is not as uplifting. The Under-Secretary and Admiral MacKenzie inform me that Ms. Barbara Catalina had been held hostage under orders from a director of the Institute for Strategic and International Studies. That individual also ordered the assassination of Lakota Elder George Morning Star, a member of the Contact Team. That director, David Kline, has been arrested by Interpol. Under extensive questioning, he has implicated Prince Heinrich Adler and several other members of the Bilderberg Executive Committee in a plot to use violence to deter the Contact Team from bringing the extraterrestrial messages to the United Nations. At the request of our Under-Secretary, Interpol is locating and detaining those involved for questioning."

The room erupted into a cacophony of shocked comments, as the delegates reacted to the announcement. After a couple minutes of allowing for reaction, the Secretary gaveled for order.

"The extortion actions by Dr. Kline and Prince Adler are deplorable. But their bad example only underscores the necessity for all of us, individuals and nations of the Earth, to abandon the old ways of seeking advantage over one another. We need now to come together and acknowledge our oneness as one people of Earth. And we need to prepare ourselves now to meet our cosmic future.

"And so, without further delay, let us resume where we left off. Let us proceed in getting ready for that future. We were about to draw lots to see who shall be the U.N.'s Special Ambassadors to meet with the delegation from the Interstellar Federation."

With a nod towards his staff, Secretary-General Kalim Salaam directed that the process of drawing lots for Special Ambassadors begin.

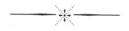

Project Epiphany

Cast of Characters

Roger P. Maguire, Ph.D.: an anthropologist in his early forties, specializing in ancient Southwest Native American astronomy and pictographic records of Star People contacts; his home is in Chatsworth, California. Divorced, has a college-aged daughter. JANUS's code name for him: "Fellow Traveler."

Melissa Maguire: Roger's daughter, a student at Cal Poly-San Luis Obispo State University.

Barbara Catalina: a part-Ojibway professional psychic in her latter thirties from Boulder, Colorado. Divorced, has an adult son; JANUS's code name for her: "Princess Leia."

Jason Catalina: Barbara's son, a graphics designer in Denver.

Major Bryce Eberhardt/Zeta One: Supervising officer at Kirtland Air Force Base's Office of Special Investigations (AFOSI); head of NSA's PANDORA Unit surveillance team.

Timmy O'Connell/Zeta Two: Nominally an intelligence analyst at Kirtland AFB's Air Force Intelligence office; under AFOSI cover, a frequent "black jobs" operative for the National Reconnaissance Organization; member of NSA's PANDORA Unit.

Judah Preston/Zeta Three: the gray-bearded oldest member of NSA's PANDORA Unit surveillance team.

Captain José DiGiorgio/Zeta Four: attached to Kirtland AFB's Security Operations Division, Directorate of Counter-Intelligence (CI), Air Force Office of Special Investigations; member, PANDORA Unit surveillance team.

Juanita Cuerno: José DiGiorgio's wife.

Robin "Ice" Miller/Zeta Five: contract pilot freelancer; former combat pilot for CIA's Air America; member, PANDORA Unit surveillance team.

Harley Clarke/Zeta Six: short, obese member of PANDORA Unit's surveillance team.

Colonel Jack Partridge: Colonel in the Army Intelligence and Security Command, a cover for his official position as director of PANDORA, a compartmentalized Special Access Program within the National Security Agency (NSA); headquartered under Sandia National Laboratories, Albuquerque; Radio code name: Eagle One.

General Hal Beardsley: Partridge's putative superior within the Army Intelligence and Security Command.

Arica: the main extraterrestrial who communicates with Barbara Catalina; almost five feet tall, with a large head, enormous slanted almond-shaped eyes, mushroom-white skin, very thin body, and delicate hands with three long fingers. Zeta System ambassador.

Timothy Katoya: 70-year-old Native American Elder of the Hopi village of Hotevilla, Arizona; member, Project Epiphany Contact Team.

Henri Fournier, Ph.D.: octagenarian chairman of JANUS; theoretical physicist on BDM Corporation's Board of Directors; on indefinite loan to the Joint Chiefs of Staff as their Science and Technology Advisor.

Nathaniel Brown, M.D., Ph.D.: Director of the Medical Sciences Department, AT&T- Bell Labs; member of JANUS.

Roderick Birdsall: Chief of Special Projects within the Directorate of Operations, CIA; member of JANUS.

Hubert Tarnsworth, Ph.D.: high-energy physicist with the Edgerton, Germhausen & Greer Corporation (EG&G); member of JANUS.

Air Force Major-General Robert "Ramrod" Lazarus, Ph.D.: nominally assigned to Haystack USAF Laboratory beneath Edwards Air Force Base; the director of a military-compartment UFO Working Group at Laboratory QQ at Los Alamos; member of JANUS.

Morris Solomon, Ph.D.: retired Harvard economist; chief consultant to the Federal Reserve Board; financial advisor to one of the three richest families in America; member of JANUS.

Senator John Knapp: Chairman of the Senate Intelligence Committee; member of JANUS.

Admiral Jordan Clannon: U.S Navy (retired); Director of the Center for Comparative Psychophysical Studies at Batelle Memorial Institute; member of JANUS.

Eleanor: Hopi proprietor of the Hotevilla general store.

Don Cortlan: a free-lance reporter and stringer for the *Baltimore Sun,* and dilettante of insider UFO information.

Project Epiphany: a small group, consisting of internationally-known UFO researchers and highly placed governmental officials, who seek pre-planned official contact with extraterrestrials.

Commander Jacques Stone, USN (ret.), Ph.D.: A former Navy pilot; former intelligence officer at the Defense Intelligence Agency, Army Intelligence, the Defense Nuclear Agency, Defense's Advanced Research Projects Agency, and Naval Intelligence; former contract Stanford Research Institute investigator into paranormal phenomena for the National Security Agency; member of Project Epiphany.

Lucy Stone: Jacques Stone's wife.

Dr. Robert Bowen: noted psychologist and investigator of UFOs, ETs, and the UFO Cover-Up; Chairman, Project Epiphany.

Sister Lisieux: French nun, foundress of a band of religious sisters who minister to Third World poor; member, Project Epiphany.

Alberta de Oliveira: Brazilian UFO investigator; member of Project Epiphany.

Dr. Leena Virtanen: ET encounters researcher; Surgeon-General of Norway; member, Project Epiphany Contact Team

Dr. Ivana Kheraskov: Russian cosmonaut; witness to numerous UFO contacts in orbit; member of Project Epiphany.

Claudia Hill: UFO investigative journalist from Zimbabwe; member of Project Epiphany.

U.N. Secretary Kalim Salaam: former member of Project Epiphany.

Leila Salaam: apolitical Tunisian wife of the UN Secretary-General; UFO information hobbyist; member of Project Epiphany Contact Team.

Former U.S. President, Earl James: member of Project Epiphany.

Lama Dharam: head Lama of Nepal; member of Project Epiphany.

Donald Cameron: noted Australian UFOlogist; member of Project Epiphany.

George Morning Star *(Anpo Wie)*: Lakota (Sioux) medicine man; member of Project Epiphany Contact Team

Professor Yat-sen Yuan: head of Beijing UFO investigation society; member of Project Epiphany.

Karl von Reuter: German anthropologist and publisher of UFO reports; member of Project Epiphany.

Gilbert Murray: head of British Close Encounters Society; member of Project Epiphany.

Manuel Gutierrez: Mexican television producer; member of Project Epiphany.

Dr. Ian McCormack: Professor of Psychiatry at Princeton and researcher into alien abductions; member of Project Epiphany.

Dr. Leonard Spruance: retired University of Idaho Psychology professor; researcher of extraterrestrial encounters; member of Project Epiphany Contact Team.

Dr. Stewart Golden: Knoxville physician; head of the Interstellar Friendship and Exchange Committee; member of Project Epiphany Contact Team.

Dr. Brent O'Hara: astronaut from Hawaii and lecturer on UFOs and New Physics; member of Project Epiphany.

Air Force Colonel Duane Warwick: former USAF Blue Light Special Forces commander; member of Project Epiphany Contact Team.

Army Major Roscoe Dent: former Chief of Intelligence to SEATO; member of Project Epiphany Contact Team.

Sojourner Dent: Roscoe Dent's wife.

Shep Gorton: dying transient casualty to Pneumonic Hemorrhagic Fever.

Saquasohuh: the Blue Star Kachina; also the seven-foot-tall, female extraterrestrial upon whom the Hopi Kachina was modeled.

Patusung-ala: The Hopi Spirits of the Four Directions.

Norbert Collier: experiencer and former Naval Intelligence officer, operating under cover as a modest Navy Chief.

John Draper: Director, Central Intelligence Agency.

Eduardo "Sewer" Sodoma: Former CIA contract "wet jobs" agent; freelance clandestine "dirty-tricks" operative.

Reid Linker: FBI Director.

Lieutenant Gaylord Littey: Former UFO recovery team specialist; member of the Blue Light cordon guarding the JANUS "flying saucer."

Jonathan Gracie: National Security Agency special agent.

Admiral Malcolm MacKenzie: Commander, U.S. Navy Seals, Team Six.

David Kline, Ph.D.: member of the Bilderberg Executive Committee; a board director of the Institute for Strategic and International Studies at Georgetown University

---

Glossary of Acronyms and Foreign Words

CIA: Central Intelligence Agency

NSA: National Security Agency

JANUS: Joint Agencies Nucleus for Unconventional Situation

UFO: Unidentified Flying Object (extraterrestrial spacecraft)

AFOSI: Air Force Office of Special Investigations (Intelligence)

CI: Counter-Intelligence, a branch of spycraft specializing in spying on other spies and infiltrators

bahana: Hopi term for the white man; also, *Bahana*, a special fair-skinned individual predicted to come to Hopi lands in the end times

PHF: Pneumonic Hemorrhagic Fever

DoD: Department of Defense

ATS: Above Top Secret, a high-level security classification

inipi: (Lakota) Stone People Lodge: sweat lodge

NRO-1: National Reconnaissance Office, an agency which commands and control space surveillance satellites; also,

NRO-2: National Reconnaissance Organization, a super-secret, multi-jurisdictional, compartmentalized group whose mission is to retrieve downed UFOs and extraterrestrials, and conduct UFO Cover-Up domestic psychological operations, including disinformation and intimidation

EMP: Electromagnetic pulse; specifically, a type of Star Wars weapon employing a directed, extreme-voltage, trillion-watt, pulsed energy field

ELINT: Electronic intelligence

ARV: Alien Reproduction Vehicle, a manmade antigravity craft retro-engineered from confiscated UFO technology

ECM: Electronic Counter-Measures (aircraft anti-detection devices)

USGS: U. S. Geological Survey, a governmental mapping agency

USFS: U.S. Forest Service

LZ: landing zone

JCS: Joint Chiefs of Staff: the top commanders of the Armed Services branches

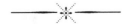

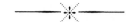

R ichard Boylan, Ph. D.

Richard is a Ph.D. behavioral scientist, Clinical Hypno-therapist, consultant, researcher, and author of four books and numerous articles. He is a consultant to persons exploring personal growth and transformation issues, ET and other anomalous experiences. His research investigations have included: human encounters with extraterrestrials, parapsychological/psychic experiences, lifestage growth factors, and societal implications of contact with cosmic cultures.

Dr. Boylan recently retired from a quarter-century career as a family and marriage counselor, clinical psychologist and social worker, and from an academic career as Lecturer at the University of California, Davis, Sacramento State University, and Sierra College.

Dr. Boylan in 1989 began to investigate the phenomenon of human-extraterrestrial contacts, and in 1992 began continuing research into these encounters. Dr. Boylan has presented papers on his research at the 1992 M.I.T. Abduction Study Conference, and at the 1995 Cosmic Cultures International Conference, Washington, DC. He has written four books, Extraterrestrial Contact and Human Responses (1992), Close Extraterrestrial Encounters (1994), Labored Journey To the Stars (1996), Project Epiphany, and has over 30 articles published.

He has conducted numerous workshops for mental health professionals on specialized counseling for experiencers of ET contact, and is a Founding Director of the Academy of Clinical Close Encounter Therapists (ACCET) Inc., an educational, networking and research organization.

Dr. Boylan has lectured widely at national and regional conferences, and has been interviewed on numerous radio and television programs, including twice on NBC/UPN's "Sightings," and on UPN's "Paranormal Borderline."

Dr. Boylan is a member of national and regional counseling, hypnotherapy and psychological associations, and is Past-President of the Sacramento Valley Psychological Association. His wife, Judith Lee Boylan, MBA and he have four adult children.